THE EDINBURGH EDITION OF
THE WAVERLEY NOVELS

EDITOR-IN-CHIEF
Dr David Hewitt

VOLUME FOUR [A]
THE BLACK DWARF

EDINBURGH EDITION OF THE
WAVERLEY NOVELS

to be complete in thirty volumes

Each volume will be published separately but original conjoint publication
of certain works is indicated in the EEWN volume numbering [4a, b; 7a, b,
etc.]. Where EEWN editors have been appointed, their names are listed

WALTER SCOTT

THE BLACK DWARF

Edited by
P. D. Garside

EDINBURGH
University
Press

COLUMBIA
University
Press

© The University Court of the University of Edinburgh 1993
Edinburgh University Press
22 George Square, Edinburgh
Columbia University Press
562 West 113th Street, New York

Typeset in Linotronic Ehrhardt
by Speedspools, Edinburgh
and first printed in Great Britain
by The Alden Press Ltd, Oxford,
on acid-free paper, and bound
by Hunter & Foulis Ltd, Edinburgh

ISBN 0 7486 0451 0 (Edinburgh edition)

British Library Cataloguing in Publication Data
Waverley Novels
Fiction
Scott, Sir Walter 1771–1832
New Edition
Hewitt, David, Editor-in-chief
The Black Dwarf
P.D. Garside, editor

ISBN 0231-08474-9 (Columbia edition)

Library of Congress Cataloging-in-Publication Data
available on request

LC Card Number 93-11343

FOREWORD

THE PUBLICATION of *Waverley* in 1814 marked the emergence of the modern novel in the western world. It is difficult now to recapture the impact of this and the following novels of Scott on a readership accustomed to prose fiction either as picturesque romance, 'Gothic' quaintness, or presentation of contemporary manners. For Scott not only invented the historical novel, but gave it a dimension and a relevance that made it available for a great variety of new kinds of writing. Balzac in France, Manzoni in Italy, Gogol and Tolstoy in Russia, were among the many writers of fiction influenced by the man Stendhal called 'notre père, Walter Scott'.

What Scott did was to show history and society in motion: old ways of life being challenged by new; traditions being assailed by counter-statements; loyalties, habits, prejudices clashing with the needs of new social and economic developments. The attraction of tradition and its ability to arouse passionate defence, and simultaneously the challenge of progress and 'improvement', produce a pattern that Scott saw as the living fabric of history. And this history was rooted in *place*; events happened in localities still recognisable after the disappearance of the original actors and the establishment of new patterns of belief and behaviour.

Scott explored and presented all this by means of stories, entertainments, which were read and enjoyed as such. At the same time his passionate interest in history led him increasingly to see these stories as illustrations of historical truths, so that when he produced his final *Magnum Opus* edition of the novels he surrounded them with historical notes and illustrations, and in this almost suffocating guise they have been reprinted in edition after edition ever since. The time has now come to restore these novels to the form in which they were presented to their first readers, so that today's readers can once again capture their original power and freshness. At the same time, serious errors of transcription, omission, and interpretation, resulting from the haste of their transmission from manuscript to print can now be corrected.

DAVID DAICHES

EDINBURGH
University
Press

CONTENTS

ACKNOWLEDGEMENTS

The Scott Advisory Board and the editors of the Edinburgh Edition of the Waverley Novels wish to express their gratitude to The University Court of the University of Edinburgh *and its Press Committee for their vision in initiating and supporting the preparation of the first critical edition of Walter Scott's fiction. Those Universities which employ the editors have also contributed greatly in paying the editors' salaries, and awarding research leave and grants for travel and materials. Particular thanks are due to* The University of Aberdeen *for its grant towards the development of an electronic concordance of the Waverley Novels, and to the University of Wales (Cardiff) for its support of the editor of* The Black Dwarf *throughout.*

Although the edition is the work of scholars employed by universities, the project could not have prospered without the help of the sponsors cited below. Their generosity has met the direct costs of the initial research and of the preparation of the text of the first six novels to appear in this edition.

BANK OF SCOTLAND
The collapse of the great Edinburgh publisher Archibald Constable in January 1826 entailed the ruin of Sir Walter Scott who found himself responsible for his own private debts, for the debts of the printing business of James Ballantyne and Co. in which he was co-partner, and for the bank advances to Archibald Constable which had been guaranteed by the printing business. Scott's largest creditors were Sir William Forbes and Co., bankers, and the Bank of Scotland. On the advice of Sir William Forbes himself, the creditors did not sequester his property, but agreed to the creation of a trust to which he committed his future literary earnings, and which ultimately repaid the debts of over £120,000 for which he was legally liable.

In the same year the Government proposed to curtail the rights of the Scottish banks to issue their own notes; Scott wrote the 'Letters of Malachi Malagrowther' in their defence, arguing that the measure was neither in the interests of the banks nor of Scotland. The 'Letters' were so successful that the Government was forced to withdraw its proposal and to this day the Scottish Banks issue their own notes.

A portrait of Sir Walter appears on all current bank notes of the Bank of Scotland because Scott was a champion of Scottish banking, and because he was an illustrious and honourable customer not just of the Bank of Scotland itself, but also of three other banks now incorporated within it—the British Linen Bank which continues today as the merchant banking arm of the Bank of Scotland, Sir William Forbes and Co., and Ramsays, Bonars and Company.

Bank of Scotland's *support of the EEWN continues its long and fruitful involvement with the affairs of Walter Scott.*

P.F. CHARITABLE TRUST
The P.F. Charitable Trust is the main charitable trust of the Fleming family which founded and still has a controlling interest in the City firm of Robert Fleming Holdings Limited. *It was started in 1951 by Philip Fleming and has since been added to by his son, Robin, who is now Managing Trustee. The Board and the editors are most grateful to the Trust and Mr Robin Fleming for their generosity to the Edition.*

EDINBURGH UNIVERSITY DEVELOPMENT TRUST
The Edinburgh University General Council Trust, now incorporated within the Edinburgh University Development Trust, derived its funds from the contributions of graduates of the University. To the trustees, and to all whose gifts allowed the Trust to give a generous grant to the EEWN, the Board and the editors express their thanks.

The Board and editors also wish to thank Sir Gerald Elliot *for a gift from his charitable trust, and the British Academy and the Carnegie Trust for the Universities of Scotland for grants to facilitate specific aspects of EEWN research.*

LIBRARIES
Without the generous assistance of the two great repositories of Scott manuscripts, the National Library of Scotland *and the* Pierpont Morgan Library, New York, *it would not have been possible to have undertaken the editing of Scott's novels, and the Board and editors cannot overstate the extent to which they are indebted to their Trustees and staffs. In particular they wish to pay tribute to the late* Professor Denis Roberts, *Librarian of the National Library, who served on the Scott Advisory Board, who persuaded many of his colleagues in Britain and throughout the world to assist the Edition, and whose determination brought about the repatriation in 1986 of the Pforzheimer Library's Scott manuscripts and of the Interleaved Set of the Waverley Novels.*

THE BLACK DWARF
Editing Scott requires knowledge and expertise beyond the capacity of any one person, and many people have assisted the editor of The Black Dwarf. *He is especially indebted to Dr Michael J. H. Robson for invaluable guidance on matters relating to Border history and topography, as well as to Miss Margaret A. Tait and Mr Robin Moffet for their selfless assistance in tracking down more general annotatory materials. Thanks are also due to: Mr David Angus, Dr Iain G. Brown, Professor David Buchan, Dr Ian Clark, the late Dr James C. Corson, Mr Thomas Crawford, Mr Walter Elliot (Ettrick and Lauderdale Museum Service), Mr John Ellis, Mrs Gillian Garside, Dr David Groves, Dr Gillian Hughes, Professor Jane Millgate, Mrs Virginia Murray, Professor*

Melvyn New, Professor David Nokes, Dr Elaine Petrie, Professor David Skilton, Sheriff J.Aikman Smith, Ms Gillean Somerville, Professor Mark Weinstein.

To help editors solve specific problems, the Edinburgh Edition of the Waverley Novels has appointed the following as consultants: Professor David Nordloh, Indiana University (editorial practice); Dr Alan Bruford, University of Edinburgh, (popular beliefs and customs); Dr John Cairns, University of Edinburgh (Scots Law); Professor Thomas Craik, University of Durham (Shakespeare); Mr John Ellis, University of Edinburgh (medieval literature); Dr Caroline Jackson-Houlston, Oxford Polytechnic (popular song); Mr Roy Pinkerton, University of Edinburgh (classical literature); Mrs Mairi Robinson (language); Professor David Stevenson, University of St Andrews (history). Of these the editor of The Black Dwarf *has called especially on the advice of Dr Alan Bruford, Dr John Cairns, Professor Thomas Craik, Mr Roy Pinkerton, Mrs Mairi Robinson and Professor David Stevenson.*

The following libraries have provided assistance either by supplying information or allowing access to their Scott holdings: Bodleian Library, Oxford; Bristol University Library; Brotherton Library; Leeds University; Edinburgh Public Library; Edinburgh University Library; Exeter University Library; Houghton Library, Harvard University; Hull University Library; Keele University Library; National Library of Scotland; Trinity College, Cambridge; University of Stirling Library; University of Wales College of Cardiff Library. The editor is also indebted to John Murray (Publishers) Ltd for permission to work with the Murray Archives at Albemarle Street, London.

GENERAL INTRODUCTION

The Edinburgh Edition of the Waverley Novels is the first authoritative edition of Walter Scott's fiction. It is the first to return to what Scott actually wrote in his manuscripts and proofs, and the first to reconsider fundamentally the presentation of his novels in print. In the light of comprehensive research, the editors decided in principle that the text of the novels in the new edition should be based on the first editions, but that all those manuscript readings which had been lost through accident, error, or misunderstanding should be restored. As a result each novel in the Edinburgh Edition differs in thousands of ways from the versions we have been accustomed to read, and many hundreds of readings never before printed have been recovered from the manuscripts. The individual differences are often minor, but are cumulatively telling. The return to the original Scott produces fresher, less formal and less pedantic novels than we have known.

Scott was the most famous and prestigious novelist of his age, but he became insolvent in 1826 following the bankruptcy of his publishers, Hurst, Robinson and Co. in London and Archibald Constable and Co. in Edinburgh. In 1827 Robert Cadell, who had succeeded Constable as Scott's principal publisher, proposed the first collected edition of the complete Waverley Novels as one way of reducing the mountain of debt for which Scott was legally liable. Scott agreed to the suggestion and over the next few years revised the text of his novels and wrote introductions and notes. The edition was published in 48 monthly volumes from 1829 to 1833. The full story of the making of the Magnum Opus, as it was familiarly christened by Scott, is told in Jane Millgate's *Scott's Last Edition* (Edinburgh, 1987), but for present purposes what is significant is that the Magnum became the standard edition of Scott, and since his death in 1832 all editions of the Waverley Novels, with the single exception of Claire Lamont's *Waverley* (Oxford, 1981), have been based on it.

Because Scott prepared the Magnum Opus it has long been felt that it represented his final wishes and intentions. In a literal sense this must be so, but all readers who open the pages of any edition published since 1832 and are confronted with the daunting clutter of introductions, prefaces, notes, and appendices, containing a miscellaneous assemblage of historical illustration and personal anecdote, must feel that the creative power which took Britain, Europe and America by storm in the preceding decades is cabin'd, cribb'd, confin'd by its Magnum context. Just as the new matter of 1829–33 is not integral to the novels as they were originally conceived, neither are the revisions and additions to the text.

'Scholarly editors may disagree about many things, but they are in general agreement that their goal is to discover exactly what an author wrote and to determine what form of his work he wished the public to have.' Thus Thomas Tanselle in 1976 succinctly and memorably defined the business of textual editing. The editors of the Edinburgh Edition have made this goal their own, and have returned to the original manuscripts, to the surviving proofs, and to other textually relevant material to determine exactly what Scott wrote; they have also investigated each British edition and every relevant foreign edition published in Scott's lifetime. They have discovered that ever since they were written, the Waverley Novels have suffered from textual degeneration.

The first editions were derived from copies of Scott's manuscripts, but the pressure to publish quickly was such that they are not wholly reliable representations of what he wrote. Without exception, later editions were based on a preceding printed version, and so include most of the mistakes of their predecessors while adding their own, and in most cases Scott was not involved. There was an accumulation of error, and when Scott came to prepare the Magnum Opus he revised and corrected an earlier printed text, apparently unaware of the extent to which it was already corrupt. Thus generations of readers have read versions of Scott which have suffered significantly from the changes, both deliberate and accidental, of editors, compositors and proof-readers.

A return to authentic Scott is therefore essential. The manuscripts provide the only fully authoritative state of the texts of the novels, for they alone proceed wholly from the author. They are for the most part remarkably coherent; the shape of Scott's narratives seems to have been established before he committed his ideas to paper, although a close examination of what he wrote shows countless minor revisions made in the process of writing, and usually at least one layer of later revising. We are closest to Scott in the manuscripts, but they could not be the sole textual basis for the new edition. They give us his own words, free of non-authorial interventions, but they do not constitute the 'form of his work he wished the public to have'.

Scott expected his novels to be printed, usually in three volumes, and he structured his stories so that they fitted the three-volume division of the printed books. He expected minor errors to be corrected, words repeated in close proximity to each other to be removed, spelling to be normalised, and a printed-book style of punctuation, amplifying and replacing the marks he had provided in manuscript, to be inserted. There are no written instructions to the printers to this effect, but his acceptance of what was done implies approval, even although the imposition of the conventions of print had such a profound effect on the evolution of his text that the conversion of autograph text into print was less a question of transliteration than of translation.

This assumption of authorial approval is better founded for Scott than for any other writer. Walter Scott was in partnership with James Ballantyne in a firm of printers which Ballantyne managed and for which Scott generated much of the work. The contracts for new Scott novels were unusual, in that they always stipulated that the printing would be undertaken by James Ballantyne and Co., and that the publishers should have the exclusive right only to purchase and to manage the sales of an agreed number of copies. Thus production was controlled not by the publishers but by James Ballantyne and his partner, Walter Scott. The textually significant consequence of this partnership was a mutual trust to a degree uncommon between author and printer. Ballantyne was most anxious to serve Scott and to assist him in preparing the novels for public presentation, and Scott not only permitted this but actively sought it. Theirs was a unique business and literary partnership which had a crucial effect on the public form of the Waverley Novels.

Scott expected his novels to appear in the form and format in which they did appear, but in practice what was done was not wholly satisfactory because of the complicated way in which the texts were processed. Until 1827, when Scott acknowledged his authorship, the novels were published anonymously and so that Scott's well-known handwriting should not be seen in the printing works the original manuscripts were copied, and it was these copies, not Scott's original manuscripts, which were used in the printing house. Not a single leaf is known to survive but the copyists probably began the tidying and regularising. The compositors worked from the copies, and, when typesetting, did not just follow what was before them, but supplied punctuation, normalised spelling, and corrected minor errors. Proofs were first read in-house against the transcripts, and in addition to the normal checking for mistakes these proofs were used to improve the punctuation and the spelling.

When the initial corrections had been made, a new set of proofs went to James Ballantyne. He acted as editor, not just as proof-reader. He drew Scott's attention to gaps in the text and pointed out inconsistencies in detail; he asked Scott to standardise names; he substituted nouns for pronouns when they occurred in the first sentence of a paragraph, and inserted the names of speakers in dialogue; he changed incorrect punctuation, and added punctuation he thought desirable; he corrected grammatical errors and removed close verbal repetitions; he told Scott when he could not follow what was happening; and when he particularly enjoyed something he said so.

These annotated proofs were sent to the author, who sometimes accepted Ballantyne's suggestions and sometimes rejected them. He made many more changes; he cut out redundant words, and substituted the vivid for the pedestrian; he refined the punctuation; he sometimes reworked and revised passages extensively, and in so doing made the proofs a stage in the composition of the novels.

When Ballantyne received Scott's corrections and revisions, he transcribed all the changes on to a clean set of proofs so that the author's hand would not be seen by the compositors. Further revises were prepared. Some of these were seen and read by Scott but by and large he seems to have trusted Ballantyne to make sure that the earlier corrections and revisions had been correctly executed. When doing this Ballantyne did not just read for typesetting errors, but continued the process of punctuating and tidying the text. A final proof allowed the corrections to be inspected and the imposition of the type to be checked prior to printing.

One might imagine that after all this activity the first editions would be perfect, but this is far from being the case. There are usually in excess of 50,000 variants in the first edition of a three-volume novel when compared with the manuscript. The great majority are in accordance with Scott's general wishes as described above. But the intermediaries, as the copyist, compositors, proof-readers, and James Ballantyne are collectively known, made mistakes; they misread the manuscripts from time to time, and they did not always understand what Scott had written. This would not have mattered had there not also been procedural failures. The transcripts were not thoroughly checked against the original manuscripts. Scott himself does not seem to have read the proofs against the manuscripts and thus did not notice transcription errors which made sense in their context. And James Ballantyne continued his editing in post-authorial proofs; his changes may have been in the spirit of Scott's own critical proof-reading, but it is probable that his efforts were never inspected by the author.

The editors of the Edinburgh Edition of the Waverley Novels have studied every single variant in the first editions of all the novels they have worked on to date. There are a large number of small verbal differences, and the editors have come to the conclusion that the words originally written by Scott, though subsequently changed by the intermediaries, are nearly always justified by colloquial, dialect, or period usage. Similarly the punctuation supplied at times misinterprets the sense of the manuscript or the rhythm of speech, and the substitution of synonyms for repeated words was often effected too mechanically, changing meaning or spoiling rhetoric. It is not surprising that the intermediaries should make mistakes when translating the manuscripts into print. Even James Ballantyne's knowledge of language and history was limited compared to Scott's. He was a trusted and competent editor; he was honest about his likes and dislikes and was useful to Scott in giving voice to them. But his annotations and suggestions show that he did not appreciate the full variety of Scott's language, objected to any suggestion of the indelicate, and tidied the text by rule. Above all, his comments were made as Scott wrote, and without knowing the outcome of the story, and thus he was inevitably unaware of the architectonics of the complete work of art. His views were sometimes wrong, and Scott was sometimes wrong to give way to them.

The editors have normally chosen the first edition of a novel as base-text, for the first edition usually represents the culmination of the initial creative process, and, local failings excepted, usually seems closest to the form of his work he wished his public to have. After the careful collation of all pre-publication materials, and in the light of their invest-igation into the factors governing the writing and printing of the Waver-ley Novels, they have incorporated into the base-text readings which were lost in the production process through accident, error or mis-understanding. In certain cases they have also introduced into the base-texts revisions from printed texts which they believe to have emanated from Scott, or are consistent with the spirit of his own revision during the initial creative process. Only revisions which belong to the process and period of initial creation have been adopted. In addition, they have corrected various kinds of error, such as typographical and copy-editing mistakes including the misnumbering of chapters, inconsistencies in the naming of characters, egregious errors of fact that are not part of the fiction, and failures of sense which a simple emendation can restore. The result is an ideal text, which the first readers of the Waverley Novels would have read had the production process been less pressurised and more considered.

The 'new' Scott will be visible not only in the text but also in the context. The Magnum introductions and notes are not integral to the novels as they were originally conceived, and are therefore reserved for separate publication in the final volumes of the edition where they will be treated as a distinct, final phase of Scott's involvement in his fiction. Thus the novels appear as they were first presented. The Edinburgh Edition of the Waverley Novels offers a clean text; there are no foot-notes or superscripts to detract from the pleasure of reading. It does not remove Scott's own introductions only to replace them with those of modern editors; the textual essays appear at the end, where they will be encountered only after reading Scott. The essays present a detailed history of the genesis and composition of the novel, a history of the evolution of the old text, and a description of the distinguishing features of the new. The textual apparatus does not include a full list of variants because for one of the major early works there would be at least 100,000 to record. Instead, the textual essays analyse and illustrate the evidence gleaned from the collation of the manuscripts and proofs (where these are extant) and of all relevant editions published in Scott's lifetime. All variants from the base-text are listed in the emendation list (but as variants from the Magnum are not, the scale of the change from old editions to the new is not immediately apparent).

And finally, there are explanatory notes and a glossary. Scott's read-ing was wide and voluminous, he was immensely knowledgeable in a range of disciplines, and he had a considerable understanding of the social organisation, customs and beliefs of contemporary and historical societies. Few readers are likely to appreciate the full extent of his learning without some assistance, and the notes at the end of this volume draw on a greater variety of expertise, and are more comprehensive, than any previously published. They are informative rather than expository; for instance, they identify all quotations, from the most obvious passages in the Bible and Shakespeare through to the truly recondite, but they leave the reader to consider their significance in each context. And the glossary for the first time attempts to cover comprehensively all Scott's period, dialectal, foreign, and obscure words.

The Edinburgh Edition of the Waverley Novels aims to provide an authoritative text of Scott's fiction, to give the reader the support required to appreciate the intellectual richness of his work, and to allow a new audience to share the excitement that the novels generated when they were first published. The editors are confident of fulfilling the first two aims. The reader must be judge of their success in the third.

DAVID HEWITT

TALES OF MY LANDLORD,

COLLECTED AND REPORTED

BY

JEDIDIAH CLEISHBOTHAM,

PARISH-CLERK AND SCHOOLMASTER OF GANDERCLEUGH.

> Hear, Land o' Cakes and brither Scots,
> Frae Maidenkirk to Jonny Groats',
> If there's a hole in a' your coats,
>   I rede ye tent it,
> A chiel's amang you takin' notes,
>   An' faith he'll prent it.

BURNS.

IN FOUR VOLUMES.

VOL. I.

EDINBURGH:

PRINTED FOR WILLIAM BLACKWOOD, PRINCE'S STREET:
AND JOHN MURRAY, ALBEMARLE STREET, LONDON.

1816.

Ahora bien, dixo el Cura, traedme, senor huésped, aquesos libros, que los quiero ver. Que me place, respondió el, y entrando, en su aposento, sacó dél una maletilla vieja cerrada con una cadenilla, y abriéndola, halló en ella tres libros grandes y unos papeles de muy buena letra escritos de mano.—DON QUIXOTE, Parte I. Capitulo 32.

It is mighty well, said the priest; pray, landlord, bring me those books, for I have a mind to see them. With all my heart, answered the host; and, going to his chamber, he brought out a little old cloke-bag, with a padlock and chain to it, and opening it, he took out three large volumes, and some manuscript papers written in a fine character.—JARVIS'S *Translation.*

TO

HIS LOVING COUNTRYMEN,

WHETHER THEY ARE DENOMINATED

MEN OF THE SOUTH,

GENTLEMEN OF THE NORTH,

PEOPLE OF THE WEST,

OR

FOLK OF FIFE;

THESE TALES,

ILLUSTRATIVE OF ANCIENT SCOTTISH MANNERS,

AND

OF THE TRADITIONS OF THEIR RESPECTIVE DISTRICTS,

ARE RESPECTFULLY INSCRIBED,

BY THEIR FRIEND AND LIEGE FELLOW-SUBJECT,

JEDIDIAH CLEISHBOTHAM.

TALES OF MY LANDLORD;

COLLECTED AND REPORTED BY

JEDIDIAH CLEISHBOTHAM,

PARISH-CLERK AND SCHOOLMASTER OF GANDERCLEUGH.

INTRODUCTION.

As I MAY, *without vanity, presume that the name and official description prefixed to this Proem will secure it, from the sedate and reflecting part of mankind, to whom only I would be understood to address myself, such attention as is due to the sedulous instructor of youth, and the careful performer of my Sabbath duties, I will forbear to hold up a candle to the day-light, or to point out to the judicious those recommendations of my labours which they must necessarily anticipate from the perusal of the title-page. Nevertheless, I am not unaware, that, as Envy always dogs Merit at the heels, there may be those who will whisper, that albeit my learning and good principles cannot (lauded be the Heavens) be denied by any one, yet that my situation at Gandercleugh hath been more favourable to my acquisitions in learning than to the enlargement of my views of the ways and works of the present generation. To the which objection, if, peradventure, any such shall be started, my answer shall be threefold:*

First, *Gandercleugh is, as it were, the central part,—the navel (*si fas sit dicere*) of this our native realm of Scotland; so that men, from every corner thereof, when travelling on their concernments of business, either towards our metropolis of law, by which I mean Edinburgh, or toward our metropolis of commerce and mart of gain, whereby I insinuate Glasgow, are frequently led to make Gandercleugh their abiding stage and place of rest for the night. And it must be acknowledged by the most sceptical, that I, who have sat in the leathern arm-chair, on the left-hand side of the fire, in the common room of the Wallace Inn, winter and summer, for every evening in my life, during forty years by-past, (the Christian Sabbaths only excepted) must have seen more of the manners and customs of various tribes and people than if I had sought them out by my own painful travel and bodily labour. Even so doth the tollman at the well-frequented turnpike on the Wellbrae-head, sitting at his ease in his own dwelling, gather more receipt of custom than if, moving forth upon the road, he* *were to require a contribution from each person whom he chanced to meet in his journey, when, according to the vulgar adage, he might possibly be greeted with more kicks than halfpence.*

But, secondly, supposing it again urged that Ithacus, the most wise of the Greeks, acquired his renown, as the Roman poet hath assured us, by visiting states and men, I reply to the Zoilus who shall adhere to this objection, that, de facto, *I have seen states and men also; for I have visited the famous cities of Edinburgh and Glasgow, the former twice, the latter three times, in the course of my earthly pilgrimage. And, moreover, I had the honour to sit in the General Assembly, (meaning, as an auditor in the galleries thereof) and have heard as much goodly speaking on the law of patronage, as, with the fructification thereof in mine own understanding, hath made me be considered as an oracle upon that doctrine ever since my safe and happy return to Gandercleugh.*

Again—and thirdly—If it be nevertheless pretended that my information and knowledge of mankind, however extensive, and however painfully acquired, by constant domestic enquiry, and by foreign travel, is, natheless, incompetent to the task of recording the pleasant narratives of my Landlord, I will let those critics know, to their own eternal shame and confusion, as well as to the abashment and discomfiture of all who shall rashly take up a song against me, that I am NOT *the writer, redacter, or compiler of the Tales of my Landlord; nor am I, in one single iota, answerable for their contents, more or less. And now, ye generation of vipers, who raise yourselves up as if it were brazen serpents, to hiss with your tongues, and to smite with your stings, bow yourselves down to your native dust, and acknowledge that yours have been the thoughts of ignorance, and the words of vain foolishness. Lo! ye are caught in your own snare, and your own pit hath yawned for you. Turn, then, aside from the task that is too heavy for you; destroy not your teeth by gnawing a file; waste not your strength in spurning against a castle-wall; nor spend your breath in contending in swiftness with a fleet steed; and let those weigh the Tales of my Landlord who shall bring with them the scales of candour cleansed from the rust of prejudice by the hands of intelligent modesty. For these alone they were compiled, as will appear from a brief narrative which my zeal for truth compelleth me to make supplementary to the present Proem.*

It is well known that my Landlord was a pleasing and a facetious man, acceptable unto all the parish of Gandercleugh, excepting only the Laird, the Exciseman, and those for whom he refused to draw liquor upon trust. Their causes of dislike I will touch separately, adding my own refutation thereof.

His honour, the Laird, accused our Landlord, deceased, of having encouraged, in various times and places, the destruction of hares, rabbits, fowls black and grey, partridges, moor-pouts, and other birds and quadrupeds, in unlawful seasons, and contrary to the laws of this realm, which hath secured, in their wisdom, the slaughter of such animals for the great of the earth, whom I have remarked to take an uncommon (though, to me, an unintelligible) pleasure therein. Now, in humble deference to his honour, and in defence of my friend deceased, I reply to this charge, that howsoever the form of such animals might appear to be similar to those so protected by the law, yet it was a mere deceptio visus; *for those which resembled hares were, in fact,* hill-kids, *and those partaking of the appearance of moor-fowl, were truly* wood-pigeons, *and consumed and eaten* eo nomine, *and not otherwise.*

Again, the Exciseman pretended, that my deceased Landlord did encourage that species of manufacture called distillation, without having an especial permission from the Great, technically called a licence, for doing so. Now I stand up to confront this falsehood; and, in defiance of him, his gauging-stick, and pen and inkhorn, I tell him, that I never saw, or tasted, a glass of unlawful aqua vitæ in the house of my Landlord; nay, that, on the contrary, we needed not such devices in respect of a pleasing and somewhat seductive liquor, which was vended and consumed at the Wallace Inn, under the name of mountain dew. If there is a penalty against manufacturing such a liquor, let him show me the statute; and, when he does, I'll tell him if I will obey it or no.

Concerning those who came to my Landlord's for liquor, and went thirsty away, for lack of present coin, or future credit, I cannot but say it has grieved my bowels as if the case had been mine own. Nevertheless, my Landlord considered the necessities of a thirsty soul, and would permit them in extreme need, and when their soul was impoverished for lack of moisture, to drink to the full value of their watches and wearing apparel, exclusively of their inferior habiliments, which he was uniformly inexorable in obliging them to retain for the credit of the house. As to mine own part, I may well say, that he never refused me that modicum of refreshment with which I am wont to recruit nature after the fatigues of my school. It is true, I taught his five sons English and Latin, writing, book-keeping, with a tincture of mathematics, and that I instructed his daughter in psalmody. Nor do I remember me of any fee or honorarium received from him on account of these my labours, except the compotations aforesaid. Nevertheless, this compensation suited my humour well, since it is a hard sentence to bid a dry throat wait till quarter-day.

But, truly, were I to speak my simple conceit and belief, I think my Landlord was chiefly moved to waive in my behalf the usual requisition of a symbol, or reckoning, by the pleasure he was wont to take in my conversation, which, though solid and edifying on the main, was like a well-built palace, decorated with facetious narratives and devices, tending much to the enhancement and ornament thereof. And so pleasant was my Landlord of the Wallace in his replies during such colloquies, that there was no district in Scotland, yea, and no peculiar, and, as it were, distinctive custom therein practised, but what was discussed betwixt us, insomuch, that those who stood by were wont to say, it was worth a bottle of ale to hear us communicate with each other. And not a few travellers, from distant parts, as well as from the remote districts of our kingdom, were wont to mingle in the conversation, and to tell news that had been gathered in foreign lands, or preserved from oblivion in this our own.

Now I chanced to have contracted for teaching the lower classes, with a young person called Peter, or Patrick, Pattieson, who had been educated in our Holy Kirk, yea, had, by the licence of presbytery, his voice opened therein as a preacher, who delighted much in the collection of olden tales and legends, and in garnishing them with the flowers of poesy, whereof he was a vain and frivolous professor. For he followed not the example of those strong poets whom I proposed to him as a pattern, but formed versification of a flimsy and modern texture, to the compounding whereof was necessary small pains and less thought. And hence I have chid him as being one of those who bring forward the fatal revolution prophesied by Mr Thomas Carey, in his vaticination on the death of the celestial Dr John Donne:

> *Now thou art gone, and thy strict laws will be*
> *Too hard for libertines in poetry;*
> *Till verse (by thee refined) in this last age*
> *Turn ballad rhime.*

I had also disputations with him touching his indulging rather a flowing and redundant than a concise and stately diction in his prose exercitations. But notwithstanding symptoms of inferior taste, and a humour of contradicting his betters upon passages of dubious construction in Latin authors, I did grievously lament when Peter Pattieson was removed from me by death, even as if he had been the offspring of my own loins. And in respect his papers had been left in my care, (to answer funeral and death-bed expences,) I conceived myself entitled to dispose of one parcel thereof, entitled, "Tales of my Landlord," to one cunning in the trade (as it is called) of bookselling. He was a mirthful man of small stature, cunning in counterfeiting of voices, and in making facetious tales and responses, and whom I have to laud for the truth of his dealings towards me.

Now, therefore, the world may see the injustice that charges me with incapacity to write these narratives, seeing, that though I have proved that I could have written them if I would, yet, not having done so, the censure will deservedly fall, if it is at all due, upon the memory of Mr Peter Pattieson; whereas I must be justly entitled to the praise, when any is due, seeing that, as the Dean of St Patrick's wittily and logically expresseth it,

> *That without which a thing is not,*
> *Is* Causa sine qua non.

The work, therefore, is unto me as a child is to a parent; through which child, if it proveth worthy, the parent hath honour and praise; but, if otherwise, the disgrace will deservedly attach to itself alone.

I have only further to intimate, that Mr Peter Pattieson, in arranging these legends for the press, hath more consulted his own fancy than the accuracy of the narration; nay, that he hath sometimes blended two or three together for the mere grace of his plot. Of which infidelity, although I disapprove and enter my testimony against it, yet I have not taken it upon me to correct the same, in respect it was the will of the deceased, that his manuscripts should be submitted to the press without diminution or alteration. A fanciful nicety it was on the part of my deceased friend, who, if thinking wisely, ought rather to have conjured me, by all the tender ties of our friendship and common pursuits, to have carefully revised, altered, and augmented, at my judgment and discretion. But the will of the dead must be scrupulously obeyed, even when we weep over their pertinacity and self-delusion. So, gentle reader, I bid you farewell, recommending you to such fare as the mountains of your own country produce. And I will only farther premise, that each Tale is preceded by a short introduction, mentioning the persons by whom, and the circumstances under which, the materials thereof were collected.

JEDIDIAH CLEISHBOTHAM.

THE BLACK DWARF

Chapter One

PRELIMINARY

Hast any philosophy in thee, Shepherd?
As You Like it

IT WAS a fine April morning (excepting that it had snowed hard the
night before, and the ground remained covered with a dazzling mantle
of six inches in depth) when two horsemen rode up to the Wallace
Inn. The first was a strong, tall, powerful man, in a grey riding-coat,
having a hat covered with wax-cloth, a huge silver-mounted horse-
whip, boots, and dreadnought overalls. He was mounted on a large
strong brown mare, rough in coat, but well in condition, with a saddle
of the yeomanry cut, and a double-bitted military bridle, somewhat
rusted. The man who accompanied him was apparently his servant;
he rode a shaggy little grey poney, had a blue bonnet over his head,
and a large check napkin folded about his neck, wore a pair of long
blue hose instead of boots, had his gloveless hands much stained with
tar, and observed an air of deference and respect towards his companion, but without any of those indications of precedence and punct-
ilio which are preserved between the gentry and their domestics. On
the contrary, the two travellers entered the court-yard abreast, and the
concluding sentence of the conversation which had been carrying on
betwixt them was a joint ejaculation, "Lord guide us, an' this weather
last, what will come o' the lambs!"

The hint was sufficient to my Landlord, who, advancing to take the
horse of the principal person, and holding him by the rein as he
dismounted, while his ostler rendered the same service to the attendant, welcomed the stranger to Gandercleugh, and, in the same breath,
enquired, what news from the south hie-lands?

"News?" said the farmer, "bad eneugh news, I think;—an' we can carry through the yowes it will be a' we can do; we maun e'en leave the lambs to the Black Dwarf's care."

"Aye, aye," subjoined the old shepherd, (for such he was) shaking his head, "he'll be unco busy amang the morts this season."

"The Black Dwarf!" said *my learned friend and patron*,* Mr Jedidiah Cleishbotham, "and what sort of a personage may he be?"

"Hout awa, man, ye'll hae heard o' Canny Elshie the Black Dwarf, or I am muckle mista'en—A' the warld tell tales about him, but it's but daft nonsense after a'—I dinna believe a word o't frae beginning to end."

"Your father believed it unco stievely, though," said the old man, to whom the scepticism of his master gave obvious displeasure.

"Aye, very true, Bauldie, but that was in the time o' the blackfaces— they believed a hantle queer things in thae days, that naebody heeds since the lang sheep came in."

"The mair's the pity, the mair's the pity," said the old man. "Your father, and sae I have aften tell'd ye, maister, wad hae been sair vexed to hae seen the auld peel-house wa's pu'd doun to make park dykes, and the bonny broomy knowe, where he liked sae weel to sit at e'en, wi' his plaid about him, and look at the kye as they came doun the loaning,—ill wad he hae liked to hae seen that braw sunny knowe a' riven out wi' the pleugh in the fashion it is this day."

"Hout, Bauldie," replied the principal, "take ye that dram the land-lord's offering ye, and never fash your beard about the changes o' the warld, sae lang as ye're blythe and bien yoursel."

"Wussing your health, sirs," said the shepherd; and, having taken off his glass, and observed the whiskey was the right thing, he con-tinued, "It's no for the like o' us to be judging, to be sure; but it was a bonny knowe that broomy knowe, and an unco braw shelter for the lambs in a severe morning like this."

"Aye, but ye ken we maun hae turnips for the lang sheep, billie, and muckle hard wark to get them, baith wi' the pleugh and the howe; and that wad sort ill wi' sitting on the broomy knowe and cracking about Black Dwarfs, and siccan clavers, as was the gate lang syne, when the short sheep were in the fashion."

"Aweel, aweel, maister," said the attendant, "short sheep had short rents, I am thinking."

Here my *worthy and learned* patron again interposed, and observed,

* Note by the publisher.—We have in this, and other instances, printed in italics some few words which the worthy editor, Mr Jedidiah Cleishbotham, seems to have interpolated upon the text of his deceased friend, Mr Pattieson. We must observe, once for all, that such liberties appear only to have been taken by the learned gentleman when his own character and conduct are concerned; and surely he must be the best judge of the style in which his own character and conduct should be treated of.

"that he could never perceive any material difference, in point of longitude, between one sheep and another."

This occasioned a loud horse laugh on the part of the farmer, and an astonished stare on that of the shepherd. "It's the woo', man,—it's the woo', and no the beasts themsels, that makes them be ca'd lang or short. I believe, if ye were to measure their backs, the short sheep wad be rather the langer-bodied o' the twa; but it's the woo' that pays the rent in thae days, and it had muckle need. Odd, Bauldie says very true, —short sheep *did* make short rents—my father paid for our steeding just threescore punds, and it stands me in three hunder, plack and bawbee.—And that's very true—I haenna time to be standing here clavering—Landlord, get us our breakfast, and see get the yauds fed —I am for doun to Christy Wilson's, to see if him and me can gree about the luckpenny I am to gie him for his year-aulds. We had drank sax mutchkins to the making the bargain at St Boswells fair, and some gate we canna gree upon the particulars preceesely, for as muckle time as we took about it—I doubt we draw to a plea.—But hear ye, neighbour," addressing my *worthy and learned* patron, "if ye want to hear ony thing about lang or short sheep, I will back here again to my kail against ane o'clock; or, if ye want ony auld-warld stories about the Black Dwarf, and sic like, if ye'll ware a half mutchkin upon Bauldie there, he'll crack t'ye like a pen-gun. And I'se gie ye a mutchkin mysel, man, if I can settle weel wi' Christy Wilson."

The farmer returned at the hour appointed, and with him came Christy Wilson, their difference having been fortunately settled without an appeal to the gentlemen of the long robe. My *learned and worthy* patron failed not to attend, both on account of the refreshment promised to the mind and to the body, *although he is known only to partake of the latter in a very moderate degree;* and the party with which my Landlord was associated continued to sit till late in the evening, seasoning their liquor with many choice tales and songs. The last incident which I recollect, was my *learned and worthy* patron falling from his chair, just as he concluded a long lecture upon temperance, by reciting, from the Gentle Shepherd, a couplet, which he *right happily* transferred from the vice of avarice to that of ebriety:—

> He that has just enough may soundly sleep,
> The owercome only fashes folk to keep.

It hath indeed been observed of my learned and worthy patron that he can never recite these verses, especially in the evening, without evincing in some such way his overpowering sense of their merit.

In the course of the evening the Black Dwarf was not forgotten, and the old shepherd, Bauldie, told so many stories of him, that they

excited a good deal of interest. It also appeared, though not till the
third punch-bowl was emptied, that much of the farmer's scepticism
on the subject was affected, as evincing a liberality of thinking, and a
freedom from ancient prejudices, becoming a man who paid three
hundred pounds a-year of rent, while, in fact, he had a lurking belief
in the traditions of his forefathers. After my usual manner, I made
farther enquiries of other persons connected with the wild and pastoral district in which the scene of the following narrative is placed,
and I was fortunate enough to recover many links of the story, not
generally known, and which account, at least in some degree, for the
circumstances of exaggerated marvel with which superstition has
attired it in the more vulgar traditions.

Chapter Two

Will none but Hearne the Hunter serve your turn?
Merry Wives of Windsor

IN ONE of the most remote districts of the south of Scotland, where an
ideal line, drawn along the tops of lofty and bleak mountains, separ-
ates that land from her sister kingdom, a young man, called Halbert, or
Hobbie Elliot, a substantial farmer, who boasted his descent from old
Martin Elliot of the Preakin-tower, noted in Border story and song,
was on his return from deer-stalking. The deer, once so numerous
among those solitary wastes, were now reduced to a very few herds,
which, sheltering themselves in the most remote and inaccessible
recesses, rendered the task of pursuing them equally toilsome and
precarious. Still, however, there were found many of the youth of the
country ardently attached to this sport, with all its dangers and
fatigues. The sword had been sheathed upon the Borders for more
than a hundred years, by the peaceful union of the crowns in the reign
of James the First of Great Britain. Still the country retained traces of
what it had been in former days; the inhabitants, their more peaceful
avocations having been repeatedly interrupted by the civil wars of the
preceding century, were scarce yet broken in to the habits of regular
industry, sheep-farming had not been introduced upon any considerable scale, and the feeding of black cattle was the chief purpose to
which the hills and vallies were applied. Near to the farmer's house he
usually contrived to raise such a crop of oats, or barley, as afforded
meal for his family; and the whole of this slovenly and imperfect mode
of cultivation left much time upon his own hands, and those of his
domestics. This was usually employed by the young men in hunting
and fishing; and the spirit of adventure, which formerly led to *raids*

and *forays* in the same districts, was still to be discovered in the eagerness with which they pursued these rural sports.

The more high-spirited among the youth were, about the time that our narrative begins, expecting, rather with hope than apprehension, an opportunity of emulating their fathers in their military achievements, the recital of which formed the chief part of their amusement within doors. The passing of the Scottish Act of Security had given the alarm to England, as it seemed to point at a separation of the two British kingdoms, after the decease of Queen Anne, the reigning monarch. Godolphin, then at the head of the English administration, foresaw that there was no other mode of avoiding the probable extremity of a civil war, but by carrying through an incorporating union. How that treaty was managed, and how little it seemed for some time to promise the beneficial results which have since taken place to such extent, may be learned from the history of the period. It is enough for our purpose to say, that all Scotland was indignant at the terms on which their legislature had surrendered their national independence. The general resentment led to the strangest leagues and to the wildest plans. The Cameronians were about to take arms for the restoration of the house of Stuart, whom they regarded, with justice, as their oppressors; and the intrigues of the period present the strange picture of papists, prelatists, and presbyterians, caballing against the same government, out of a common feeling that their country had been treated with injustice. The fermentation was universal; and, as the population of Scotland had been generally trained to arms, under the Act of Security, they were not indifferently prepared for war, and waited but the declaration of some of the nobility to break out into open hostility. It was at this period of public confusion that our story opens.

The cleugh, or wild ravine, into which Hobbie Elliot had followed the game, was already far behind him, and he was considerably advanced on his return homeward, when the night began to close upon him. This would have been a circumstance of great indifference to the experienced sportsman, who could have walked blindfold over every inch of his native heaths, had it not happened near a spot, which, according to the traditions of the country, was in extremely bad fame as haunted by supernatural appearances. To tales of this kind Hobbie had, from his childhood, lent an attentive ear; and as no part of the country afforded such a variety of legends, so no man was more deeply read in their fearful lore than Hobbie of the Heugh-foot, for so our gallant was called, to distinguish him from a round dozen of Elliots who bore the same christian name. It cost him no effort, therefore, to call to memory the terrific incidents connected with the extensive

waste upon which he was now entering. In fact, they presented themselves with a readiness which he felt to be somewhat dismaying.

This dreary common was called Meikle-stane-Moor, from a huge
column of unhewn granite, which raised its massy head on a knoll near
the centre of the heath, perhaps to tell of the mighty dead who slept
beneath, or to preserve the memory of some bloody skirmish. The real
cause of its existence had, however, passed away; and tradition, who is
as frequently an inventor of fiction as a preserver of truth, had supplied its place with a supplementary legend of her own, which now
came full upon Hobbie's memory. The ground about the pillar was
strewed, or rather encumbered, with many large fragments of stone of
the same consistence with the column, which, from their appearance
as they lay scattered on the waste, were popularly called the Grey
Geese of Meikle-stane-Moor. The legend accounted for this name
and appearance by the catastrophe of a noted and most formidable
witch who frequented these hills in former days, causing the ewes to
keb, and the kine to cast their calves, and performing all the feats of
mischief ascribed to these evil beings. On this moor she used to hold
her revels with her sister hags; and rings were still pointed out on
which no grass nor heath ever grew, the turf being, as it were, calcined
by the scorching hoofs of their diabolical partners.

Once upon a time this old hag is said to have crossed the moor,
driving before her a flock of geese, which she proposed to sell to
advantage at a neighbouring fair;—for it is well known that the fiend,
however liberal in imparting his powers of doing mischief, ungener-
ously leaves his allies under the necessity of performing the meanest
rustic labours for subsistence. The day was far advanced, and her
chance of obtaining a good price depended on her being first at the
market. But the geese, which had hitherto preceded her in a pretty
orderly manner, when they came to this wide common, interspersed
with marshes and pools of water, scattered in every direction, to
plunge into the element in which they delighted. Incensed at the
obstinacy with which they defied all her efforts to collect them, and
not remembering the terms of the contract by which the fiend was
bound to obey her commands for a certain space, the sorceress
exclaimed, "Deevil, that neither I nor they ever stir from this spot
more!" The words were hardly uttered, when, by a metamorphosis as
sudden as any in Ovid, the hag and her refractory flock were converted into stone, the angel whom she served grasping eagerly at an
opportunity of completing the ruin of her body and soul by a literal
obedience to her orders. It is said, that when she perceived and felt the
transformation which was about to take place, she exclaimed to the
treacherous fiend, "Ah! thou fause thief—lang hast thou promised

me a grey gown, and now I am getting ane that will last for ever." The
dimensions of the pillar, and of the stones, were often appealed to, as a
proof of the superior stature and size of old women and of geese in the
days of other years, by those praisers of the past who held the comfortable opinion of the gradual degeneracy of mankind.

All particulars of this legend Hobbie called to mind as he paced
along the moor. He also remembered, that, since the catastrophe had
taken place, the scene of it had been avoided, at least after night-fall,
by all human beings, as being the ordinary resort of kelpies, spunkies,
and other demons, once the companions of the witches' diabolical
revels, and now continuing to rendezvous upon the same spot, as if
still in attendance on their transformed mistress. Hobbie's natural
hardihood, however, manfully combatted with those intrusive sensa-
tions of awe. He summoned to his side the brace of large greyhounds,
who were the companions of his sports, and who were wont, in his own
phrase, to fear neither dog nor devil; he looked at the priming of his
piece, and, like the clown in Hallowe'en, whistled up the warlike ditty
of Jock of the Side, as a general causes his drums be beat to inspirit the
doubtful courage of his soldiers.

In this state of mind, he was very glad to hear a friendly voice shout
in his rear, and propose to him a partner on the road. He slackened his
pace, and was speedily joined by a youth well known to him, a gentleman of some fortune in that remote country, and who had been abroad
upon the same errand with himself. Young Earnscliff, "of that ilk,"
had lately come of age, and succeeded to a moderate fortune, a good
deal dilapidated, from the share his family had taken in the disturb-
ances of the period. They were much and generally respected in the
country, a reputation which this young gentleman seemed likely to
sustain, as he was well educated, and of excellent dispositions.

"Wow! Earnscliff," exclaimed Hobbie, "I am glad to meet your
honour ony gait, and company's blithe on a bare moor like this—it's an
unco bogilly bit—Where hae ye been sporting?"

"Up the Caillie Cleugh, Hobbie," answered Earnscliff, returning
his greeting. "But will our dogs keep the peace, think you?"

"De'il a fear o' mine," said Hobbie, "they have scarce a leg to stand
on.—Odd! the deer's fled the country, I think! I have been as far as
Inger-fell-foot, and de'il a horn has Hobbie seen, excepting three
red-wud raes, that never let me within shot of them, though I gaed a
mile round to get up the wind to them, an' a'.—De'il o' me wad care
mickle, only I wanted some venison to our auld gude-dame.—The
carline, she sits in the neuk yonder, upbye, and cracks about the grand
shooters and hunters lang syne—Odd, I think they hae killed a' the
deer in the kintra, for my part."

"Well, Hobbie, I have shot a fat buck, and sent him to Earnscliff this morning—you shall have half of him for your grandmother."

"Mony thanks to ye, Mr Patrick, ye're kend to a' the kintra for a kind heart. It will do the auld wife's heart gude—mair be token, when she kens it comes frae you—and maist of a', gin ye'll come up and take your share, for I reckon ye are lonesome now in the auld tower, and a' your folk at that weary Edinburgh. I wonder what they can find to do amang a wheen ranks o' stane-houses, wi' slate on the tap o' them, that might live on their ain bonny green hills."

"My education and my sisters' has kept my mother much in Edinburgh for several years," said Earnscliff, "but I promise you I propose to make up for lost time."

"And ye'll rig out the auld tower a bit," said Hobbie, "and live hearty and neighbour-like wi' the auld family friends, as the Laird o' Earnscliff should. I can tell ye, my mother—my grandmother I mean —but, since we lost our ain mother, we ca' her sometimes the tane, and sometimes the tother—but, ony gate, she thinks hersel no that distant connected wi' you."

"Very true, Hobbie, and I will come to the Heugh-foot to dinner to-morrow with all my heart."

"Weel, that's kindly said! We are auld neighbours, an' we were nae kin—and my gude-dame's fain to see you—she clavers aye about your father that was killed lang syne."

"Hush, hush, Hobbie—not a word about that—it's a story better forgotten."

"I dinna ken—if it had chanced amang our folk, we wad hae keepit it in mind mony a day till we got some mends for it—But ye ken your ain ways best, ye lairds—I have heard say that Ellieslaw's friend stickit your sire after the laird himsel had mastered his sword."

"Fie, fie, Hobbie; it was a foolish brawl, occasioned by wine and politics—many swords were drawn—it is impossible to say who struck the blow."

"At ony rate, auld Ellieslaw was aiding and abetting, and I am sure if ye were sae disposed as to take amends on him, naebody could say it was wrang, for your father's blood is beneath his nails—and besides there's naebody else left that was concerned to take amends upon, and he's a prelatist and a jacobite into the bargain—I can tell ye the kintra looks for something atween ye."

"O for shame, Hobbie! you that profess religion to stir your friend up to break the law, and take vengeance at his own hand, and in such a bogilly bit too, where we know not what beings may be listening to us!"

"Hush, hush!" said Hobbie, drawing nearer to his companion, "I was na thinking o' the like o' them—But I can guess a wee bit what keeps your hand up, Mr Patrick; we a' ken it's no lack o' courage, but the twa grey een of a bonnie lass, Miss Isbel Vere, that keeps you sae sober."

"I assure you, Hobbie," said his companion, rather angrily, "I assure you you are mistaken; and it is extremely wrong in you, either to think of, or to utter, such an idea; I have no idea of permitting freedoms to be carried so far as to connect my name with that of any young lady."

"Why, there now—there now!" retorted Elliot; "did not I say it was nae want o' spunk that made ye sae mim?—Weel, weel, I meant nae offence—but there's just ae thing ye may notice frae a friend. The auld Laird of Ellieslaw has the auld riding blood far hetter at his heart than ye hae—troth, he kens naething about thae new-fangled notions o' peace and quietness—he's a' for the auld-warld doings o' lifting and laying on, and he has a wheen stout lads at his back too, and keeps them weel up in heart, and as fu' o' mischief as young colts. Where he gets the gear to do't nane can say—he lives high, and far abune his rents here—however, he pays his way—Sae, if there's ony outbreak in the country, he's likely to break out wi' the first—and weel does he mind the auld quarrels between ye. I'm surmizing he'll be for a touch at the auld tower at Earnscliff."

"Well, Hobbie, if he should be so ill advised, I shall try to make the old tower good against him, as it has been made good by my betters against his betters many a day ago."

"Very right—very right—that's speaking like a man now—and, if sae should be that this be sae, if ye'll just gar your servant jow out the great bell in the tower, there's me, and my twa brothers, and little Davie o' the Stenhouse, will be wi' you, wi' a' the power we can make, in the snapping of a flint."

"Many thanks, Hobbie; but I hope we shall have no war of so unnatural and unchristian a kind in our time."

"Hout, sir, hout; it wad be but a wee bit neighbour war, and Heaven and earth would make allowances for it in this uncultivated place—it's just the nature o' the folk and the land—we canna live quiet like Loudon folk—we hae nae sae muckle to do."

"Well, Hobbie, for one who believes so deeply as you do in super-natural appearances, I must own you take Heaven in your own hand rather audaciously, considering where we are walking."

"What needs I care for the Meikle-stane-Moor ony mair than ye do yoursel, Earnscliff? to be sure they say there's a sort o' worricows and lang-nebbit things about the land, but what need I care for them? I hae a good conscience, unless it be about a rant amang the lasses, or a splore at a fair, and that's no muckle to speak of. I am, though I say it mysel, as quiet a lad and as peaceable"——

"And Dick Turnbull's head that you broke, and Willie of Winton whom you shot at?"

"Hout, Earnscliff, ye keep a record of a' men's misdoings—Dick's head's healed again, and we're to fight out the quarrel at Jeddart, on the Rood-day, so that's like a thing settled in a peaceable way; and than I am friends wi' Willie again, puir chield—it was but twa or three hail-draps after a'.—I wad let ony body do the like o't to me for a pint o' brandy. But Willie's lowland bred, puir fallow, and soon frighted for himsel.—And, for the worricows, were we to meet ane on this very bit"——

"As is not unlikely," said young Earnscliff, "for there stands your old witch, Hobbie."

"I say," continued Elliot, as if indignant at this hint—"I say, if the auld carline hersel was to get up out of the grund just before us here, I would think nae mair——But, gude preserve us, Earnscliff, what can yon be?"——

Chapter Three

Brown dwarf, that o'er the moorland strays,
    Thy name to Keeldar tell!
"The Brown Man of the moor, that stays
    Beneath the heather-bell."
               JOHN LEYDEN

THE OBJECT which alarmed the young farmer in the middle of his valorous protestations, startled for a moment even his less-prejudiced companion. The moon, which had arisen during their conversation, was, in the phrase of that country, wading or struggling with clouds, and shed only a doubtful and occasional light. By one of her beams, which streamed upon the great granite column, to which they now approached, they discovered a form, apparently human, but of a size much less than ordinary, which moved slowly among the large grey stones, not like a person intending to journey onward, but with the slow, irregular, flitting movement of a being who hovers around some spot of melancholy recollection, uttering also, from time to time, a sort of indistinct muttering sound. This so much resembled his idea of the motions of an apparition, that Hobbie Elliot, making a dead pause, while his hair erected itself upon his scalp, whispered to his companion—"It's auld Ailie hersel! Shall I gi'e her a shot, in the name of God?"

"For Heaven's sake, no," said his companion, holding down the weapon which he was about to raise to the aim—"for Heaven's sake, no; it's some poor distracted creature."

"Distracted yoursel, for thinking of going sae near to her," said Elliot, holding his companion, in his turn, as he prepared to advance. "We'll aye hae time to pit ower a bit prayer (an' I could but mind ane) afore she comes this length—God! she's in nae hurry," continued he, growing bolder from his companion's confidence, and the little notice the apparition seemed to take of them. "She hirples like a hen on a het girdle—I redd ye, Earnscliff," (this he added in a gentle whisper,) "let us take a cast about, as if to draw the wind on a buck—the bog is no abune knee-deep, and better a saft road as bad company."

Earnscliff, however, in spite of his companion's resistance and remonstrances, continued to advance on the path they had originally pursued, and soon confronted the object of their investigation.

The height of the object, which seemed even to decrease as they approached it, appeared to be under four feet, and its form, so far as the imperfect light afforded them the means of discerning, was very nearly as broad as long, or rather of a spherical shape, which could only be occasioned by some strange personal deformity. The young sportsman hailed this extraordinary appearance twice, without receiving any answer, or attending to the pinches by which his companion endeavoured to intimate that their best course was to walk on, without giving farther disturbance to a being of such singular and preternatural exterior. To the third repeated demand of "Who are you? What do you do here at this hour of night?"—a voice replied, whose shrill, uncouth, and dissonant tones made Elliot step two paces back, and startled even his companion, "Pass on your way, and ask nought at them that ask nought at you."

"What do you do here so far from shelter? Are you benighted on your journey? Will you follow us home, ('God forbid,' ejaculated Hobbie Elliot, involuntarily) and I will give you a lodging."

"I would sooner lodge by mysel in the deepest of the Tarras-flow," again whispered Hobbie.

"Pass on your way," rejoined the figure, the harsh tones of his voice still more exalted by passion. "I want not your guidance—I want not your lodging—it is five years since my head was under a human roof, and I trust it was for the last time."

"He is mad," said Earnscliff—"He has a look of auld Humphrey Ettercap, the tinkler, that perished in this very moss about five years syne," answered his superstitious companion; "but Humphrey was a thought bigger in the bouk."

"Pass on your way," reiterated the object of their curiosity, "the breath of your human bodies poisons the air around me—the sound of your human voices goes through my ears like sharp bodkins."

"Lord safe us!" said Hobbie, "that the dead should bear sic fearfu' ill-will to the living!—his saul maun be in a puir way, I am jealous."

"Come, my friend," said Earnscliff, "you seem to suffer under some strong affliction; common humanity will not allow us to leave you here."

"Common humanity!" exclaimed the being, with a scornful laugh that sounded like a shriek, "where got ye that catch-word—that noose for woodcocks—that common disguise for man-traps—that bait which the wretched idiot who swallows, will soon find covers a hook with barbs ten times sharper than those you lay for the animals which you murder for your luxury!"

"I tell you, my friend," again replied Earnscliff, "you are incapable to judge of your own situation—you will perish in this wilderness, and we must, in compassion, force you along with us."

"I'll hae neither hand nor foot in it," said Hobbie; "let the ghaist take his ain way, for God's sake."

"My blood be on my own head, if I perish here," said the figure; and, observing Earnscliff meditated laying hold on him, he added, "and your blood be upon yours, if you touch but the skirt of my garment to infect me with the taint of mortality!"

The moon shone more brightly as he spoke thus, and Earnscliff observed that he held out his right hand armed with some weapon of offence, which glittered in the cold ray like the blade of a long knife, or the barrel of a pistol. It would have been madness to persevere in his attempt upon a being thus armed, and holding such desperate language, especially as it was plain he would have little aid from his companion, who had fairly left him to settle matters with the apparition as he could, and had proceeded a few paces on his way homeward. Earnscliff, therefore, turned and followed Hobbie, often looking back towards the supposed maniac, who, as if raised to frenzy by the interview, roamed wildly around the great stone, exhausting his voice in shrieks and imprecations that thrilled wildly along the waste heath.

The two sportsmen moved on some time in silence, until they were out of hearing of these uncouth sounds, which was not ere they had gained a considerable distance from the pillar which gave name to the moor. Each made his private comments on the scene they had witnessed, until Hobbie Elliot suddenly exclaimed, "Weel, I'll uphaud that yon ghaist, if it be a ghaist, has baith done and suffered muckle evil in the flesh, that gars him rampauge in that way after he is dead and gane."

"It seems to me the very madness of misanthropy," said Earnscliff, following his own current of thought.

"And ye didna think it was a spiritual creature, then?" asked Hobbie at his companion.

"Who, I?—No, surely."

"Weel, I am partly of the mind mysel that it may be a live thing—and yet I dinna ken, I wadna wish to see ony thing look liker a bogle."

"At any rate," said Earnscliff, "I will ride over to-morrow, and see what has become of that unhappy being."

"In fair day-light?" queried the yeoman, "then, grace o' God, Earnscliff, I'se be wi' ye. But here we are nearer to Heugh-foot than to your house by twa mile. Hadna ye better e'en gae hame wi' me, and we'll send the callant on the powney to tell them that you are wi' us, though I believe there's naebody at hame to wait for you but the servants and the cat."

"And I would not willingly have either the servants be anxious, or puss forfeit her supper, in my absence. I'll be obliged to you to send the boy as you propose."

"And you'll gae hame to Heugh-foot. They'll be right blithe to see you, that will they."

This affair settled, they walked briskly on a little farther, when, coming to the ridge of a pretty steep hill, Hobbie Elliot exclaimed, "Now, Earnscliff, I am aye glad when I come to this very bit—Ye see the light below, that's in the ha' window, where grannie, the gash auld carline, is sitting birling at her wheel—and ye see yon other light that's gaun whiddin' back and forrit through amang the windows? that's my cousin, Grace Armstrong,—she's twice as clever about the house as my sisters, and sae they say themsels, for they're good-natured lasses as ever trod on heather; but they confess themsels, and sae does grannie, that she has far maist action—is the best goer in the toun— now that grannie is off the foot hersel—My brothers, ane o' them's awa to wait upon the Chamberlain, and ane's at Mossphadraig, that's our led farm—he can see after the stock as weel as I can do."

"You are lucky, my good friend, in having so many valuable relations."

"Troth am I—grace make me thankful, I'se never deny it.—But will ye tell me now, Earnscliff, that has been at college, and the high-school of Edinburgh, and got a' sort o' lair where it was to be best gotten—will you tell me—no that it's ony concern of mine in particular, but I heard the priest of St John's, and our minister, bargaining about it at the Winter fair, and troth they baith spake very weel—Now, the priest says it's unlawful to marry ane's cousin; but I canna say I thought he brought out the Gospel authorities half sae weel as our minister—our minister is thought the best divine and the best preacher atween this and Edinburgh—Dinna ye think he was likely to be right?"

"Certainly marriage, by all protestant Christians, is held to be as free as God made it by the Levitical law; so, Hobbie, there can be no bar, legal or religious, betwixt you and Miss Armstrong."

"Hout awa wi' your daffing, Earnscliff—ye are sae angry yoursel if ane touches you a bit, man, on the sooth side of the jest—No that I was asking the question about Grace, for ye maun ken she's no my cousin-german out and out, but the daughter of my uncle's wife by her first marriage, so she's nae kith nor kin to me—only a connection like.— But now we are at the sheeling-hill—I'll fire off my gun, to let them ken I'm coming, that's aye my way; and if I hae a deer I gie them twa shots, ane for the deer and ane for mysel."

He fired off his piece accordingly, and a number of lights were seen to traverse the house, and even to gleam before it. Hobbie Elliot pointed out one of these to Earnscliff, which seemed to glide from the house towards some of the out-houses—"That's Grace, hersel," said Hobbie. "She'll no meet me at the door, I'se warrant her—but she'll be awa', for a' that, to see if my hounds' supper be ready, puir tykes."

"Love me, love my dog," answered Earnscliff. "Ah, Hobbie, you are a lucky young fellow."

This observation was uttered with something like a sigh, which apparently did not escape the ear of his companion.

"Hout, other folk may be as lucky as I am—O how I have seen Miss Isbel Vere's head turn after somebody when they passed ane another at the Carlisle races! Wha kens how things come round in this world?"

Earnscliff muttered something like an answer; but whether in assent of the proposition, or rebuking the application of it, could not easily be discovered; and it seems probable that the speaker himself was willing to leave his meaning in doubt and obscurity. They had now descended the broad loaning, which, winding round the foot of the steep bank, or heugh, brought them in front of the thatched, but comfortable, farm-house, which was the dwelling of Hobbie Elliot and his family.

The door-way was thronged with joyful faces; but the appearance of a stranger blunted many a jibe which had been prepared on Hobbie's lack of success in the deer-stalking. There was a little bustle among three handsome young women, each endeavouring to devolve upon another the task of ushering the stranger into the apartment, while probably all were anxious to escape to make some little personal arrangements before presenting themselves to a young gentleman in a dishabille only intended for brother Hobbie.

Hobbie, in the meanwhile, bestowing some hearty and general abuse upon them all, (for Grace was not of the party,) snatched the candle from the hand of one of the rustic coquettes, as she stood playing pretty with it in her hand, and ushered his guest into the family parlour, or rather hall; for the place having been a house of defence in former times, the sitting apartment was a vaulted and paved room, damp and dismal enough compared with the lodgings of the yeomanry of our days, but which, when well lighted up with a large sparkling fire of turf and bog-wood, seemed to Earnscliff a most comfortable exchange for the darkness and bleak blast of the hill. Kindly and repeatedly was he welcomed by the venerable old dame, the mistress of the family, who, dressed in her coif and pinners, her close and decent gown of home-spun wool, but with a large gold necklace and ear-rings, looked, what she really was, the lady as well as the farm house-wife, as, seated in her chair of wicker, by the corner of the great chimney, she directed the evening occupations of the young women, and of two or three stout serving wenches, who sate plying their distaffs behind the backs of their young mistresses.

As soon as Earnscliff had been duly welcomed, and hasty orders issued for some addition to the evening meal, his grandame and sisters opened their battery upon Hobbie Elliot for his lack of success against the deer.

"Jenny needna have kept up her kitchen fire for a' that Hobbie has brought hame," said one sister.

"Troth no, lass," said another; "the gathering peat, if it was weel blawn, wad dress a' our Hobbie's venison."

"Aye, or the low of the candle if the wind wad let it bide steady," said a third; "if I were him I would bring hame a black craw, rather than come back three times without a buck's horn to blaw on."

Hobbie turned from the one to the other, regarding them alternately with a frown on his brow, the augury of which was confuted by the good-humoured laugh on the lower part of his countenance. He then strove to propitiate them, by mentioning the intended present of his companion.

"In my young days," said the old lady, "a man wad hae been ashamed to come back frae the hill without a buck hanging on each side o' his horse, like a cadger carrying calves."

"I wish they had left some for us then, grannie," retorted Hobbie; "they've cleared the country o' them, thae auld friends o' yours, I'm thinking."

"Ye see other folk can find game, though you cannot, Hobbie," said the eldest sister, glancing a look at young Earnscliff.

"Weel, weel, woman, has nae every dog his day, begging Earns-cliff's pardon for the auld saying—Mayna I hae his luck, and he mine, another time?—It's a braw thing for a man to be out a' day, and frighted—na, I winna say that neither—but mistrysted wi' bogles in the hame coming, and then to hae to flyte wi' a wheen women that hae been doing naething in the live-lang day but whirling a bit stick, wi' a thread trailing at it, or boring at a clout."

"Frighted wi' bogles!" exclaimed the females, one and all, for great was the regard then paid, and perhaps still paid, in these glens to all such fantasies.

"I did not say frighted, now—I only said mis-set wi' the thing—And there was but ae bogle, neither—Earnscliff, you saw it as weel as I did."

And he proceeded, without very much exaggeration, to detail, in his own way, the meeting they had with the mysterious being at Meikle-stane-Moor, concluding, he could not conjecture what on earth it could be, unless it was either the Enemy himsel, or some of the auld Peghts that held the country lang syne.

"Auld Peght!" exclaimed the grandame; "na, na—bless thee frae scathe, my bairn, it's been nae Peght that—it's been the Brown Man of the Moors! O weary fa' thae evil days!—what can evil beings be coming for to distract a poor country, now it's peacefully settled, and living in luve and law?—O weary on him! he ne'er brought gude to these lands or the indwellers. My father aften tauld me he was seen in the year o' the bluidy fight at Marston-Moor, and than again in Mont-rose's troubles, and again before the rout o' Dunbar, and, in my ain time, he was seen about the time o' Bothwell-Brigg, and they said the second-sighted Laird of Benarbuck had a communing wi' him some time afore Argyle's landing, but that I canna speak to sae preceesely—it was far in the west.—O, bairns, he's never permitted but in an ill time, sae mind ilka ane o' ye to draw to Him that can help in the day of trouble."

Earnscliff now interposed, and expressed his firm conviction that the person they had seen was some poor maniac, and had no commission from the invisible world to announce either war or evil. But his opinion found a very cold audience, and all joined to deprecate his purpose of returning to the spot the next day.

"O, my bonnie bairn," said the old dame, (for, in the kindness of her heart, she extended her parental style to all in whom she was interested)—"You should beware mair than other folk—there's been a heavy breach made in your house wi' your father's bloodshed, and wi' law-pleas and losses sinsyne—and you are the flower of the flock, and the lad that will build up the auld bigging again (if it be HIS will)

to be an honour to the country, and a safeguard to those that dwell in it
—and you by others are called on to put yoursel in no rash ventures—
for yours was aye ower venturesome a race, and muckle they got by it."

"But I am sure, my good friend, you would not have me be afraid of
going to an open moor in broad day-light?"

"I dinna ken—I wad never bid son or friend o' mine haud their
hand back in a gude cause, whether it were a friend's or their ain—that
suld be by nae bidding of mine, or of ony body that's come of a gentle
kindred—But it winna gang out of a grey pow like mine, that to gang
to seek for evil that's no fashing wi' you, is clean against law and
Scripture."

Earnscliff resigned an argument which he saw no prospect of main-
taining with good effect, and the entrance of supper broke off the
conversation. Miss Grace had by this time made her appearance, and
Hobbie, not without a conscious glance at Earnscliff, placed himself
by her side. Mirth and lively conversation, in which the old lady of the
house took the good-humoured share which so well becomes old age,
restored to the cheeks of the damsels the roses which their brother's
tale of the apparition had chaced away, and they danced and sung for
an hour after supper as if there were no such things as goblins in the
world.

Chapter Four

I am Misanthropos, and hate mankind;
For thy part, I do wish thou wert a dog,
That I might love thee something.
        Timon of Athens

ON THE MORNING, after breakfast, Earnscliff took leave of his hos-
pitable friends, promising to return in time to partake of the venison,
which had arrived from his house. Hobbie, who apparently took leave
of him at the door of his habitation, slunk out, however, and joined
him at the top of the hill.

"Ye'll be gaun yonder, Mr Patrick; feind o' me will mistryst you for
a' my mother says. I thought it best to slip out quietly though, in case
she should mislippen something of what we're gaun to do—we
maunna vex her at nae rate—it was amaist the last word my father said
to me on his death-bed."

"By no means, Hobbie," said Earnscliff; "she well merits all your
attention."

"Troth, for that matter, she would be as sair vexed amaist for you as
for me—but d'ye really think there's nae presumption in venturing

back yonder?—We hae nae special commission, ye ken."

"If I thought as you do, Hobbie, I would not perhaps enquire farther into this business; but as I am of opinion that preternatural visitations are either ceased altogether, or become very rare in our days, I am unwilling to leave a matter uninvestigated which may concern the life of a poor distracted being."

"Aweel, aweel, if ye really think that," answered Hobbie doubtfully —"And it's for certain the very fairies—I mean the very good neighbours themsells (for they say folk suldna ca' them fairies) that used to be seen on every green knowe at e'en, are nae half sae often visible in our days. I canna depone to having ever seen ane mysel, but I ance heard ane whistle ahint me in the moss, as like a whaup as ae thing could be like anither. And mony ane my father saw when he used to come hame frae the fairs at e'en, wi' a drap drink in his head, honest man."

Earnscliff was somewhat entertained with the gradual declension of superstition from one generation to another, which was inferred in this last observation; and they continued to reason on such subjects, until they came in sight of the upright stone which gave name to the moor.

"As I shall answer," says Hobbie, "yonder's the creature creeping about yet!—But it's day-light, and you have your gun, and I brought out my wee-bit whinger—I think we may venture upon him."

"By all manner of means," said Earnscliff; "but, in the name of wonder, what can he be doing there?"

"Biggin a dry-stane dyke, I think, wi' the grey geese, as they ca' thae great loose stanes—Odd, that passes a' thing I e'er heard tell of."

As they approached nearer, Earnscliff could not help agreeing with his companion. The figure they had seen the night before seemed slowly and toilsomely labouring to pile the large stones one upon another, as if to form a small inclosure. Materials lay around him in great plenty, but the labour of carrying on the work was immense, from the size of some of the stones; and it seemed astonishing that he should have succeeded in moving several which already formed the foundation of his edifice. He was struggling to remove a fragment of great size, when the two young men came up, and was so intent upon executing his purpose, that he did not perceive them until they were close upon him. In straining and heaving at the stone, in order to arrange it in his own way, he displayed a degree of strength which seemed inconsistent with his size and apparent deformity. Indeed, to judge from the difficulties he had already surmounted, he must have been of Herculean powers; for some of the stones he had succeeded in raising must apparently have required two men's strength to move them. Hobbie's suspicions began to revive, on seeing the preter-natural strength he had exerted.

"I am amaist persuaded it's the ghaist of a stane-mason—see siccan band-stanes as he's laid—An' it be a man, after a', I wonder what he wad take by the rood to build my march-dyke. There's ane sair wanted between Cringlehope and the Shaws.—Honest man, (raising his voice,) ye make gude firm wark there."

The being whom he addressed raised his eyes with a ghastly stare, and getting up from his stooping posture, stood before them in all his native deformity. His head was of immense size, covered with a fell of shaggy black hair, partly grizzled with age; his eye-brows, shaggy and prominent, overhung a pair of small, dark, piercing eyes, set far back in their sockets, that rolled with a portentous wildness, indicative of partial insanity. The rest of his features were of the coarse, rough-hewn stamp with which a painter would equip a giant in a romance, to which was added, the wild, irregular, and peculiar expression so often seen in the countenances of those whose persons are deformed. His body, thick and round, like that of a man of middle size, was mounted upon two large feet; but nature seemed to have forgotten the legs and the thighs, or they were so very short as to be hidden by the dress which he wore. His arms were long and brawny, furnished with two muscular hands, and where uncovered in the eagerness of his labour, were shagged with coarse black hair. It seemed as if nature had origin-ally intended the separate parts of his body to be the members of a giant, but had afterward capriciously assigned them to the person of a dwarf, so ill did the length of his arms and the iron strength of his frame correspond with the shortness of his stature. His cloathing was a sort of coarse brown tunic, like a monk's frock, girt round him with a belt of seal-skin. On his head he had a cap made of badger's skin, or some other rough fur, which added considerably to the grotesque effect of his whole appearance, and overshadowed features, whose habitual expression seemed that of sullen malignant misanthropy. This remarkable Dwarf gazed on the two youths in silence, with a dogged and irritated look, until Earnscliff, willing to sooth him into better temper, observed—"You are hard tasked, my friend; allow us to assist you."

Elliot and he accordingly placed the stone, by their joint efforts, upon the rising wall. The Dwarf watched them with the eye of a taskmaster, and testified, by petted gestures, his impatience at the time which they took in adjusting the stone. He pointed to another —they raised it also——to a third—to a fourth—they continued to humour him, though with some trouble, for he assigned them, as if intentionally, the heaviest fragments which lay near. "And now, friend," said Elliot, as the unreasonable Dwarf indicated another stone larger than any they had yet moved, "Earnscliff may do as he likes; but be ye man, or be ye waur, de'il be in my fingers if I break my back wi' heaving thae stanes ony langer like a barrow-man, without getting sae muckle as thanks for my pains."

"Thanks!" exclaimed the Dwarf, with a motion expressive of the utmost contempt—"There—take them, and fatten upon them!—take them, and may they thrive with you as they have done with me—as they have done with every mortal worm that ever heard the word spoken by his fellow reptile!—Hence—either labour or begone."

"This is a fine reward we have, Earnscliff, for building a tabernacle for the devil, and prejudicing our ain souls into the bargain, for what I ken."

"Our presence," answered Earnscliff, "seems only to irritate his frenzy; we had better leave him, and send some one to provide him with food and necessaries."

They did so. The servant dispatched for this purpose found the Dwarf still labouring at his wall, but could not extract a word from him. The lad, infected with the superstitions of the country, did not long persist in an attempt to intrude questions or advice on so singular a figure, but placing the articles which he had brought for his use on a stone at some distance, left them at the misanthrope's disposal.

The Dwarf proceeded in his labours, day after day, with an assiduity so incredible as to appear almost supernatural. In one day he often seemed to have done the work of two men, and his building soon assumed the appearance of the walls of a hut, which, though very small, and constructed only of stones and turf, without any mortar, exhibited, from the unusual size of the stones employed, an appearance of solidity very uncommon for a cottage of such narrow dimensions and rude construction. Earnscliff, attentive to his motions, no sooner perceived to what they tended, than he sent down a number of spars of wood suitable for forming the roof, which he caused to be left in the neighbourhood of the spot, resolving next day to send workmen to put them up. But his purpose was anticipated, for in the evening, during the night, and early in the morning, the Dwarf had laboured so hard, and with such ingenuity, that he had nearly completed the adjustment of the rafters. His next labour was to cut rushes and thatch his dwelling, a task which he performed with singular dexterity. As he seemed so averse to receive any aid beyond the occasional assistance of a passenger, materials suitable to his purpose, and tools, were supplied to him, in the use of which he proved to be skilful. He constructed the door and window of his cot, he adjusted a rude bed-stead, and a few shelves, and appeared to become somewhat soothed in his temper as his accommodations increased.

His next task was to form a strong inclosure, and to labour the land within it to the best of his power, until, by transporting mould and working up what was upon the spot, he formed a patch of garden-ground. It must be naturally supposed, that, as above hinted, this solitary being received assistance occasionally from such travellers as crossed the moor by chance, as well as from several who went from curiosity to visit his works. It was, indeed, impossible to see a human being, so unfitted by nature for hard labour, toiling with such unremitting assiduity, without aiding him in his task; and, as no one of his occasional assistants was acquainted with the help which the Dwarf had received from others, the celerity of his progress lost none of its marvels in their eyes. The strong and compact appearance of the cottage and its garden, formed in so very short a space and by such a being, the superior skill which he displayed in mechanics, and in other arts, gave suspicion to the surrounding neighbours. They insisted, that, if he was not a phantom,—an opinion which was now abandoned, since he had plainly appeared a being of blood and bone with themselves,—yet he must be in close league with the invisible world, and have chosen that sequestered spot to carry on his communication with them undisturbed. They insisted, that, though in a different sense from the philosopher's application of the phrase, he was never less alone than when alone; and that from the heights which commanded the moor at a distance, passengers often discovered a person at work along with this dweller of the desert, but who regularly disappeared as soon as they approached closer to the cottage. Such a figure was also said to have been occasionally seen sitting beside him at the door, walking with him on the moor, or assisting him in fetching the water from his fountain. Earnscliff explained this phænomenon by supposing it to be the Dwarf's shadow.

"De'il a shadow has he," replied Hobbie Elliot, who was a strenuous defender of the general opinion; "he's ower far in wi' the Auld Ane to have a shadow. Besides," he argued more logically, "whaever heard of a shadow that came between a body and the sun? and this thing, be it what it will, is bigger and taller than the body himsel, and has been seen to come between him and the sun mair than anes or twice either."

These suspicions, which, in any other part of the country, would have been attended with investigations a little inconvenient to the supposed wizard, were here only productive of respect and awe. The recluse being seemed somewhat gratified by the marks of timid veneration with which the wanderer approached his dwelling, the look of startled surprise with which he surveyed his person and his premises, and the hurried step with which he pressed his retreat as he passed the awful spot. The bolder only stopped to gratify their curiosity by a hasty glance at the walls of his cottage and garden, apologized for by a courteous salutation, which the inmate sometimes deigned to return by a word or a nod. Earnscliff often passed that way, and seldom without enquiring after the Solitary, who seemed now to have arranged his establishment for life.

No efforts could engage him in any conversation on his own personal affairs; nor was he communicative or accessible in talking on any other subject whatsoever, although he seemed to have considerably relented in the extreme ferocity of his misanthropy, or rather to be less frequently visited with the fits of derangement of which this was a symptom. No argument could prevail upon him to accept any thing beyond the simplest necessaries, although much was offered, by Earnscliff out of charity, and by his more superstitious neighbours from other motives. The benefits of these last he repaid by advice, when consulted on their diseases, or those of their cattle. He often furnished them with medicines also, and seemed possessed, not only of such as are the produce of the country, but of foreign drugs. He gave these persons to understand that his name was Elshender the Recluse; but his popular epithet soon came to be Canny Elshie, or the Wise Wight of Meikle-stane. Some extended their queries beyond their bodily complaints, and requested advice upon other matters, which he delivered with an oracular shrewdness that greatly confirmed the opinion of his possessing preternatural skill. The querists usually left some offering upon a stone, at a distance from his dwelling; if it was money, or any article which did not suit him to accept, he either threw it away, or suffered it to remain where it was left without making use of it. On all these occasions his manners were rude and unsocial; and his words, in number, just sufficient to express his meaning as briefly as possible, and he shunned all communication that went a syllable beyond the matter in hand. When winter had passed away, and his garden began to afford him herbs and vegetables, he confined himself almost entirely to these articles of food. He accepted, notwithstanding, a pair of she-goats from Earnscliff, which fed on the moor, near his dwelling, and supplied him with milk.

When Earnscliff found his gift had been received, he soon afterwards paid the hermit a visit. The old man was seated on a broad flat stone near his garden-door, which was the seat of science he usually occupied when disposed to receive his patients or clients. The inside of his hut, and that of his garden, he kept as sacred from human intrusion as the natives of Otaheite do their Morai. Apparently he would have deemed it polluted by the step of any human being. When he shut himself up in his habitation, no entreaty could prevail upon him to make himself visible, or to give audience to any one whomsoever.

Earnscliff had been fishing in a small river at some distance. He had his rod in his hand, and his basket with his trouts at his shoulder. He sate down upon a stone nearly opposite to the Dwarf, who, familiarized with his presence, took no farther notice of him than by elevating his huge mis-shapen head for the purpose of staring at him, and then again sinking it upon his bosom, as if in profound meditation. Earnscliff looked around him, and observed that the hermit had increased his accommodations by the construction of a shed for the reception of his goats.

"You labour hard, Elshie," said he, willing to lead this singular being into conversation.

"Labour," re-echoed the Dwarf, "is the mildest evil of a lot so miserable as that of mankind; better to labour like me, than sport like you."

"I cannot defend the humanity of our ordinary rural sports, Elshie, and yet"——

"And yet," interrupted the Dwarf, "they are better than your ordinary business; better exercise idle and wanton curiosity on mute fishes than on your fellow-creatures. Yet why should I say so? Why should not the whole human herd butt, gore, and gorge upon each other, till all are extirpated but one huge and over-fed Behemoth, and he, when he had throttled and gnawed the bones of all his fellows—he, when his prey failed him, to lie roaring whole days for lack of food, and, finally, to die inch by inch of famine—it were a consummation worthy of the race!"

"Your deeds are better, Elshie, than your words," answered Earnscliff; "you assist to preserve the race that your misanthropy slanders."

"I do; but why?—Hearken. You are one on whom I look with the least loathing, and I care not, if, contrary to my wont, I waste a few words in compassion to your infatuated blindness. If I cannot send disease into families, and murrain among the herds, can I attain the same end so well as by prolonging the lives of those who can serve the purpose of destruction as effectually?—If Alice of Bower had died in winter, would young Ruthwin have been slain for her love this last spring?—Who thought of penning their cattle beneath the tower when the Red Reiver of Westburnflat lay on his death-bed?—My draughts, my skill recovered him. And, now, who dare leave his herd upon the lea without a watch, or go to sleep without unchaining the sleuth-hound?"

"True," answered Earnscliff, "you did little good to society by the last of these cures. But, to balance the evil, there is my friend Hobbie, honest Hobbie of the Heugh-foot, your skill relieved him last winter in a fever that might have cost his life."

"Thus think the children of clay in their ignorance," said the Dwarf, smiling maliciously, "and thus they speak in their folly. Have you marked the young cub of a wild-cat that has been domesticated, how sportive, how gamesome, how gentle,—but trust him with your game, your lambs, your poultry, his inbred ferocity breaks forth; he gripes, tears, ravages, and devours."

"Such is the animal's instinct," answered Earnscliff; "but what has that to do with Hobbie?"

"It is his emblem—it is his picture," rejoined the Recluse. "He is at present tame, quiet, and domesticated, for lack of opportunity to exercise his inborn propensities; but let the trumpet of war sound— let the young blood-hound snuff blood, he will be as ferocious as the wildest of his Border ancestors that ever fired a helpless peasant's hay-stack. Can you deny, that even at present he often urges you to take bloody revenge for an injury received when you were a boy?" (Earnscliff started; the Recluse appeared not to observe his surprise, and proceeded.) "And the trumpet *will* blow, the young blood-hound shall lap blood, and I will laugh and say, For this I preserved thee!" He paused, and continued,—"Such are my cures;—their object—their purpose, perpetuating the mass of misery, and playing even in this desert my part in the general tragedy. Were *you* on your sick-bed, I might, in compassion, send you a cup of poison."

"I am much obliged to you, Elshie, and certainly shall not fail to consult you with so comfortable a hope from your assistance."

"Do not flatter yourself too far," replied the Hermit, "with the hope that I will positively yield to the frailty of pity. Why should I snatch a dupe, so well fitted to endure the miseries of life as you are, from the wretchedness which his own visions, and the villainy of the world, are preparing for him?—Why should I play the compassionate Indian, and, knocking out the brains of the captive with my tomahawk at once, spoil the three days' amusement of my kindred tribe, at the very moment when the brands were lighted, the pincers heated, the cauldrons boiling, the knives sharpened, to tear, scorch, seethe, and scarify the intended victim?"

"A dreadful picture you present to me of life, Elshie, but I am not daunted by it," returned Earnscliff. "We are sent here in one sense to bear and to suffer, but in another to do and to enjoy. The active day has its evening of repose; even patient sufferance has its alleviations where there is a consolatory sense of duty discharged."

"I spurn at the slavish and bestial doctrine," said the Dwarf, his eyes kindling with insane fury,—"I spurn at it as worthy only of the beasts that perish—But I will waste no more words with you."

He rose hastily; but, ere he withdrew into the hut, he added, with great vehemence, "Yet, lest you still think my apparent benefits to mankind flow from the stupid and servile source, called love of our fellow-creatures, know, that were there a man who had annihilated my soul's dearest hope—who had torn my heart to mammocks, and seared my brain till it glowed like a volcano, and were that man's fortune and life in my power as completely as this frail pot-sherd," (he snatched up an earthen cup which stood beside him,) "I would not dash him into atoms thus—" (he flung the vessel with fury against the wall.) "No!" (he spoke more composedly, but with the utmost bitterness,) "I would pamper him with wealth and power to inflame his evil passions, and to fulfil his evil designs; he should lack no means of vice and villainy; he should be the centre of a whirlpool that should itself know neither rest nor peace, but boil with unceasing fury, while it wrecked every goodly ship that approached its limits! he should be an earthquake capable of shaking the very land in which he dwelt, and rendering all its inhabitants childless, outcast, and miserable, as I am!"

The wretched being rushed into his hut as he uttered these last words, shutting the door with furious violence, and rapidly drawing two bolts, one after another, as if to exclude the intrusion of any one of that hated race, who had thus lashed his soul to frenzy. Earnscliff left the moor with a mingling sensation of pity and horror, pondering what strange and melancholy cause could have reduced to such a miserable state of mind, a man whose language argued him to be of rank and education much superior to the vulgar. He was also surprised to see how much particular information a person who had lived in that country so short a time, and in so recluse a manner, had been able to collect about the dispositions and private affairs of the inhabitants.

"It is no wonder," he said to himself, "that with such extent of information, such a mode of life, so uncouth a figure, and sentiments so virulently misanthropic, this unfortunate should be regarded by the vulgar as in league with the Enemy of Mankind."

Chapter Five

The bleakest rock upon the loneliest heath
Feels, in its barrenness, some touch of spring;
And, in the April dew, or beam of May,
Its moss and lichen freshen and revive;
And thus the heart, most seared to human pleasure,
Melts at the tear, joys in the smile of woman.

BEAUMONT

AS THE SEASON advanced, the weather became more genial, and the Recluse was more frequently found occupying the broad flat stone in the front of his mansion. As he sate there one day, about the hour of noon, a party of gentlemen and ladies, well mounted, and numerously attended, swept across the heath at some distance from his dwelling. Dogs, hawks, and led-horses, swelled the retinue, and the air resounded at intervals with the cheer of the hunters, and the sound of horns blown by the attendants. The Solitary was about to retire into his mansion at the sight of a train so joyous, when three young ladies, with their attendants, who had made a circuit, and detached themselves from their party, in order to gratify their curiosity by a sight of the Wise Wight of Meikle-stane, came suddenly up ere he could effect his purpose. The first shrieked, and put her hands before her eyes, at sight of an object so unusually deformed. The second, with a hysterical giggle, which she intended should disguise her terrors, asked the Recluse, whether he could tell their fortune. The third, who was best mounted, best dressed, and incomparably the best-looked of the three, advanced, as if to cover the incivility of her companions.

"We have lost the right path that leads through these morasses, and our party have gone forward without us," said the young lady. "Seeing you, father, at the door of your house, we turned this way"——

"Hush!" interrupted the Dwarf; "so young and already so artful? You came—you know you came, to exult in the conscience of your own youth, wealth, and beauty, by contrasting them with age, poverty, and deformity. It is a fit employment for the daughter of your father, but how unlike the child of your mother!"

"Did you, then, know my parents, and do you know me?"

"Yes; this is the first time you have crossed my waking eyes, but I have seen you in my dreams."

"Your dreams?"

"Aye, Isabel Vere. What hast thou, or thine, to do with my waking thoughts?"

"Your waking thoughts, sir," said the second of Miss Vere's companions, with a sort of mock gravity, "are fixed, doubtless, upon wisdom; folly can only intrude on your sleeping moments."

"Over thine," retorted the Dwarf, more splenetically than became a philosopher, or hermit, "folly exercises an unlimited empire, asleep or awake."

"Lord bless us!" said the lady, "he's a prophet, sure enough."

"As surely," continued the Recluse, "as thou art a woman—a woman!—I should have said a lady—a fine lady. You asked me to tell your fortune—it is a simple one; an endless chase through life after follies not worth catching, and which, when caught, are successively thrown away—a chase, pursued from the days of tottering infancy to those of old age upon her crutches. Toys and merry-makings in childhood—lovers and dupes in youth—spadille and basto in age, shall succeed each other as objects of pursuit—flowers and butterflies in spring—butterflies and thistle-down in summer—withered leaves in autumn and winter—all pursued, all caught, all flung aside.— Stand apart; your fortune is said."

"All *caught*, however," retorted the laughing fair one, who was a cousin of Miss Vere's; "that's something, Nanny," she continued, turning to the timid damsel who had first approached the Dwarf; "will you not ask your fortune?"

"Not for worlds," said she, drawing back, "I have heard enough of yours."

"Well, then," said Miss Ilderton, offering money to the Dwarf, "I'll pay for mine, as if it were spoken by an oracle to a princess."

"Truth," said the Soothsayer, "can neither be bought nor sold," and he pushed back her proffered offering with morose disdain.

"Well, then," said the lady, "I'll keep my money, Mr Elshender, to assist me in the chase I am to pursue."

"You will need it," replied the cynic; "without it, few pursue successfully, and fewer are themselves pursued.—Stop!" he said to Miss Vere, as her companions moved off, "with you I have more to say. You have what your companions would wish to have, or to be thought to have,—beauty, wealth, station, accomplishment."

"Forgive my following my companions, father; I am proof both to flattery and fortune-telling."

"Stay," continued the Dwarf, with his hand on her horse's rein, "I am no common soothsayer, and I am no flatterer. All the advantages I have detailed, all and each of them have their corresponding evils— unsuccessful love, crossed affections, the gloom of a convent, or an odious alliance. I, who wish ill to all mankind, cannot wish more evil to you, so much is your course of life already crossed by it."

"And if it be, father," said Miss Vere, "let me enjoy the readiest solace of adversity while prosperity is in my power. You are old; you are poor; your habitation is far from human aid, were you ill or in want; your situation, in many respects, exposes you to the suspicions of the vulgar, which are too apt to break out into actions of brutality. Let me think I have mended the lot of one human being; accept of such assistance as I have power to offer; do this for my sake, if not for your own, that, when these evils arise, which you prophesy perhaps too truly, I may not have to reflect, that the hours of my happier time have been passed altogether in vain."

The old man answered with a broken voice, and almost without addressing himself to the young lady.

"Yes, 'tis thus thou should'st think—'tis thus thou should'st speak, if ever human speech and thought kept touch with each other! They do not—they do not—Alas! they cannot. And yet—wait here an instant—stir not till my return." He went to his little garden, and returned with a half-blown rose. "Thou hast made me shed a tear—the first tear which has wet my eye-lid for many a year—for that good deed receive this token of gratitude. It is but a common rose; preserve it, however, and do not part with it. Come to me in your hour of adversity. Show me that rose, and if thy hope be withered as my heart is—if it should be in my wildest and fiercest movements of rage against a hateful world, still it will recal gentler thoughts to my bosom, and perhaps happier prospects to thine. But no message," he exclaimed, rising into his usual mood of misanthropy,—"no message —no go-between! Come thyself; and the heart and the doors that are shut against every other earthly being, shall open to thee and to thy sorrows. And now pass on."

He let go the bridle-rein, and the young lady rode on, after expressing her thanks to this singular being, as well as her surprise at the extraordinary nature of his address would permit, often turning back to look at the Dwarf, who still remained at the door of his habitation, and watched her progress over the moor towards her father's castle of Ellieslaw, until the brow of the hill hid them from his sight.

The ladies, mean time, jested with Miss Vere on the strange interview they had just had with the far-famed Wizard of the Moor. "Isabella has all the luck at home and abroad; her hawk strikes down the black-cock; her eyes wound the gallant; no chance for her poor companions and kinswomen; even the conjurer cannot escape the force of her charms. You should, in compassion, cease to be such an engrosser, my dear Isabel, or at least set up shop and sell off all the goods you do not mean to keep for your own use."

"You shall have them all," replied Miss Vere, "and the conjurer to boot, at a very easy rate."

"No! Nancy shall have the conjurer," said Miss Ilderton, "to supply deficiencies; she's not quite a witch herself, you know."

"Lord, sister," answered the younger Miss Ilderton, "what could I do with so frightful a monster? I kept my eyes shut after once glancing at him; and, I protest, I thought I saw him still, though I winked as close as ever I could."

"That's a pity," said her sister; "ever while you live, Nanny, chuse an admirer whose faults can be hid by winking at them.—Well, then, I must take him myself, I suppose, and put him into mamma's Japan cabinet, in order to shew that Scotland can produce a specimen of mortal clay, moulded into a form ten thousand times uglier than the imaginations of Canton and Pekin, fertile as they are in monsters, have immortalized in porcelain."

"There is something," said Miss Vere, "so melancholy in the situation of this poor man, that I cannot enter into your mirth, Lucy, so readily as usual. If he has no resources, how is he to exist in this waste country, living, as he does, at such a distance from mankind? and, if he has the means of securing occasional assistance, will not the very suspicion that he is possessed of them, expose him to plunder and assassination by some of our unsettled neighbours?"

"But you forget that they say he is a warlock," said Nancy Ilderton.

"And, if his magic diabolical should fail him," rejoined her sister, "I would have him trust to his magic natural, and thrust his enormous head, and most preternatural visage, out at his door or window, full in view of the assailants. The boldest robber that ever rode would hardly bide a second glance of him. Well, I wish I had the use of that Gorgon's head of his only one half hour."

"For what purpose, Lucy?" said Miss Vere.

"O! I would frighten out of the castle that dark, stiff, and stately Sir Frederick Langley, that is so great a favourite with your father, and so little a favourite of your's. I protest I shall be obliged to the Wizard as long as I live, if it were only for the half hour's relief from that man's company which we have gained by deviating from the party to visit Elshie."

"What would you say, then," said Miss Vere, in a low tone, so as not to be heard by the younger sister, who rode before them, the narrow path not admitting of their moving all three abreast; "what would you say, my dearest Lucy, if it were proposed to you to endure his company for life?"

"Say? I would say no, *no*, N O, three times, each louder than another, till they should hear me to Carlisle."

"And Sir Frederick would say then, nineteen nay-says are half a grant."

"That," replied Miss Lucy, "depends entirely on the manner in which the nay-says are said. Mine should have no one grain of concession in them, I promise you."

"But if your father," said Miss Vere, "were to say, Thus do— *or*——"

"I would stand to the consequences of his *or*, were the most cruel father that ever was recorded in romance to fill up the alternative."

"And what if he threatened you with a catholic aunt, an abbess, and a cloister?"

"Then," said Miss Ilderton, "I would threaten him with a protestant son-in-law, and be glad of an opportunity to disobey him for conscience sake. And now that Nanny has cantered on, let me really say, I think you would be excuseable before God and man for resisting this preposterous match by every means in your power. A proud, dark, ambitious man—a caballer against the state—infamous for his avarice and severity—a bad son—a bad brother—unkind and ungenerous to all his relatives—Isabel, I would die rather than have him."

"Don't let my father hear you give me such advice," said Miss Vere, "or adieu to Ellieslaw-Castle."

"And adieu to Ellieslaw-Castle, with all my heart," said Lucy, "if I once saw you fairly out of it, and settled under some kinder protector than he whom nature has given you. O, if my poor father had been in his former health, how gladly would he have received and sheltered you, till this ridiculous and cruel persecution was blown over!"

"Would to God it had been so, my dear Lucy," answered her friend; "but I fear, that, in your father's weak state of health, he would be altogether unable to protect me against the means which would be immediately used for reclaiming the poor fugitive."

"I fear so, indeed," replied Miss Ilderton, "but we will consider and devise something. Now that your father and his guests seem so deeply engaged in some mysterious plot, to judge from the passing and returning of messages, from the strange faces which appear and disappear without being announced by their names, from the collecting and cleaning of arms, and the anxious gloom and bustle which seems to agitate every male in the castle, it may not be impossible for us (always in case matters be driven to extremity) to shape out some little supplemental conspiracy of our own. I hope the gentlemen have not kept all the policy to themselves; and there's one associate that I would gladly admit to our councils."

"Not Nanny?"

"O, no!" said Miss Ilderton; "Nancy, though an excellent good girl, and fondly attached to you, would make a dull conspirator—as dull as Elliot and all the other subordinate plotters in Venice Preserved. No;

this is a Jaffeir, or a Pierre, if you like the character better; and yet, though I know I shall please you, I am afraid to mention his name to you lest I vex you at the same time. Can you not guess? Something about an eagle and a rock; it does not begin with eagle in English, but something very like it in Scotch."

"You cannot mean young Earnscliff, Lucy?" said Miss Vere, blushing deeply.

"And whom else should I mean?" said Lucy. "Jaffeirs and Pierres are very scarce in this country, I take it, though one could find Renaults and Bedamars enow."

"How can you talk so wildly, Lucy? Your plays and romances have positively turned your brain. You know, that, independent of my father's consent, without which I never will marry any one, and which, in the case you point at, would never be granted; independent, too, of our knowing nothing of young Earnscliff's inclinations, but by your own wild conjectures and fancies—besides all this, there is the fatal brawl!"

"When his father was killed?" said Lucy. "But that was very long ago; and I hope we have outlived the time of bloody feud, when a quarrel was carried down between two families from father to son, like a Spanish game at chess, and a murder or two committed in every generation just to keep the matter from going to sleep. We do with our quarrels now-a-days as with our clothes; cut them out for ourselves, and wear them out in our own day, and should no more think of resenting our fathers' feuds, than of wearing their slashed doublets and trunk-hose."

"You treat this far too lightly, Lucy," answered Miss Vere.

"Not a bit, my dear Isabella," said Lucy. "Consider, your father, though present in the unhappy affray, is never supposed to have struck the fatal blow; besides, in former times, in case of mutual slaughter between clans, subsequent alliances were so far from being excluded, that the hand of a daughter, or a sister, was the most frequent gage of reconciliation. You laugh at my skill in romance; but, I assure you, should your history be written, like that of many a less distressed and less deserving heroine, the well-judging reader would set you down for the lady and the love of Earnscliff, from the very obstacle which you suppose so insurmountable."

"But these are not the days of romance, but of sad reality, for there stands the castle of Ellieslaw."

"And there stands Sir Frederick Langley at the gate, waiting to assist the ladies from their palfreys. I would as lief touch a toad; I will disappoint him, and take old Horsington the groom for my master of the horse."

So saying, the lively young lady switched her palfrey forward, and, passing Sir Frederick with a familiar nod as he stood ready to take her horse's rein, she cantered forward and jumped into the arms of the old groom. Fain would Isabella have done the same had she dared; but her father stood near, displeasure already darkening on a countenance peculiarly qualified to express the harsher passions, and she was compelled to receive the unwelcome assiduities of her detested suitor.

Chapter Six

Let not us that are squires of the night's body be called
thieves of the day's beauty: let us be Diana's foresters,
gentlemen of the shade, minions of the moon.
                    Henry the Fourth, Part I

THE SOLITARY had consumed the remainder of the day in which he had the interview with the young ladies, within the precincts of his garden. Evening again found him seated on his favourite stone. The sun setting red, and among seas of rolling clouds, threw a gloomy lustre over the moor, and gave a deeper purple to that broad outline of heathy mountains which surrounded this desolate spot. The Dwarf sate watching the clouds as they towered above each other in masses of conglomerated vapours, and, as a strong lurid beam of the sinking luminary darted full on his solitary and uncouth figure, he might well have seemed the demon of the storm which was gathering, or some gnome summoned forth from the recesses of the earth by the subterranean signals of its approach. As he sate thus, with his dark eye turned toward the scowling and blackening heaven, a horseman rode rapidly towards him, and stopping, as if to let his horse breathe for an instant, made a sort of obeisance to the anchoret, with an air betwixt effrontery and embarrassment.

The figure of the rider was thin, tall, and slender, but remarkably athletic, bony, and sinewy; like one who had all his life followed those violent exercises which prevent the human form from increasing in bulk, while they harden and confirm by habit its muscular powers. His face, thin, sun-burnt, and freckled, had a sinister expression of violence, impudence, and cunning, each of which seemed alternately to predominate over the others. Sandy-coloured hair, and reddish eyebrows, from under which looked forth his sharp grey eyes, completed the inauspicious outline of the horseman's physiognomy. He had pistols in his holsters, and another pair peeped from his belt, though he had taken some pains to conceal them by buttoning his doublet. He wore a rusted steel head-piece, a buff jacket of rather an antique cut,

gloves, of which that for the right hand was covered with small scales
of iron, like an ancient gauntlet; and a long broadsword completed his
equipage.

"So——" said the Dwarf, "rapine and murder once more on horseback."

"On horseback?" said the bandit; "aye, aye, Elshie, your leech-
craft has set me on the bonny bay again."

"All those promises of amendment which you made during your
illness forgotten?" continued Elshender.

"All passed away with the water-saps and panada," returned the
unabashed convalescent. "Ye ken, Elshie, for they say ye are weel
acquent wi' that gentleman,

> When the devil was sick, the devil a monk would be,
> When the devil was well, the devil a monk was he."

"Thou say'st true," said the Solitary; "as well divide a wolf from his
appetite for carnage, or a raven from her scent of slaughter, as thee
from thy accursed propensities."

"What would you have me do?—It's born with me—lies in my very
blude and bane. Why, man, the lads of Westburnflat, for ten lang
descents, have been livers and lifters. They have all drunk hard, lived
high, taken deep revenge for light offence, and never wanted gear for
the winning."

"Right; and thou art as thorough-bred a wolf," said the Dwarf, "as
ever leapt a lamb-fold at night. On what hell's errand art thou bound
now?"

"Can your skill not guess?"

"Thus far I know," said the Dwarf, "that thy purpose is bad, thy
deed will be worse, and the issue worst of all."

"And you like me the better for it?—eh?" said Westburnflat; "you
always said you did."

"I have cause to like all," said the Solitary, "that are scourges to
their fellow-creatures, and thou art a bloody one."

"No—I say not guilty to that—never bluidy unless there's resistance, and that sets a man's bluid up, ye ken.—And this is nae great
matter, after a'; just to cut the comb of a young cock that has been
crawing a little ower crousely."

"Not young Earnscliff?" said the Solitary, with some emotion.

"No! not young Earnscliff—not young Earnscliff *yet;* but his time
may come, if he will not take warning, and get him back to the
burrows-town that he's fit for, and no keep skelping about here,
destroying the few deer that are left in the country, and pretending to
act as a magistrate, and writing letters to the great folks at Auld Reekie

about the disturbed state of the land. Let him take care o' himsel!"

"Then it must be Hobbie of the Heugh-foot. What harm has the lad done you?"

"Harm! nae great harm; but I hear he says I staid away from the Ba'-spiel on Fastern's E'en, for fear of him; and it was only for fear of the Country Keeper, for there was a warrant against me. I'll stand Hobbie's feud, and a' his clan's. But it's no so much for that, as to gi'e him a lesson no to let his tongue gallop ower freely about his betters. I trow he will hae lost the best pen-feather o' his wing before to-morrow morning.—Farewell, Elshie; there's some canny boys waiting for me down amang the shaws, owerbye; I will see you as I come back, and bring ye a blythe tale in return for your leech-craft."

Ere the Dwarf could collect himself to reply, the Reiver of West-burnflat set spurs to his horse. The animal, starting at one of the stones which lay scattered about, flew from the path. The rider exercised his spurs and whip without moderation or mercy. The horse became furious, reared, kicked, plunged and bolted like a deer, with all his four feet off the ground at once. It was in vain; the unrelenting rider sate as if he had been a part of the horse which he bestrode; and, after a short but most furious contest, compelled the subdued animal to proceed upon the path at a rate which soon carried him out of sight of the Solitary.

"The villain," exclaimed the Dwarf,—"the cool-blooded, hardened, unrelenting ruffian,—the wretch, whose every thought is infected with crimes, has thewes and sinews, limbs, strength, and activity enough to compel a nobler animal than himself to carry him to the place where he is to perpetrate his wickedness; while I, had I the weakness to wish to put his wretched victim on his guard, and to save the helpless family, would see my good intentions frustrated by the decrepitude which chains me to the spot.—Why should I wish it were otherwise? What has my screech-owl voice, my hideous form, and my mis-shapen features, to do with the fairer workmanship of nature? Do not men receive even my benefits with shrinking horror and ill-suppressed disgust? And why should I interest myself in a race who account me a prodigy and an outcast, and who have treated me as such? No; by all the ingratitude with which I have been repaid—by all the wrongs which I have sustained—by my imprisonment—my stripes—my chains—I will wrestle down my feelings of rebellious humanity. I will not be the fool I have been, to swerve from my principles whenever there was an appeal, forsooth, to my feelings, as if I, towards whom none show sympathy, ought to have sympathy with any one. Let Destiny drive forth her scythed car through the overwhelmed and trembling mass of humanity! Shall I be the idiot to throw this decrepid form, this mis-shapen lump of mortality, under her wheels, that the dwarf—the wizard—the hunch-back might save from destruction some fair form or some active frame, and all the world clap their hands at the exchange? No, never!—And yet this Elliot—this Hobbie, so young and gallant, so frank, so—I will think of it no longer. I cannot aid him if I would, and I am resolved—firmly resolved, that I would not aid him, if a wish were the pledge of his safety!"

Having thus ended his soliloquy, he retreated into his hut for shelter from the storm which was fast approaching, and now began to burst in large and heavy drops of rain. The last rays of the sun now disappeared entirely, and two or three claps of distant thunder followed each other at brief intervals, echoing and re-echoing among the range of heathy fells like the sound of a distant engagement.

Chapter Seven

Proud bird of the mountain, thy plume shall be torn!—
*   *   *
Return to thy dwelling; all lonely, return;
For the blackness of ashes shall mark where it stood,
And a wild mother scream o'er her famishing brood.
CAMPBELL

THE NIGHT continued to be sullen and stormy; but morning rose as if refreshed by the rains. Even the Meikle-stane-Moor, with its broad bleak swells of barren grounds, interspersed with marshy pools of water, seemed to smile under its serene influence, just as good-humour can spread a certain inexpressible charm over the plainest human countenance. The heath was in its thickest and deepest bloom. The bees, which the Solitary had added to his rural establishment, were abroad and on the wing, and filled the air with the murmurs of their industry. As the old man crept out of his little hut, his two she-goats came to meet him, and licked his hands in gratitude for the vegetables with which he supplied them from his garden. "You, at least," he said—"you, at least, see no differences in form which can alter your feelings to a benefactor—to you, the finest shape that ever statuary moulded would be an object of indifference or of alarm, should it present itself instead of the mutilated trunk to whose services you are accustomed. While I was in the world, did I ever meet with such a return of gratitude?—No—the domestic whom I had bred from infancy made mouths at me as he stood behind my chair—the friend whom I had supported with my fortune, and for whose sake I had even stained——(he stopped with a strong convulsive shudder) even he thought me more fit for the society of lunatics—for their disgraceful restraint, for their cruel privations, than for communication with the rest of humanity—Hubert alone—and Hubert too will one day abandon me—all of a piece—one mass of wickedness, selfishness, and ingratitude—wretches, who sin even in their devotions; and such is their hardness of heart, that they do not even, without hypocrisy, thank the Deity himself for his warm sun and pure air."

As he was plunged in these gloomy soliloquies, he heard the tramp of a horse on the other side of his inclosure, and a strong clear bass voice singing with the liveliness inspired by a light heart,

> Canny Hobbie Elliot, canny Hobbie now,
> Canny Hobbie Elliot, I'se gang alang wi' you.

At the same moment, a large deer greyhound sprung over the Hermit's fence. It is well known to the sportsmen in these wilds, that the appearance and scent of the goat so much resembles that of their usual objects of chase, that the best broke greyhounds will sometimes fly upon them. The dog in question instantly pulled down and throttled one of the Hermit's she-goats, while Hobbie Elliot, who came up, and jumped from his horse for the purpose, was unable to extricate the harmless animal from the fangs of his attendant until it was expiring. The Dwarf eyed, for a few moments, the convulsive starts of his dying favourite, until the poor goat stretched out her limbs with the twitches and shivering fit of the last agony. He then started into an access of frenzy, and, unsheathing a long sharp knife, or dagger, which he wore under his coat, he was about to launch it at the dog, when Hobbie, perceiving his purpose, interposed, and caught hold of his hand, exclaiming, "Let a be the hound, man—let a be the hound—na, na, Killbuck manna be guided that gate, neither."

The Dwarf turned his rage on the young farmer; and, by a sudden effort, far more powerful than Hobbie expected from such a person, freed his wrist from his grasp, and offered the dagger at his heart. All this was done in the twinkling of an eye, and the incensed Recluse might have completed his vengeance by plunging the weapon in Elliot's bosom, had he not been checked by an internal impulse which made him hurl the knife to a distance.

"No," he exclaimed, as he thus voluntarily deprived himself of the means of gratifying his rage; "not again—not again!"

Hobbie retreated a step or two in great surprise, discomposure, and disdain, at having been placed in such danger by an object apparently so contemptible.

"The de'il's in the body for strength and bitterness!" were the first words that escaped him, which he followed up with an apology for the accident that had given rise to their disagreement. "I am na justifying

Killbuck a'thegether neither, and I am sure it was a vexing thing to you, Elshie, that the mischance should hae happened; but I'll send you twa gaits and twa fat gimmers, man, to make a' straight again. A wise man like you shouldna bear malice against a poor dumb thing; ye see that a gait's like first cousin to a deer, sae he acts but according to his nature after a'. Had it been a pet-lamb, there wad hae been mair to be said. Ye suld keep sheep, Elshie, and no gaits, where there's sae mony deer-hounds about—but I'll send ye baith."

"Wretch!" said the Hermit, "your cruelty has destroyed one of the only creatures in existence that would look on me with kindness."

"Dear! Elshie, I'm wae ye suld hae cause to say sae; I am sure it was na wi' my will.—And yet, it's true, I should hae minded your gaits, and coupled up the dogs. I am sure I would rather they had worried the primest wether in my faulds.—Come, man, forget and forgi'e. I am e'en as vexed as ye can be—But I am a bridegroom, ye see, and that puts a' things out o' my head, I think. There's the marriage dinner, or gude part o't, that my twa brithers are bringing on a sled round by the Riders' Slack, three goodly bucks as ever ran on Dallom-lea, as the sang says; they couldna come the straight road for the saft grund. I wad send ye a bit venison, but ye wadna take it weel maybe, for Killbuck catched it."

During this long speech, in which the good-natured Borderer endeavoured to propitiate the offended Dwarf by every argument he could think of, he heard him with his eyes bent on the ground, as if in the deepest meditation, and at length broke forth—"Nature?—yet it is indeed in the usual beaten path of Nature. The strong gripe and throttle the weak; the rich depress and despoil the needy; the happy— those who are idiots enough to think themselves happy insult the misery and diminish the consolation of the wretched.—Go hence, thou who hast contrived to give an additional pang to the most miserable of human beings—thou who hast deprived me of what I half considered as a source of comfort—go hence, and enjoy the happiness prepared for thee at home!"

"Never stir," said Hobbie, "if I wadna take you wi' me, man, if ye wad but say it wad divert ye to be at the bridal on Monday. There will be a hundred strapping Elliots to ride the brouze—the like's no been seen sin the days of auld Martin of the Preakin-tower—I wad send the sled for ye wi' a canny powny."

"Is it to me you propose once more to mix in the society of the common herd?"

"Commons!" retorted Hobbie, "nae siccan commons neither; the Elliots hae been lang kenn'd a gentle race."

"Hence! begone!" reiterated the Dwarf; "may the same evil luck attend thee that thou hast left behind with me! If I go not with you myself, see if you can escape what my attendants, Wrath and Misery, have sent to thy threshold before thee."

"I wish ye wadna speak that gate," said Hobbie. "Ye ken yoursel, Elshie, naebody judges you to be ower canny; now I'll tell ye just ae word for a'—ye hae spoken as muckle as wussing ill to me and mine; now, if ony mischance happen to Grace, which God forbid, or to mysel, or to the poor dumb tyke; or if I be skaithed and injured in body, gudes, or gear, I'll no forget wha it is that it's owing to."

"Out, hind!" exclaimed the Dwarf; "home! home to your dwelling, and think on me when you find what has befallen there."

"Aweel, aweel," said Hobbie, mounting his horse, "it serves naething to strive wi' cripples, they are aye cankered; but I'll just tell ye ae thing, neighbour, that, if things be otherwise than weel wi' Grace Armstrong, I'se gi'e you a scouther if there be a tar-barrel in the five parishes."

So saying, he rode off; and Elshie, after looking at him with a scornful and indignant laugh, took spade and mattock, and occupied himself in digging a grave for his deceased favourite.

A low whistle, and the words, "Hist, Elshie, hist!" disturbed him in this melancholy occupation. He looked up, and the Red Reiver of Westburnflat was before him. Like Banquo's murderer, there was blood on his face, as well as upon the rowels of his spurs and the sides of his over-ridden horse.

"How now, ruffian?" demanded the Dwarf, "is thy job chared?"

"Aye, aye! doubt not that, Elshie," answered the freebooter; "when I ride, my foes may moan. They have had mair light than comfort at the Heugh-foot this morning; there's a toom byre and a wide, and a wail and a cry for the bonny bride."

"The bride?"

"Aye; Charlie Cheat-the-Woodie, as we ca' him, that's Charlie Forster of Finning-beck, has promised to keep her in Cumberland till the blast blaw bye. She saw me, and kenn'd me in the splore, for the mask fell frae my haffits for a blink. I am thinking it wad concern my safety if she were to come back here, for there's mony o' the Elliots, and they band weel thegither for right or wrang. Now, what I chiefly came to ask your rede in, is, how to make her sure?"

"Would'st thou murder her, then?"

"Umph! no—no—That I would not do, if I could help it. But they say they can whiles get folk cannily away to the plantations from some of the outports, and something to boot for them that brings a bonny wench. They're wanted beyond seas thae female cattle, and they're no that scarce here. But I think o' doing better for this lassie. There's a ladye, that, unless she be a better bairn, is ganging to foreign parts whether she will or no—Now, I think of sending Grace to wait on her —she's a bonny lass—Hobbie will hae a merry morning when he comes hame, and misses baith bride and gear."

"Aye; and do you not pity him?"

"Wad he pity me were I gaeing up the Castle-hill at Jeddart?* And yet I rue something for the bit lassie; but he'll get anither, and little skaith dune—ane is as gude as anither. And now, you that like to hear o' splores, heard ye ever o' a better ane than I hae had this morning?"

"Air, ocean, and fire," said the Dwarf, speaking to himself, "the earthquake, the tempest, the volcano, are all mild and moderate, compared to the wrath of man. And what is this fellow, but one more skilled than others in executing the end of his existence?—Hear me, felon, go again where I before sent thee."

"To the steward?"

"Aye; and tell him, Elshender the Recluse commands him to give thee gold. But hear me—let the maiden be discharged free and unin-jured—return her to her friends—let her swear not to discover thy villainy."

"Swear?" said Westburnflat, "but what if she break her aith? Women are not famous for keeping their plight. A wise man like you should ken that.—And uninjured—wha kens what may happen were she to be left lang at Finning-beck? Charlie Cheat-the-Woodie is a rough customer. But if the gold could be made up to twenty pieces, I think I could insure her being wi' her friends within the twenty-four hours."

The Dwarf took his tablets from his pocket, marked a line in them, and tore out the leaf. "There," he said, giving the robber the leaf— "But, mark me; thou knowest I am not to be fooled by thy treachery; if thou darest to disobey my directions, thy wretched life, be sure, shall answer it."

"I know," said the fellow, looking down, "that you have power on earth, however ye came by it; you can do what nae other man can do, baith by physic and foresight; and the gold is shelled down when ye command, as fast as I have seen the ash-keys fall in a frosty morning in October. I will not disobey you."

"Begone, then, and relieve me of thy hateful presence."

The robber set spurs to his horse, and rode on without reply.

Hobbie Elliot, in the meanwhile, had pursued his journey rapidly, harassed by those oppressive and indistinct fears that all was not right at home, which men usually term a presentiment of misfortune. Ere

---

* The place of execution at that ancient burgh, where many of Westburnflat's profession have made their final exit.

he reached the top of the bank from which he could look down on his own habitation, he was met by his nurse—a person then of great consequence in all families in Scotland, whether of the higher or middling classes. The connection between them and their foster-children was accounted a tie far too dearly intimate to be broken; and it usually happened, in the course of years, that the nurse became a resident in the family of her foster-son, assisting in the domestic duties, and receiving all marks of attention and regard from the heads of the family. So soon as Hobbie recognized the figure of Annaple, in her red cloak and black hood, he could not help exclaiming to himself, "What ill luck can hae brought the auld nurse sae far frae hame, her that never stirs a gun-shot frae the door-stane for ordinar?—Hout, it will just be to get crane-berries, or whortle-berries, or some such stuff, out of the moss, to make the pyes and tarts for the feast on Monday.—I cannot get the words of that cankered, auld, cripple de'il's-buckie out o' my head—the least thing makes me dread some ill news.—O, Killbuck, man! were there nae deer and gaits eneuch in the country, but ye behoved to gang and worry his creature, bye a' other folks'?"

By this time Annaple, with a brow like a tragic volume, had hobbled towards him, and caught his horse with the bridle. The despair in her look was so evident as to deprive him even of the power of asking the cause. "O my bairn!" she cried, "gang na forward—gang na forward—it's a sight to kill ony body, let alane thee."

"In God's name, what's the matter?" said the astounded horseman, endeavouring to extricate his bridle from the grasp of the old woman; "for Heaven's sake, let me go and see what's the matter."

"Ohon! that I should have lived to see the day!—The steading's a' in a low, and the bonny stack-yard lying in the red ashes, and the gear a' driven. But gang na forward; it wad break your young heart, hinny, to see what my auld een hae seen this morning."

"And who has dared to do this? let go my bridle, Annaple—where is my grandmother—my sisters?—Where is Grace Armstrong?—God! —the words of the warlock are knelling in my ears!"

He sprung from his horse to rid himself of Annaple's interruption, and, ascending the hill with great speed, soon came in view of the spectacle with which she had threatened him. It was indeed a heart-breaking sight. The habitation which he had left in its seclusion, beside the mountain stream, surrounded with every evidence of rustic plenty, was now a wasted and blackened ruin. From amongst the shattered and sable walls the smoke continued to rise. The turf-stack, the barn-yard, the offices stocked with cattle, all the wealth of an upland cultivator of the period, of which poor Elliot possessed no common share, had been laid waste or carried off in a single night. He stood a moment motionless, and then exclaimed, "I am ruined now—ruined to the ground!—But curse on the warld's gear—Had it no been the very week before my bridal—But I am nae babe, to sit doun and greet about it. If I can but find Grace, and my grandmother, and my sisters weel, I can go to the wars in Flanders, as my gude-sire did wi' Buccleuch—At ony rate, I will keep up a heart, or they will lose theirs a'thegether."

Manfully strode Hobbie down the hill, resolved to suppress his own despair, and administer consolation which he did not feel. The neighbouring inhabitants of the dale, particularly those of his own name, had already assembled. The younger part were in arms and clamorous for revenge, although they knew not upon whom; the elder were taking measures for the relief of the distressed family. Annaple's cottage, which was situated down the brook, at some distance from the scene of mischief, had been hastily adapted for the temporary accommodation of the old lady and her daughters, with such articles as had been contributed by the neighbours, for very little was saved from the wreck.

"Are we to stand here a' day, sirs," exclaimed one tall young man, "and look at the burned wa's of our kinsman's house?—Every wreath of the reek is a blast of shame upon us! Let us to horse, and take the chase.—Wha has the nearest blood-hound?"

"It's young Earnscliff," answered another; "and he's been on and away wi' six horse lang syne, to see if he can track them."

"Let us follow him than, and raise the country, and make mair help as we ride, and than have at the Cumberland reivers—Take, burn, and slay—they that lie nearest us shall smart first."

"Whisht! haud your tongues, daft callants," said an old man, "ye dinna ken what ye speak about. What! wad ye raise war atween twa peacefu' countries?"

"And what signifies deaving us wi' tales about our fathers," retorted the young man, "if we're to sit and see our friends' houses burned ower their heads, and no put out a hand to revenge them? Our fathers didna do that, I trow."

"I am no saying ony thing against revenging Hobbie's wrang, puir chield; but we maun take the law wi' us in thae days, Simon," answered the more prudent elder.

"And, besides," said another old man, "I dinna believe there's ane living now that kens the lawful mode of following a fray across the Border. Tam o' Whittram kenn'd a' about it, but he died in the hard winter."

"Ay," said a third, "he was at the great gathering when they chased as far as Thirlwall—it was the year after the fight at Philiphaugh."

"Hout!" exclaimed another of these discording counsellors, "there's nae great skill needed; just put a lighted peat on the end of a spear, or hay-fork, or something, and blaw a horn, and cry the gathering-word, and than it is lawful to follow gear into England, and recover it by the strong hand, or to take gear frae some other Englishman, providing ye lift nae mair than's been lifted frae you,—that's the auld Border law, made at Dundrennan, in the days of the Black Douglas. De'il ane need doubt it."

"Come away, then, lads," cried Simon, "get to your geldings, and we'll take auld Cuddy the muckle tasker wi' us; he kens the value o' the stock and plenishing that's been lost. Hobbie's stalls and stakes shall be fou again or night; and if we canna big up the auld house sae soon, we'se lay an English ane as low as Heugh-foot is—and that's fair play, a' the warld ower."

This animating proposal was received with great applause by the younger part of the assemblage, when a whisper ran among them, "There's Hobbie himsel, puir fallow; we'll be guided by him."

The principal sufferer, having now reached the bottom of the hill, pushed on through the crowd, unable, from the tumultuous state of his feelings, to do more than receive and return the grasps of the friendly hands by which his neighbours and kinsmen mutely expressed their sympathy in his misfortune. While he pressed Simon of Hackburn's hand, his anxiety at length found words. "Thank ye, Simon—thank ye, neighbours—I ken what ye wad a' say—But where are they?—Where are——" He stopped, as if afraid even to name the objects of his enquiry; and, with a similar feeling, his kinsman, without reply, pointed to the hut, into which Hobbie precipitated himself with the desperate air of one who is resolved to know the worst at once. A general expression of sympathy accompanied him.—"Ah, puir fallow—puir Hobbie!"

"He'll learn the warst o't, now!"

"But I trust Earnscliff will get some speerings o' the puir lassie."

Such were the exclamations of the group, which, having no acknowledged leader to direct their motions, passively awaited the return of the sufferer, and determined to be guided by his directions.

The meeting between Hobbie and his family was in the highest degree affecting. His sisters threw themselves upon him, and almost stifled him with their caresses, as if to prevent his looking round to distinguish the absence of one yet more beloved.

"God help thee, my son! He can help, when worldly trust is a broken reed."—Such was the welcome of the matron to her unfortunate grandson. He looked eagerly round, holding two of his sisters by the hand, while the third hung around his neck—"I see you—I count you—My grandmother, Lilias, Jean, and Annot; but where is——" (he hesitated, and then continued, as if with an effort,) "Where is Grace? Surely this is not a time to hide hersel frae me—there's nae time for daffing now."

"O brother!" and "O our poor Grace!" was the only answer his questions could procure, till his grandmother rose up, and gently extricating him from the weeping girls, led him to a seat, and, with the affecting serenity which sincere piety, like oil sprinkled on the waves, can throw over the most acute feelings, she said, "My bairn, when thy grandfather was killed in the wars, and left me with six orphans around me, with scarce bread to eat, or a roof to cover us, I had strength,—not of mine own—but I had strength given me to say, The Lord's will be done! My son, our peaceful house was last night broken into by moss-troopers, armed and masked; they have taken and destroyed all, and have carried off our dear Grace;—pray for strength to say, HIS will be done."

"Mother! mother! urge me not—I cannot—not now—I am a sinful man, and of a hardened race.—Masked—armed—Grace carried off! Gi'e me my sword, and my father's knapscap—I will have vengeance, if I should go to the pit of darkness to seek it!"

"O my bairn, my bairn! be patient under the rod. Who knows when He may lift his hand off from us? Young Earnscliff, Heaven bless him, has ta'en the chase, with Davie of Stenhouse, and the first comers. I cried to let house and plenishing burn, and follow the reivers to recover Grace, and Earnscliff and his men were ower the Fell within three hours after the deed. God bless him; he's a real Earnscliff—his father's son—a leal friend."

"A true friend, indeed; God bless him!" exclaimed Hobbie; "let us on and away, and take the chase after him."

"O, my child, before you run on danger, let me hear you but say, His will be done!"

"Urge me not, mother—not now." He was rushing out, when, looking back, he observed his grandmother make a mute attitude of affliction. He returned hastily, threw himself into her arms, and said, "Yes, mother, I *can* say, His will be done, since it will comfort you."

"May He go forth—may He go forth with you, my dear bairn; and O, may He give you cause to say on your return, His name be praised!"

"Farewell, mother!—farewell, my dear sisters!" exclaimed Elliot, and rushed out of the house.

Chapter Eight

Now horse and hattock, cried the laird,—
Now horse and hattock, speedilie;
They that winna ride for Telfer's kye,
Let them never look in the face o' me.
Border Ballad

"HORSE! horse! and spear!" exclaimed Hobbie to his kinsmen.—
Many a ready foot was in the stirrup; and, while Elliot hastily collected
arms and accoutrements, no easy matter in such a confusion, the glen
resounded with the approbation of his younger friends.

"Hae ye ony tidings?—Hae ye ony speerings, Hobbie?" said old
Dick of the Dingle. "O, callans, dinna be ower hasty."

"Ay, ay!" exclaimed Simon of Hackburn, "that's the gate to take it,
Hobbie. Let women sit and greet at hame, men must do as they have
been done by; it's the Scripture says't."

"Haud your tongue, sir," said the senior, "ye dinna ken what ye
speak."

"What signifies preaching to us e'enow," said Simon; "if ye canna
make help yoursel, dinna keep them at hame that can."

"Whisht, sir! what do ye ken wha's wrang'd ye?"

"D'ye think we dinna ken the road to England as weel as our fathers
before us?—All evil comes out o' thereaway—it's an auld saying and a
true; and we'se e'en away there, as if the devil was blawing us south."

"We'll follow the track o' Earnscliff's horses ower the waste," cried
one Elliot.

"I'll prick them out through the blindest moor in the Border an'
there had been a fair held there the day before," said Hugh, the
blacksmith of Ringleburn, "for I aye shoe his horse wi' my ain hand."

"Lay on the deer-hounds," cried another; "where are they?"

"Hout, man, the sun's been lang up, and the dew is aff the grund—
the scent will never lie."

Hobbie instantly whistled on his hounds, which, roving about the
ruins of their old habitation, were filling the air with their doleful
howls.

"Now, Killbuck," said Hobbie, "try thy skill this day"—and then, as
if a light had suddenly broke on him,—"that ill-fa'ard goblin spake
something o' this. He may ken mair o't, either by villains on earth, or
devils below—I'll hae it frae him, if I should cut it out o' his mis-
shapen bouk wi' my whinger." He then hastily gave directions to his
comrades. "Four o' ye, wi' Simon, haud right forward to Græme's-

gap. If they're English, they'll be for being back that way. The rest disperse by twasome and threesome through the waste, and meet me at the Trysting-pool. Tell my brothers, when they come up, to follow and meet us there—Poor lads, they will hae hearts weel nigh as sair as mine—little think they what a sorrowful house they are bringing their venison to—I'll ride ower Meikle-stane-Moor mysel."

"And if I were you," said Dick of the Dingle, "I would speak to Canny Elshie. He can tell ye whate'er betides in this land, if he's sae minded."

"He shall tell me," said Hobbie, who was busy putting his arms in order, "what he kens o' this night's job, or I shall right weel ken wherefore he does not."

"Ay, but speak him fair, my bonny man—speak him fair, Hobbie; the like o' him will no bear thrawing. They converse sae muckle wi' thae fractious ghaists and evil spirits, that it clean spoils their temper."

"Let me alane to guide him," answered Hobbie; "there's that in my breast this day, that would ower-maister a' the warlocks on earth, and a' the devils in hell."

And being now fully equipped, he threw himself on his horse, and spurred him at a rapid trot against the steep ascent.

Elliot speedily surmounted the hill, rode down the other side at the same rate, crossed a wood of copse, and traversed a long glen, ere he at length regained Meikle-stane-Moor. As he was obliged, in the course of his journey, to relax his speed in consideration of the labour which his horse might still have to undergo, he had time to consider more maturely in what manner he should address the Dwarf, in order to extract from him the knowledge which he supposed him to be in possession of concerning the authors of his misfortunes. Hobbie, though blunt, plain of speech, and hot of disposition, like most of his countrymen, was by no means deficient in the shrewdness which is also their characteristic. He reflected, that from what he had observed on the memorable night when the Dwarf was first seen, and from the conduct of that mysterious being ever since, he was likely to be rendered even more obstinate in his sullenness by threats and violence.

"I'll speak him fair," he said, "as auld Dickon advised me. Though folk say he has a league wi' Satan, he canna be sic an incarnate devil as no to take some pity in a case like mine; and folk threep he'll whiles do good, charitable sort o' things. I'll keep my heart doun as weel as I can, and stroke him wi' the hair; and if the warst come to the warst, it's but wringing the head o' him about at last."

In this disposition of accommodation he approached the hut of the Solitary.

The old man was not upon his seat of audience, nor could Hobbie perceive him in his garden, or enclosures.

"He's gotten into his very Keep," said Hobbie, "maybe to be out o' the gate, but I'se pu' it doun about his lugs, if I canna win at him otherwise."

Having thus communed with himself, he raised his voice, and invoked Elshie in a tone as supplicating as his conflicting feelings would permit. "Elshie, my gude friend." No reply. "Elshie, Canny Father Elshie." The Dwarf remained mute. "Sorrow be in the crooked carcase of thee," said the Borderer between his teeth, and then again attempting a soothing tone; "good Father Elshie, a most miserable creature desires some counsel of your wisdom."

"The better!" answered the shrill and discordant voice of the Dwarf through a very small window, resembling an arrow-slit, which he had constructed near the door of his dwelling, and through which he could see any one who approached it, without the possibility of their looking in upon him.

"The better!" said Hobbie impatiently; "what is the better, Elshie? Do you not hear me tell you I am the most miserable wretch alive?"

"And do you not hear me tell you it is so much the better? and did I not tell you this morning, when you thought yourself so happy, what an evening was coming upon you?"

"That ye did e'en," replied Hobbie, "and that gars me come to you for advice now; they that foresaw the trouble maun ken the cure."

"I know no cure for earthly trouble," returned the Dwarf; "or, if I did, why should I help others, when none hath aided me? Have I not lost wealth, that would have bought all thy barren hills a hundred times over? rank, to which thine is but as that of a peasant? society, where there was an interchange of all that was amiable—of all that was intellectual? Have I not lost all this? Am I not residing here, the veriest outcast on the face of Nature, in the most hideous and most solitary of her retreats, myself more hideous than all that is around me? And why should other worms complain to me when they are trodden on, since I am myself lying crushed and writhing under the chariot-wheel?"

"Ye may have lost all this," answered Hobbie, in the bitterness of emotion; "land and friends, goods and gear; ye may hae lost them a', —but ye ne'er can hae sae sair a heart as mine, for ye ne'er lost nae Grace Armstrong. And now my last hopes are gane, and I shall ne'er see her mair."

This he said in the tone of deepest emotion—and there followed a long pause, for the mention of his bride's name had overcome the more angry and irritable feelings of poor Hobbie. Ere he had again addressed the Solitary, the bony hand and long fingers of the latter, holding a large leathern bag, was thrust forth at the small window, and as it unclutched the burden, and let it drop with a clang upon the ground, his harsh voice again addressed Elliot.

"There—there lies a salve for every human ill; so, at least, each human wretch willingly thinks.—Begone; return twice as wealthy as thou wert before yesterday, and torment me no more with questions, complaints, or thanks; they are alike odious to me."

"It is a' gowd, by Heaven!" said Elliot, having glanced at the contents; and then again addressing the Hermit, "Muckle obliged for your good-will; and I wad blythely gi'e ye a band for some o' the siller, or a wadset ower the lands o' Wideopen. But I dinna ken, Elshie; to be free wi' you, I dinna like to use siller unless I kenn'd it was decently come by; and maybe it might turn into sclate-stanes, and cheat some poor man."

"Ignorant idiot!" retorted the Dwarf, "the trash is as genuine poison as ever was dug out of the bowels of the earth. Take it—use it, and may it thrive with you as it hath done with me!"

"But I tell ye," said Elliot, "it was na about the gear that I was consulting you,—it was a braw barn-yard, doubtless, and thirty head of finer cattle there were na on this side of the Cat-rail; but let the gear gang,—if I could but hear—if ye could but gi'e me speerings o' puir Grace, I would be content to be your slave for life, in ony thing that didna touch my salvation. O Elshie, speak, man, speak!"

"Well, then," answered the Dwarf, as if worn out by his importunity, "since thou hast not enough of woes of thine own, but must needs seek to burden thyself with those of a partner. Seek her whom thou hast lost in the *West*."

"In the *West*? That's a wide word."

"It is the last," said the Dwarf, "which I design to utter;" and he drew the shutter of his window, leaving Hobbie to make the most of the hint he had given.

The west! the west!—thought Elliot; the country is pretty quiet down that way, unless it were Jock o' the Tod-holes; and he's ower auld now for the like o' thae jobs.—West!—By my life, it must be Westburnflat. "Elshie, just tell me one word. Am I right? Is it Westburnflat? If I am wrang, say sae. I wadna like to wyte an innocent neighbour wi' violence—No answer—It must be the Red Reiver—I didna think he wad hae ventured on me, neither, and sae mony kin as there is o' us—I am thinking he'll hae some better backing than his Cumberland friends.—Fareweel to you, Elshie, and mony thanks—I downa be fashed wi' the siller e'en now, for I maun awa' to meet my friends at the trysting place—Sae, if ye carena to open the window, ye can fetch it in after I am awa'."

Still there was no reply.

"He's deaf, or he's daft, or he's baith; but I hae nae time to stay to claver wi' him."

And off rode Hobbie Elliot towards the place of rendezvous which he had named to his friends.

Four or five riders were already gathered at the Trysting-pool. They stood in close consultation together, while their horses were permitted to graze among the poplars which overhung the broad still pool. A more numerous party were seen coming from the southward. It proved to be Earnscliff and his party, who had followed the track of the cattle as far as the English border, but had halted on the information that a considerable force was drawn together under some of the jacobite gentlemen in that district, and there were tidings of insurrection in different parts of Scotland. This took away from the act which had been perpetrated, the appearance of private animosity, or love of plunder; and Earnscliff was now disposed to regard it as a symptom of civil war. The young gentleman greeted Hobbie with the most sincere sympathy, and informed him of the news he had received. "Then, may I never stir frae the bit," said Elliot, "if auld Ellieslaw is not at the bottom o' the hale villainy! Ye see he's leagued wi' the Cumberland Catholics; and that agrees weel wi' what Elshie hinted about Westburnflat, for Ellieslaw aye protected him, and he will want to harry and disarm the country about his ain hand before he breaks out."

Some now remembered that the party of ruffians had been heard to say they were acting for James VIII., and were charged to disarm all rebels. Others had heard Westburnflat boast that Ellieslaw would soon be in arms for the jacobite cause, and that he himself was to hold a command under him, and that they would be bad neighbours to young Earnscliff, and all that stood out for the established government. The result was a strong belief that Westburnflat had headed the party under Ellieslaw's orders, and they resolved to proceed instantly to the house of the former, and, if possible, to secure his person. They were by this time joined by so many of their dispersed friends, that their number amounted to upwards of twenty horsemen, well mounted, and tolerably, though variously, armed.

A brook, which issued from a narrow glen among the hills, entered, at Westburnflat, upon the open morassy level, which, expanding about half a mile in every direction, gives name to the spot. In this place the character of the stream becomes changed, and, from being a lively brisk-running mountain-torrent, it stagnates, like a blue swollen snake, in dull deep windings through the swampy level. On the side of the stream, and nearly about the centre of the plain, arose the Tower of Westburnflat, one of the few remaining strong-holds formerly so numerous upon the Borders. The ground upon which it stood was gently elevated above the marsh for about a hundred yards, affording an esplanade of dry turf, which extended immediately around the foundations of the tower; but, beyond that space, the surface presented to strangers was that of an impassable and dangerous bog. The owner of the tower and his intimates alone knew the winding and intricate paths; which, leading over ground that was comparatively sound, admitted visitors to his residence. But among the party who were assembled under Earnscliff's directions, there was more than one person qualified to act as a guide. For although the owner's character and habits of life were generally known, yet the laxity of feeling with respect to property prevented his being looked on with the abhorrence with which he must have been regarded in a more civilized country. He was considered, among his more peaceable neighbours, pretty much as a gambler, cock-fighter, or horse-jockey, would be regarded at the present day; a person, of course, whose habits were to be condemned, and his society, in general, avoided, yet who could not be considered as marked with the indelible infamy attached to his profession, where laws have been habitually observed. And their indignation was awaked against him upon this occasion, not so much on account of the general nature of the transaction, which was just such as was to be expected from this marauder, but because the violence had been perpetrated upon a neighbour against whom he had no cause of quarrel, against a friend of their own,—above all, against one of the name of Elliot, to which clan most of them belonged. It was not, therefore, wonderful that there should be several in the band pretty well acquainted with the locality of his habitation, and capable of giving such directions and guidance as soon placed the whole party on the open space of firm ground in front of the Tower of Westburn-flat.

Chapter Nine

So spak the knicht; the geaunt sed,
Lead forth with the, the sely maid,
    And mak me quite of the and sche;
For glaunsing ee, or brow so brent,
Or cheek with rose and lilye blent,
    Me lists not ficht with the.
        Romaunce of the Falcon

THE TOWER, before which the party now stood, was a small square building, of the most gloomy aspect. The walls were of great thickness, and the windows, or slits which served the purpose of windows, seemed rather calculated to afford the defenders the means of employing missile weapons than for admitting air or light to the apartments within. A small battlement projected over the walls on every side, and afforded farther advantage of defence by its niched parapet, within which arose a steep roof, flagged with grey stones. A single turret at one angle, defended by a door studded with huge iron nails, rose above the battlement, and gave access to the roof from within, by the spiral stair-case which it enclosed. It seemed to the party that their motions were watched by some one concealed within this turret; and they were confirmed in their belief, when, through a narrow loophole, a female hand was seen to wave a handkerchief, as if by way of signal to them. Hobbie was almost out of his senses with joy and eagerness. "It was Grace's hand and arm," he said; "I can swear to it amang a thousand. There's not the like of it on this side of the Lowdens—We'll have her out, lads, if we should carry off the Tower of Westburnflat stane by stane."

Earnscliff, though he doubted the possibility of recognizing a fair maiden's hand at such a distance from the eye of the lover, would say nothing to damp his friend's animated hopes, and it was resolved to summon the garrison.

The shouts of the party, and the winding of one or two horns, at length brought to a loop-hole, which flanked the entrance, the haggard face of an old woman.

"That's the Reiver's mother," said one of the Elliots; "she's ten times waur than himsel, and is wyted for muckle of the ill he does about the country."

"Wha are ye? What d'ye want here?" were the queries of the respectable progenitor.

"We are seeking William Græme of Westburnflat," said Earnscliff.

"He is no at hame," returned the old dame.

"When did he leave home?" pursued Earnscliff.

"I canna tell," said the portress.

"When will he return?" said Hobbie Elliot.

"I dinna ken naething about it," replied the inexorable guardian of the Keep.

"Is there any body within the tower with you?" again demanded Earnscliff.

"Naebody but mysel and Baudrons," said the old woman.

"Then open the gate and admit us," said Earnscliff; "I am a justice of peace, and am in search of the evidence of a felony."

"De'il be in their fingers that draws a bolt for ye," retorted the portress; "for mine shall never do it. Think na ye shame o' yoursels, to come here siccan a band o' ye, wi' your swords and spears, and steel-caps, to frighten a lone widow woman?"

"Our information," said Earnscliff, "is positive; we are seeking goods which have been forcibly carried off, to a great amount."

"And a young woman, that's been cruelly made prisoner, that's worth mair than a' the gear, twice told," said Hobbie.

"And I warn you," continued Earnscliff, "that your only way to prove your son's innocence is to give us quiet admittance to search the house."

"And what will ye do, if I carena to thraw the keys, or draw the bolts, or open the grate to sic a clam-jamfarie?" said the old dame, scoffingly.

"Force our way wi' the king's keys, and break the neck of every living soul we find in the house, if ye dinna gi'e it ower forthwith!" menaced Hobbie.

"Threatened folks live lang," said the hag, in the same tone of irony; "there's the iron grate,—try your skeel on it, lads—it has kept out as gude men as you or now."

So saying, she laughed, and withdrew from the aperture through which she had held the parley.

The besiegers now had a serious consultation. The immense thickness of the walls, and the small size of the windows, might even, for a time, have resisted cannon-shot. The entrance was secured, first, by a strong grated door, entirely of hammered iron, of such ponderous strength as seemed calculated to resist any force they could bring against it. "Pinches or forehammers will never pick upon it," said Hugh, the blacksmith of Ringleburn; "ye might as weel batter it wi' pipe-stapples."

Within the door-way, and at the distance of nine feet, which was the solid thickness of the wall, there was a second door of oak, crossed, both breadth and lengthways, with clenched bars of iron, and studded full of broad-headed nails. Besides all these defences, they were by no means confident in the truth of the old dame's assertion, that she alone composed the garrison. The more knowing of the party had observed hoof-marks in the track by which they approached the tower, which seemed to intimate that several persons had very lately passed in that direction. This was doubted by others, who pretended to trace the same hoof-marks out of the morass, and receding from the tower in a southern direction.

To all these difficulties were added their slender means of attacking the place. There was no hope of procuring ladders long enough to reach the battlements, and the windows, besides being very narrow, were secured with iron bars—scaling was therefore out of the question. Mining was still more so, for want of tools and of gunpowder. Neither were the besiegers provided with food, means of shelter, or other conveniences, which might have enabled them to convert the siege into a blockade; and there would, at any rate, have been a risk of relief from some of the marauder's comrades. Hobbie grinded and gnashed his teeth, as, walking round the fastness, he could devise no means of making a forcible entry. At length he suddenly exclaimed, "But what for no do as our fathers did lang syne?—Put hand to the wark, lads. Let us cut up bushes and briars, pile them before the door and set fire to them, and smoke that auld devil's dam as if she were to be reested for bacon."

All immediately closed with this proposal, and some went to work with swords and knives to cut down the alder and hawthorn bushes which grew by the side of the sluggish stream, many of which were sufficiently decayed and dry for their purpose, while others began to collect them in a large stack properly disposed for burning as close to the iron grate as they could be piled. Fire was speedily obtained from one of their guns, and Hobbie was already advancing to the pile with a kindled brand, when the surly face of the robber, and the muzzle of a musquetoon, were partially shewn at a shot-hole which flanked the entrance. "Mony thanks to ye," he said scoffingly, "for collecting sae muckle winter eilding for us; but if ye step a foot nearer it wi' that lunt, it's be the dearest step ye ever made in your days."

"We'll sune see that," said Hobbie, advancing fearlessly with the torch.

The marauder snapped his piece at him, which, fortunately for our honest friend, did not go off; while Earnscliff, firing at the same moment at the narrow aperture and slight mark afforded by the robber's face, grazed the side of his head with a bullet. He had apparently calculated upon his post affording him more security, for he no sooner felt the wound, though a very slight one, than he requested a parley, and demanded to know what they meant by attacking in this fashion a peaceable honest man, and shedding his blood in that lawless manner?

"We want your prisoner," said Earnscliff, "to be delivered up to us in safety."

"But what concern have you with her?" replied the marauder.

"That," retorted Earnscliff, "you, who are detaining her by force, have no right to enquire."

"Aweel, I think I can gi'e a guess," said the robber. "Weel, sirs, I am laith to enter into deadly feud with you by spilling ony of your bluid, though Earnscliff hasna stopped to shed mine—and ye can hit a mark to a groat's breadth—so, to prevent mair skaith, I am willing to deliver up the prisoner, since nae less will please you."

"And Hobbie's gear?" cried Simon of Hackburn. "D'ye think

you're to be free to plunder our faulds and byres, as if it were an auld wife's hen-cavey?"

"As I live by bread," replied Willie of Westburnflat, "as I live by bread, I have not a single cloot o' them; they're a' ower the march lang syne; there's no a horn o' them about the tower. But I'll see what o' them can be gotten back, and I'll take this day twa days to meet Hobbie at the Castleton wi' twa friends on ilka side, and see to make an agreement about a' the wrang that he can wyte me wi'."

"Ay, ay," said Elliot, "that will do weel aneugh."—And then aside to his kinsman, "Murrain on the gear! Lord's sake, man! say nought about them. Let us but get puir Grace out o' that auld hellicat's clutches."

"And ye gie me your word, Earnscliff," said the marauder, who still lingered at the shot-hole, "your faith and troth, with hand and glove, that I am free to come and free to gae, wi' five minutes to open the grate, and five minutes to steek it and draw the bolts? less winna do, for they want creishing sairly."

"You shall have full time," said Earnscliff, "I plight my faith and troth, my hand and my glove."

"Wait there a moment, then," said Westburnflat; "or, hear ye, I wad rather ye wad fa' back a pistol-shot from the door. It's no that I mistrust your word, Earnscliff, but it's best to be secure."

"O, friend," thought Hobbie to himself, as he drew back, "an' I had you but on Turner's-holm, and naebody bye but twa honest lads to see fair play, I wad make ye wish ye had broken your leg ere ye had touched beast or body that belanged to me."

"He has a white feather in his wing this same Westburnflat after a'," said Simon of Hackburn, somewhat scandalized by his ready surrender. "He'll ne'er fill his father's boots."

In the meanwhile, the inner door of the tower was opened, and the mother of the freebooter appeared in the space betwixt that and the outer grate. Willie himself was next seen leading forth a female, and the old woman, carefully bolting the grate behind them, remained on the post as a sort of centinel.

"Ony ane or twa o' ye come forward," said the outlaw, "and take her frae my hand hale and sound."

Hobbie advanced eagerly to meet his betrothed bride. Earnscliff followed more slowly to guard against treachery. Suddenly Hobbie slackened his pace in the deepest mortification, while that of Earnscliff was quickened by impatient surprise. It was not Grace Armstrong, but Miss Isabella Vere, whose liberation had been effected by their appearance before the tower.

"Where is Grace? Where is Grace Armstrong?" exclaimed

Hobbie, in the extremity of wrath and indignation.

"Not in my hands," answered Westburnflat; "ye may search the tower, if ye misdoubt me."

"You fause villain, ye sall account for her, or die on the spot," said Elliot, presenting his gun.

But his companions, who now came up, instantly disarmed him of his weapon, exclaiming, all at once, "Hand and glove! faith and troth! Haud a care, Hobbie, we maun keep our word wi' Westburnflat, were he the greatest rogue ever rode."

Thus protected, the outlaw recovered his audacity, which had been somewhat daunted by the menacing gesture of Elliot.

"I have keepit my word," he said, "sirs! and I look to have nae wrang amang ye.—If this is na the prisoner ye sought," he said, addressing Earnscliff, "ye'll render her back to me again. I am answerable for her to those that aught her."

"For God's sake, Mr Earnscliff, protect me!" said Miss Vere, clinging to her deliverer; "do not you abandon one whom the whole world seems to have abandoned."

"Fear nothing," whispered Earnscliff, "I will protect you with my life." Then turning to Westburnflat, "Villain!" he said, "how dared you to insult this lady?"

"For that matter, Earnscliff," answered the freebooter, "I can answer to them that has better right to ask me than you have; but if you come with an armed force, and take her awa' from them that her friends lodged her wi', how will you answer that?—But it's your ain affair—Nae man can keep a tower against twenty—A' the men o' the Mearns downa do mair than they dow."

"He lies most falsely," whispered Isabella; "he carried me off by violence from my father."

"Maybe he only wanted ye to think sae, hinny; but it's nae business o' mine, let it be as it may.—So ye winna resign her back to me?"

"Back to you, fellow? Surely no," answered Earnscliff; "I will protect Miss Vere, and escort her safely wherever she is pleased to be conveyed."

"Ay, ay, maybe you and her hae settled that already."

"And Grace?" interrupted Hobbie, shaking himself loose from the friends who had been preaching to him the sanctity of the safe conduct, upon the faith of which the freebooter had ventured from his tower. "Where's Grace?" and he rushed on the marauder, sword in hand. Westburnflat thus pressed, after calling out, "God's sake, Hobbie, hear me a gliff!" fairly turned his back and fled. His mother stood ready to open and shut the grate; but Hobbie struck at the freebooter as he entered with so much force, that the sword made a considerable cleft in the lintel of the vaulted door, which is still shewn as a memorial of the superior strength of those who lived in the days of yore. Ere Hobbie could repeat the blow, the door was shut and secured, and he was compelled to retreat to his companions, who were now preparing to break up the siege of Westburnflat. They insisted upon his accompanying them in their return.

"Ye hae broken truce already," said old Dick of the Dingle; "an' we take na gude care, ye'll play mair gowk's tricks, and make yoursel the laughing-stock o' the hale country, besides having your friends charged with slaughter under trust. Bide till the meeting at Castleton, as ye hae greed; and if he doesna make ye amends, then we'll hae it out o' his very heart's blood. But let us gang reasonably to wark and keep our tryst, and I'se warrant we get back Grace, and the kye an' a'."

This cold-blooded reasoning went ill down with the unfortunate lover; but, as he could only obtain the assistance of his neighbours and kinsmen on their own terms, he was compelled to acquiesce in their notions of good faith and regular procedure.

Earnscliff now requested the assistance of a few of the party to convey Miss Vere to her father's castle of Ellieslaw, to which she was peremptory in desiring to be conducted. This was readily granted; and five or six young men agreed to attend him as an escort. Hobbie was not of the number. Almost heart-broken by the events of the day, and his final disappointment, he returned moodily home to take such measures as he could for the sustenance and protection of his family, and to arrange with his neighbours the farther steps which should be adopted for the recovery of Grace Armstrong. The rest of the party dispersed in different directions, as soon as they had crossed the morass. The outlaw and his mother watched them from the tower until they entirely disappeared.

Chapter Ten

> I left my ladye's bower last night—
> It was clad in wreaths of snaw,—
> I sought it when the sun was bright,
> And sweet the roses blaw.
> *Old Ballad*

INCENSED at what he deemed the coldness of his friends, in a cause which interested him so nearly, Hobbie had shaken himself free of their company, and was now upon his solitary road homeward. "The fiend founder thee!" he said, as he spurred impatiently his over-fatigued and stumbling horse; "thou art like a' the rest o' them. Hae I not fed thee, and bred thee, and dressed thee wi' mine ain hand, and wouldst snapper now and break my neck at my utmost need? But thou'rt e'en like the laive—the farthest off o' them a' is my cousin ten times removed; and day or night I wad hae served them wi' my best blood; and now, I think they shew mair regard to the common thief of Westburnflat than to their ain kinsman. But I should see the lights now in the Heugh-foot—Waes me!" he continued, recollecting himself, "there will neither coal nor candle-light shine in the Heugh-foot ony mair! An' it were na for my mother and sisters, and poor Grace, I could find in my heart to put spurs to the beast, and loup ower the scaur into the water to make an end o't a'."—In this disconsolate mood, he turned his horse's bridle towards the cottage in which his family had found refuge.

As he approached the door, he heard whispering and tittering amongst his sisters. "The devil's in the women," said poor Hobbie; "they would nicker, and laugh, and giggle, if their best friend was lying a corp—and yet I am glad they can keep up their heart sae weel, poor silly things; but the dirdum fa's on me, to be sure, and no on them."

While he thus meditated, he was engaged in fastening up his horse in a shed. "Thou maun do without horse-sheet and surcingle now, lad," he said, addressing the animal; "you and me hae had a downcome alike—we had better hae fa'en in the deepest pool o' Tarras."

He was interrupted by the youngest of his sisters, who came running out, and speaking in a constrained voice, as if to stifle some emotion, called out to him, "What are ye doing there, Hobbie, fiddling about the naig, and there's ane frae Cumberland been waiting here for ye this hour and mair? Haste ye in, man; I'll take aff the saddle."

"Ane frae Cumberland!" exclaimed Elliot; and putting the bridle of his horse into the hand of his sister, he rushed into the cottage. "Where is he? where is he?" he exclaimed, glancing eagerly round, and seeing only females; "Did he bring news of Grace?"

"He dought na bide an instant langer," said the elder sister, still with a suppressed laugh.

"Hout fie, bairns!" said the old lady, with something of good-humoured reproof, "ye should na vex your billy Hobbie that way. Look round, my bairn, and see if there is na ane here mair than you left this morning."

Hobbie looked eagerly round. "There's you, and the three titties."

"There's four of us now, Hobbie, lad," said the youngest, who at this moment entered.

In an instant Hobbie had in his arms Grace Armstrong, who, with one of his sisters' plaids around her, had passed unnoticed at his first entrance. "How dared you do this?" said Hobbie.

"It wasna my fault," said Grace, endeavouring to cover her face with her hands, to hide at once her blushes and escape the storm of hearty kisses with which her bridegroom punished her simple stratagem,—"It wasna my fault, Hobbie; ye should kiss Jeanie and the rest o' them, for they hae the wyte o't."

"And so I will," said Hobbie, and embraced and kissed his sisters and grandmother a hundred times, while the whole party half-laughed, half-cried, in the extremity of their joy. "I am the happiest man," said Hobbie, throwing himself down upon a seat, almost exhausted,—"I am the happiest man in this world."

"Then, O my dear bairn," said the good old dame, who lost no opportunity of teaching her lesson of religion at those moments when the heart was best opened to receive it,—"Then, O my son, give praise to Him that brings smiles out o' tears and joy out o' grief, as he brought light out o' darkness and the world out o' naething. Was it not my word, that, if ye could say His will be done, ye might soon hae cause to say His name be praised?"

"It was—it was your word, grannie; and I do praise Him for his mercy, and for leaving me a good parent when my ain were gane," said honest Hobbie, taking her hand, "that puts me in mind to think of Him, baith in happiness and distress."

There was a solemn pause of one or two minutes, employed in the exercise of mental devotions, which expressed, in purity and sincerity, the gratitude of the affectionate family to that Providence who had unexpectedly restored to their embraces the friend whom they had lost.

Hobbie's first enquiry was concerning the adventures which Grace had undergone. They were told at length, but amounted in substance to this:—That she was awaked by the noise which the ruffians made in breaking into the house, and by the resistance offered by one or two of the servants, which was soon overpowered; that, dressing herself hastily, she ran down stairs, and in the scuffle having seen Westburn-flat's vizard drop off, she imprudently named him by his name, and besought him for mercy; that the ruffian instantly stopped her mouth, dragged her from the house, and placed her on horseback, behind one of his associates.

"I'll break the accursed neck of him," said Hobbie, "if there were na another Græme in the land but himsel!"

She proceeded to say, that she was carried southward along with the party, and the spoil which they drove before them, until they had crossed the Border. Suddenly a person, known to her as a kinsman of Westburnflat, came riding very fast after the marauders, and told their leader, that his cousin had learnt from a sure hand that no luck would come of it, unless the lass was restored to her friends. After some discussion, the chief of the party seemed to acquiesce. Grace was placed behind her new guardian, who pursued in silence, and with great speed, the least-frequented path to the Heugh-foot, and ere evening closed set down the fatigued and terrified damsel within a quarter of a mile of the dwelling of her friends. Many and sincere were the congratulations which passed on all sides.

As these emotions subsided, less pleasing considerations began to intrude themselves.

"This is a miserable place for ye a'," said Hobbie, looking around him; "I can sleep weel aneugh mysel out-bye beside the naig, as I hae done mony a lang night in the hills. But how ye are to put yoursels up, I canna see; and, what's waur, I canna mend it—And, what's waur than a', the morrow may come, and the day after that, without your being a bit better off."

"It was a cowardly, cruel thing," said one of the sisters, looking round, "to harry a puir family to the bare wa's this gate."

"And leave us neither stirk nor stot," said the youngest brother, who now entered, "nor sheep nor lamb, nor aught that eats grass and corn."

"If they had ony quarrel at us," said Harry, the second brother, "were we na ready to have fought it out? And that we should have been a' frae hame, too,—ane and a' upon the hill—Odd, an' we had been at hame, Will Græme's stomach shouldna hae wanted its morning; but it's biding him yet, is it na, Hobbie?"

"Our neighbours hae ta'en a day at the Castleton to gree wi' him at the sight o' men," said Hobbie mournfully; "they behoved to have it a' their ain gate, or there was nae help to be got at their hand."

"To gree wi' him!" exclaimed both his brothers at once, "after siccan an act of stouthrief as hasna been heard o' in the country since the auld riding days!"

"Very true, billies, and my blood was e'en boiling at it; but the sight o' Grace Armstrong has settled it brawly."

"But the stocking, Hobbie?" said John Elliot; "we're utterly ruined. Harry and I hae been to gather what was on the out-bye land, and there's scarce a cloot left. I kenna how we're to carry on—We maun a' gang to the wars, I think. Westburnflat hasna the means, e'en if he had the will, to make up our loss; there's nae mends to be got out o' him, but what ye take out o' his banes. He has nae a four-fitted thing but the bay naig he rides on, and that's but a washy beast and has the mallenders to boot. We are ruined stoop and roop."

Hobbie cast a mournful glance on Grace Armstrong, who returned it with a downcast look and a gentle sigh.

"Dinna be cast down, bairns," said the grandmother, "we hae gude friends that winna forsake us in adversity. There's Sir Thomas Kittle-loof is my third cousin by the mother's side, and he has come by a hantle siller, and been made a knight-baronet into the bargain, for being ane o' the commissioners at the Union."

"He wadna gi'e a boddle to save us frae famishing," said Hobbie; "and, if he did, the bread that I bought wi't would stick in my throat when I thought it was part of the price of puir auld Scotland's crown and independence."

"There's the Laird o' Dunder, ane o' the auldest families in Tiviot-dale."

"He's in the tolbooth, mother—he's in the heart of Mid-Lowden for a thousand merk he borrowed from Saunders Wyliecoat the writer."

"Poor man!" exclaimed Mrs Elliot, "can we no send him some-thing, Hobbie?"

"Ye forget, grannie, ye forget we want help oursels," said Hobbie, somewhat peevishly.

"Troth did I, hinny," replied the good-humoured lady, "just at the instant; it's sae natural to think o' ane's blude relations before them-sels.—But there's young Earnscliff."

"He has ower little o' his ain; and siccan a name to keep up, it wad be a shame," said Hobbie, "to burden him wi' our distress. And I'll tell ye, grannie, it's needless to sit rhyming ower the stile of a' your kith, kin, and allies, as if there was a charm in their braw names to do us gude; the grandees hae forgotten us, and those of our ain degree hae just little aneugh to gang on wi' themsels; ne'er a friend hae we that can, or will, help us to stock the farm again."

"Then, Hobbie, we maun trust in Him that can raise up friends and fortune out o' the bare moor, as they say."

Hobbie sprung upon his feet. "Ye are right, grannie!" he exclaimed; "ye are right. I do ken a friend on the bare moor, that baith can, and will, help us—The turns o' this day hae dung my head clean hirdie girdie. I left as much gowd lying on Meikle-stane-Moor this morning as would plenish the house and stock the Heugh-foot twice ower, and I am sure Elshie wadna grudge us the use of it."

"Elshie!" said his grandmother in astonishment; "what Elshie do you mean?"

"What Elshie suld I mean, but Canny Elshie, the Wise Wight o' Meikle-stane," replied Hobbie.

"God forefend, my bairn, you should gang to fetch water out o' broken cisterns, or seek for relief to them that deal wi' the Evil One! There was never luck in their gifts, nor grace in their paths. And the hale country kens that that body Elshie's an unco man. O, if there was the law, and the douce quiet administration of justice, that makes a kingdom flourish in righteousness, the like o' them suldna be suffered to live! The wizard and the witch are the abomination and the evil thing in the land."

"Troth, mother," answered Hobbie, "ye may say what ye like, but I am in the mind that witches and warlocks havena half the power they had lang syne; at least, sure I am that ae ill-deviser, like auld Ellieslaw, or ae ill-doer, like that d—d villain, Westburnflat, is a greater plague and abomination in a country-side than a hale curnie o' the warst witches that ever capered on a broomstick, or played cantrips on Fastern's E'en. It wad hae been lang or Elshie had burned down my house and barns, and I am determined to try if he will do aught to build them up again. He's weel kenn'd a skilfu' man ower a' the country, as far as Brough under Stanmore."

"Bide a wee, my bairn; mind his benefits havena thriven wi' a' body. Jock Howden died o' the very same disorder Elshie pretended to cure him of, about the fa' o' the leaf; and though he helped Lambside's cow weel out o' the moor-ill, yet the louping-ill's been sairer amang his sheep than ony season before. And then I hear he uses sic words abusing human nature, that it's like a flying in the face of Providence; and ye mind ye said yoursel, the first time ye ever saw him, that he was mair like a bogle than a living thing."

"Hout, mother," said Hobbie, "Elshie's no that bad a chield; he's a grewsome spectacle for a crooked disciple, to be sure, and a rough talker, but his bark is waur than his bite; sae, if I had anes something to eat, for I havena had a morsel ower my throat this day, I wad streek mysel down for twa three hours aside the beast, and be on and awa' to Meikle-stane wi' the first skreigh o' morning."

"And what for no the night, Hobbie?" said Harry, "and I'll ride wi' ye."

"My naig is tired," said Hobbie.

"Ye may take mine, then," said John.

"But I am a wee thing wearied mysel."

"You wearied?" said Harry, "shame on ye! I have kenn'd ye keep the saddle twenty-four hours thegither, and ne'er sic a word as weariness in your wame."

"The night is very dark," said Hobbie, rising and looking through the casement of the cottage; "and, to speak truth, and shame the de'il, though Elshie's a real honest fallow, yet somegate I would rather take day-light wi' me when I gang to visit him."

This frank avowal put a stop to farther argument; and Hobbie, having thus compromised matters between the rashness of his brother's counsel, and the timid cautions which he received from his grandmother, refreshed himself with such food as the cottage afforded; and, after a cordial salutation all round, retired to the shed, and stretched himself beside his trusty palfrey. His brothers shared between them some trusses of clean straw, disposed in the stall usually occupied by old Annaple's cow; and the females arranged themselves for repose as well as the accommodations of the cottage would permit.

With the first dawn of morning, Hobbie arose; and, having rubbed down and saddled his horse, he set forth to Meikle-stane-Moor. He avoided the company of either of his brothers, from an idea, that the Dwarf was most propitious to those who visited him alone.

"The creature," said he to himself, as he went along, "is na neigh-bourly; ae body at a time is fully mair than he weel can abide. I wonder if he's looked out o' the crib o' him to gather up the bag o' siller. If he hasna done that, it will maybe hae been a braw windfa' for somebody, and I'll be finely flung.—Come, Tarras," said he to his horse, striking him at the same time with the spur, "make mair fit, man; we maun be first on the field if we can."

He was now on the heath, which began to be illuminated by the beams of the rising sun; the gentle declivity which he was descending presented him a distinct, though distant, view of the Dwarf's dwelling. The door opened, and Hobbie witnessed with his own eyes that phænomenon which he had frequently heard mentioned. Two human figures (if that of the Dwarf could be termed such) issued from the solitary abode of the Recluse, and stood as if in converse together in the open air. The taller form then stooped, as if taking something up which lay beside the door of the hut, then both moved forward a little way, and again halted, as in deep conference. All Hobbie's supersti-tious terrors revived on witnessing this spectacle. That the Dwarf would open his dwelling to mortal guest, was as improbable as that any one would choose voluntarily to be his nocturnal visitor; and, under the full conviction that he beheld a wizard holding intercourse with his familiar spirit, Hobbie pulled in at once his breath and his bridle, resolved not to incur the indignation of either by a hasty intrusion on their conference. They were probably aware of his approach, for he had not halted for a moment before the Dwarf returned to his cottage; and the taller figure who had accompanied him, glided round the inclosure of the garden, and seemed to disappear from the eyes of the admiring Hobbie.

"Saw ever mortal the like o' that!" said Elliot; "but my case is desperate, sae, if he were Beelzebub himsel, I'se venture down the brae on him."

Yet, notwithstanding his assumed courage, he slackened his pace when, nearly upon the very spot where he had last seen the tall figure, he discerned, as if lurking among the long heather, a small black rough-looking object, like a terrier dog. "He has nae dog that ever I heard of," said Hobbie, "but mony a de'il about his hand! Lord forgi'e me for saying sic a word—It keeps its grund, be what it like—I am judging it's a badger; but whae kens what shapes thae bogles will take to fright a body—it will maybe start up like a lion or a crocodile when I come nearer—I'se e'en drive a stane at it, for if it change its shape when I am ower near, Tarras will never stand it, and it will be ower muckle to hae him and the de'il to fight wi' baith at ance."

He therefore cautiously threw a stone at the object, which continued motionless. "It's nae living thing, after a'," said Hobbie, "but the very bag o' siller that he flung out o' window yesterday! and that other queer lang creature has just brought it sae muckle farther on the way to me."

He then advanced and lifted the heavy fur pouch, which was quite full of gold. "Mercy on us!" said Hobbie, whose heart fluttered between glee at the revival of his hopes and prospects in life, and suspicion of the purpose for which this assistance was afforded him— "Mercy on us! it's an awfu' thing to touch what has been sae lately in the claws of something no canny. I canna shake mysel loose o' the belief that there has been some jookery-packery of Satan's in a' this; but I am determined to conduct mysel like an honest man and a gude Christian, come o't what will."

He advanced accordingly to the cottage door, and having knocked repeatedly without receiving any answer, he at length elevated his voice and addressed the inmate of the hut. "Elshie! Father Elshie! I ken ye're within doors, and wauking, for I saw ye at the door-cheek as I came ower the bent; will ye come out and speak just a gliff to ane that has mony thanks to con ye?—It was a' true ye tell'd me about Westburnflat; but he's sent back Grace safe and skaithless, sae there's nae ill suffered yet but what may be sowthered or sustained.—Wad ye but come out a gliff, man, or but say ye're listening?—Aweel, since ye winna answer, I'se e'en proceed wi' my tale. Ye see I hae been thinking it wad be a sair thing on twa young folk, like Grace and me, to put aff our marriage for mony years till I was abroad and came back again wi' some gear; and they say folk manna take booty in the wars as they did lang syne, and the pay's a sma' matter; there's nae gathering gear on that—and than there's my gude-dame's auld—and my sisters wad sit pinging by the ingle-side for want o' me to ding them about—and Earnscliff, or the neighbourhood, or maybe your ain sell, Elshie, might want some gude turn that Hob Elliot could do ye—and it's a pity that the auld house o' the Heugh-foot should be wrecked a'thegither

—Sae I was thinking—But de'il hae me, that I should say sae," continued he, checking himself, "if I can bring mysel to ask a favour of ane
that winna sae muckle as ware a word on me, to tell me if he hears me
speaking till him."

"Say what thou wilt—do what thou wilt," answered the Dwarf from
his cabin, "but begone, and leave me at peace."

"Weel, weel," replied Elliot, "since ye are content to hear me, I'se
make my tale short.—Since ye are sae kind as to say ye are content to
lend me as muckle siller as will stock and plenish the Heugh-foot, I am
content, on my part, to accept the courtesy wi' mony kind thanks; and
troth, I think it will be as safe in my hands as yours, if ye leave it flung
about in that gate for the first loon body to lift, forbye the risk o' bad
neighbours that can win through steekit doors and lock-fast places, as
I can tell to my cost. I say, since ye hae sae muckle consideration for
me, I'se be blythe to accept your kindness; and my mother and me
(she's liferenter and I am fiar o' the lands o' Wideopen) would grant
you a wadset, or an heritable band, for the siller, and to pay the annual
rent half yearly; and Saunders Wyliecoat to draw the band, and you to
be at nae charge wi' the writings."

"Cut short thy jargon, and begone," said the Dwarf; "thy loquac-
ious bull-headed honesty makes thee a more intolerable plague than
the light-fingered courtier who would take a man's all without troub-
ling him with either thanks, explanation, or apology. Hence, I say!
thou art one of those tame slaves whose word is as good as their bond.
Keep the money, principal and interest, until I demand it of thee."

"But," continued the pertinacious Borderer, "we are a' life-like and
death-like, Elshie, and there really should be some black and white on
this transaction. Sae just make me a minute, or missive, as they ca't at
Jeddart, in ony form ye like, and I'se write it fair ower, and subscrive it
before famous witnesses. Only, Elshie, I wad wuss ye to pit naething
in't that may be prejudicial to my salvation; for I'll hae the minister to
read it ower, and it wad be only exposing yoursel to nae purpose. And
now I am ganging awa', for ye'll be wearied o' my cracks, and I am
wearied wi' cracking without an answer—and I'se bring ye a bit o'
bride's-cake ane o' thae days, and maybe bring Grace to see ye. Ye
wad like to see Grace, man, for as dour as ye are—Eh, Lord! I wish he
may be weel, that was a sair grane! or, maybe, he thought I was
speaking of heavenly grace, and no of Grace Armstrong. Poor man, I
am very doubtfu' o' his condition; but I am sure he is as kind to me as if
I were his son, and a queer-looking father I wad hae had, if that had
been e'en sae."

Hobbie now relieved his benefactor of his presence, and rode
blythely home to display his treasure, and consult upon the means of

repairing the damage which his fortune had sustained through the aggression of the Red Reiver of Westburnflat.

Chapter Eleven

> Three ruffians seized me yester morn,
> Alas! a maiden most forlorn;
> They choked my cries with wicked might,
> And bound me on a palfrey white:
> As sure as Heaven shall pity me,
> I cannot tell what men they be.
> *Christabelle*

THE COURSE of our story must here revert a little, to detail the circumstances which had placed Miss Vere in the unpleasant situation from which she was unexpectedly, and indeed unintentionally, liberated, by the appearance of Earnscliff and Elliot, with their friends and followers, before the Tower of Westburnflat.

On the morning preceding the night in which Hobbie's house was plundered and burnt, Miss Vere was requested by her father to accompany him in a walk through a distant part of the romantic grounds which lay around his Castle of Ellieslaw. "To hear was to obey," in the true style of oriental despotism; but Isabella trembled in silence while she followed her father through rough paths, now winding by the side of the river, now ascending the cliffs which serve for its banks. A single servant, selected perhaps for his stupidity, was the only person who attended them. From her father's silence, Isabella little doubted that he had chosen this distant and sequestered scene to resume the argument which they had so frequently maintained upon the subject of Sir Frederick's addresses, and that he was meditating in what manner he should most effectually impress upon her the necessity of receiving him as her suitor. But her fears seemed for some time to be unfounded. The only sentences which her father from time to time addressed to her, respected the beauties of the romantic landscape through which they strolled, and which varied its features at every step and turning. To these observations, although they seemed to come from a heart occupied by more gloomy as well as more important cares, Isabella endeavoured to answer in a manner as free and unconstrained as it was possible for her to assume, amid the involuntary apprehensions which crowded upon her imagination.

Sustaining, with mutual difficulty, a desultory conversation, they at length gained the centre of a small wood, composed of large old oaks, intermingled with birches, mountain-ashes, hazel, holly, and a variety of underwood. The boughs of the tall trees met closely above, and the underwood filled up each interval between their trunks below. The spot on which they stood was rather more open; still, however, embowered under the natural arcade of tall trees, and darkened on the sides for a space around by a great and lively growth of copse-wood and bushes.

"And here, Isabella," said Mr Vere, as he pursued the conversation, so often resumed, so often dropped, "here I would erect an altar to Friendship."

"To Friendship, sir?" said Miss Vere, "and why in this gloomy and sequestered spot, rather than elsewhere?"

"O, the propriety of the *locale* is easily vindicated," replied her father with a sneer. "You know, Miss Vere, (for you, I am well aware, are a learned young lady,) you know, that the Romans were not satisfied with embodying, for the purpose of worship, each useful quality and moral virtue to which they could give a name, but they, moreover, worshipped the same under each variety of titles and attributes which could give a distinct shade, or individual character, to the virtue in question. Now, for example, the Friendship to whom a temple should be here dedicated, is not Masculine Friendship, which abhors and despises duplicity, art, and disguise; but Female Friendship, which consists in little else than a mutual disposition on the part of the friends, as they call themselves, to abet each other in obscure fraud and petty intrigue."

"You are severe, sir," said Miss Vere.

"Only just," said her father; "a humbler copier I am from nature, with the advantage of contemplating two such excellent studies as Lucy Ilderton and yourself."

"If I have been unfortunate enough to offend you, sir, I can conscientiously excuse Miss Ilderton from being either my counsellor, or confidante."

"Indeed! how came you, then," said Mr Vere, "by the flippancy of speech, and pertness of argument, by which you have disgusted Sir Frederick, and given me of late such deep offence?"

"If my manner has been so unfortunate as to displease you, sir, it is impossible for me to apologize too deeply, or too sincerely; but I cannot profess the same contrition for having answered Sir Frederick flippantly when he pressed me rudely. Since he forgot I was a lady, it was time to shew him that I am at least a woman."

"Reserve then your pertness for those who press you on the topic, Isabella," said her father coldly; "for my part, I weary of the subject, and will never speak upon it again."

"God bless you, my dear father," said Isabella, seizing his reluctant hand; "there is nothing you can impose on me, save the task of listening to this man's persecutions, that I will call, or think, a hard-ship."

"You are very obliging, Miss Vere, when it happens to suit you to be dutiful," said her unrelenting father, forcing himself at the same time from the affectionate grasp of her hand; "but henceforward, child, I will save myself the trouble of offering you unpleasant advice on any topic.—You must look to yourself."

At this moment four ruffians rushed upon them. Mr Vere and his servant drew their hangers, which it was the fashion of the time to wear, and attempted to defend themselves and protect Isabella. But while each of them was engaged by an antagonist, she was forced into the thicket by the two remaining villains, who placed her and them-selves on horses which stood ready behind the copse-wood. They mounted at the same time, and, placing her between them, set off at a round gallop, holding the reins of her horse on each side. By many an obscure and winding path, over dale and down, through moss and moor, she was conveyed to the tower of Westburnflat, where she remained strictly watched, but not otherwise ill treated, under the guardianship of the old woman, to whose son that retreat belonged. No entreaties could prevail upon the hag to give Miss Vere any information on the object of her being carried forcibly off and con-fined in this secluded place. The arrival of Earnscliff, with a strong party of horsemen before the tower, alarmed the robber. As he had already directed Grace Armstrong to be restored to her friends, it did not occur to him that this unwelcome visit was on her account; and seeing at the head of the party, Earnscliff, whose attachment to Miss Vere was whispered in the country, he doubted not that her liberation was the sole object of the attack upon his fastness. The dread of personal consequences compelled him to deliver up his prisoner in the manner we have already narrated.

At the moment the tramp of the horses was heard which carried off the daughter of Ellieslaw, her father fell to the ground, and his ser-vant, a stout young fellow, who was gaining ground on the ruffian with whom he had been engaged, left the combat to come to his master's assistance, little doubting that he had received a mortal wound. Both the villains immediately desisted from farther combat, and retreating into the thicket, mounted their horses, and went off at full speed after their companions. Mean time, Dixon had the satisfaction to find Mr Vere not only alive but unwounded. He had overreached himself, and stumbled, it seemed, over the root of a tree in making too eager a blow at his antagonist. The despair he felt at his daughter's disappearance, was, in Dixon's phrase, such as would have melted the heart of a whin-stane, and he was so much exhausted by his feelings, and the vain researches which he made to discover the track of the ravishers, that a considerable time elapsed ere he reached home, and communicated the alarm to his domestics.

All his conduct and gestures were those of a desperate man.

"Speak not to me, Sir Frederick," he said impatiently; "you are no father—she was my child—an ungrateful one, I fear, but still my child —my only child. Where is Miss Ilderton? she must know something of this. It corresponds with what I was informed of her schemes. Go, Dixon, call Ratcliffe here instantly—Let him come without a minute's delay."

The person he had named at this moment entered the room.

"I say, Dixon," continued Mr Vere in an altered tone, "let Mr Ratcliffe know, I beg the favour of his company on particular business. —Ah! my dear sir," he proceeded, as if noticing him for the first time, "you are the very man whose advice can be of the utmost service in this cruel extremity."

"What has happened, Mr Vere, to discompose you?" said Mr Ratcliffe gravely; and while the Laird of Ellieslaw details to him, with the most animated gestures of grief and indignation, the singular adventure of the morning, we will take the opportunity to inform our readers of the relative circumstances in which these gentlemen stood to each other.

In early youth Mr Vere of Ellieslaw had been remarkable for a career of dissipation, which, in advanced life, he had exchanged for the no less destructive career of dark and turbulent ambition. In both cases, he had gratified the predominant passion without respect to the diminution of his private fortune, although, where such inducements were awanting, he was deemed close, avaricious, and grasping. His affairs being much embarrassed by his earlier extravagance, he went to England, where he was understood to have formed a very advantageous matrimonial connection. He was many years absent from his family estate. Suddenly and unexpectedly he returned a widower, bringing with him his daughter, then a girl of about ten years old. From this moment his expence seemed unbounded in the eyes of the simple inhabitants of his native mountains. It was supposed he must necessarily have plunged himself deeply in debt. Yet he continued to live in the same lavish expence, until some months before the commencement of our narrative, when the public opinion of his embarrassed circumstances was confirmed, by the residence of Mr Ratcliffe at Ellieslaw Castle, who, by the tacit consent, though obviously to the great displeasure, of the lord of the mansion, seemed, from the moment of his arrival, to assume and exercise a predominant and unaccountable influence in the management of his private affairs.

Mr Ratcliffe was a grave, steady, reserved man, in an advanced period of life. To those with whom he had occasion to speak upon business, he appeared uncommonly well versed in all its forms. With others he held little communication; but in any casual intercourse, or conversation, displayed the powers of an active and well-informed mind. For some time before taking up his final residence at the castle, he had been an occasional visitor there, and was at such times treated by Mr Vere (contrary to his general practice towards those who were inferior to him in rank) with marked attention, and even deference. Yet his arrival always appeared to be an embarrassment to his host, and his departure a relief; so that, when he became a constant inmate of the family, it was impossible not to observe indications of the displeasure with which Mr Vere regarded his presence. Indeed, their intercourse formed a singular mixture of confidence and constraint. Mr Vere's most important affairs were regulated by Mr Ratcliffe; and although he was none of those indulgent men of fortune, who, too indolent to manage their own business, are glad to devolve it upon another, yet, in many instances, he was observed to give up his own opinion, and submit to the contradictions which Mr Ratcliffe did not hesitate distinctly to express.

Nothing seemed to vex Mr Vere more than when strangers seemed to observe the state of tutelage under which he appeared to labour. When it was noticed by Sir Frederick, or any of his intimates, he sometimes repelled their remarks haughtily and indignantly, sometimes endeavoured to evade them, by saying, with a forced laugh, "That Ratcliffe knew his own importance, but that he was the most honest and skilful fellow in the world, and it would be impossible for him to manage his English affairs without his advice and assistance." Such was the person who entered the room at the moment Mr Vere was summoning him to his presence, and who now heard with surprise, mingled with obvious incredulity, the hasty narrative of what had befallen Miss Vere.

Her father concluded, addressing Sir Frederick, and the other gentlemen, who stood around in astonishment, "And now, my friends, you see the most unhappy father in Scotland. Lend me your assistance, gentlemen—give me your advice, Mr Ratcliffe. I am incapable of acting, or thinking, under the unexpected violence of such a blow."

"Let us take our horses, call our attendants, and scour the country in pursuit of the villains," said Sir Frederick.

"Is there no one whom you can suspect," said Ratcliffe, gravely, "of having some motive for this strange crime? These are not the days of romance, when ladies are carried off merely for their beauty."

"I fear," said Mr Vere, "I can too well account for this strange incident. Read this letter, which Miss Lucy Ilderton thought fit to address from my house of Ellieslaw to young Mr Earnscliff, whom, of all men, I have a hereditary right to call my enemy. You see she writes to him as the confidante of a passion which he has the assurance to entertain for my daughter; tells him she serves his cause with her friend very ardently, but that he has a friend in the garrison who serves him yet more effectually. Look particularly at the pencilled passages, Mr Ratcliffe, where this meddling girl recommends bold measures, with an assurance that his suit would be successful any where beyond the bounds of the barony of Ellieslaw."

"And you argue, from this romantic letter of a very romantic young lady, Mr Vere," said Ratcliffe, "that young Earnscliff has carried off your daughter, and committed a very great and criminal act of violence, on no better advice and assurance than that of Miss Lucy Ilderton?"

"What else can I think?" said Ellieslaw.

"What else can any one think?" said Sir Frederick; "or who else could have any motive for committing such a crime?"

"Were that the best mode of fixing the guilt," said Mr Ratcliffe, calmly, "others might easily be pointed out, to whom such actions are more congenial, and who had also sufficient motives of instigation. Supposing it were judged advisable to remove Miss Vere to some place in which constraint might be exercised upon her inclinations to a degree which cannot at present be attempted under the roof of Ellieslaw-Castle—What says Sir Frederick Langley to that supposition?"

"I say," returned Sir Frederick, "that although Mr Vere may choose to endure in Mr Ratcliffe freedoms totally inconsistent with his situation in life, I will not permit such license of inuendo, by word or look, to be extended to me, with impunity."

"And I say," said young Marischal of Marischal-Wells, who was also a guest at the castle, "that you are all stark-mad to stand wrangling here, instead of going in pursuit of the ruffians."

"I have ordered off the domestics already in the track most likely to overtake them," said Mr Vere; "if you will favour me with your company, we will follow them and assist their search."

The efforts of the party were totally unsuccessful, probably because Ellieslaw directed the pursuit to proceed in the direction of Earnscliff-Tower, under the supposition that the owner would prove to be the author of the violence, so that they followed a direction diametrically opposite to that in which the ruffians had actually proceeded. In the evening they returned, harassed and out of spirits. But other guests had, in the meanwhile, arrived at the castle; and, after the recent loss sustained by the owner had been narrated, wondered at, and lamented, recollection of it was, for the present, drowned in the discussion of deep political intrigues, of which the crisis and explosion were momentarily expected.

Several of the gentlemen who took part in this divan were catholics, and all of them were staunch jacobites, whose hopes were at present at the highest pitch, as an invasion, in favour of the Pretender, was daily expected from France, which Scotland, between the defenceless state of its garrisons and fortified places, and the general disaffection of the inhabitants, was rather prepared to welcome than to resist. Ratcliffe, who neither sought to assist at their consultations on this subject, nor was invited to do so, had, in the meanwhile, retired to his own apartments. Miss Ilderton was sequestered from society by a sort of honourable confinement, "until," said Mr Vere, "she should be safely conveyed home to her father's house," an opportunity for which occurred on the following day.

The domestics could not help thinking it remarkable how soon the loss of Miss Vere, and in so strange a manner, seemed to be forgotten by the other guests at the castle. They knew not, that those the most interested in her fate were well acquainted with the cause of her being carried off and the place of her retreat; and that the others, in the anxious and doubtful moments which precede the breaking forth of a conspiracy, were little accessible to any feelings but what arose immediately out of their own machinations.

Chapter Twelve

Some one way, some another—Do you know
Where we may apprehend her?

THE RESEARCHES after Miss Vere were (for the sake of appearances, perhaps) resumed on the succeeding day, with similar bad success, and the party were returning towards Ellieslaw in the evening.

"It is singular," said Marischal to Ratcliffe, "that four horsemen and a female prisoner should have passed through the country without leaving the slightest trace of their passage. One would think they had traversed the air, or sunk through the ground."

"Men may often," answered Ratcliffe, "arrive at a knowledge of that which *is*, from discovering that which is *not*. We have now scoured every road, path, and track leading from the castle, in all various points of the compass, saving only that intricate and difficult pass which leads southward down the Westburn, and through the morasses at Westburnflat."

"And why have we not examined that?" said Marischal.

"O, Mr Vere and Sir Frederick can best answer that question," replied his companion, drily.

"Then I will ask it at them instantly," said Marischal; and, addressing Mr Vere, "I am informed, sir, there is a path we have not yet examined, leading by Westburnflat."

"O," said Sir Frederick, laughing, "we know the owner of Westburnflat well—a wild lad, that knows little difference between his neighbour's goods and his own; but, withal, very honest to his principles: He would disturb nothing belonging to Ellieslaw."

"Besides," said Mr Vere, smiling mysteriously, "he had other tow on his distaff last night. Have you not heard young Elliot of the Heugh-foot has had his house burnt, and his cattle driven, because he refused to give up his arms to some honest men that think of starting for the king?"

The company smiled upon each other, as at hearing of an exploit which favoured their own views.

"Yet, nevertheless," resumed Marischal, "I think we ought to ride in this direction also, otherwise we shall certainly be blamed for our negligence."

No reasonable objection could be offered to this proposal, and the party turned their horses' heads towards Westburnflat.

They had not proceeded very far in that direction when the trampling of horses was heard, and a small body of riders were perceived advancing to meet them.

"There comes Earnscliff," said Marischal. "I know his bright bay with the star in his front."

"And there is my daughter along with him," exclaimed Vere, furiously. "Who shall call my suspicions false or injurious now? Gentlemen—friends—lend me the assistance of your swords for the recovery of my child."

He unsheathed his weapon, and was imitated by Sir Frederick and several of the party, who prepared to charge those that were advancing towards them. But the greater part hesitated.

"They come to us in all peace and security," said young Marischal-Wells; "let us first hear what account they give us of this mysterious affair—if Miss Vere has sustained the slightest insult or injury from Earnscliff, I will be the first to revenge her—but let us hear what they say."

"You do me wrong by your suspicions, Marischal," continued Vere; "you are the last I would have expected to hear express them."

"You injure yourself, Ellieslaw, by your violence, though the cause may excuse it."

He then advanced a little before the rest, and called out, with a loud voice,—"Stand, Mr Earnscliff, or do you and Miss Vere advance alone to meet us. You are charged with having carried that lady off from her father's house, and we are here in arms to shed our best blood for her recovery, and for bringing to justice those who have injured her."

"And who would do that more willingly than I, Mr Marischal?" said Earnscliff, haughtily,—"than I who had the satisfaction this morning to liberate her from the dungeon in which I found her confined, and who am now escorting her back to the Castle of Ellieslaw?"

"Is this so, Miss Vere?" said Marischal.

"It is," answered Isabella, eagerly,—"it is so; for Heaven's sake, sheathe your swords. I will swear by all that is sacred, that I was carried off by ruffians, whose persons and object were alike unknown to me, and am now restored to freedom by means of this gentleman's gallant interference."

"By whom, and wherefore, could this have been done?" pursued Marischal.—"Had you no knowledge of the place to which you were conveyed?—Earnscliff, where did you find the lady?"

But ere either question could be answered, Ellieslaw advanced, and, returning his sword to the scabbard, cut short the conference.

"When I know," he said, "exactly how much I owe to Mr Earnscliff, he may rely on suitable acknowledgments; mean time," taking the bridle of Miss Vere's horse, "thus far I thank him for replacing my daughter in the power of her natural guardian."

A sullen bend of the head was returned by Earnscliff with equal haughtiness; and Ellieslaw, turning back with his daughter upon the road to his own house, appeared engaged with her in a conference so earnest, that the rest of the company judged it improper to intrude by approaching them too nearly. In the mean time, Earnscliff, as he took leave of the other gentlemen belonging to Ellieslaw's party, said aloud, "Although I am unconscious of any circumstance in my conduct that can authorize such a suspicion, I cannot but observe, that Mr Vere seems to believe that I have had some hand in the atrocious violence which has been offered to his daughter. I request you, gentlemen, to take notice of my explicit denial of a charge so dishonourable; and that, although I can pardon the bewildering feelings of a father in such a moment, yet, if any other gentleman," (he looked hard at Sir Frederick Langley,) "thinks my word and that of Miss Vere, with the evidence of my friends who accompany me, too slight for my exculpation, I will be happy—most happy—to repel the charge as becomes a man who counts his honour dearer than his life."

"And I'll be his second," said Simon of Hackburn, "and take up ony twa o' ye, gentle or semple, laird or loon, it's a' ane to Simon."

"Who is that rough-looking fellow?" said Sir Frederick Langley, "and what has he to do with the quarrel of gentlemen?"

"I'se a lad frae the Hie Te'iot," said Simon, "and I'll quarrel wi' ony body I like, except the King or the Laird I live under."

"Come," said Marischal, "let us have no brawls.—Mr Earnscliff, although we do not think alike in some things, I trust we may be opponents, even enemies, if fortune will have it so, without losing our respect for truth, fair-play, and each other. I believe you as innocent of this matter as I am myself; and I will pledge myself that my cousin, Ellieslaw, so soon as the perplexity attending these sudden events has left his judgment to its free exercise, shall handsomely acknowledge the very important service you have this day rendered him."

"To have served your cousin is a sufficient reward in itself—Good evening, gentlemen," continued Earnscliff, "I see most of your party are already on their way to Ellieslaw."

Then saluting Marischal with courtesy, and the rest of the party with indifference, Earnscliff turned his horse and rode towards the Heugh-foot, to concert measures with Hobbie Elliot for farther researches after his bride, of whose restoration to her friends he was still ignorant.

"There he goes," said Marischal, "he is a fine, gallant, young fellow, upon my soul, and yet I should like well to have a thrust with him on the green turf. I was reckoned at college nearly his equal with the foils, and I should like to try him at sharps."

"In my opinion," answered Sir Frederick Langley, "we have done very ill in having suffered him, and those men who are with him, to go off without taking away their arms; for the whigs are very likely to draw to a head under such a young fellow as that."

"For shame, Sir Frederick," exclaimed Marischal; "do you think that Ellieslaw could, in honour, consent to any violence being offered to Earnscliff, when he entered his bounds only to bring back his daughter? or, if he were to be of your opinion, do you think that I, and the rest of these gentlemen, would disgrace ourselves by assisting in such a transaction? No, no, fair-play and auld Scotland for ever. When the sword is drawn, I will be as ready to use it as any man; but while it is in the sheath, let us behave like gentlemen and neighbours."

Soon after this colloquy they reached the castle, where Ellieslaw, who had been arrived a few minutes before, met them in the court-yard.

"How is Miss Vere? and have you learned the cause of her being carried off?" asked Marischal hastily.

"She is retired to her apartment greatly fatigued, and I cannot expect much light upon her adventure till her spirits are somewhat recruited," replied her father. "She and I are not the less obliged to you, Marischal, and to my other friends, for their kind enquiries. But I must suppress the father's feelings for a while to give myself up to those of the patriot. You know this is the day fixed for our final decision—time presses—our friends are arriving, and I have opened house, not only for the gentry, but for the under-spur-leathers whom we must necessarily employ. We have, therefore, little time to prepare to meet them—look over these lists, Marchie, (an abbreviation by which Marischal-Wells was known among his friends)—Do you, Sir Frederick, read these letters from Lothian and the west—all is ripe for the sickle, and we have but to summon out the reapers."

"With all my heart," said Marischal; "the more mischief the better sport."

Sir Frederick looked grave and discontented.

"Walk aside with me, my good friend," said Ellieslaw to the sombre Baronet, "I have something for your private ear, with which I know you will be gratified."

They walked into the house, leaving Ratcliffe and Marischal standing together in the court.

"And so," said the former to the latter, "the gentlemen of your political persuasion think the downfall of this government so certain, that they disdain even to throw a decent disguise over the machinations of their party?"

"Faith, Mr Ratcliffe," answered Marischal, "the actions and sentiments of *your* friends may require to be veiled, but I am better pleased that ours can go bare-faced."

"And is it possible," continued Ratcliffe, "that you, who, notwithstanding your thoughtlessness and heat of temper, (I beg pardon, Mr Marischal, I am a plain man)—that, who, notwithstanding these constitutional defects, possess natural good sense and acquired information, should be infatuated enough to embroil yourself in such desperate proceedings? How does your head feel when you are engaged in these dangerous conferences?"

"Not quite so secure on my shoulders," answered Marischal, "as if I were talking of hunting and hawking. I am not of so indifferent a mould as my cousin Ellieslaw, who speaks treason as if it were child's nursery rhymes, and loses and recovers that sweet girl, his daughter, with a good deal less emotion on both occasions, than would have affected me had I lost and recovered a greyhound puppy. My temper is not quite so inflexible, nor my hate against government so inveterate, as to blind me to the full danger of the attempt."

"Then why involve yourself in it?" said Ratcliffe.

"Why, I love this poor exiled king with all my heart; and my father was an old Gilliecrankie-man, and I long to see some amends on the courtiers that have bought and sold old Scotland, whose crown has been so long independent."

"And for the sake of these shadows," said his monitor, "you are going to involve your country in war, and yourself in trouble?"

"*I* involve? No!—but, trouble for trouble, I had rather it came to-morrow than a month hence. Come, I know it will; and, as our country folks say, better soon than syne—it will never find me younger—and, as for hanging, as Sir John Falstaff says, I can become a gallows as well as another. You know the old end of the ballad;

> Sae dauntonly, sae wantonly,
> Sae rantingly gaed he,
> He play'd a spring, and danced a round,
> Beneath the gallows tree."

"Mr Marischal, I am sorry for you," said his grave adviser.

"I am obliged to you, Mr Ratcliffe; but I would not have you judge of our enterprise by my vindication of it; there are wiser heads than mine at the work."

"Wiser heads than yours may lie as low," said Ratcliffe, in a warning tone.

"Perhaps so; but no lighter heart shall; and, to prevent its being made heavier by your remonstrances, I will bid you adieu, Mr Ratcliffe, till dinner time, when you shall see that my apprehensions have not spoiled my appetite."

Chapter Thirteen

> To face the garment of rebellion
> With some fine colour, that may please the eye
> Of fickle changelings, and poor discontents,
> Which gape and rub the elbow at the news
> Of hurly-burly innovation.
> *Henry the Fourth, Part I*

THERE had been great preparations made at Ellieslaw-Castle for the entertainment of this important day, when not only the gentlemen of note in the neighbourhood, attached to the jacobite interest, were expected to rendezvous, but also many subordinate malcontents, whom difficulty of circumstances, love of change, resentment against England, or any of the numerous causes which inflamed men's passions at the time, rendered apt to join in perilous enterprise. The men of rank and substance were not many in number, for almost all the large proprietors stood aloof, and most of the smaller gentry and yeomanry were of the presbyterian persuasion, and, therefore, however displeased with the Union, unwilling to engage in a jacobite conspiracy. But there were some gentlemen of property, who, either from early principle, from religious motives, or sharing the ambitious views of Ellieslaw, had given countenance to his scheme; and there were, also, some fiery young men, like Marischal, desirous of signalizing themselves, by engaging in a dangerous enterprise, by which they hoped to vindicate the independence of their country. The other members of the party were men of inferior rank and desperate fortunes, who were now ready to rise in that part of the country, as they did afterwards in the year 1715, under Forster and Derwentwater, when a troop, commanded by a Border gentleman, named Douglas, consisted almost entirely of freebooters, among whom the notorious Luck-in-a-Bag, as he was called, held a distinguished command. We think it necessary to mention these particulars, applicable solely to the province in which our scene lies, because, unquestionably, the jacobite party in other parts of the kingdom consisted of more formidable, as well as more respectable, materials.

One long table extended itself down the ample hall of Ellieslaw Castle, which was still left much in the state in which it had been one hundred years before, stretching, that is, in gloomy length, through the whole side of the castle, vaulted with ribbed arches of freestone, the groins of which sprung from projecting figures, which, carved into all the wild forms that the fantastic imagination of a Gothic architect could devise, grinned, frowned, and gnashed their tusks at the assembly below. Long, narrow windows lighted the banqueting-room on both sides, filled up with stained glass, through which the sun emitted a dusky and discoloured light. A banner, which tradition averred to have been taken from the English at the battle of Sark, waved over the chair in which Ellieslaw presided, as if to inflame the courage of the guests, by reminding them of ancient victories over their neighbours. He himself, a portly figure, dressed upon this occasion with uncommon care, and with features, which, though of a stern and sinister expression, might well be termed handsome, looked the old feudal baron extremely well. Sir Frederick Langley was placed on his right hand, and Mr Marischal of Marischal-Wells upon his left. Some gentlemen of consideration, with their sons, brothers, and nephews, occupied the upper end of the table, and amongst these Mr Ratcliffe had his place. Beneath the salt-cellar (a massive piece of plate which occupied the midst of the table) sate the *sine nomine turba*, men whose vanity was gratified by occupying even this subordinate space at the social board, while the distinction observed in ranking them was a salvo to the pride of their superiors. That the lower-house was not very select must be admitted, since Willie of Westburnflat was one of the party. The unabashed audacity of this fellow, in daring to present himself in the house of a gentleman, to whom he had just offered so flagrant an insult, can only be accounted for by supposing him conscious that his share in carrying off Miss Vere was a secret, safe in her possession and that of her father.

Before this numerous and miscellaneous party was placed a dinner, consisting, not indeed of all the delicacies of the season, as the newspapers express it, but of viands, ample, solid, and sumptuous, under which the very board groaned. But the mirth was not in proportion to the good cheer. The lower end of the table was, for some time, chilled by constraint and respect upon finding themselves members of so august an assembly, and those who were placed around it had those feelings of awe with which P.P., Clerk of this Parish, describes himself as impressed, when he first uplifted the psalm in presence of those persons of high worship, the wise Mr Justice Freeman, the good Lady Jones, and the great Sir Thomas Truby. This ceremonious frost, however, soon gave way before the incentives to merriment, which were liberally supplied and as liberally consumed by the guests of the lower description. They became talkative, loud, and even clamorous in their mirth.

But it was not in the power of wine or brandy to elevate the spirits of those who held the higher places at the banquet. They experienced the chilling revulsion of spirits, which often takes place when men are called upon to take a desperate resolution, after having placed themselves in circumstances where it is alike difficult to advance or to recede. The precipice looked deeper and more dangerous as they approached to the brink, and each waited with an inward emotion of awe, expecting which of his confederates would set the example by plunging himself down. This inward sensation of fear and reluctance acted differently, according to the various habits and characters of the company. One looked grave, one looked silly, one gazed with apprehension on the empty seats at the higher end of the table, placed for members of the conspiracy, whose prudence had prevailed over their political zeal, and who had absented themselves from their consultations at this critical period, and some seemed to be reckoning up in their minds the comparative rank and prospects of those who were present and absent. Sir Frederick Langley looked moody and discontented. Ellieslaw himself made such forced efforts to raise the spirits of the company as plainly marked the flagging of his own. Ratcliffe watched the scene with the composure of a vigilant but uninterested spectator. Marischal alone, true to the thoughtless vivacity of his character, eat and drank, laughed and jested, and seemed even to find amusement in the embarrassment of the company.

"What has damped our noble courage this morning!" he exclaimed; "we seem to be met at a funeral, where the chief mourners must not speak above their breath, while the mutes and the saulees (looking to the lower end of the table) are carousing below. Ellieslaw, when will you *lift?* where sleeps your spirit, man? and what has quelled the high hope of the Knight of Langley-dale?"

"You speak like a madman," said Ellieslaw; "Do you not see how many are absent?"

"And what of that? Did you not know before, that one-half of the world are better talkers than doers? For my part, I am much encouraged by seeing at least two-thirds of our friends true to the rendezvous, though I suspect one-half of these came to secure the dinner in case of the worst."

"There is no news from the coast which can amount to certainty of the King's arrival," said another of the company, in that tone of subdued and tremulous whisper which implies a failure of resolution.

"Not a line from the Earl of D——, nor a single gentleman from the southern side of the Border."

"What's he that wishes for some men from England?"

exclaimed Marischal, in a theatrical tone of affected heroism,

> "My cousin Ellieslaw? No, my fair cousin,
> If we are doomed to die"——

"For God's sake," said Ellieslaw, "spare us your folly at present, Marischal."

"Well, then," said his kinsman, "I'll bestow my wisdom upon you instead, such as it is. If we have gone forward like fools, do not let us go back like cowards. We have done enough to draw upon us both the suspicion and vengeance of the government; do not let us give up before we have done something to deserve it.—What, will no one speak? Then I'll leap the ditch the first." And, starting up, he filled a beer glass to the brim with claret, and, waving his hand, commanded all to follow his example, and to rise up from their seats. All obeyed— the more qualified guests as if passively, the others with enthusiasm. "Here, my friends, I give you the pledge of the day,—The Independence of Scotland, and the Health of our lawful Sovereign, King James the Eighth, now landed in Lothian, and, as I trust and believe, in full possession of his ancient capital!"

He quaffed off the wine, and threw the glass over his head.

"It should never," he said, "be profaned by a meaner toast."

All followed his example, and, amid the crash of glasses and the shouts of the company, pledged themselves to stand or fall with the principles and political interest which their toast expressed.

"You have leaped the ditch with a witness," said Ellieslaw, apart to Marischal; "but I believe it is all for the best; at all events, we cannot now retreat from our undertaking. One man alone," (looking at Ratcliffe) "has refused the pledge; but of that by and by."

Then, rising up, he addressed the company in a style of inflammatory invective against the government and its measures, especially the Union, a treaty, by means of which, he affirmed, Scotland had been at once cheated of her independence, her commerce, and her honour, and laid as a fettered slave at the foot of the rival, against whom, through such a length of ages, through so many dangers, and by so much blood, she had honourably defended her rights. This was touching a theme which found a responsive chord in the bosom of every man present.

"Our commerce is destroyed," hollowed old John Rewcastle, a Jedburgh smuggler, from the lower end of the table.

"Our agriculture is ruined," said the Laird of Broken-girth-flow, a territory, which, since the days of Adam, had borne nothing but ling and whortleberries.

"Our religion is cut up, root and branch," said the pimple-nosed pastor of the Episcopal meeting-house at Kirkwhistle.

"We shall shortly neither dare shoot a deer or kiss a wench, without a certificate from the presbytery and kirk-treasurer," said Marischal-Wells.

"Or make a brandy Jeroboam on a frosty morning, without licence from a commissioner of excise," said the smuggler.

"Or ride over the fell on a moonless night," said Westburnflat, "without asking leave of young Earnscliff, or some Englified justice of the peace; thae were gude days on the Border when there was neither peace nor justice heard of."

"Let us remember our wrongs at Darien and Glencoe," continued Ellieslaw, "and take arms for protection of our rights, our fortunes, our lives, and our families."

"Think upon genuine episcopal ordination, without which there can be no lawful clergy," said the divine.

"Think of the piracies committed on our East-Indian trade by Green and the English thieves," said William Wilieson, half-owner and sole skipper of a brig that made four voyages annually between Cockpool and Whitehaven.

"Remember your liberties," rejoined Marischal, who seemed to take a mischievous delight in precipitating the movements of the enthusiasm which he had excited, like a roguish boy, that, having lifted the sluice of a mill-dam, enjoys the clatter of the wheels which he has put into motion, without thinking of the mischief he may have occasioned. "Remember your liberties," he exclaimed, "confound cess, press, presbytery and the memory of old Willie that first brought them upon us!"

"Damn the gauger," echoed old John Rewcastle; "I'll cleave him wi' my ain hand."

"And confound the Country-Keeper and the constable," re-echoed Westburnflat; "I'll weize a brace of balls through them ere morning."

"We are agreed, then," said Ellieslaw, when the shouts had something subsided, "to bear this state of things no longer?"

"We are agreed to a man," answered his guests.

"Not literally so," said Mr Ratcliffe; "for though I cannot hope to assuage the violent symptoms which seem so suddenly to have seized upon the company, yet I beg to observe, that as far as the opinion of a single member goes, I do not entirely coincide in the list of grievances which has been announced, and that I do utterly protest against the frantic measures which you seemed disposed to adopt for removing them. I can easily suppose much of what has been spoken may have arisen out of the heat of the moment, or be said perhaps in jest. But there are some jests of a nature very apt to transpire; and you ought to remember, gentlemen, that stone walls have ears."

"Stone walls may have ears," returned Ellieslaw, eyeing him with a look of triumphant malignity, "but domestic spies, Mr Ratcliffe, will soon find themselves without any, if any such dares to continue his abode in a family where his coming was an unauthorized intrusion, where his conduct has been that of a presumptuous meddler, and from which his exit shall be that of a baffled knave, if he does not know how to take a hint."

"Mr Vere," returned Ratcliffe, with calm contempt, "I am fully aware that as soon as my presence becomes useless to you, which it must through the rash step you are about to adopt, it will immediately become unsafe to myself, as it has always been hateful to you. But I have one protection, and it is a strong one; for you would not willingly hear me detail before gentlemen, and men of honour, the singular circumstances in which our connection took its rise. As to the rest, I rejoice at its conclusion; and as I think that Mr Marischal and some other gentlemen will guarantee the safety of my ears and of my throat (for which last I have more reason to be apprehensive) during the course of the night, I shall not leave your castle till to-morrow morning."

"Be it so, sir," replied Vere; "you are entirely safe from my resentment, because you are beneath it, and not because I am afraid of your disclosing any family secrets, although, for your own sake, I warn you to beware how you do so. Your agency and intermediation can be of little consequence to one who will win or lose all, as lawful right or unjust usurpation shall succeed in the struggle that is about to ensue. Farewell, sir."

Ratcliffe cast upon him a look, which Vere seemed to sustain with difficulty, and, bowing to those around him, arose and left the room.

This conversation made an impression on many of the company, which Ellieslaw hastened to dispel, by entering upon the business of the day. Their hasty deliberations went to organize an immediate insurrection. Ellieslaw, Marischal, and Sir Frederick Langley, were chosen leaders, with power to direct their farther measures. A place of rendezvous was appointed, at which all agreed to meet early on the ensuing day, with such followers and friends to the cause as each could collect around him. Several of the guests retired to make the necessary preparations; and Ellieslaw made a formal apology to the others, who with Westburnflat and the old smuggler continued to ply the bottle staunchly, for leaving the head of the table, as he must necessarily hold a separate and sober conference with the coadjutors whom they had associated with him in the command. The apology was the more readily accepted, as he prayed them, at the same time, to continue to amuse themselves with such refreshments as the cellars of the castle afforded. Shouts of applause followed their retreat; and the names of Vere, Langley, and, above all, of Marischal, were thundered forth in chorus, and bathed with copious bumpers repeatedly, during the remainder of the evening.

When the principal conspirators had retired into a separate apartment, they gazed on each other for a minute with a sort of embarrassment, which, in Sir Frederick's dark features, amounted to an expression of discontented sullenness. Marischal was the first to break the pause, saying, with a loud burst of laughter,—"Well! we are fairly embarked now, gentlemen—*vogue la galère!*"

"We may thank you for the plunge," said Ellieslaw.

"Yes; but I don't know how far you will thank me," answered Marischal, "when I shew you this letter which I received just before we sat down. My servant told me it was delivered by a man he had never seen, who went off at the gallop after charging him to put it into my own hands."

Ellieslaw impatiently opened the letter, and read aloud.—

Edinburgh,——

"HOND. SIR,

Having obligations to your family, which shall be nameless, and learning that you are one of the company of adventurers doing business for the house of James and Company, late merchants in London, now at Dunkirk, I think it right to send you this early and private information, that the vessels you expected have been driven off the coast, without having been able to break bulk, or to land any part of their cargo; and that the west-country partners have resolved to withdraw their name from the firm, as it must prove a losing concern. Having good hope you will avail yourself of this early information, to do the needful for your own security, I rest your humble servant,

NIHIL NAMELESS."

For RALPH MARISCHAL, *of Marischal-Wells*
—*These, with care and speed.*

Sir Frederick's jaw dropped, and his countenance blackened as the letter was read, and Ellieslaw exclaimed,—"Why, this affects the very main-spring of our enterprize. If the French fleet, with the King on board, has been chased off by the English, as this d—d scrawl seems to intimate, where are we?"

"Just where we were this morning, I think," said Marischal, still laughing.

"Pardon me, and a truce to your ill-timed mirth, Mr Marischal; this morning we were not committed publicly, as we now stand committed, by your own mad act, when you had a letter in your pocket apprizing you our undertaking was desperate."

"Aye, aye, I expected you would say so. But, in the first place, my friend Nihil Nameless and his letter may be all a flam; and, moreover, I would have you know I am tired of a party that does nothing but form bold resolutions over night, and sleep them away with their wine before morning. The government are now unprovided of men and ammunition; in a few weeks they will have enough of both; the country is now in a flame against them; in a few weeks, betwixt the effects of self-interest, of fear, and of lukewarm indifference, which are already so visible, this first fervour will be as cold as Christmas. So, as I was determined to go the vole, I have taken care you should dip as deep as I—it signifies nothing plunging—you are fairly in the bog, and must struggle through."

"You are mistaken with respect to one of us, Mr Marischal," said Sir Frederick Langley, and, applying himself to the bell, desired the attendant who entered to order his servants and horses instantly.

"You must not leave us, Sir Frederick," said Ellieslaw; "we have our musters to go over."

"I will go to-night, Mr Vere," said the knight, "and write you my intentions in this matter when I am at home."

"Ay," said Marischal, "and send them I suppose by a troop of horse from Carlisle to make us prisoners. Look ye, Sir Frederick, I for one will neither be deserted nor betrayed; and if you leave Ellieslaw-Castle to-night, it shall be by passing over my dead body."

"For shame! Marischal," said Mr Vere, "how can you so hastily misinterpret our friend's intentions? I am sure Sir Frederick can only be jesting with us; for, were he not too honourable to dream of deserting the cause, he cannot but remember the full proofs we have of his accession to it, and his eager activity in advancing it. He cannot but be conscious, besides, that the first information will be readily received by government, and that if the question be, which can first lodge intelligence of the affair, we can easily save a few hours on him."

"You should say *you*, not *we*, when you talk of priority in such a race of treachery; for my part, I won't enter my horse for such a plate," said Marischal; and added, betwixt his teeth, "a pretty pair of fellows to trust a man's neck with!"

"I am not to be intimidated from doing what I think proper," said Sir Frederick Langley; "and my first step shall be to leave Ellieslaw. I have no reason to keep faith with one (looking at Vere) who has kept none with me."

"In what respect?" said Ellieslaw, silencing, with a motion of his hand, his impetuous kinsman,—"how have I disappointed you, Sir Frederick?"

"In the nearest and most tender point—you have trifled with me concerning our proposed alliance, which you well knew was the gage of our political undertaking. This carrying off and this bringing back of Miss Vere,—the cold reception I have met with from her, and the excuses with which you cover it, I believe to be mere evasions, that you may yourself retain possession of the estates which are her's by right, and make me, in the meanwhile, a tool in your desperate enterprize, by holding out hopes and expectations which you are resolved never to realize."

"Sir Frederick, I protest by all that is sacred"——

"I will listen to no protestations; I have been cheated with them too long," answered Sir Frederick.

"If you leave us," said Ellieslaw, "you cannot but know both your ruin and ours is certain; all depends on our adhering together."

"Leave me to take care of myself," returned the knight; "but were what you say true, I would rather perish than be fooled any farther."

"Can nothing—no surety convince you of my sincerity?" said Ellieslaw, anxiously; "this morning I should have repelled your unjust suspicions as an insult, but situated as we now are"——

"You feel yourself compelled to be sincere?" retorted Sir Frederick. "If you would have me think so, there is but one way to convince me of it—let your daughter bestow her hand on me this evening."

"So soon?—impossible," answered Vere, "think of her late alarm —of our present undertaking."

"I will listen to nothing but to her consent, plighted at the altar— You have a chapel in the castle—Doctor Hobbler is present among the company—this proof of your good faith to-night, and we are again joined in heart and hand. If you refuse me now when it is so much for your advantage to consent, how shall I trust you to-morrow, when I shall stand committed in your undertaking, and unable to retract?"

"And I am to understand, that, if you can be made my son-in-law to-night, our friendship is renewed?" said Ellieslaw.

"Most infallibly, and most inviolably," replied Sir Frederick.

"Then," said Vere, "though what you ask is premature, indelicate, and unjust towards my character, yet, Sir Frederick, give me your hand—my daughter shall be your wife."

"This night?"

"This very night," replied Ellieslaw, "before the clock strikes twelve."

"With her own consent, I trust," said Marischal; "for I promise you both, gentlemen, I will not stand tamely by, and see any violence put on the will of my pretty kinswoman."

"Another pest in this hot-headed fellow," muttered Ellieslaw; and then aloud, "With her own consent! For what do you take me, Marischal, that you should suppose your interference necessary to protect my daughter against her father? Depend upon it, she has no repugnance to Sir Frederick Langley."

"Or rather to be called Lady Langley? faith, like enough—there are many women might be of her mind; and I beg your pardon, but these sudden demands and concessions alarmed me a little on her account."

"It is only the suddenness of the proposal that embarrasses me," said Ellieslaw; "but perhaps if she is found intractable, Sir Frederick will consider"——

"I will consider nothing, Mr Vere—your daughter's hand to-night, or I depart, were it at midnight—there is my ultimatum."

"I embrace it," said Ellieslaw; "and I will leave you to talk upon our military preparations, while I go to prepare my daughter for so sudden a change of condition."

So saying, he left the company.

Chapter Fourteen

He brings Earl Osmond to receive my vows.
O dreadful change! for Tancred, haughty Osmond.
Tancred and Sigismunda

MR VERE, whom long practice of dissimulation had enabled to model his very gait and footsteps to aid the purpose of deception, walked along the stone passage, and up the first flight of steps towards Miss Vere's apartment, with the alert, firm, and steady pace of one, who is bound, indeed, upon important business, but who entertains no doubt he can terminate his affairs satisfactorily. But when out of hearing of the gentlemen whom he had left, his step became so slow and irresolute, as to correspond with his doubts and his fears. At length he paused in an anti-chamber to collect his ideas, and form his plan of argument before approaching his daughter.

"In what more hopeless and inextricable dilemma was ever an unfortunate man involved?"—Such was the tenor of his reflections.—"If we now fall to pieces by disunion, there can be little doubt that the government will take my life as the prime agitator of the insurrection. Or, grant I could stoop to save myself by a hasty submission, am I not, even in that case, utterly ruined? I have broken irreconcileably with Ratcliffe, and can have nothing to expect from that quarter but insult and persecution. I must wander forth an impoverished and dishonoured man, without even the means of sustaining life, far less wealth sufficient to counterbalance the infamy which my countrymen, both those whom I desert and those whom I join, will attach to the name of the political renegade. It is not to be thought of. And yet, what choice remains between this lot and the ignominious scaffold? Nothing can save me but reconciliation with these men; and, to accomplish this, I have promised to Langley that Isabella shall marry him ere midnight, and, to Marischal, that she shall do so without compulsion. I have but one remedy betwixt me and ruin—her consent to take a suitor whom she dislikes, upon such short notice as would disgust her, even were he a favoured lover—But I must trust to the romantic generosity of her disposition; and let me paint the necessity of obedience ever so strongly, I cannot overcharge its reality."

Having finished this sad chain of reflections upon his perilous condition, he entered his daughter's apartment, with every nerve bent up to the support of the argument which he was about to sustain. Though a deceitful and ambitious man, he was not so devoid of natural affection but that he was shocked at the part he was about to act, in practising on the feelings of a dutiful and affectionate child; but the recollection, that, if he succeeded, his daughter would only be trepanned into an advantageous match, and that, if he failed, he himself was a lost man, was quite sufficient to drown all scruples.

He found Miss Vere seated by the window of her dressing-room, her head reclining on her hand, and either sunk in slumber, or so deeply engaged in meditation, that she did not hear the noise he made at his entrance. He approached with his features composed to a deep expression of sorrow and sympathy, and, sitting down beside her, solicited her attention by quietly taking her hand, a motion which he did not fail to accompany with a deep sigh.

"My father?—" said Isabella, with a sort of start which expressed at least as much fear, as joy or affection.

"Yes, Isabella," said Vere, "your unhappy father, who comes now as a penitent to crave forgiveness of his daughter for an injury done to her in the excess of his affection, and then to take leave of her for ever."

"Sir?—Offence to me?—Take leave for ever?—What does all this mean?" said Miss Vere.

"Yes, Isabella, I am serious. But first let me ask you, have you no suspicion that I may have been privy to the strange chance which befel you yesterday morning?"

"You, sir?" answered Isabella, stammering, between a consciousness that he had guessed her thoughts justly, and the shame as well as fear which forbade her to acknowledge a suspicion so degrading and so unnatural.

"Yes!" he continued, "your hesitation confesses that you entertained such an opinion, and I have now the painful task of confessing that your suspicions have done me no injustice. But listen to my motives. In an evil hour I countenanced the addresses of Sir Frederick Langley, conceiving it impossible that you could have any permanent objections to a match where the advantages were, in most respects, on your side. In a worse, I entered with him into measures calculated to restore our banished monarch, and the independence of my country. He has taken advantage of my unguarded confidence, and now has my life at his disposal."

"Your life, sir?" said Isabella, faintly.

"Yes, Isabella, the life of him who gave life to you. So soon as I foresaw the excesses into which his headlong passion (for, to do him justice, I believe his unreasonable conduct arises from excess of attachment to you) was like to hurry him, I endeavoured, by finding a plausible pretext for your absence for some weeks, to extricate myself from the dilemma in which I am placed. For this purpose I would, in case your objections to the match continued insurmountable, have sent you privately for a few months to the convent of your maternal aunt at Paris. By a series of mistakes you have been brought from the place of secrecy and security which I had destined for your temporary abode. Fate has baffled my last chance of escape, and I have only to give you my blessing, and send you from the castle with Mr Ratcliffe, who now leaves it—my own fate will soon be decided."

"Good Heaven, sir! can this be possible?" exclaimed Isabella. "O, why was I freed from the restraint in which you placed me? or why did you not impart your pleasure to me?"

"Think an instant, Isabella. Would you have had me prejudice in your opinion the friend I was most desirous of serving, by communicating to you the injurious eagerness with which he pursues his object? Could I do so honourably, having promised to assist his suit?—But it is all over. I and Marischal have made up our minds to die like men; it only remains to send you from hence under a safe escort."

"Great powers! and is there no remedy?"

"None, my child," answered Vere, gently, "unless one which you would not advise your father to adopt—to be the first to betray his friends."

"O, no! no!" she answered abhorrently yet hastily, as if to reject the temptation which the alternative presented to her. "But is there no other hope—through flight—through mediation—through supplication?—I will bend my knee to Sir Frederick!"

"It would be fruitless degradation; he is determined on his course, and I am equally resolved to stand the hazard of my fate.—On one condition only he will turn aside from his purpose, and that condition my lips shall never utter to you."

"Name it, I conjure you, my dear father! What can he ask that we ought not to grant, to prevent the hideous catastrophe with which you are threatened?"

"That, Isabella," said Vere, solemnly, "you shall never know until your father's head has rolled on the bloody scaffold; then indeed you will learn there was one sacrifice by which I might have been saved."

"And why not speak it now? Do you fear I would flinch from the sacrifice of fortune for your preservation? or would you bequeath me the bitter legacy of live-long remorse so oft as I shall think that you perished while there remained one mode of preventing the dreadful misfortune that overhangs you?"

"Then, my child," said Vere, "since you press me to name what I would a thousand times rather leave in silence, I must inform you that he will accept for ransom nothing but your hand in marriage, and that conferred before midnight this very evening!"

"This evening, sir?—and to such a man!—a man?—a monster,

who could wish to win the daughter by threatening the life of the father—it is impossible!"

"You say right, my child," answered her father, "it is indeed impossible; nor have I either the right or the wish to exact such a sacrifice— It is the course of nature that the old should die and be forgot, and the young should live and be happy."

"My father die? and his child can save him?—but no—no—my dear father, pardon me, it is impossible; you only wish to guide me to your wishes. I know your object is what you think my happiness, and this dreadful tale is only told to influence my conduct and subdue my scruples."

"My daughter," replied Ellieslaw, in a tone where offended authority seemed to struggle with parental affection, "my child suspects me of inventing a false tale to work upon her feelings! Even this I must bear, and even from this unworthy suspicion I must descend to vindicate myself. You know the stainless honour of your cousin Marischal— mark what I shall write to him, and judge from his answer, if the danger in which we stand is not real, and whether I have not used every means to avert it."

He sate down, wrote a few lines hastily, and handed them to Isabella, who, after repeated and painful efforts, cleared her eyes and head sufficient to discern their purport.

"Dear Cousin," said the billet, "I find my daughter, as I expected, in despair at the untimely and premature urgency of Sir Frederick Langley. She cannot even comprehend the peril in which we stand, or how much we are in his power—Use your influence with him, for Heaven's sake, to modify proposals to the acceptance of which I cannot, and will not, urge my child against all her own feelings, as well as those of delicacy and propriety, and oblige your loving Cousin,— R.V."

In the agitation of the moment, when her swimming eyes and dizzy brain could hardly comprehend the sense of what she looked upon, it is not surprising that Miss Vere should have omitted to remark that this letter seemed to rest her scruples rather upon the form and time of the proposed union, than on a rooted dislike to the suitor proposed to her. Mr Vere rang the bell, and gave the letter to a servant to be delivered to Mr Marischal, and, rising from his chair, continued to traverse the apartment in silence and in great agitation until the answer was returned. He glanced it over, and wrung the hand of his daughter as he gave it to her. The tenor was as follows:—

"MY DEAR KINSMAN,
I have already urged the knight on the point you mention, and I find

him as fixed as Cheviot. I am truly sorry my fair cousin should be pressed to give up any of her maidenly rights. Sir Frederick consents, however, to leave the castle with me the instant the ceremony is performed, and we will raise our followers and begin the fray. Thus there is great hope the bridegroom may be knocked on the head before he and the bride can meet again, so Bell has a fair chance to be Lady Langley *à très bon marché*. For the rest, I can only say, that if she can make up her mind to the alliance at all—it is no time for mere maiden ceremony—my pretty cousin must needs consent to marry in haste, or we shall all repent at leisure, or rather have very little leisure to repent, which is all at present from him who rests your affectionate kinsman,—R.M."

"P.S. Tell Isabella that I would rather cut the knight's throat after all, and end the dilemma that way, than see her constrained to marry him against her will."

When Isabella had read this letter, it dropped from her hand, and she would, at the same time, have fallen from her chair, had she not been supported by her father.

"My God, my child will die!" exclaimed Vere, the feelings of nature overcoming, even in *his* breast, the sentiments of selfish policy; "look up, Isabella—look up, my child—come what will, you shall not be the sacrifice—I will fall myself with the consciousness I leave you happy —My child may weep on my grave, but she shall not—not in this instance—reproach my memory." He called a servant.—"Go, bid Mr Ratcliffe come hither directly."

During this interval, Miss Vere became deadly pale, clenched her hands, pressing the palms strongly together, closed her eyes, and drew her lips together with strong compression, as if the severe constraint which she put upon her internal feelings extended even to her muscular organization.—Then raising her head, and drawing in her breath strongly ere she spoke, she said, with firmness,—"Father, I consent to the marriage."

"You shall not—you shall not, my child—my dear child—you shall not embrace certain misery to free me from uncertain danger."

So exclaimed Ellieslaw; and, strange and inconsistent beings that we are! he expressed the real though momentary feelings of his heart.

"Father," repeated Isabella, "I will consent to the marriage."

"No, my child, no—not now at least—we will humble ourselves to obtain delay from him; and yet, Isabella, could you overcome a dislike which has no real foundation, think, in other respects, what a match— wealth—rank—importance."

"Father!" reiterated Isabella, "I have consented."

It seemed as if she had lost the power of saying any thing else, or even of varying the phrase which, with such effort, she had compelled herself to utter.

"Heaven bless thee, my child!—Heaven bless thee!—And it will bless with riches, with pleasure, with power."

Miss Vere faintly entreated to be left by herself for the rest of the evening.

"But will you not receive Sir Frederick?" said her father anxiously.

"I will meet him," she replied, "I will meet him—when I must—and where I must—but spare me now."

"Be it so, my dearest; you shall know no restraint that I can save you from. Do not think too hardly of Sir Frederick for this, it is an excess of passion."

Isabella waved her hand impatiently.

"Forgive me, my child—I go—Heaven bless thee. At eleven—if you call me not before—at eleven I come to seek you."

When he left Isabella she dropped upon her knees—"Heaven aid me to support the resolution I have taken—Heaven only can—O, poor Earnscliff! who shall comfort him? and with what contempt he will pronounce her name who listened to him to-day and gave herself to another at night. But let him despise me—better so than that he should know the truth—Let him despise me—if it will but lessen his grief, I should feel comfort in the loss of his esteem."

She wept bitterly; attempting in vain, from time to time, to commence the prayer for which she had sunk on her knees, but unable to calm her spirits sufficiently for the exercise of devotion. As she remained in this agony of mind the door of her apartment was slowly opened.

Chapter Fifteen

The darksome cave they enter, where they found
The woful man, low sitting on the ground,
Musing full sadly in his sullen mind.
                                        Faery Queen

THE INTRUDER on Miss Vere's sorrows was Ratcliffe. Ellieslaw had, in the agitation of his mind, forgotten to countermand the order he had given to call him thither, so that he opened the door with the words, "You sent for me, Mr Vere." Then looking around—"Miss Vere, alone! on the ground! and in tears!"

"Leave me—leave me, Mr Ratcliffe," said the unhappy young lady.

"I must not leave you," said Ratcliffe; "I have been repeatedly requesting admittance to take my leave of you, and have been refused, until your father himself sent for me. Blame me not, if I am bold and intrusive; I have a duty to discharge which makes me so."

"I cannot listen to you—I cannot speak to you, Mr Ratcliffe; take my best wishes, and, for God's sake, leave me."

"Tell me only, is it true that this monstrous match is to go forwards, and this very night? I heard the very servants proclaim it as I was on the great stair-case—I heard directions given to clear out the chapel."

"Spare me, Mr Ratcliffe; and, from the state in which you see me, judge of the cruelty of these questions."

"Married? to Sir Frederick Langley? and this night? It must not—cannot—shall not be."

"It *must* be so, Mr Ratcliffe, or my father is ruined."

"Ah! I understand," answered Ratcliffe; "and you have sacrificed yourself to save him who—but let the virtue of the child atone for his faults—What *can* be done? Time presses—I know but one remedy—with four-and-twenty hours I might find many—Miss Vere, you must implore the protection of the only human being who has it in his power to controul the course of events which threatens to hurry you before it."

"And what human being," answered Miss Vere, "has such power?"

"Start not when I name him," said Ratcliffe, coming near her, and speaking in a low but distinct voice. "It is he who is called Elshender the Recluse of Meikle-stane-Moor."

"You are mad, Mr Ratcliffe, or you mean to insult my misery by an ill-timed jest!"

"I am as much in my senses, young lady, as you are; and I am no idle jester, far less with misery, least of all with your misery. I swear to you that this being (who is other far than what he seems) actually possesses the means of redeeming you from this hateful union."

"And of insuring my father's safety?"

"Yes! even that," said Ratcliffe, "if you plead his cause with him—yet how to obtain admittance?"

"Fear not that," said Miss Vere, suddenly recollecting the incident of the rose; "I remember he desired me to call upon him for aid in my extremity, and gave me this flower as a token. Ere it faded away entirely, I would need, he said, his assistance; is it possible his words can have been aught but the ravings of insanity?"

"Doubt it not—fear it not—but, above all," said Ratcliffe, "let us lose no time—Are you at liberty and unwatched?"

"I believe so," said Isabella; "but what would you have me do?"

"Leave the castle instantly, and throw yourself at the feet of this extraordinary man, who, in circumstances that seem to argue the extremity of the most contemptible poverty, possesses yet almost an absolute influence over your fate.—Guests and servants are deep in their carouse—the leaders sitting in conclave on their treasonable schemes—my horse stands ready in the stable—I will saddle one for you, and meet you at the little garden-gate—O, let no doubt of my prudence or fidelity prevent your taking the only step in your power to escape the dreadful fate which must attend the wife of Sir Frederick Langley!"

"Mr Ratcliffe," said Miss Vere, "you have always been esteemed a man of honour and probity, and a drowning wretch will catch at the feeblest twig—I will trust you—I will follow your advice—I will meet you at the garden-gate."

She bolted the outer-door of her apartment as soon as Mr Ratcliffe left her, and descended to the garden by a separate stair of communication which opened to her dressing-room. On the way she felt inclined to retract the consent she had so hastily given to a plan so hopeless and extravagant. But as she passed in her descent a private door which entered to the chapel from the back-stair, she heard the voice of the female-servants as they were employed in the task of cleaning it. They spoke in a tone of commiseration.

"Married! and to sae bad a man—Ewhow, sirs! ony thing rather than that."

"They are right—they are right," said Miss Vere, "any thing rather than that."

She hurried to the garden. Mr Ratcliffe was true to his appointment—the horses stood saddled at the garden-gate, and in a few minutes they were advancing rapidly towards the hut of the Solitary.

While the ground was favourable, the speed of their journey was such as to prevent much communication; but when a steep ascent compelled them to slacken their pace, a new cause of apprehension occurred to Miss Vere's mind.

"Mr Ratcliffe," she said, pulling up her horse's bridle, "let us prosecute no farther a journey, which nothing but the extreme agitation of my mind can vindicate my having undertaken—I am well aware that this man passes among the vulgar as being possessed of supernatural powers, and carrying on an intercourse with beings of another world—I would have you aware I am neither to be imposed on by such follies, nor, were I to believe in their existence, durst I, with my feelings of religion, apply to this being in my distress."

"I should have thought, Miss Vere," replied Ratcliffe, "my character and habits of thinking were so well known to you, that you might have held me exculpated from crediting such absurdity."

"But in what other mode can a being so miserable himself in

appearance possess the power of assisting me?"

"Miss Vere," said Ratcliffe, after a momentary pause, "I am bound by a solemn oath of secrecy—You must, without farther explanation, be satisfied with my pledged assurance, that he does possess the power, if you can inspire him with the will, and that I doubt not."

"Mr Ratcliffe," said Miss Vere, "you may yourself be mistaken; you ask an unlimited degree of confidence from me."

"Recollect, Miss Vere," he replied, "that when, in your humanity, you asked me to interfere with your father in favour of Haswell and his ruined family—when you requested me to prevail on him to do a thing most abhorrent to his nature—to forgive an injury and remit a penalty —I stipulated that you should ask me no questions concerning the sources of my influence—You found no reason to distrust me then, do not distrust me now."

"But the extraordinary mode of life of this man," said Miss Vere; "his seclusion—his figure—the deepness of misanthropy which he is said to express in his language—Mr Ratcliffe, what can I think of him if he really possesses the powers you ascribe to him?"

"This man, young lady," replied Ratcliffe gravely, "was bred a catholic, a sect which affords a thousand instances of men who have retired from power and affluence to voluntary privations more strict even than his."

"But he avows no religious motive."

"No," replied Ratcliffe; "disgust with the world has operated his retreat from it without assuming the veil of superstition. Thus far I may tell you—He was born to great wealth, which his parents designed should become greater by his union with a kinswoman, whom for that purpose they bred up in their own house—You have seen his figure; judge what the young lady must have thought of the lot to which she was destined—Yet, habituated to his appearance, she showed no reluctance, and the friends of —— of the person of whom I speak, doubted not that the excess of his attachment, the various acquisitions of his mind, his many and amiable qualities, had over-come the natural horror which his destined bride must have enter-tained at an exterior so dreadfully inauspicious."

"And did they judge truly?"

"You shall hear. He at least was fully aware of his own deficiency; the sense of it haunted him like a phantom. 'I am,' was his own expression to me,—I mean to a man whom he trusted, 'I am, in spite of what you would say, a poor miserable outcast, fitter to have been smothered in the cradle, according to the wise law of the ancient Spartans, than to have been brought up to scare the world in which I crawl.' The person whom he addressed in vain endeavoured to

impress him with the indifference to external form, which is the natural result of philosophy, or entreat him to recal the superiority of
mental talents to the more attractive attributes that are merely personal. 'I hear you,' he would reply; 'but you speak the voice of cold-
blooded Stoicism, or, at best, of friendly partiality. But look at every
book which we have read, those excepted of that abstract philosophy
which feels no responsive voice in our natural feelings. Is not personal
form, such as at least can be tolerated without horror and disgust,
always represented as essential to our ideas of a friend, far more a
lover? Is not such a mutilated monster as I am, excluded, by the very
fiat of Nature, from her fairest enjoyments? What but my wealth
prevents all—perhaps even Letitia, or you, from shunning me as
something foreign to your nature, and more odious, by bearing that
distorted resemblance to humanity which we remark in the animals
that are most hateful to man because they seem his caricature?'"

"You repeat the sentiments of a madman," said Miss Vere.

"No," replied her conductor, "unless a morbid and excessive sensibility on such a subject can be termed insanity. Yet I will not deny that
this governing feeling and apprehension carried the person who
entertained it, to lengths which indicated a deranged imagination. He
appeared to think that it was necessary for him, by exuberant, and not
always well-chosen instances of liberality, and even profusion, to unite
himself to the human race, from which he conceived himself naturally
dissevered. The benefits which he bestowed, from a disposition
naturally philanthropical in an uncommon degree, were exaggerated
by the influence of the goading reflection, that more was necessary
from him than from others, as if it were to reconcile mankind to
receive him into their class. It is scarce necessary to say, that the
bounty which flowed from a source so capricious was often abused,
and his confidence frequently betrayed. These disappointments
which occur to all, more or less, and most to such as confer benefits
without just discrimination, his diseased fancy set down to the hatred
and contempt excited by his personal deformity. But I fatigue you,
Miss Vere."

"No—by no means—I—I could not prevent my attention from
wandering an instant; pray proceed."

"He became at length," continued Ratcliffe, "the most ingenious self-tormentor of whom I have ever heard; the scoff of the
rabble, and the sneer of the yet more brutal vulgar of his own
rank, was to him agony and breaking on the wheel. He registered
the laugh of the carman whom he passed in the street, and the
suppressed titter, or yet more offensive terror, of the girl of
quality to whom he was introduced in company, as proofs of the

true sense which the world entertained of him, as a prodigy unfit to be received among them on the usual terms of society, and as vindicating the wisdom of his purpose in withdrawing himself from among them. On the faith and sincerity of two persons alone, he seemed to rely implicitly—on that of his betrothed bride, and of a friend eminently gifted in personal accomplishments, who seemed, and indeed was probably, sincerely attached to him. He ought to have been so, at least, for he was literally loaded with benefits by him whom you now are about to see. The parents of the subject of my story died within a short space of each other. Their death postponed the marriage, for which the day had been fixed. The lady did not seem greatly to mourn this delay; perhaps that was not to have been expected, but she intimated no change of intention, when, after a decent interval, a second day was named for their union. The friend of whom I spoke was then a constant resident at the Hall. In an evil hour, at the earnest request and entreaty of this friend, they joined a general party where men of different political opinions were mingled, and where they drank deep. A quarrel ensued; the friend drew his sword with others, and was thrown down and disarmed by a more powerful antagonist. They fell in the struggle at the feet of the Recluse, who, maimed and truncated as his form appears, possesses, nevertheless, great strength, as well as strong passions. He caught up a sword, pierced the heart of his friend's antagonist, was tried, and his life, with difficulty, redeemed from justice at the expence of a year's close imprisonment, the punishment of manslaughter. The incident affected him most deeply, the more that the deceased was a man of excellent character, and had sustained gross insult and injury ere he drew his sword.—I think, from that moment, I observed—I beg pardon—the fits of morbid sensibility which had tormented this unfortunate gentleman, were rendered henceforth more acute by remorse, which he, of all men, was least capable of having willingly incurred, or of sustaining when it became his unhappy lot. His paroxysms of agony could not be concealed from the lady to whom he was betrothed; and it must be confessed they were of an alarming and fearful nature. He comforted himself, that, at the expiry of his imprisonment, he would form with his wife and friend a society, encircled by which he might dispense with more extensive communication with the world. He was deceived. Before that term elapsed, his friend and his betrothed bride were man and wife. The effect of a shock so dreadful on an ardent temperament, and a disposition already soured by bitter remorse and loosened by the indulgence of a gloomy imagination from the rest of mankind, I cannot describe to you; it was as if the last cable at which the vessel rode had suddenly parted, and left her abandoned to the wild fury of the tempest. He was placed under restraint. As a temporary measure this might have been justifiable; but his hard-hearted friend, who, in consequence of his marriage, was now his nearest ally, prolonged his confinement, in order to enjoy the management of his immense estates. There was one who owed his all to the sufferer, an humble friend, but grateful and faithful. By unceasing exertion, and repeated invocation of justice, he at length succeeded in obtaining his patron's freedom, and re-instatement in the management of his own property, to which was soon added that of his intended bride, who, having died without male issue, her estates reverted to him, as heir of entail. But freedom and wealth were unable to restore the equipoize of his mind; the first he despised, the last only served him as far as it afforded him the means of indulging his strange and wayward fancy. He had renounced the Catholic religion, but perhaps some of its doctrines continued to influence his mind, over which remorse and misanthropy now assumed, in appearance, an unbounded authority. His life has since been that of alternately a pilgrim and a hermit, suffering the most severe privations, not indeed in ascetic devotion, but in abhorrence of mankind. Yet no man's words and actions have been at such a wide difference, nor has any hypocritical wretch ever been more ingenious in assigning good motives for his most vile actions, than this unfortunate in reconciling to his abstract principles of misanthropy, a conduct which flows from his natural generosity and kindliness of feeling."

"Still, Mr Ratcliffe—still you describe the inconsistencies of a madman."

"By no means," replied Ratcliffe. "That the imagination of this gentleman is disordered, I will not pretend to dispute; and I have already told you that it has sometimes broke out into paroxysms approaching to real mental alienation. But it is of his common state of mind which I speak; it is irregular, but not deranged; the shades which distinguish the maniac from the man of a sound mind are as gradual as those that divide the light of noon-day from midnight. The courtier who ruins his fortune for the attainment of a title which can do him no good, or power of which he can make no suitable or creditable use, the miser who hoards his useless wealth, and the prodigal who squanders it, are all in the eye of sound reason marked with a certain shade of insanity. To criminals who are guilty of enormities, when the temptation to a sober mind bears no proportion to the horror of the act, or the probability of detection and punishment, the same observation applies; and all violent passions, as well as anger, may be termed a short madness."

"This may be all good philosophy, Mr Ratcliffe," answered Miss Vere; "but, excuse me, it by no means emboldens me to visit, at this late hour, a person whose extravagance of imagination you yourself can only palliate."

"Rather, then," said Ratcliffe, "receive my solemn assurances that you do not incur the slightest danger. But what I have been hitherto afraid to mention for fear of alarming you, is, that now when we are within sight of his retreat, for I can discern it through the twilight, I must go no farther with you; you must proceed alone."

"Alone?—I dare not."

"You must," continued Ratcliffe; "I will remain here and wait for you."

"You will not then stir from this place," said Miss Vere; "yet the distance is so great, you could not hear me were I to cry for assistance."

"Fear nothing," said her guide; "or observe, at least, the utmost caution in suppressing every expression of timidity. Recollect that his predominant and most harassing apprehension arises from a consciousness of the hideousness of his appearance. Your path lies straight beside yon half-fallen willow; keep the left side of it; the marsh lies on the right. Farewell for a time. Remember what you are threatened with, and let it overcome at once your fears and scruples."

"Mr Ratcliffe," said Isabella, "Farewell; if you have deceived an unfortunate like myself, you have forfeited the fair character for probity and honour to which I have trusted."

"On my life—on my soul," continued Ratcliffe, raising his voice as the distance between them increased, "you are safe—perfectly safe."

Chapter Sixteen

> ———'Twas time and griefs
> That framed him thus: Time, with his fairer hand,
> Offering the fortunes of his former days,
> The former man may make him—Bring us to him,
> And chance it as it may.

THE SOUNDS of Ratcliffe's voice had died on Isabella's ear; but as she frequently looked back, it was some encouragement to her to discern his form now darkening in the gloom. Ere, however, she went much farther, she lost the object in the increasing shade. The last glimmer of the twilight placed her before the hut of the Solitary. She twice extended her hand to the door, and twice she withdrew, and when she did at length make the effort, the knock did not equal in violence the throb of her own bosom. Her next effort was louder; her third was reiterated, for the fear of not obtaining the protection from which Ratcliffe promised so much, began to overpower the terrors of his presence from whom she was to request it. At length, as she still received no answer, she repeatedly called upon the Dwarf by his assumed name, and requested him to answer and open to her.

"What miserable being is reduced," said the appalling voice of the Solitary, "to seek refuge here? Go hence; when the heath-fowl need shelter, they seek it not in the nest of the night-raven."

"I come to you, father," said Isabella, "in my hour of adversity, even as you yourself commanded, when you promised your heart and your door should be open to my distress; but I fear"——

"Ha!" said the Solitary, "then thou art Isabella Vere; give me a token that thou art she."

"I have brought you back the rose which you gave me; alas, it has not had time to fade ere the hard fate you foretold has come upon me!"

"And if thou hast thus redeemed thy pledge," said the Dwarf, "I will not forfeit mine. The heart and the door that are shut against every other earthly being shall be open to thee and to thy sorrows."

She heard him move in his hut, and presently afterwards strike a light. One by one, bolt and bar were then withdrawn, the heart of Isabella throbbing higher as these obstacles to their meeting were successively removed. The door opened, and the Solitary stood before her, his uncouth form and features illuminated by the iron lamp which he held in his hand.

"Enter, daughter of affliction," he said,—"enter the house of misery."

She entered; and, with a precaution which increased her trepidation, the Recluse's first act, after setting the lamp upon the table, was to replace the numerous bolts which secured the door of his hut. She shrunk as she heard the noise which accompanied this ominous operation, yet remembered Ratcliffe's caution, and endeavoured to suppress all appearance of apprehension. The light of the lamp was weak and uncertain; but the Recluse, without taking immediate notice of Isabella, otherwise than by motioning her to sit down on a small settle beside the fire-place, made haste to kindle some dry furze, which presently cast a blaze through the cottage. Wooden shelves, which bore a few books, some bundles of dried herbs, and one or two cups and platters, were on one side of the fire; on the other were placed the ordinary tools of field-labour, mixed with those used by mechanics. Where the bed should have been, there was a wooden frame, strewed with withered moss and rushes, the couch of the ascetic. The whole space of the cottage did not exceed ten feet by six within the walls; and its only furnit-

ure, besides what we have mentioned, were a table and two stools
formed of rough deal.

Within these narrow precincts Isabella now found herself enclosed
with a being whose history had nothing to reassure her, and the fearful
conformation of whose hideous countenance inspired an almost
superstitious terror. He occupied the seat opposite to her, and drooping his huge and shaggy eyebrows over his piercing black eyes, gazed at
her in silence, as if agitated by a variety of contending feelings. On the
other side sate Isabella, pale as death, her long hair uncurled by the
evening damps, and falling over her shoulders and breast, as the wet
streamers of a vessel droop from the mast when the storm has passed
away and left her stranded on the beach. The Dwarf first broke the
silence with the sudden, abrupt, and alarming question,—"Woman,
what evil fate has brought thee hither?"

"My father's danger, and your own command," she replied faintly,
but firmly.

"And you hope for aid from me?"

"If you can bestow it," she replied, still in the same tone of mild
submission.

"And how should I possess that power?" continued the Dwarf, with
a bitter sneer; "Is mine the form of a redresser of wrongs? Is this the
castle in which one powerful enough to be sued to by fair suppliants is
likely to hold his residence? I but mocked thee, girl, when I said I
could relieve thee."

"Then, must I depart, and face my fate as I best may?"

"No!" said the Dwarf, rising, interposing between her and the
door, and motioning to her sternly to resume her seat—"No! you
leave me not in this way; we must have farther conference. Why
should one being desire aid of another? Why should not each be
sufficient to itself? Look round you—I, the most despised and most
decrepid outcast on Nature's common, have required sympathy and
help from no one. These stones are of my own piling; these utensils I
framed with my own hands; and with this"——and he laid his hand
with a fierce smile on the long dagger which he always wore beneath
his garment, and unsheathed it so far that the blade glimmered clear
in the fire-light—"With this," he pursued, as he thrust the weapon
back into the scabbard, "I can, if necessary, defend the vital spark
enclosed in this poor trunk, against the strongest and fairest that shall
threaten me with injury."

It was with difficulty Isabella refrained from screaming out aloud;
but she *did* refrain.

"This," continued the Recluse, "is the life of nature, solitary, self-
sufficing, and independent. The wolf calls not the wolf to aid him in

forming his den; and the vulture invites not another to assist her in striking down her prey."

"And when they are unable to procure themselves support," said Isabella, judiciously thinking that he would be most accessible to argument couched in his own metaphorical style, "what is then to befal them?"

"Let them starve, die, and be forgotten; it is the common lot of humanity."

"It is the lot of the wild tribes of nature," said Isabella, "but chiefly of those who are destined to support themselves by rapine, which brooks no partner; but it is not the law of nature in general; even the lower orders have confederacies for mutual defence. But mankind—the race would perish did they cease to aid each other. From the time that the mother binds the child's head, till the moment that some kind assistant wipes the death-damp from the brow of the dying, we cannot exist without mutual help. All, therefore, that need aid, have right to ask it of their fellow-mortals; no one who has the power of granting can refuse it without guilt."

"And in this simple hope, poor maiden," said the Solitary, "thou hast come into the desert, to seek one whose wish it were that the league thou hast spoken of were broken for ever, and that, in very truth, the whole race should perish! Wert thou not frightened?"

"Misery," said Isabella, firmly, "is superior to fear."

"Hast thou not heard it said in thy mortal world, that I have leagued myself with other powers, deformed to the eye and malevolent to the human race as myself? Hast thou not heard this? And doest thou seek my cell at midnight?"

"The Being I worship supports me against such idle fears," said Isabella; but the increasing agitation of her bosom belied the courage which her words expressed.

"Ho! ho!" said the Dwarf, "thou vauntest thyself a philosopher? Yet, should'st thou not have thought of the danger of entrusting thyself, young and beautiful, in the power of one so spited against humanity, as to place his chief pleasure in defacing, destroying, degrading her fairest works?"

Isabella, much alarmed, continued to answer, with firmness, "Whatever injuries you may have sustained in the world, you are incapable of revenging them on one who never wronged you, nor, wilfully, any other."

"Ay, but maiden," he continued, his dark eyes flashing with an expression of malignity which communicated itself to his wild and distorted features, "Revenge is like the hungry wolf, which asks only

to tear flesh and lap blood. Think you the lamb's plea of innocence
would be listened to?"

"Man!" said Isabella, rising and expressing herself with much dig-
nity, "I fear not the horrible ideas with which you would impress me. I
cast them from me with disdain. Be you mortal or fiend, you would not
offer injury to one who sought you as a suppliant in her utmost need
—you would not—you durst not."

"Thou say'st truly, maiden," rejoined the Solitary; "I dare not—I
would not. Begone to thy dwelling. Fear nothing with which they
threaten thee. Thou hast asked my protection—thou shalt find it
effectual."

"But, father, this very night I have consented to wed the man that I
abhor, or I must put the seal to my father's ruin."

"This night?—at what hour?"

"Ere midnight."

"And twilight," said the Dwarf, "has already passed away. But fear
nothing, there is ample time to protect thee."

"And my father?" continued Isabella, in a suppliant tone.

"Thy father," replied the Dwarf, "has been, and is, my most bitter
enemy. But fear not; thy virtue shall save him. And now, begone; were
I to keep thee longer by me, I might again fall into the stupid dreams
concerning human worth from which I have been so fearfully
awakened. But fear nothing—at the very foot of the altar I will redeem
thee. Adieu, time presses, and I must act!"

He led her to the door of the hut, which he opened for her departure. She remounted her horse, which had been feeding in the outer
enclosure, and pressed him forward by the light of the moon, which
was now rising, to the spot where she had left Ratcliffe.

"Have you succeeded?" was his first eager question.

"I have obtained promises from him to whom you sent me; but how
can he possibly accomplish them?"

"Thank God!" said Ratcliffe; "doubt not his power to fulfil his
promise."

At this moment a shrill whistle was heard to resound along the
heath.

"Hark!" said Ratcliffe, "he calls me—Miss Vere, return home, and
leave unbolted the postern-door of the garden; to that which opens on
the back-stairs I have a private key."

A second whistle was heard yet more shrill and prolonged than the
first.

"I come, I come," said Ratcliffe; and, setting spurs to his horse,
rode over the heath in the direction of the Recluse's hut. Miss Vere
returned to the castle in less than half an hour after she parted with

Ratcliffe, though the distance was five long miles, so much had the mettle of the animal on which she rode, and her own anxiety of mind, combined to accelerate her journey.

She obeyed Ratcliffe's directions, though without well apprehending their purpose, and leaving her horse at large in a paddock near the garden, hurried to her own apartment, which she reached without observation. She now unbolted her door, and rang her bell for lights. Her father appeared along with the servant who answered her summons.

"He had been twice," he said, "listening at her door during the two hours which had elapsed since he left her, and, not hearing her speak, had become apprehensive that she was taken ill."

"And now, my dear father," she said, "permit me to claim the promise you so kindly gave; let the last moments of freedom which I am to enjoy be mine without interruption; and protract to the last moment the respite which is allowed me."

"I will," said her father; "nor shall you be again interrupted. But this disordered dress—this dishevelled hair—do not let me find you thus when I call on you again; the sacrifice to be beneficial must seem voluntary."

"Must it be so?" she replied, "then fear not, my father, the victim shall be adorned."

Chapter Seventeen

This looks not like a nuptial.
Much Ado about Nothing

THE CHAPEL in the castle of Ellieslaw, destined to be the scene of this ill-omened union, was a building of much older date than the castle itself, though that claimed considerable antiquity. Before the wars between England and Scotland had become so common and of such long duration, that the buildings along both sides of the Border were chiefly dedicated to warlike purposes, there had been a small settlement of monks at Ellieslaw, a dependency, it is believed by antiquaries, upon the rich Abbey of Jedburgh. Their possessions had long passed away under the changes introduced by war and mutual ravage. A feudal castle had arisen on the ruins of their cells, and their chapel was included within its precincts.

The edifice, in its round arches and massive pillars, the simplicity of which referred their date to what has been called the Saxon architecture, presented at all times a dark and sombre appearance, and had been frequently used as the cemetery of the family of the feudal lords, as well as formerly of the monastic brethren. But it looked doubly gloomy by the effect of the few and smoky torches which were used to enlighten it upon the present occasion, and which, spreading a glare of yellow light in their immediate vicinity, were surrounded beyond by a red and purple halo reflected from their own smoke, and beyond that again by a zone of darkness which magnified the extent of the chapel, while it rendered it impossible for the eye to ascertain its limits. Some injudicious ornaments, adopted in haste for the occasion, rather added to the dreariness of the scene. Old fragments of tapestry, torn from the walls of other apartments, had been hastily and partially disposed around those of the chapel, and mingled inconsistently with scutcheons and funeral emblems of the dead, which they elsewhere exhibited. On each side of the stone altar was a monument, the appearance of which formed an equally strange contrast. On the one was the figure, in stone, of some grim hermit, or monk, who had died in the odour of sanctity; he was represented as recumbent, in his cowl and scapulaire, with his face turned upward as in the act of devotion, and his hands folded, from which his string of beads was dependent. On the other side was a tomb, in the Italian taste, composed of the most beautiful statuary marble, and accounted a model of modern art. It was erected to the memory of Isabella's mother, the late Mrs Vere of Ellieslaw, who was represented as in a dying posture, while a weeping cherub, with eyes averted, seemed in the act of extinguishing a dying lamp as emblematic of her speedy dissolution. It was, indeed, a masterpiece of art, but misplaced in the rude vault to which it had been consigned. Many were surprised, and even scandalized, that Ellieslaw, not remarkable for attention to his lady while alive, should erect after her death such a costly mausoleum in affected sorrow; others cleared him from the imputation of hypocrisy, and averred that the monument was constructed under the direction and at the sole expence of Mr Ratcliffe.

Before these monuments the wedding guests were assembled. They were few in number; for many had left the castle to prepare for the ensuing political explosion, and Ellieslaw was, in the circumstances of the case, far from being desirous to extend invitations farther than to those near relations whose presence the custom of the country rendered indispensable. Next to the altar stood Sir Frederick Langley, dark, moody, thoughtful, even beyond his wont, and near him, Marischal, who was to play the part of bridesman, as it was called. The thoughtless humour of this young gentleman, on which he never deigned to place the least restraint, added to the cloud which overhung the brows of the bridegroom.

"The bride is not yet come out of her chamber," he whispered to

Sir Frederick; "I trust that we must not have recourse to the violent expedients of the Romans which I read of at college. It would be hard upon my pretty cousin to be run away with twice in two days, though I know none better worth such a violent compliment."

Sir Frederick attempted to turn a deaf ear to this discourse, humming a tune and looking another way, but Marischal proceeded in the same wild manner.

"This delay is hard upon Dr Hobbler, who was disturbed to accelerate preparations for this joyful event just when he had successfully extracted the cork of his third bottle. I hope you will keep him free of the censure of his superiors, for I take it this is beyond canonical hours.—But here comes Ellieslaw and my pretty cousin—prettier than ever, I think, were it not she seems so faint and so deadly pale— Hark ye, Sir Knight, if she says not YES with right good will, it shall be no wedding for all that has come and gone yet."

"No wedding, sir?" returned Sir Frederick, in a loud whisper, the tone of which indicated his angry feelings were suppressed with difficulty.

"No—no marriage," replied Marischal, "there's my hand and glove on't."

Sir Frederick Langley took his hand, and as he wrung it hard, said in a much lower whisper, "Marischal, you shall answer this," and then flung his hand from him.

"That I will readily do," said Marischal, "for never word escaped my lips that my hand was not ready to guarantee—So, speak up, my pretty cousin, and tell me if it be your free and unbiassed resolution to accept of this gallant knight for your lord and husband; for if you have a tenth part of a scruple upon the subject, fall back, fall edge, he shall not have you."

"Are you mad, Mr Marischal?" said Ellieslaw, who, having been this young man's guardian during his minority, often employed a tone of authority to him. "Do you suppose I would drag my daughter to the foot of the altar, were it not her own free choice?"

"Tut, Ellieslaw," retorted the young gentleman, "never tell me of the contrary; her eyes are full of tears, and her cheek is whiter than her white dress. I must insist, in the name of common humanity, that the ceremony be adjourned till to-morrow."

"She shall tell you herself, thou incorrigible intermeddler in what concerns thee not, that it is her wish the ceremony should go on.—Is it not, Isabella, my dear?"

"It is," said Isabella, half fainting—"since there is no help either in God or man."

The first word alone was distinctly audible. Marischal shrugged his shoulders and stepped back. Ellieslaw led, or rather supported, his daughter to the altar. Sir Frederick moved forward and placed himself by her side. The clergyman opened his prayer-book, and looked to Mr Vere for the signal to commence the service.

"Proceed," said the latter.

But a voice, as if proceeding from the tomb of his deceased wife, called, in such loud and harsh accents as wakened every echo in the vaulted chapel, "Forbear!"

All were mute and motionless, till a distant rustle, and the clash of swords, or something resembling it, was heard from the remote apartments. It ceased almost instantly.

"What new device is this?" said Sir Frederick, fiercely, eyeing Ellieslaw and Marischal with a glance of malignant suspicion.

"It can be but the frolic of some intemperate guest," said Ellieslaw, though greatly confounded; "we must make large allowance for the excess of this evening's festivity. Proceed with the service."

Before the clergyman could obey, the same prohibition which they had before heard, was repeated from the same spot. The female attendants screamed, and fled from the chapel; the gentlemen laid their hands on their swords. Ere the first moment of surprise had passed by, the Dwarf stepped from behind the monument, and placed himself full in front of Mr Vere. The effect of so strange and hideous an apparition, in such time, place, and circumstances, appalled all present, but seemed to annihilate the Laird of Ellieslaw, who, dropping his daughter's arm, staggered against the nearest pillar, and, clasping it with his hands as if for support, laid his brow against the column.

"Who is this fellow?" said Sir Frederick; "what can he mean by this intrusion?"

"It is one who comes to tell you," said the Dwarf, with the peculiar acrimony which usually marked his manner, "that, in marrying that young lady, you wed neither the heiress of Ellieslaw, nor of Mauley-Hall, nor of Polverton, nor of one furrow of land, unless she marries with MY consent; and to thee that consent shall never be given. Down —down on thy knees, and thank Heaven that thou art prevented from wedding qualities with which thou hast no concern—portionless truth, virtue, and innocence.—And thou, base ingrate," he continued, addressing himself to Ellieslaw, "what is thy wretched subterfuge now? Thou, who would'st sell thy daughter to relieve thee from danger, as in famine thou would'st have slain and devoured her to preserve thy own vile life!—Ay, hide thy face with thy hands; well may'st thou blush to look on him whose body thou did'st consign to chains, his hand to guilt, and his soul to misery. Saved once more by the virtue of her who calls thee father, go hence, and may the pardon and benefits that I confer on thee prove literal coals of fire, till thy brain is seared and scorched like mine."

Ellieslaw left the chapel with a gesture of mute despair.

"Follow him, Hubert Ratcliffe," said the Dwarf, "and inform him of his destiny. He will rejoice—for to breathe air and to handle gold is for him happiness."

"I understand nothing of all this," said Sir Frederick Langley; "but we are here a body of gentlemen in arms and authority for King James; and whether you really, sir, be that Sir Edward Mauley, who has been so long supposed dead in confinement, or whether you be an impostor assuming his name and title, we will use the freedom of detaining you till your appearance here, at this moment, is better accounted for; we will have no spies among us—Seize on him, my friends."

But the domestics shrunk back in doubt and alarm. Sir Frederick himself stepped forward towards the Recluse, as if to lay hands on his person, when his progress was suddenly stopped by the glittering point of a partizan, which the sturdy hand of Hobbie Elliot presented against his bosom.

"I'll gar day-light shine through ye, if ye offer to steer him. Naebody shall lay a finger on Elshie; he's a canny neighbourly man, aye ready to make a friend help; and, though ye may think him a lamiter, yet, grippie for grippie, friend, I'll wad a wether he'll make the blude spin frae under your nails. He's a tough carle, Elshie! he grips like a smith's vice."

"What has brought you here, Elliot?" said Marischal, "who called on you for interference?"

"Troth, Marischal-Wells," answered Hobbie, "I am just come here, wi' twenty or thretty mair o' us, in my ain name and the King's— or Queen's, ca' they her? and Canny Elshie's into the bargain, to keep the peace, and pay back some ill usage Ellieslaw has gi'en me. A bonnie breakfast the loons gae me the ither morning, and him at the bottom o't; and trow ye I was na ready to supper him up?—Ye needna lay your hands on your swords, gentlemen, the house is ours wi' little din; for the doors were open, and there had been ower muckle punch amang your folk; we took their swords and pistols as easily as ye wad shiel peascods."

Marischal rushed out, and immediately re-entered the chapel.

"By Heaven! it is true, Sir Frederick; the house is filled with armed men, and our drunken beasts are all disarmed. Draw, and let us fight our way."

"Binna rash—binna rash," exclaimed Hobbie, "hear me—hear me

a bit—we mean ye nae harm; but, as ye are in arms for King James, as ye ca' him, and the prelates, we thought it right to keep up the auld neighbour-war, and stand up for the t'other ane and the Kirk. But we'll no hurt a hair o' your heads, if ye like to gang hame quietly. And it will be your best way, for there's sure news come frae Loudoun, that him they ca' Bang, or Byng, or what is't, has bang'd the French ships and the new king aff the coast howsomever; sae, ye had best bide content wi' auld Nanse for want of a better Queen."

Ratcliffe, who at this moment re-entered, confirmed these accounts, so unfavourable to the Jacobite interest. Sir Frederick, almost instantly, and without taking leave of any one, left the castle, with such of his attendants as were able to follow him.

"And what will you do, Mr Marischal?" said Ratcliffe.

"Why, faith," answered he, smiling, "I hardly know; my spirit is too great, and my fortune too small, for me to follow the example of the doughty bridegroom. It is not in my nature, and it is not worth my while."

"Well, then, disperse your men, and remain quiet, and this will be overlooked, as there has been no overt act."

"Hout, ay," said Elliot, "just let byganes be byganes, and a' friends again; de'il ane I bear malice at but Westburnflat, and I hae gi'en him baith a het skin and a cauld ane. I hadna changed three blows of the broadsword wi' him before he lap the window into the castle-moat, and swattered through it like a wild-duck. He's a clever fallow, indeed! maun kilt awa wi' ae bonnie lass in the morning, and another at night, less wadna serve him! but if he doesna kilt himsel out o' the country I'se kilt him wi' a tow, for the Castleton meeting's clean blawn ower; his friends will no countenance him."

During the general confusion, Isabella had thrown herself at the feet of her kinsman, Sir Edward Mauley, for so we must now call the Solitary, to express at once her gratitude, and to beseech forgiveness for her father. The eyes of all began to be fixed on them, as soon as their own agitation and the bustle of the attendants had somewhat abated. Miss Vere kneeled beside the tomb of her mother, to whose statue her features exhibited a marked resemblance. She held the hand of the Dwarf, which she kissed repeatedly and bathed with tears. He stood fixed and motionless, excepting that his eyes glanced alternately on the marble figure and the living suppliant. At length, the large drops which gathered on his eye-lashes compelled him to draw his hand across them.

"I thought," he said, "that tears and I had done; but we shed them at our birth, and their spring dries not until we are in our graves. But no melting of the heart shall dissolve my resolution. I part here, at once, and for ever, with all of which the memory," (looking to the tomb,) "or the presence," (he pressed Isabella's hand,) "is dear to me. —Do not speak to me! do not thwart my determination! it will avail nothing; you will hear of and see this lump of deformity no more. I will be dead to you ere I am actually in my grave, and you will think of me as a friend disencumbered from the toils and crimes of existence."

He kissed Isabella on the forehead, impressed another kiss on the brow of the statue by which she knelt, and left the chapel followed by Ratcliffe. Isabella, almost exhausted with the emotions of the day, was carried to her apartment by her women. Most of the other guests dispersed, after having separately endeavoured to impress on all who would listen to them their disapprobation of the plots formed against the government, or their regret for having engaged in them. Hobbie Elliot assumed the command of the castle for the night, and mounted a regular guard. He boasted not a little of the alacrity with which his friends and he had obeyed a hasty summons received from Elshie through the faithful Ratcliffe. And it was a lucky chance, he said, that, on the very day, they had got notice that Westburnflat did not intend to keep his tryste at Castleton, but to hold them at defiance. A considerable party had assembled at the Heugh-foot with the intention of paying a visit to the robber's tower on the ensuing morning, and their course was easily directed to Ellieslaw Castle.

Chapter Eighteen

————Last scene of all,
To close this strange eventful history.
As You Like it

ON THE NEXT morning, Mr Ratcliffe presented Miss Vere with a letter from her father, of which the following is the tenor:—

"MY DEAREST CHILD,

"The malice of a persecuting government will compel me, for my own safety, to retreat abroad, and to remain for some years in foreign parts. I do not ask you to accompany, or follow me; you will attend to my interest and your own more effectually by remaining where you are. It is unnecessary to enter into a minute detail concerning the causes of the strange events which yesterday took place. I think I have reason to complain of the usage I have received from Sir Edward Mauley, who is your nearest kinsman by the mother's side; but, as he has declared you his heir, and is to put you in immediate possession of a large part of his fortune, I account it a full atonement. I am aware he has never forgiven the preference which your mother gave to my addresses, instead of complying with the terms of a sort of family compact which absurdly and tyrannically destined her to wed her deformed relative. The shock was even sufficient to unsettle his wits, (which, indeed, were never over-well arranged;) and I had, as the husband of his nearest kinswoman and heir, the delicate task of taking care of his person and property, until he was reinstated in the management of the latter by those who, no doubt, thought they were doing him justice; although, if some parts of his subsequent conduct be examined, it will appear that he ought, for his own sake, to have been left under the influence of a mild and salutary restraint.

"In one particular, however, he shewed a sense of the ties of blood, as well as of his own frailty; for while he sequestered himself closely from the world, under various names and disguises, and insisted on spreading a report of his own death, (in which to gratify him I unwillingly acquiesced,) he left to my disposal the rents of a great proportion of his estates, and especially all those, which, having belonged to your mother, reverted to him as a male fief. In this he may have thought that he was acting with extreme generosity, while, in the opinion of all impartial men, he will only be considered as having fulfilled a natural obligation, seeing that, in justice, if not in strict law, you must be considered as the heir of your mother, and I as your legal administrator. Instead, therefore, of considering myself as loaded with obligations to Sir Edward on this account, I think I had reason to complain that these remittances were only doled out to me at the pleasure of Mr Ratcliffe, who, moreover, exacted from me mortgages over my paternal estate of Ellieslaw for any sums which I required as an extra advance; and thus may be said to have insinuated himself into the absolute management and controul of my property. Or, if all this seeming friendship was employed by Sir Edward for the purpose of obtaining a complete command of my affairs, and acquiring the power of ruining me at his pleasure, I feel myself, I must repeat, still less bound by the alleged obligation.

"About the autumn of last year, as I understand, either his own crazed imagination, or the accomplishment of some such scheme as I have hinted, brought him down to this country. His alleged motive, it seems, was a desire of seeing a monument which he had directed to be raised in the chapel over the tomb of your mother. Mr Ratcliffe, who at this time had done me the honour to make my house his own, had the complaisance to introduce him secretly into the chapel. The consequence, as he informs me, was a frenzy of several hours, during which the poor man fled into the neighbouring moors, in one of the wildest spots of which he chose, when he was somewhat recovered, to fix his mansion, and set up for a sort of country empiric, a character, which, even in his best days, he was fond of assuming. It is remarkable, that, instead of informing me of these circumstances that I might have had the relative of my late wife taken such care of as his calamitous condition required, Mr Ratcliffe seems to have had such culpable indulgence for his irregular plans as to promise and even swear secrecy concerning them. He visited Sir Edward often, and assisted in the fantastic task he had taken upon him of constructing a hermitage. Nothing they appear to have dreaded more than a discovery of their intercourse.

"The ground was open in every direction around, and a small soutterain, probably sepulchral, which their researches had detected near the great granite pillar, served to conceal Ratcliffe when any one approached his master. I think you will be of opinion, my love, that this secrecy must have had some strong motive. It is also remarkable, that while I thought my unhappy friend was residing among the monks of La Trappe, he should have been actually living, for many months, in this bizarre disguise, within five miles of my house, and obtaining regular information of my most private movements, either by Ratcliffe, or through Westburnflat and others, whom he had the means to bribe to any extent. He makes it a crime against me that I endeavoured to establish your marriage with Sir Frederick. I acted for the best; but if he thought otherwise, why did he not step manfully forwards, express his own purpose of becoming a party to the settlements, and take that interest which he is entitled to claim in you as heir to his great property?

"Even now, though he is somewhat tardy in announcing his purpose, I am far from opposing my authority against his wishes, although the person he desires you to regard as your future husband be young Earnscliff, the very last whom I should have thought likely to be acceptable to him. But I give my free and hearty consent, providing the settlements are drawn in such an irrevocable form as may secure my child from suffering by that state of dependence, and the sudden and causeless revocation of allowances, of which I have so much reason to complain. Of Sir Frederick Langley, I augur, you will hear no more. He is not likely to claim the hand of a dowerless maiden. I therefore commit you, my dear Isabella, to the wisdom of Providence and to your own prudence, begging you to lose no time in securing those advantages which the fickleness of your kinsman has withdrawn from me to shower upon you.

"Mr Ratcliffe mentioned Sir Edward's intention to settle a considerable sum upon me yearly, for my maintenance in foreign parts; but this my heart is too proud to accept from them. I told him I had a dear child, who, while in affluence herself, would never suffer me to be in poverty. I thought it right to intimate this to them pretty roundly, that whatever income be settled upon you, it may be calculated so as to cover this necessary and natural encumbrance. I will willingly settle upon you the castle and manor of Ellieslaw, to shew my parental affection and disinterested zeal for promoting your settlement in life. The annual interest of debts charged on the estate somewhat exceeds the income, even after a reasonable rent has been put upon the mansion and the mains. But as all the debts are in the person of Mr Ratcliffe, as your kinsman's trustee, he will not be a troublesome creditor. And here I must make you aware, that though I have to complain of Mr Ratcliffe's conduct to me personally, I, nevertheless, believe him a just and upright man, with whom you may safely consult on your affairs, not to mention that to cherish his good opinion will be the best way to retain that of your kinsman. Remember me to Marchie —I hope he will not be troubled on account of late matters. I will write more fully from the Continent. Meanwhile, I rest your loving father,

RICHARD VERE."

The above letter throws the only additional light which we have been able to procure upon the earlier part of our story. It was Hobbie's opinion, and may be that of most of our readers, that the Recluse of Meikle-stane-Moor had but a kind of a gloaming, or twilight understanding; and that he probably had neither very clear views as to what he himself wanted, nor was apt to pursue his ends by the clearest and most direct means: so that to seek the clew of his conduct, was likened, by Hobbie, to looking for a straight path through a common, in which are a hundred devious tracks, but not one distinct line of road.

When Isabella had perused the letter, her first enquiry was after her father. He had left the castle early in the morning, after a long interview with Mr Ratcliffe, and was already far on his way to the next port, where he might expect to find shipping for the Continent.

"Where was Sir Edward Mauley?"

No one had seen the Dwarf since the eventful scene of the preceding evening.

"Odd, if ony thing has befa'en puir Elshie," said Hobbie Elliot, "I wad rather I were harried ower again."

He immediately rode to his dwelling, and the remaining she-goat came bleating to meet him, for her milking hour was long past. The Solitary was no where to be seen; his door, contrary to wont, was open, his fire extinguished, the whole hut left in the state which it exhibited on Isabella's visit to him. It was pretty clear that the means of conveyance which had brought the Dwarf to Ellieslaw on the preceding evening, had removed him from it to some other place of abode. Hobbie returned disconsolate to the castle.

"I am doubting we hae lost Canny Elshie for gude an' a'."

"You have, indeed," said Ratcliffe, producing a paper, which he put into Hobbie's hands; "but read that, and you will perceive you have been no loser by having known him."

It was a short deed of gift, by which "Sir Edward Mauley, otherwise called Elshender the Recluse, endowed Halbert, or Hobbie Elliot, and Grace Armstrong, in full property, with a considerable sum borrowed by Elliot from him."

Hobbie's joy was mingled with feelings which drew tears down his rough cheeks.

"It's a queer thing," he said; "but I canna joy in the gear unless I kenn'd the puir body was happy that gave it me."

"Next to enjoying happiness ourselves," said Ratcliffe, "is the consciousness of having bestowed it on others. Had all my master's benefits been conferred like the present, what a different return they would have produced! But the indiscriminate profusion that would glut avarice, or supply prodigality, neither does good, nor is rewarded by gratitude. It is sowing the wind to reap the whirlwind."

"And that wad be a sair har'st," said Hobbie; "but, wi' my young leddy's leave, I wad fain take down Elshie's skeps o' bees, and set them in Grace's bit flower-yard at the Heugh-foot—they sall ne'er be smeekit by ony o' huz. And the puir goat, she would be negleckit about a great town like this; and she could feed bonnily on our lily lea by the burn side, and the hounds wad ken her in a day, and never fash her, and Grace wad milk her ilka morning wi' her ain hand, for Elshie's sake; for though he was thrawn and cankered in his converse, he liket dumb creatures weel."

Hobbie's requests were readily granted, not without some wonder at the natural delicacy of feeling which pointed out to him this mode of displaying his gratitude. He was delighted when Ratcliffe informed him that his benefactor should not remain ignorant of the care which he took of his favourite.

"And mind be sure and tell him that grannie and the titties, and, abune a', Grace and mysel, are weel and thriving, and that it is a' his doing—that canna but please him, ane wad think."

And Elliot and the family at Heugh-foot were, and continued to be, as fortunate and happy as his undaunted honesty, tenderness, and gallantry, so well merited.

All bar between the marriage of Earnscliff and Isabella was now removed, and the settlements which Ratcliffe produced on the part of

Sir Edward Mauley, might have satisfied the cupidity of Mr Vere himself. But Miss Vere and Ratcliffe thought it unnecessary to mention to Earnscliff that one great motive of Sir Edward in thus loading the young pair with benefits, was to expiate his having, many years before, shed the blood of his father in a hasty brawl. If it be true, as Ratcliffe asserted, that the Dwarf's extreme misanthropy seemed to relax somewhat, under the consciousness of having diffused happiness among so many, the recollection of this circumstance might probably be one of his chief motives for refusing obstinately ever to witness their state of contentment.

Marischal hunted, shot, and drank claret—tired of the country, went abroad, served three campaigns, came home, and married Lucy Ilderton.

Years fled over the heads of Earnscliff and his wife, and found and left them contented and happy. The scheming ambition of Sir Frederick Langley engaged him in the unfortunate insurrection of 1715. He was made prisoner at Preston, in Lancashire, with the Earl of Derwentwater and others. His defence, and the dying speech which he made on the occasion, may be found in the State Trials. Mr Vere, furnished by his daughter with an ample income, continued to reside abroad, engaged deeply in the affair of Law's bank during the regency of the Duke of Orleans, and was at one time supposed to be immensely rich. But, on the bursting of that famous bubble, he was so much chagrined at being again reduced to a moderate annuity, (although he saw thousands of his companions in misfortune absolutely starving) that vexation of mind brought on a paralytic stroke, of which he died, after lingering under its effects a few weeks.

Willie of Westburnflat fled from the wrath of Hobbie Elliot, as his betters did from the pursuit of the law. His patriotism urged him to serve his country abroad, while his reluctance to leave the native soil pressed him rather to remain in the beloved island, and collect purses, watches, and rings on the highroads at home. Fortunately for him, the first impulse prevailed, and he joined the army under Marlborough; obtained a commission, to which he was recommended by his services in collecting cattle for the commissariat; returned home after many years, with some money, (how come by Heaven only knows)—demolished the peel-house at Westburnflat, and built, in its stead, a high narrow *onstead*, of three stories, with a chimney at each end—drank brandy with the neighbours, whom, in his younger days, he had plundered—spoke much of the Duke of Marlborough, and very little of Charlie Cheat-the-Woodie—died in his bed, and is recorded upon his tombstone at Kirkwhistle, (still extant) as having played all the parts of a brave soldier, a discreet neighbour, and a sincere Christian.

Mr Ratcliffe resided usually with the family at Ellieslaw; but regularly every spring and autumn he absented himself for about a month. On the direction and purpose of his periodical journey he remained steadily silent; but it was well understood that he was then in attendance on his unfortunate patron. At length, on his return from one of these visits, his grave countenance, and deep mourning dress, announced to the Ellieslaw family that their benefactor was no more. Sir Edward's death made no addition to their fortune, for he had divested himself of his property during his lifetime, and chiefly in their favour. Ratcliffe, his sole confidant, died at a good old age, but without ever uttering the place to which his master had finally retired, or the manner of his death, or the place of his burial. It was supposed that on all these particulars his patron had enjoined him secrecy.

The sudden disappearance of Elshie from his extraordinary hermitage corroborated the reports which the common people had spread concerning him. Many believed that, having ventured to enter a consecrated building, contrary to his paction with the Evil One, he had been bodily carried off while on his return to his cottage; but most are of opinion that he only disappeared for a season, and continues to be seen from time to time among the hills. And retaining, according to custom, a more vivid recollection of his wild and desperate language, than of the benevolent tendency of most of his actions, he is usually identified with the malignant dæmon called the Man of the Moors, whose feats were quoted by Mrs Elliot to her grandson; and, accordingly, is generally represented as bewitching the sheep, causing the ewes to *keb*, that is, to cast their lambs, or seen loosening the impending wreath of snow to precipitate down on such as take shelter, during the storm, beneath the bank of a torrent, or under the shelter of a steep glen. In short, the evils most dreaded and deprecated by the inhabitants of that pastoral country, are ascribed to the agency of the Black Dwarf.

ESSAY ON THE TEXT

1. THE GENESIS OF *THE BLACK DWARF*   2. THE COMPOSITION OF *THE BLACK DWARF:* the Manuscript; preparing the First Edition; changes between manuscript and First Edition   3. THE LATER EDITIONS: Second Edition; Third Edition; Fourth Edition; Fifth/Sixth Edition; octavo *Novels and Tales*; duodecimo *Novels and Tales*; eighteenmo *Novels and Tales*; the Interleaved Set and the Magnum   4. THE PRESENT TEXT: punctuation and orthography; verbal emendations (misreadings, misunderstandings, wrong insertions, wrong omissions, wrong substitutions or alterations, wrong rearrangements, misguided corrections, problems with names, transferences between English and Scots); later editions; preliminaries.

The following conventions are used in transcriptions from Scott's manuscript: deletions are enclosed ⟨thus⟩ and insertions ↑thus↓; an insertion within an insertion is indicated by double arrows ↑↑thus↓↓: superscript letters are lowered without comment; the letters 'NL' (new line) are Scott's own, and indicate that he wished a new paragraph to be opened, in spite of running on the text, whereas the words '[new paragraph]' are editorial and indicate that Scott opened a new paragraph on a new line. The same conventions are used as appropriate for indicating variants between the printed editions.

1. THE GENESIS OF *THE BLACK DWARF*

The Black Dwarf was originally published as the first story in *Tales of my Landlord*, which appeared in the beginning of December 1816. Initially it had been planned that the *Tales* would comprise four Scottish regional stories, each filling a volume of the four-volumed work. *The Black Dwarf* was written and printed before the end of August 1816. But the next, *The Tale of Old Mortality*, expanded to fill the remaining three volumes, as Scott effectively reverted to the more familiar three-decker novel form. *The Black Dwarf* is thus something of an anomaly, the sole survivor of a scheme which was never implemented. At the same time, its genesis can never be entirely separated from the larger conceptual framework of *Tales of my Landlord*.

Negotiations for the contract of *Tales of my Landlord* were conducted between James Ballantyne, Scott's printer and partner, and William Blackwood, the Edinburgh publisher, in the spring of 1816. On 12 April an excited Blackwood wrote to his London associate, John Murray, describing the offer of 'a work of fiction in four volumes, such as Waverley, &c'. Pressed by Blackwood to disclose that the author was 'the author of *Waverley*', commonly held to be Scott, Ballantyne had retreated ('he was not at liberty to mention its title, nor was he at liberty to give the author's name'). The terms, however, clearly followed a formula used for Scott's preceding works of fiction. The author was to be paid half profits after the deduction of production costs; £600 worth of John Ballantyne's stock of books must be purchased immediately; the first two volumes would be made available in six or eight weeks, and if not acceptable the contract was to be terminated; an edition of 2000 would be ready by 1 October.[1] The item about John Ballantyne's stock— the remnants of a disastrous publishing adventure that had involved Scott—left little doubt in Blackwood's mind as to what was being offered. On 13 April James Ballantyne presented an estimate of £584 for printing a first edition of 2000, the price to include £30 for 'transcribing the whole, from the Author's orig[inal] MS' and £25 for corrections ('which are likely to be *extremely* heavy').[2] Again it would have been difficult for Ballantyne to have slanted his message more pointedly. Further letters from Blackwood pressed Murray for an early response; while at the same time Blackwood's appetite was whetted with snippets from *The Antiquary*, Scott's third novel, which was fast approaching publication. When Murray's answer finally arrived, on 20 April, Blackwood felt elated at having wrested Scott from the clutches of his rival publisher, Archibald Constable: 'I have been occupied with this for years, and I hope have now accomplished what will be of immense service to us'.[3] The deal could not be concluded immediately, however, since Ballantyne needed to consult with the author. In the meantime, Blackwood entered into the less scintillating business of ordering items from John Ballantyne's unwanted stock.

It is not difficult to sense the invisible hand of Scott behind the negotiations, which began when *The Antiquary* was nearing completion at press, and just as Scott left Edinburgh for a month's stay at Abbotsford. Before departing, he almost certainly composed the preliminary 'Advertisement' to *The Antiquary* announcing the retirement of 'the author of *Waverley*' after a trilogy of novels dealing with Scotland from 1745 to the close of the eighteenth century. The decision to change publishers thus coincided with an important juncture in Scott's artistic career. At the same time, financial considerations were never far from view. A change of publisher would, at the very least, provide a useful way of testing the market. John Murray, financially sound, patron of a literary circle at Albemarle Street, and the publisher of Byron, undoubtedly represented Scott's main target. Blackwood, who had become Murray's agent in Scotland in 1811, was regarded more as a go-between, the extent of his ambition unsuspected by both Murray and Scott. The change of publisher also probably dictated Scott's decision not to use John Ballantyne, his usual literary agent: John was distrusted by Blackwood and Murray alike, whereas Blackwood had been cultivating James with printing work for several years. In fact, James's inexperience evidently led to his offering Blackwood softer terms than had been intended. Writing to John on 29 April, Scott listed the items which needed to be firmed up or added by his brother. Only 6000 copies should be offered, not the copyright; bills were to be accepted by both publishers ('I will have London Bills as well as Blackwoods'); paper and print was to be supplied by James Ballantyne & Co. for all editions. Furthermore, inspection copies were not to go out to the publishers: 'He talks of volumes being put into the publishers hands to consider & decide on. No such thing—a bare perusal at St. John Street only'. If Blackwood hesitated, John must treat instantly with Constable.[4]

The new terms were accepted by Blackwood, at James Ballantyne's office, on the afternoon of 30 April. The contract, dated that day, offered the right to print up to 6000 copies, either as one or in successive editions. In addition to items mentioned above, it stipulated that the publishers were to accept bills at 12 months for print and paper on completion, when the author was to also receive payment for his half-profits in the (more advantageous) form of bills at 6 months. The last item concerned the right of inspection before the contract became binding: 'You are to have the liberty of perusing a volume of the Work at my house in St. John Street; and if, upon such perusal you shall disapprove of the speculation, you shall have it in your option to annul the bargain; such option to be signified to me within twenty-four hours after perusing the volume'.[5] In justifying to Murray what he had done Blackwood confided that Ballantyne had promised to keep him in touch from the start: 'he assured me however that he would give me such information while the first volume was going on as would put both your mind and mine quite at rest'. He also gave notice that he intended to take full advantage of the right of inspection: 'I should have mentioned that I am to go to Ballantyne's house, and be shut up by myself, or have it read to me in company with William Erskine. Now I mean to do both.' Ballantyne had also told him that 1000 copies of *The Antiquary* 'were just shipped' to Longman & Co., and that publication was planned for Saturday, 4 May.[6]

One notable omission from the agreement was a deadline, though the provisional terms had apparently mentioned 1 October. Blackwood by his own account was given plenty of verbal assurances, Ballantyne claiming to have 'read a considerable part of it' and promising 'to put to press immediately'.[7] Confirmation of a sort came when Murray was pressed for his share of payment on John's stock: 'In the course of a month, I think, a great part of the M.S. will be put into my hands'.[8] Ballantyne then lowered his profile. A new note of anxiety is perceptible in Blackwood's letters to Murray in May. By 21 June this had turned to something closer to despair: 'my own belief is that at the time he made such solemn promises to me that the first volume would be in my hands in a month, he had not the smallest expectation of this being the case'.[9] On 2 July Blackwood took an early morning ride to gather his thoughts. 'Sitting, walking, or riding is all the same', he told Murray. 'I feel as much puzzled as ever, and undetermined whether or not to cut this Gordian knot.' An open rupture might, he felt, prove counter-productive in the light of Scott's usefulness as a contributor to Murray's *Quarterly Review* and his own imminent move to Princes Street in the fashionable New Town.[10] On 31 July, having received no full answer to a letter of protest to Ballantyne on 24 June, Blackwood issued a veiled ultimatum:

> It surely will not to be thought unreasonable that Mr Murray and I should, at a distance of three months from the period at which we granted our acceptances for six hundred pounds, feel rather impatient at hearing nothing whatever of the Work of Fiction of which you assured me the first volume would be printed and put into my hands upwards of two months ago.[11]

This time Ballantyne answered by return with assurances, supposedly straight from the author: 'He says . . . that I shall have the first vol. in my hands by the end of August, and that the whole work will, as he all along said, be ready for publication by Christmas'.[12]

From this point Ballantyne was armed with more tangible evidence of progress. After a 'decisive conversation' on Saturday, 3 August, he responded with two letters of 5 August in an effort to forestall the threatened withdrawal. The first reported a message received from the author, promising publication in November: 'His words are these: "The work is now ready to go to the press; and you will have the copy in two days."' The second ended by recording the actual receipt of copy: 'I ought to add that I have this moment received a considerable portion of the MS'.[13] On the following day, according to Ballantyne, the process of setting the work had already begun: 'The work is now actually in the press,—at least in the hands of the Compositors'.[14] However by 14 August the volume was still 'not yet quite ready'. 'I find that what I have received will make about 200 or 250 pages'.[15] Blackwood could either see this shortly, or wait for completion. In his reply of 16 August Blackwood expressed his willingness to see either 'the portion of 250 pages or the whole of the first volume', while pressing an earlier request about a copy being made available for a final decision in London.[16] The author's refusal was relayed by Ballantyne on Wednesday, 21 August: 'Nothing shall induce me to allow the book to go out of your hands. . . . Mr Blackwood's taste is as competent as that of any man to enable him to come to a just conclusion'. Softening the blow, Ballantyne announced his possession of printed copy: 'I have myself read it with the greatest admiration and delight. The remainder, I think, will be ready for your inspection about the beginning of next week'.[17]

Blackwood was delighted with the news. By working late, Ballantyne was able to send eight sheets on the evening of 22 August. His covering note, apparently for the first time, mentioned the title as 'Tales of My Landlord'. He also outlined the plan of the whole work: 'Each volume contains a Tale; so there will be four in all. The next relates to the period of the Covenanters'.[18] At midnight, having run though the 192 pages of text, Blackwood began a letter to Murray detailing how the narrative had made such 'strong & most favourable impression' on him.

> The title is "Tales of My Landlord;" collected and reported by Jedidiah Cleisbotham [*sic*], Parish-Clerk and Schoolmaster of Gandercleugh". The introduction consisting of 20 pages is finely given in the character of a Scotch Dominie, whose style is scriptural pedantic and tautological interlarded with scraps of Latin—

After supplying a few extracts from Jedidiah's preamble, Blackwood moved to the main story ('The title of the tale which will occupy this volume is "The Black Dwarf"'), peppering his account with quotations which for the most part accurately match the published first edition. Having reached as far as page 82, with the watchman 'crying past 3 Oclock', he went to bed. The letter was taken up again at 2 p.m. in the following afternoon, when Blackwood hurriedly completed his résumé without further quotation. He also disclosed that he had written early in morning to tell Ballantyne he was 'perfectly satisfied'.[19] Before leaving for London at the end of the month, Blackwood must have authorised the advance advertisement of *Tales of my Landlord*, 'collected and reported by Jedediah Cleishbotham', which appeared in the *Edinburgh Evening Courant* on 31 August 1816.

There is no direct evidence of when Scott began writing *Tales of my Landlord*. Ballantyne's reported claim on 12 April that he had 'read a considerable part of it' probably originated in his desire to capture Blackwood's interest. On the other hand, the idea of a new manifestation under a different pseudonym was probably established in Scott's mind when he wrote the 'Advertisement' to *The Antiquary*. Writing to John Ballantyne on 29 April he talked positively of 'a 4 volume work a Romance totally different in stile and structure from the others'.[20] In fact, the stimulus for a series of tales 'reported' by a pedantic schoolmaster could have arrived at Abbotsford while negotiations were taking place. Joseph Train, an excise officer who had recently entered into an antiquarian correspondence with Scott, later traced the origin of Jedidiah Cleishbotham to his own unfulfilled plan for a 'History of Galloway', which had involved the circularisation of a questionnaire amongst 'the Parish Clerks and Schoolmasters of Galloway'. One communication, from a Mr Broadfoot, was humorously 'signed Clashbottom, a professional appellation—derived I suppose from his using the Birch'. 'This facetious gentleman', Train added, 'was very nearly related to the celebrated "Jedediah of Gandercleugh"—and like him frequently tastes the Mountain dew with the Exciseman and the Landlord not in the Wallace Inn at Gandercleugh but at the sign of the "Shoulder of Mutton" in Newton Stewart.'[21] Train's story was given wide currency by its inclusion in J.G. Lockhart's *Life of Scott*, which

adds the detail of Train handing over Broadfoot's response during a
seminal visit in May to Scott's Edinburgh residence at Castle Street.[22]
The inception of the scheme, however, can be pushed a significant
degree earlier. A printed leaflet (headed 'NEWTONSTEWART, 25th
March, 1816'), soliciting 'Parochial Schoolmasters' for information
concerning 'any Legends or Traditions' in their parishes, was enclosed
by Train in a letter addressed to Scott at Abbotsford on 27 April 1816.
Train added in his own hand at the bottom: 'I have scattered these
Queries over this quarter solely for the purpose of obtaining Local
Information for you and I hope I will not be disappointed'.[23] Train's
letter arrived just as Scott was briefing John Ballantyne about terms, and
might well have been instrumental in establishing the pattern for a series
of regional tales 'illustrative of ancient Scottish manners'. More generally the 'Introduction' to *Tales* contains a number of allusions to domestic issues in Scotland during the spring and early summer of 1816, and
is manifestly a document of that period.

The opening framework of *The Black Dwarf*, involving the arrival of
two Border hill farmers at Gandercleugh, could also have been conceived and possibly written up during Scott's spring stay at Abbotsford.
In his capacity as Sheriff of Selkirkshire, Scott attended the Circuit
Court held at Jedburgh from 15-17 April. Here his old friend Robert
Shortreed identified for him a Border farmer, Jamie Davidson, tenant in
Hyndlee (some 15 km south-west of Jedburgh). The meeting was
recalled by Shortreed almost a decade later, when denying the popular
report that Davidson was the original of Dandie Dinmont in *Guy Man-
nering* (1815):

> I myself pointed Jamie out to him [Sir Walter] as the supposed
> Dandie Dinmont as he was standin glowrin' amang the crowd on
> Jethart Street ae market day to see the Judge pass.—I saw him
> . . . amang the fouk wi' his glazed hat on and asked Sir W if he
> wad like to see Dandie Dinmont! . . . short tho' their interview was,
> it was during it that he pencilled off . . . Jamie Davidson the store-
> farmer who is represented as coming up with his shepherd Bauldie
> to the Wallace Inn in the beginning of the First Tales of my Land-
> lord which appeared shortly after—Young Mr Pringle of White-
> bank was present at the Interview and he told me that great part of
> what Jamie Davidson then said . . . is there not only in substance
> merely but that we have the actual words & phrases he made use of.
> So much Mr P said is this the case that on my first reading the Black
> Dwarf the moment I saw the farmer's ejaculation about the ill
> plight of 'the yowes' & the lambs I knew him to be Jamie Davidson
> and felt assured that I was about to read what I had heard before
> —in short I was prepared for the whole scene.[24]

Shortreed's account is confirmed by a letter of Scott's to his actor friend
Daniel Terry on 18 April, which remarks on his finding Dinmont in 'a
man whom I never saw in my life before'. In the same letter he reported

the bad weather—a pattern which was to continue through the year—
and the ominous outlook for sheep-farming: 'it is snowing and hailing
eternally, and will kill all the lambs to a certainty, unless it changes in a
few hours'.[25] The words are echoed in the opening words of the Border
farmers in *The Black Dwarf*: 'Lord guide us, an' this weather last, what
will come o' the lambs!'

Scott's short visit to Jedburgh would also have jogged his mind about
past Border events, confirming or even initiating his choice of a 'southern' location for the first of his tales. Writing to Margaret Clephane,
Lady Compton, he compared the present case facing the court—
'whether two poor caitiffs who had committed some paltry thefts should
be sent to Botany Bay or no'—with the days when 'Jeddart Justice' ruled
on the Borders: 'See how much Jedburgh is fallen off wherever the
criminals came in so fast that they were fain to execute them first and
afterwards try them at leisure'.[26] Meeting Robert Shortreed, too, would
have reminded Scott of the Border 'raids' into Liddesdale, in southern
Roxburghshire, which the two had made made together in search of
ballads. Through Shortreed Scott had met descendants of the Elliot
clan who still farmed the area, now mostly as tenants of the Duke of
Buccleuch. On their first 'raid' in Autumn 1792 they had first visited
Milburnholm, near Hermitage Castle, which was farmed by William
and Walter Elliot, sons of Robert Elliot, who in the mid-eighteenth
century had been tenant of several farms in the upper Hermitage Water
part of the valley. They then rode to spend the night with Dr John Elliot
at Cleughhead (close to the present settlement of Steele Road, approximately 4 km south-east of Hermitage Castle). Elliot was Scott's leading
informant about the Liddesdale ballads, which were to play a crucial
part in the development of *Minstrelsy of the Scottish Border* (1802–03).
Most of Scott's subsequent 'raids' took place in autumn, though Shortreed remembered one spring visit 'for the express purpose o' hearing
the air of the Fray of Suport'. Later expeditions cut deeper into the
valley to the banks of Liddel Water, down to the border with England at
Kershopefoot. From John Elliot, the Laird of Whithaugh, Scott heard
the music of 'Dick o' the Cow' and 'Jock o' the Side'; though, according
to Shortreed, they had also ridden six miles to see Thomas Elliot tenant
in Twislehope 'for no other reason than to see gin I had the right *lilt* o'
Dick o' the Cow, for Whithaugh wasna vera sure about it'. Shortreed's
account gives a great sense of a physical familiarisation with the terrain,
as Scott linked events in the ballads with present-day 'manners' and
topography: 'we rade about visiting the scenes of remarkable occurrences & roved away amang the fouk, haill days at a time'.[27]

In his self-review of *Tales of my Landlord* in the *Quarterly Review* for
January 1817 (published in mid-May), Scott clearly identified *The Black
Dwarf* as a story set in Liddesdale. He also pointed to another major
inspiration, whose roots again lay in the 1790s, in hinting at a prototype

for the central, eponymous figure of the 'Black Dwarf':

> He once resided (and perhaps still lives) in the vale formed by the
> Manor-water which falls into the Tweed near Peebles, a glen long
> honoured by the residence of the late venerable Professor Fer-
> guson.[28]

The hint prompted an inevitable chase for the living original, leading to
the discovery within months of David Ritchie (1740–1811), a real-life
dwarf, who had lived in a cottage on the farm of Woodhouse, in the
Parish of Manor, in Peeblesshire. It was through his friendship with
Captain Adam Ferguson, eldest son of the distinguished philosopher of
the same name, that Scott had come into contact with Ritchie. Professor
Ferguson had retired with his family to the neighbouring mansion of
Hallyards, about a kilometre from Ritchie's cottage. Scott's Introduction (1830) to *The Black Dwarf* in the Magnum Opus edition of the
Waverley Novels fixes his meeting with Ritchie in autumn 1797; though
a letter to Shortreed dated 16 October 1796 from 'Halyards' indicates
that it might have taken place a year earlier.[29] An account of the interview, purportedly communicated by Captain Ferguson, later appeared
in *Chambers' Edinburgh Journal*. It indicates a traumatic experience for
Scott, engendered by Ritchie's recognition of a kindred spirit in the
'limping youth' before him:

> '*He has poo'er*', said the dwarf, in a voice which made the flesh of the
> hearers thrill within them . . . 'My, *he* has poo'er', repeated the
> recluse; and then, going to his usual seat, he sat for some minutes
> grinning horribly, as if enjoying the impression he had made; while
> not a word escaped from any of the party. Mr Ferguson at length
> plucked up his spirits, and called to David to open the door, as they
> must now be going. The dwarf slowly obeyed; and when they had
> got out, Mr Ferguson observed, that his friend was as pale as ashes,
> while his person was agitated in every limb.[30]

By the time of the Magnum, after several catchpenny publications by
William and Robert Chambers, Ritchie had become something of a
cult figure, making it difficult now to distinguish genuine biographical
material from the broader influence of Scott's imaginative creation. It
seems probable, however, that Scott was indebted to the Ritchie experience for his description of the Dwarf's cottage and garden, some of his
character's misanthropy and local reputation for supernatural knowledge, and (if the above account is to be believed) the fraught interview
with Isabella near the end of the story.

There are also indications that Scott was reminded about Ritchie by
events in 1816. After the death of Professor Ferguson in February 1816,
Scott took an almost paternal interest in the three Ferguson daughters,
Isabella, Mary and Margaret. In a letter to Adam on 12 March, he
proposed a refuge at Kaeside on the Abbotsford estate: 'At all events we
will see you at Abbotsford this summer'.[31] The movements of the Fergusons in 1816 are uncertain, though it seems likely that some of the

family would have visited Abbotsford to consider the offer, which eventually resulted in the lease of Huntlyburn, another house on the estate, in October 1817. Writing to an inquiring antiquary in 1831, Scott placed the Fergusons at the root of all authoritative accounts of Ritchie: 'I saw him myself, and the other reports were taken from Professor Ferguson and his family, so we are, generally speaking, secure of their accuracy'.[32] There are grounds for believing that at least one of the Ferguson sisters contributed to the extensive and influential 'Account of David Ritchie, the Original of the Black Dwarf', which appeared in the *Scots Magazine* (under its new title of the *Edinburgh Magazine*) for October 1817. This was pieced together by the editor Thomas Pringle, incorporating material from more than one source, including anecdotes from 'A lady, who knew him [Ritchie] from her infancy, and who has furnished us in the most obliging manner with some particulars respecting him'. The essay also featured an engraving of Ritchie 'from an original drawing taken some time before his death by a very accomplished person who lived for many years in habits of frequent and familiar intercourse with him'.[33] This tallies with Robert Chambers's account in a letter to Scott in 1830:

> I think I have been told that it was written by Miss Ferguson, daughter of the Professor, and one of your own most intimate friends. At least, I am pretty sure I have been informed, on good authority, that the drawing which accompanies the article was by her.[34]

On 9 September 1817 Pringle had written to Scott specifically asking for help with the October number which was later to include the 'Account of David Ritchie'.[35] Most intriguing of all is the article's quotation of a passage of 'picturesque' description, on the subject of Ritchie's intended burial-place, allegedly taken from 'A short Account of David Ritchie, with an elegy on his death: printed for the author, July 1816'. The footnote which identifies the source continues:

> This is curious, as having been in print some little time before the *Tales of my Landlord* appeared. But it was never published, and the author, whom we have conversed with, does not imagine that any of the few copies which he privately distributed could possibly have found their way to the hands either of Mr Peter Pattieson, or his learned and worthy patron, the Schoolmaster of Gandercleugh.[36]

No copy of this pamphlet appears to have survived, and its provenance remains a mystery. In the footnote, however, one senses a a fairly knowing continuation of the game concerning authorship initiated by the pseudonymous *Tales*. At the very least, it seems fair to speculate a sharing of memories about Hallyards with the Fergusons during the spring/summer of 1816.

It is possible Scott delayed writing the story until his return to Abbotsford for the summer on about 23 July 1816. Certainly Blackwood's ultimatum in early August, which threatened a financially embarrassing

return of bills, seems to have forced him into releasing material prematurely. The last portions too appear to have been written at pace, to
satisfy Blackwood's clamouring for copy. Scott later told Lady Louisa
Stuart how he had 'bungled up a conclusion as a boarding school Miss
finishes a task which she had commenced with great glee & accuracy'.[37]
Four more printed sheets were in Blackwood's hands on 28 August, by
which time Scott was asking through Ballantyne for 'some covenanting
books' to help with the next story.[38] At the end of August Ballantyne
took to his bed with an inflammatory illness. In a letter on 1 September
from Kelso, in his mother's hand, he conveyed the author's agreement
that Murray could be given sight of the first volume. Another letter on 3
September confirmed that two copies had been sent to London. By now
it was clear that *The Tale of Old Mortality* was breaking the mould: 'the
second tale will occupy the second and third volumes, and a Highland
tale will form the fourth. The second tale is already very far advanced'.[39]

The full 2000 sheets for the first edition were almost certainly pulled
while the printed text was being prepared in August. Work now began
on setting and proofing *The Tale of Old Mortality* as copy flowed from the
author through September. Early in October *The Black Dwarf* flared
momentarily into view again as a result of a request from Blackwood
(communicated as always through Ballantyne) that the author should
revise the conclusion of the story. The suggestion appears to have
originated from William Gifford, Murray's literary adviser, and pro-
voked an explosive and well-known reaction:

> My respects to the Booksellers & I belong to the Death-head
> Hussars of literature who neither *take* nor *give* criticism. I know no
> business they had to show my work to Gifford nor would I cancel a
> leaf to please all the critics of Edinburgh & London . . .[40]

Scott's assertion of authorial independence, while no doubt heartfelt,
provided a useful smoke-screen for the sheer impracticability of what
was being proposed, notwithstanding Blackwood's offer to defray ex-
penses. Revision would have involved an unprecedented return to the
manuscript, with a temporary setting aside of *The Tale of Old Mortality*;
the transcription of new material, as well as fresh setting and proofing;
and the ponderous printing of 2000 new copies of the affected sheets.
One suspects, however, that Scott's confidence in the story was not left
undented; and that his memory of the incident later found expression in
the relatively large number of deprecatory comments made by him
about the *Dwarf* in the wake of publication.

As *The Tale of Old Mortality* neared completion at the end of October,
work began on the final stages of preparing *Tales of my Landlord* for
publication. On 13 November Blackwood informed Murray that 'the
whole will be in proof in a few days & Ballantyne expects to be ready for
delivery in a fortnight'. Such was his confidence in immediate success,
that he had ordered a second edition of 2000 'to press directly'. By

Wednesday, 20 November, he was able to schedule shipment of Murray's share and make plans for co-ordinating publication in Edinburgh and London:

> Ballantyne has just been with me & informs me that the last sheet and titles of the Tales will go to press tomorrow, and I expect to be able to send you 6 complete copies by Friday's mail. He is to make every exertion to have copies ready on Tuesday so that we may ship for you by that day's smack. I will not be able to put off publication here longer than Monday se'night 2d Decr as the author is impatient to have it fairly out . . .[41]

An advertisement in the *Edinburgh Evening Courant* on November 21 set publication for 2 December. On 22 November Blackwood transmitted two copies through Ballantyne for 'the author', having already somewhat cheekily sent 'the very first copy' to Scott.[42] Ballantyne's account for paper and printing and author's half profits is dated 23 November.[43] A first consignment of 700 copies was shipped to Murray on 25 November, an advance letter sent by mail predicting arrival at the wharf on Saturday (30 November).[44] Murray's advertisements promising publication 'in a few days' appeared in the London papers from 28 November; this changed to 'this day published' in the *Morning Post* on 5 December. In Edinburgh the *Courant* announced publication on Monday, 2 December. In spite of a last-minute attempt by Ballantyne to have it raised, the price for the four volumes was £1 8s. (£1.40).

2. THE COMPOSITION OF *THE BLACK DWARF*

The Manuscript. The original manuscript of *The Black Dwarf*, which has survived in its entirety, is in the Pierpont Library, New York. The tight binding of the manuscript in its present form makes it difficult to ascertain the exact conjugation of its gatherings, though the sequence of watermarks gives some sort of guidance.[45] Scott's numbering of the leaves (from [1] to 101—the only foliation present) is also revealing, as are a number of blank rectos and repeated numbers with asterisks. These are noted in the following table illustrating foliation:

Scott	Consecutive	Features
None	[f. 1]	Title
None	[f. 2]	Dedication
None	[f. 3]	Introduction starts
2–5	[ff. 4–7]	to end of Introduction
None	[f. 8]	blank recto; verso additions to f. 9r
6	[f. 9]	*The Black Dwarf* starts
*6	[f. 10]	
7–20	[ff. 11–24]	
*21	[f. 25]	blank recto; verso additions to f. 26r
21–32	[ff. 26–37]	
None	[f. 38]	blank recto; verso additions to f. 39r
33–48	[ff. 39–54]	Ch. 9 ends third way down f. 54r

*48	[f. 55]	Ch. 10 begins; no additions on f. 54v
49–73	[ff. 56–80]	Ch. 13 ends two-thirds way down f. 80r
73*	[f. 81]	Ch. 14 begins; no additions on f. 80v
74–101	[ff. 82–109]	
None	[f. 110]	

The irregularities between ff. 7 and 10, though complicated, are consistent with the Introduction at one stage having been detached from the story proper. The blank rectos at f. 25 (Scott's f. *21) and f. 38 (unnumbered), on the other hand, do not coincide with any significant break in the text: f. 24r ends at 30.4 'stanes', f. 37r at 46.15 'chase, that'. However, there is a noticeable change of pen stroke at an early point on both the succeeding folios 26 and 39 (at 30.6 'Thanks', and 46.20 'The Dwarf'). In the top left margin of f. 26r, moreover, Scott has written 'Ch. IV', presumably as a marker since the fourth chapter had commenced at f. 22. The evidence in both instances indicates a conscious break in writing, consistent (say) with a temporary setting aside of the manuscript, a change of residence, or the detachment of a section for consideration by another party. It might also indicate the transmission of copy to the printing office, though there are no marks of a packet having been formed. Larger breaks, more in keeping with the latter procedure, appear at ff. 54/5 (48/*48) and ff. 80/81 (73/73*), where in each case Scott's asterisked number coincides with the beginning of a chapter (Chs 10 and 14 in the present edition). The overall impression gained from the manuscript is that Scott wrote the first nine chapters in a number of stages, possibly with interruption, but without sending material for printing. This was then followed by two relatively unbroken phases of writing, taking the novel first to the end of Chapter 13, and then on to its conclusion. These large divisions probably correspond with the batches of manuscript received by James Ballantyne during August 1816.

In composition Scott follows his usual practice of covering rectos densely, and using the facing verso for alterations and additions. The script is for the most part unbroken by large alterations, Scott apparently having constructed his story without any sudden changes of mind. A close inspection of the rectos nevertheless reveals a myriad of small alterations, many of which must have been made during the initial composition, though differing ink colours indicate that some were entered at a subsequent point. A good proportion of the latter kind are in a similar pen to that used in the following sequence, indicating that it was Scott's habit to resume work by reading over and correcting the immediately preceding batch. Another layer of correction could also have been added before copy was dispatched to the printers, and there are grounds for believing that the heading to Jedidiah's Introduction and some of the chapter numbers are interpolations made retrospectively. The manuscript thus not only offers a unique view of the primary creative urge in process, but also anticipates a number of changes made by Scott, and in some cases intermediaries in the printing-house, during the transmission of the text into its printed form.

With between 10 to 30 deletions and alterations on each recto, some of which are illegible, it is impossible to classify in detail all the different kinds of changes in evidence. A large proportion of alterations, however, fall under one of three categories.

1] A number of repetitions of words in close proximity were eliminated, both in the course of writing and retrospectively. On several occasions the resulting transference leads to a more precise or pithier term (as in the substitution of 'sinewy' for 'muscular' at 42.30, or 'snapper' for 'stumble' at 66.2). In the following instance (given here, as in other cases below, in its manuscript form) a new lilting rhythm is discovered: 'hes a ⟨true⟩ ↑real↓ Earnscliffe—his father's son—a ⟨true⟩ ↑leal↓ friend' (53.27–28). Not untypically, the above passage appears immediately before an apparently fresh phase of writing, the alterations matching the new pen stroke.

2] More apposite or contextually fluent words frequently replace relatively wooden or amorphous predecessors. Single word examples are the substitution of 'pipe-stapples' for 'tobacco-pipes' at 61.26, 'moor-ill' for 'distemper' at 70.19 and 'grewsome' for 'queer' at 70.25. Among new phrases to emerge are: 'atween ⟨the⟩ ↑twa peacefu'↓ countries' (51.30–31); 'by the ⟨water⟩ side of the sluggish stream' (62.12); and 'just ⟨send⟩ ↑make↓ me a ⟨memorandum⟩ ↑minute or missive↓' (73.28).

3] Scott often inserts single words and short phrases, thereby adding fresh detail, improving rhetorical flow, and sharpening sense. Some narrative passages are especially well worked over, as in the description of Meikle-stane-Moor in Chapter 2 or the first full physical account of the Dwarf (Ch. 4). Other insertions help steady Scott's narrative voice, or add rhetorical force to some of his 'correct' speakers. More noticeable still is his habit of adding pithy new phrases to Scots speech. Examples include: 'what news ↑from the south hie-lands↓' (11.28), 'the track o' Earnscliffes horses ↑ower the waste↓' (54.24), and (a complete sentence) '↑Murrain on the gear!↓' at 63.10. Generally speaking, the areas of Scots dialogue are among the most heavily altered in the manuscript.

A number of syntactical gaps, the product of Scott's speed in writing, are similarly filled by insertion into the main text. Pruning is less common, though Scott occasionally cuts a superfluous or indecisive phrase. Proper names replace personal pronouns on a handful of occasions, and a number of brief dialogic pointers (said-so-and-so phrases) are attached to speeches. Scott rarely intervenes for grammatical reasons alone; nor is there much evidence of his retrospectively altering punctuation. Orthography remains untouched—with one notable exception.

On approximately twenty occasions, Scott alters English words in favour of Scots equivalents. Some changes obviously occurred in the course of writing: as in '⟨kept⟩ keepit it in mind' (18.26–27), and 'the ⟨poor⟩ pure [*sic*] goat' (122.25). In the case of insertions, however, the ink colour sometimes indicates a subsequent intervention (an example is '⟨about⟩ ↑abune↓' at 21.12). Other Scots forms are superimposed, either by overwriting a whole word (e.g. 'maun' over 'may' at 56.23), or through changing single letters ('many' is altered to 'mony' at 68.12). Transferences to English, when found, normally correct an accidental slippage from adjacent Scottish speech, the product of Scott's original failure to return to an 'English' register quickly enough. An exception is the deletion of the Dwarf's opening words 'Gang on your gate' in favour of 'Pass on your way' (21.28, 35, 43), which perhaps reflects an initial uncertainty about whether he should be a Scots or English speaker.

More than 200 interventions are found on facing versos, adding in all more than 4000 words to the text. Some 40 are alterations or embellishments, with Scott seeking space for an alternative phrase or expanded sentence. The rest are insertions, ranging from routine applications such as dialogic pointers to whole new sequences of writing. Scott uses the verso, for example, to sketch in an account of Grace Armstrong's capture and recovery (see Ch. 10): a sequence of events which has to be kept separate from similar experiences suffered by Isabel Vere. No less than 50 insertions and embellishments add to Scots dialogue, introducing approximately 170 extra Scots words into the text. Some of the story's finest flourishes enter in this way, a point illustrated by the three larger insertions in the manuscript version of 73.9–14:

> ... ↑I am content on my part to accept the courtesy wi' mony kind thanks↓ & troth I think it will ↑be↓ as safe in my hands as yours if ye leave it flung about ⟨the door⟩ in that gate ↑for the first loon body to lift↓ forbye the risque of bad neighbours ↑that can win through steekit doors & lock-fast places↓ as I can tell to my cost—

Almost equally dense changes amplify the Dwarf's misanthropic outbursts, with Scott making a considerable effort to find an appropriate rhetorical pitch.

Of four chapter mottoes present in the manuscript, only that to Chapter 13 is in place on the recto; those to Chapters 2, 3 and 11 appear on facing versos and must have been added after the initial composition. The motto from John Leyden at Chapter 3 originally stood at the head of Chapter 2, but was deleted in favour of the passage from Shakespeare found in the first (as in the present) edition.

Preparing the First Edition. All the evidence points to the first edition having been prepared in a narrow space of three to four weeks, from Ballantyne's first receipt of copy from Scott early in August 1816 to Blackwood's departure to London at the end of the same month. The process would have begun with the transcription of the manuscript, necessary to preserve Scott's anonymity. In the case of *The Black Dwarf* the transcriber has not been identified. John Ballantyne, who had been closely involved in the preparation of *The Antiquary*, was absent from Edinburgh during August, and it is unlikely that James with all his other preoccupations would have taken on a relatively menial task (in fact, his letters suggest that he first read the text in proof). Since there was a need to feed the press quickly, in the light of Blackwood's importunity, a trusted employee in the printing office would have been most convenient. Once sections of the transcript were ready, the process of setting into type could begin, followed by the pulling of first proofs. These would be read against the transcript, the type corrected as necessary, then second proofs would be produced for the author. While there is no direct evidence of Scott receiving proofs of the *Dwarf*, a number of medium-size insertions made between the manuscript and first edition are clearly authorial. The longest takes up five lines in the first edition, but virtually all the rest are brief enough to have been accommodated within single pages (which, in the first edition, vary between 23 and 25 lines). In view of the rush to produce the final text, it is possible that Scott was more than usually concerned not to introduce alterations that involved re-imposing more than a page.

Clearly the first half of the story had reached a readable form by the time Ballantyne sent Blackwood the first eight sheets on the evening of Thursday, 22 August. Additional evidence is provided by Blackwood's letter to Murray, begun that night, with its detailed commentary on the text to about the middle of the fourth sheet. Blackwood's quotations leave little doubt that he was reading a text identical to the first edition, even in areas where substantive changes were made after the manuscript (as in the cases illustrated below, where Scott's foliation is followed):

Manuscript	Blackwood/First Edition
the circumstances under which it was told	the circumstances under which, the materials thereof were collected
(f. 5r)	(9.11−12)
amang a whin stane-houses wi slate on them	amang a wheen ranks o' stane-houses, wi' slate on the tap o' them
(f. 10v)	(18.8)
lookd ... the lady as well as the farm house-wife	looked ... the lady as well as the farmer's wife
(f. 16v)	(compare 25.14−15)

The third of these changes is interpretable as a deterioration which took place in the printing-house; but the second bears the hallmark of Scott, and the first would seem to go well beyond the brief of an ordinary intermediary. In the case of the earliest sheets, then, the full process of transference into print (including the incorporation of Scott's proof changes) appears to have been accomplished in little more than a fortnight.

In sending the first eight sheets, Ballantyne also drew Blackwood's attention to an unresolved difficulty: 'There is an unaccountable confusion, as you will see, betwixt the *grandmother* and *mother* of Hobbie Elliott; but the author will of course correct it in the sheets not yet thrown off'.[46] The confusion is traceable back to the manuscript, where the status of Hobbie's relation shifts as follows: 1] returning from hunting, Hobbie talks of his 'gude-dame' (grandmother) and her concern for Earnscliff (Ch. 2); 2] approaching Heugh-foot, he points out 'grannie' who is 'in the ha' window' (23.23), and in the ensuing scene in the farmhouse the same person is manifestly grandmother to the Elliot siblings (Ch. 3); but 3] when Hobbie returns to find destruction at Heugh-foot (Ch. 7), it is his 'mother' he asks for; and 4] after the recovery of Grace Armstrong, it is she who reminds her 'son' to thank Providence (Ch. 10). At stage 1 Scott further aggravated the problem by inserting an additional exchange on the facing verso, with the result that Hobbie refers to his 'mother' and 'gude-dame' in successive utterances. This idiosyncrasy was dealt with by a cancel replacing pages 47–48 in the first edition. Comparison with the pre-cancel state (discovered in a copy at Keele University)[47] illustrates the Defoe-esque ingenuity with which Scott and his coadjutors could meet a crisis.

> I can tell ye, my mother thinks hersel no that distant connected wi' you. (Keele copy)
>
> I can tell ye, my mother—my grandmother I mean—but, since we lost our ain mother, we ca' her sometimes the tane, and sometimes the tother—but, ony gate, she thinks hersel no that distant connected wi' you. (First edition: see 18.15–18)

A more general transference from mother/son to grandmother/grandson, in direct narrative, was also made at stage 3 (though, in speech, Hobbie continues to address his 'mother'). In an earlier note to Blackwood on 22 August, Ballantyne had written: 'You shall have all that is thrown off, and what is imposed, before dinner'.[48] 'Imposed' indicates that bound type for the later sheets was in a state of readiness for printing, but that copies had not yet been pulled in number. Changes then could have been made by taking down and replacing type within the printing house, though in the case of stage 4 (which commences just at the point where the batch sent to Blackwood leaves off) the hand of the author is plainly visible. The most obvious explanation is that Scott received revises for the last affected sheets. All this seems to have blown up at a very late stage. The only indication in the manuscript that Scott was aware of the problem occurs in the concluding narrative reference to 'the Man of the Moors, whose feats were quoted by Mrs Elliot to her grandson' at 124.23–24. In the manuscript the last words read 'to her Grandson Js.', the 'Js.' apparently being a signal to James Ballantyne (perhaps in jest) to get matters right.

Even with the ratification of the contract, pressure still remained to complete the volume. Blackwood's observation on 28 August that four more sheets had arrived indicates that the composition of the story was by then completed, since sheet M in the first edition leads almost to the end of the present Chapter 14 (to 99.34 'my child'), and hence well past the last perceptible division in the manuscript. In the later stages Scott almost certainly found himself correcting proofs as he continued to write. The spelling of Meikle-stane-Moor provides a useful pointer. On its first two appearances in the manuscript Scott writes 'Meikle-' in his clearest hand, apparently to signal a preferred spelling. In the first edition, however, 'Meikle' rapidly changes via 'Mickle' to 'Muckle' (Mucklestane-Moor), probably as a result of misreading or a compositorial preference for 'muckle'. Scott nevertheless continued to write 'Meikle-' (there is a particularly clear instance at 69.34) until virtually the end of the manuscript. Only at 121.22 does one find an unambiguously clear 'Mucklestane Moor'. The most likely explanation is that Scott reluctantly conceded the change on seeing that 'Muckle' had become the standard form in proofs. There is strong internal evidence, too, that as the end approached Scott was deliberately trying to minimise the risk of error in the printing house, perhaps with a view to not receiving proofs at all. Tell-tale signs in the manuscript include clearer spellings, especially for proper names, and a more marked punctuation. Furthermore, collation between the manuscript and first edition shows a considerably lower number of significant verbal changes in the final third of the novel. The last sizeable addition occurs at 91.7–9 ('This conversation . . . day'), none of those which follow exceeding four words. Signature P (the last full sheet) contains only two verbal additions of more than one word, neither of which is noticeably Scott's.

Evidence of substantive changes taking place after the incorporation of material from author's proofs has come to light through the discovery of the 'Keele' copy of *Tales of my Landlord*, which consists largely of sheets discarded during the printing of the first and second editions. In the case of the *Dwarf*, sheets M and N have no press figures, and both contain proof marks in an orthodox hand which is neither Scott's nor Ballantyne's. For the most part the corrections pick up typographical points, such as damaged letters, though closing quotation marks are also requested at one point. More significantly, at 106.18 'abhorrence to mankind' is changed to 'abhorrence of mankind'. In the manuscript Scott had written 'not indeed in devotion to God but in dislike to mankind'. What appears to have happened is that the substitution of 'abhorrence' for 'dislike' at an earlier proof stage left the somewhat ungainly 'in abhorrence to', resulting in this final alteration by an in-house reader in the last proofs before printing. Such a late intervention, presumably on grammatical grounds, offers a salutary reminder that not all the verbal emendations made for the first edition were overseen by Scott.

Changes between Manuscript and First Edition. During the process of preparing the first edition a whole new punctuational apparatus was added to Scott's original text. It is not certain at what point and by whom punctuational marks were supplied, though there is a strong possibility that much of the practical pointing was undertaken by compositors, who were regarded as highly skilled in this sphere. Most common amongst marks is the insertion of approximately 6000 commas, the influx being particularly noticeable in areas of direct narrative (where the manuscript punctuation is generally lightest). Another significant feature is the large-scale transference of Scott's dashes into a variety of points such as semicolons, full stops, exclamation and question marks—some of the heaviest changes occurring in dialogue, where the dash had previously been all-dominant. The long consecutive sequences of writing in the manuscript are also broken up through the creation of 700 'new' paragraphs (though in areas of dialogic exchange a large proportion of these are effectively signalled by the manuscript's system of using dashes with quotation marks at the end of utterances). Initial letters in words are raised and lowered in about equal proportions, hyphenation is altered to match more closely the conventions of print, and routine details such as apostrophes are supplied where required.

In orthography a primary target is Scott's use of older, quainter forms such as 'publickly' and 'quarrell'. Broad changes occur within Scots, where substitutions include 'gude' for 'guid', 'hale' for 'haill', 'kenn'd' for 'kend', and 'wheen' for 'whin'. Normally words ending 'sell(s)' (e.g. 'himsell') in the manuscript are transferred to 'sel(s)' in the first edition ('himsel'). The first edition, on the other hand, is far from being uniform in these respects. An extreme (but not untypical) instance is provided by its treatment of the affirmative 'ay/aye'. Here the manuscript's 'aye' is at first followed, but from sheet G onwards 'ay' consistently takes its place.

The transference of words between English and Scots deserves to be considered as a special category, somewhere between orthographical and verbal changes. In *The Black Dwarf* more than 240 instances are found where English words have been changed to Scots equivalents by the time of the first edition. Most common amongst the transferences (with number of occurrences in parenthesis) are: 'of' to 'o''' (34); 'you' to 'ye' (30); 'have' to 'hae' (18); 'with' to 'wi''' (13). Less frequent, but representative of the kind of change taking place, are 'came' to 'cam' (3), 'would' to 'wad' (3), 'poor' to 'puir' (3), and 'son' to 'bairn' (5). As the last instance indicates, the search for an equivalent sometimes leads to a more substantive change, but generally the shift is achieved by an 'orthographical' transference to the same word in its Scots spelling. All but a handful of these changes take place in the first ten chapters of the *Dwarf*, reflecting the much larger concentration of Scots in that part of the story. As a whole the Scots acquired after the manuscript represents slightly more than 10 per cent of the total Scots found in the first edition. The degree to which Scott was involved in the process is unclear. Evidence supplied by novels involving Scots where author's proofs have survived suggests a more localised and specific level of engagement. In *The Fortunes of Nigel*, James VI's Scots is accentuated to contrast with the more anglicised George Heriot; and the proofs of *The Bride of Lammermoor* offered an opportunity to modify some of the near-gibberish created by errors of transmission in the later stages of the story ('as war'nt' is corrected back to 'I'se warrant'). None of these proofs, however, suggest anything like a full-scale overhaul by Scott at proof stage; on the contrary, collation of proofs of *Redgauntlet* shows several instances where Scots has been added before and after Scott revised. In effect, the addition of Scots appears to have been one of the tasks undertaken by intermediaries.

Whatever the peculiar circumstances, the process of Scotification in the *Dwarf* appears to have been done consistently and with a measure of sensitivity. The large majority of transferences are matched by similar usages in the manuscript, and in some cases might be said to follow Scott's own prompting there. Scott seems to have been especially vulnerable during the initial composition when first engaging with Scots or re-entering from a different vantage point. The last sentence in Hobbie's speech at 56.37–38, which in the manuscript is found at the beginning of a verso insertion, is entirely in English: ' ↑ And now my last hopes are gone and I shall never see her more . . . ↓ '. Here the first edition introduces three Scots forms ('gane', 'ne'er' and 'mair'). Difficulties could also occur on the first introduction of Scots-speaking characters. Willie of Westburnflat's crone-like mother even betrays traces of the drawing-room in the manuscript version of 60.28–31:

"We are seeking William Græme of Westburnflat" said Earnscliffe "He is not at home" returnd the old dame "When did he leave home" pursued Earnscliffe "I cannot tell" said the portress . . .

Before the printed version someone intervened to change 'not' to 'no', 'home' to 'hame', and 'cannot' to 'canna': not only accentuating the appearance of the most atavistic character in the story, but also allowing the contrapuntal effect (here with the 'correct' Earnscliff) usually sought by Scott in such exchanges.

In contrast there are almost 70 instances of Scots words in the manuscript being transferred to English. Two are apposite corrections, stemming from the inappropriate placing of Scots in 'English' mouths. Another weeds out a Scoticism which had accidentally crept into the narrative. The remainder are more difficult to understand. Other proofs demonstrate that Scott *could* occasionally transfer to English for special rhetorical purposes. It is possible, too, that some of the Scots was subsequently considered as potentially misleading or too arcane for an English readership. But most of the disappearances are interpretable in the light of several kinds of mistake that might have been made by intermediaries: a tendency to slip back into routine English (not surprising amongst staff whose day-to-day work included sermons and school-books), simple misreading (Scott's 'doun' is almost indistinguishable from his 'down'), or unfamiliarity with a literary turn of phrase, special idiom, or regional nuance.

Between the manuscript and the first edition some 875 verbal changes took place in single words and groups of words. These can be roughly broken down into the following categories. Transferences between single words occur on approximately 370 occasions. Single words are also inserted in 140 instances, and in a further 70 cases groups of words from two upwards are added to the text. On 130 occasions words are omitted, approximately two-thirds of these consisting of one word only. Alterations involving more than single words occur about 125 times, and words are rearranged (by transposition etc.) on 40 occasions. These changes vary between embellishments which are almost certainly authorial, routine corrections which could be either by Scott or an intermediary, and palpable misreadings or misinterpretations of the manuscript. The following account is largely concerned with emendations that are either authorial or in keeping with standing orders governing intermediaries.

Most noticeable amongst routine changes is the continued ironing out of repetitions, some of which would have come into sharper relief through the integration of verso material into the main text. Valid single word transferences, on this basis, are made on about thirty occasions. Substitutions include: 'dogged' (29.34) for 'sullen', avoiding repetition with 'sullen malignant misanthropy' at the end of the preceding sentence; 'moor' (42.17) for 'heath', necessitated by 'heathy' (a recto insertion) immediately below; and 'residence' (77.39) for 'arrival', apparently to avoid a chime with 'arrival' at 77.42, itself originally part of a verso addition. Most of the changes are unexceptional, though the search for a synonym sometimes results in a slightly more inflated or orthodox term; examples are the replacement of 'heart' by 'bosom' at 46.33, and 'seen' by 'observed' at 55.31. On the other hand, substitution occasionally leads to the inclusion of a sharper word, as in the selection of 'broad-headed' as a replacement for 'iron' (nails) at 61.30 (to avoid repetition with 'bars of iron' immediately before). Repetition is also a factor in some larger alterations. At 33.35–36 'the purpose of destruction' replaces the manuscript's 'the same purpose', apparently in response to the proximity of 'the same end' (33.34–35), though one effect is to give an extra flourish to the Dwarf's rhetoric. (On other occasions, however, changes of this nature ignore more resonant echoes.) In a handful of cases, too, repetition is avoided by excision of words: at 121.22–23, for example, Scott had originally written 'twilight *kind of an* understanding' (my italics).

Other routine changes in the first edition may be divided for convenience into seven categories. 1] *Grammatical changes to achieve correctness, especially in narrative passages.* For example, at 80.3 'was momentarily expected' becomes 'were . . . expected' to tally with 'crisis and explosion'. 2] *Word replacement in favour of 'logical' or stylistically 'correct' equivalents.* A fairly routine substitution here is 'assemblage' for 'assistants' (52.17). 3] *Transferences in narrative to standard forms and idioms.* Under this category can be counted the substitution of 'as' for Scott's more Scottish 'so' (see e.g. the opening 'As' at 25.19). 4] *Antiquation of speech.* The Dwarf's 'has' is turned to 'hath' or 'hast', and 'are' to 'art', in a number of instances. On one occasion, too, 'hath' replaces 'has' in Jedidiah's Introduction. 5] *Pruning of authorial mannerisms.* Several superfluous words (as marked by italics) are usefully excised: 'rising *as it were* into his usual mood of misanthropy' (38.24); 'wi' *some* twenty ↑or thretty↓ mair o' us' (116.30). A similar phenomenon is the suppression of 'very' where it might be deemed rhetorically redundant (as in 'a *very* foolish brawl' at 18.30). 6] *Correction of factual details.* The printed text clarifies uncertainties in the manuscript about the precise number of Hobbie's brothers and sisters, and successfully negotiates Scott's dual naming of the family 'nurse' as Annaple and Elspat by opting for Annaple. 7] *Insertion of words to fill lacunae in the manuscript.* Apparently unintended gaps left in the course of composition are usefully filled on about thirty occasions (as through the addition of 'his' in 'most of his countrymen' at 55.29–30).

Scott's presence is more strongly felt in about twenty single-word insertions which either clarify meaning or add fresh detail. There is a sense of positive fine-tuning in the addition of 'check' to 'napkin' at 11.16, 'coarse' to 'black' at 29.23, 'surly' to 'face' at 62.17, and 'honest' to 'lads' at 63.24. One can reasonably assume that a considerable number of the larger insertions (if not all) came from Scott. A good proportion are categorisable as attempts to space out the rapid dialogic exchanges written by Scott in full creative flow. This includes the addition of 15 dialogic pointers, distinguishing speakers more explicitly, sometimes with an indication of tone and manner of delivery as well. Material is also placed at the beginning and end of utterances in an effort to provide clearer lines of demarcation between speeches: an example is the addition of 'Back to you, fellow?' at the beginning of Earnscliff's speech at 64.32. At one point a whole new utterance is granted to Earnscliff ('That . . . enquire' at 62.36–37), breaking up what might otherwise have seemed a rather self-involved speech by Westburnflat. On other occasions, new material serves to tie up loose ends of the narrative: the addition of 'an opportunity for which occurred on the following day' at 80.14–15, for example, successfully disposes of Lucy Ilderton for the rest of the story. Scott is found in his most creative vein, however, in several distinctive additions to vernacular dialogue (introducing in all 30 additional Scots words to the text). They include Hobbie's opportunistic 'There's ane sair wanted between Cringlehope and the Shaws' (29.5–6), Westburnflat's vulpine 'there's some canny boys . . . amang the shaws, owerbye' (44.10–11), and Hobbie's morose address to his horse ('Thou maun do without horse-sheet and surcingle . . . pool o' Tarras'), at 66.20–22. The third instance, the last full embellishment involving Scots, might even be said to define the outer limit of Scott's creativity at proof stage. In addition to these inter-textual changes, 14 mottoes are added between the manuscript and first edition. These are found at the head of the present Chapters 1, 4–10, 12 and 14–18.

The first edition of the *Dwarf* is not a stable text typographically, and there are signs of panic stations in the printing house in a number of compositorial errors and inconsistencies. Some corrections were evidently made during the course of printing. At 57.28 'last' in some copies appears as 'lat' in others; 'when the trampling of horses was heard, and a small body of riders were perceived' (81.22–23)—the manuscript form —is transposed to read 'were heard . . . was perceived' in about half the copies seen. There are also two chapters 9, yet no chapters headed 11 or 13—whether as a result of the division of the manuscript's Chapter 6 into two, confusion caused by the exchange of manuscript and printed copy, or simple error in the printing house, is uncertain. Further inconsistency is introduced by the title-page's spelling of Jedidiah as Jedediah, though there is reason to believe this arose during the preparation of preliminaries later in the year.[49]

3. THE LATER EDITIONS

The Black Dwarf went through no less than eleven different printed states in Scott's lifetime. As the first volume of *Tales of my Landlord*, first series, it appeared in five independent editions in less than three years. The second and third editions were printed and published in a narrow space between December 1816 and February 1817; the fourth was printed by April 1817, though for special reasons it was kept under wraps until the following year. A main reason for this rapid succession was Blackwood and Murray's initial uncertainty about the authorship, which prevented their risking a large first edition: a situation later complicated by a breakdown in communication between the two publishers when the second edition was ordered, and finally by problems in negotiating beyond the 6000 copies originally contracted for. The first series of *Tales* is also exceptional in that Scott eventually broke with the original publishers, allowing the right to bring out a fifth edition (1819) to Blackwood's arch rival, Constable.

After that the *Dwarf* was reset independently in five collected editions, before appearing in the Magnum Opus in February 1830. Having purchased the copyrights, Constable brought out *Novels and Tales of the Author of Waverley* (1819) in twelve octavo volumes. The same collection later appeared in two alternative formats: a sixteen-volume duodecimo (12mo) version in 1821 and a smaller octodecimo (18mo) set in twelve volumes in 1823. New editions of the octavo and duodecimo sets were brought out in 1822 and 1825 respectively. On each occasion the *Dwarf* held its place as the first of the *Tales of my Landlord*, sandwiched between Jedidiah's Introduction and *Old Mortality*, and somewhat awkwardly occupying the first part of a single volume.

As the accompanying stemma illustrates, the text of *The Black Dwarf* followed a long and complicated route on its way to the Magnum.

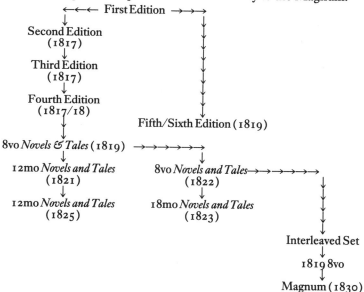

In the case of the earliest editions, the copy used for setting in Ballantyne's printing works was evidently the immediately preceding edition; alterations made in these editions thus tend to be accumulative. The text used for the fifth edition of the *Dwarf*, however, was a copy of the first edition. The 1819 octavo collected edition in turn bypassed the fifth edition by turning to the fourth for its copy text, making the fifth a dead end. Similar dead ends en route to the Magnum occur in the case of 1823 18mo and both the 1821 and 1825 duodecimo sets.

A simple collation of the Magnum *Dwarf* against the first edition reveals in the region of 1400 variants, about 25 per cent of which might be called substantive. Punctuation is heavier, grammar more 'correct', spelling nears consistency, repetitions have been largely removed. The story also appears more 'Scottish' in flavour, with 66 word changes from English to Scots forms, as opposed to only 15 in the opposite direction. A more comprehensive deconstruction, however, shows that only about a third of the total number of variants are directly attributable to the Magnum. An almost equal number of changes had been accumulated by the time of the fourth edition, including the bulk of Magnum's 'new' Scots. The proximity of the second, third, and fourth editions to the initial, rushed printing of the *Dwarf* makes the emendations found there of particular interest. Similar personnel are likely to have been employed; and the direct or indirect intervention of Scott—close at hand in Edinburgh during the winter months—cannot be discounted.

The Second Edition. Notwithstanding Blackwood's foresight in ordering a second edition (2000) on 13 November 1816, a serious shortfall of saleable copies of the first edition had developed by 20 December, with James Ballantyne unable to promise fresh deliveries before the end of the month. Ballantyne's account for the second edition (headed 31 December 1816) was sent on 1 January 1817, and is endorsed as paid by Blackwood on 3 January.[50] The new edition was announced in the *Edinburgh Evening Courant* on 2 January.

Some 240 changes from the first edition version of the *Dwarf* are found in the second. About half of these are punctuational, the most prominent feature here being a tendency to further root out Scott's dashes (nearly 50 in all), either by deletion or replacement by more conventional marks (notably, semicolons and full stops). Capitalisation and hyphenation increase, and three 'new' paragraphs are made. More than 90 per cent of these changes were ultimately absorbed into the Magnum.

There are more than 60 spelling changes, half (31) of which alter English to equivalent Scottish/colloquial forms. Substitutions include: 'doun' for 'down', 'mak' for 'make', 'sax' for 'six', 'ye' for 'you', 'ain' for 'own', 'yowes' for 'ewes'. Interestingly, in six cases the second edition reverts to the manuscript in changing to Scots. Single-word changes occur on 24 occasions, usually to avoid repetition (9 instances) or in the pursuit of grammatical or semantic correctness. Nearly all these changes are found in direct narrative or, to a lesser extent, in the mouths of 'correct' speakers. Three have the effect of restoring the manuscript: 'composedly' for 'composed' at 35.12, 'piety' for 'pity' at 53.9, and 'internal' for 'external' at 99.29. Certainly the proportion of restorations is high compared with later editions, and the last two instances might conceivably have resulted from a check against the original manuscript.

Additionally words are rearranged in three local instances, and single words omitted on four occasions. Two egregious errors in the bylines of mottoes are also corrected. 'Mucklestane-Moor' is made uniform throughout. In all, the second edition provides a more heavily punctuated, obtrusively Scottish text, with fewer formal irregularities in its direct narrative.

The Third Edition. On 10 February Blackwood wrote to Murray that copies of the third edition of *Tales* would be available for packing that evening: 'I shall keep them at it most of the night so as to ship as many as they can get ready tomorrow before the vessels sail'. Ballantyne's account for the impression of 2000, dated 10 February, was sent to Blackwood on 12 February.[51] Earlier correspondence between Blackwood and Murray indicates that work had begun early in January: this tallies with Ballantyne's subsequent claim that he had taken 'little more than five weeks' to complete.[52] The edition was first advertised in the *Edinburgh Weekly Journal* on 19 February 1817.

A complete resetting of the first volume is evident in nearly 190 variants against the second edition. Amongst almost 100 punctuational changes, the most prevalent feature is a continuing tightening of marks. More than sixty new spellings occur, with a further movement to Scots forms ('pounds' to 'punds', 'poor' to 'puir', 'hundred' to 'hunder'). Changes are also made within Scots, either to preferred forms ('scathe' to 'scaith', 'hale' to 'hail') or through simple conflation ('were na' to 'werena' etc.). Jedidiah (Cleishbotham) is regularised for the first time to Jedediah, in accordance with the title-page in previous editions. English forms are 'normalised' in a handful of cases: 'phænomenon' twice becomes 'phenomenon'; 'leapt' is preferred to 'leaped' at 43.24, inadvertently restoring the manuscript; but 'past' mindlessly replaces 'passed' at 109.11 ('when the storm has past away').

A few words are transposed in dialogue ('ye did' to 'did ye', 'he will' to 'will he'), presumably for dramatic effect. Another is added ('approaching,' after 'Hobbie,' at 72.12), to give a fuller sense of physical movement. Single-word changes (22 in all) are mostly occasioned by a desire for stylistic 'correctness', with the result that the text sometimes seems more inflated and distant. Almost half these changes occur in areas of dialogue, resulting in a slight but ominous flattening out of the text. One exception might be claimed: Hobbie's 'down my throat' becomes 'ower my throat' at 70.27. While possibly motivated by the proximity of another 'down', this nevertheless shows a capacity for extemporisation beyond standing orders.

The Fourth Edition. Negotiations between James Ballantyne and Blackwood for a new edition of *Tales*, extending the number beyond the original 6000, started on 20 January 1817.[53] With Murray clamouring for further copies, on 10 February Blackwood upped the order to 3000 copies, albeit noting to his partner that 'the demand seems to be slackening here'. On 29 March Blackwood received a note from Ballantyne, stating that the edition would be ready about 12 or 15 April.[54] Though plainly coloured by other considerations, there is little reason to doubt James Ballantyne's claim that he had taken an unrushed nine weeks to prepare the four volumes.[55] But the new edition could not be released on the market until the third edition cleared. Blackwood began advertising in the Edinburgh papers on 1 January 1818. Some title-pages are dated 1817, others 1818.

This edition introduces about 125 new variants to the *Dwarf*. A noticeable feature in about 70 punctuational changes is a temporary stemming of the tide of commas (24 deleted, only 11 added). 23 spelling alterations include 11 new Scoticisms (e.g. 'often' to 'aften', 'nag' to 'naig'), but also four cases of anglicisation. An almost equal number (20) of single word changes are made, the majority for grammatical or semantic reasons. A general flattening of direct speech, including that in Scots, is again apparent. Other changes include two single-word additions, one similar omission, and three simple transpositions—one of which ('I am' at 94.10) reverts to the manuscript state.

The fourth edition assimilates most of the changes made by the second and third editions, with the exception of sheets C and O, where emendations made by the third edition (including 6 transferences to Scots) are not carried through. The most obvious explanation is the use as a copy text of a 'mongrel' volume, mixing sheets from second and third editions.

The Fifth/'Sixth' Edition. As part of the terms for the second series of *Tales of my Landlord*, finalised on 2 October 1817, Scott handed Constable the right to publish 'the next edition of the original Tales'.[56] Subsequent correspondence between James Ballantyne and Robert Cadell, Constable's partner, reveals that it was Cadell who eventually gave the order to proceed, late in November 1818, in an effort to circumvent the author's request for a new edition of *The Heart of Mid-Lothian* (first published that summer as the second series of the *Tales*). Cadell proposed 2000, Scott upped this to 3000.[57] The edition was delivered in January 1819, though its advertisement was held back until the announcement of the third series of *Tales* (comprising *The Bride of Lammermoor* and *A Legend of Montrose*) early in May 1819. Blackwood and Murray threatened legal action on the grounds that their own stock was unexhausted, and an out-of-court settlement resulted in Constable & Co. purchasing a large number of unsold copies of the fourth edition. The only complete copy of the 'sixth' edition traced in British libraries is at Trinity College, Cambridge. Its press figures match those of the fifth edition, indicating that it consists of fifth edition sheets with a new title-page, and that it is not a true sixth edition at all.[58]

Cadell's letter to Ballantyne ordering the edition, on 24 November 1818, specifically states: 'It affords me pleasure to send with this the volumes of the Tales *first* series'.[59] The first volume of this set evidently belonged to the first edition, since the text of the *Dwarf* misses out the accreted alterations made up to the fourth. At the same time the fifth edition includes almost 200 variants of its own, comparable in character (if not quality) to any of the preceding subsequent editions. Changed words (21) include: 'hoarse laugh' to 'horse-laugh' at 13.3, 'wildly' to 'shrilly' at 22.34, 'inmate' to 'inhabitant' at 32.4; and, ingeniously when seen in context, 'words . . . were' for 'word . . . was' at 114.43. (Only the first of these, however, could claim any authority from the manuscript.) One spelling change might reflect the influence of an intervening publication: 'the heart of Mid-Lowden' at 69.12 becomes the 'the Heart of Mid-Lothian'. Loudon (Lothian) elsewhere appears as 'London'! Scots forms (14) are imposed sporadically ('comb' to 'kame', 'lawful' to 'lawfu'', 'moor' to 'muir'), some seeming distant from Scott's original usage. Hardly any of the verbal changes made in this edition are found in the Magnum.

The Octavo *Novels and Tales* (1819, 1822). More than 500 variants against the first edition had accumulated by the time of the fourth edition: 315 broadly punctuational; 125 spelling changes, almost half (59) of which are from English to Scots; and 90 other substantive changes, most involving single words. Nearly all these passed into the 1819 octavo *Novels and Tales*, which effectively became the 'base' text for subsequent collected editions. 1500 copies of the twelve-volumed set were apparently ordered from Ballantyne in Spring 1819, after pressure from Scott had prevented Constable from using the rival Edinburgh firm of Ramsay & Co.[60] The last part of the printing was done in haste and some confusion, Cadell on 22 September threatening to send volumes 9 and 10 (*The Heart of Mid-Lothian*) to another printer: 'You have thus only 6, 7 & 8 to complete—and to these do pray bend your whole force'. Shipment to Hurst, Robinson & Co. took place on 3 December 1819.[61] *The Black Dwarf*, which occupies the first part of volume 7, was presumably completed in October/November. The set was announced in the *Edinburgh Evening Courant* on 9 December 1819, priced £7 4s. (£7.20).

Notwithstanding the pressure of deadlines, collation shows a considerable overhaul of the text inherited from the fourth edition, with the generation of more than 300 new variants. Characteristic of more than 160 changes in punctuational marks is the hardening of 25 commas into semicolons. The standardisation of spelling is more sweeping than in previous editions: 'enterprize' is preferred to 'enterprise', 'shown' to 'shewn', and so on. A tendency to capitalise initial letters, particularly in the case of descriptive titles (the Tower of Westburnflat, Jacobite, Presbyterian), helps give an air of greater formality. Amongst 40 verbal changes, new words or phrases are inserted on 13 occasions—a process obviously encouraged by the change of format. These include the addition of a short sentence ('It's impossible', at the end of Hobbie's speech at 19.36), and the insertion of one dialogic pointer ('said he', after 'sir', at 81.4). The same freedom of space allowed the creation of six 'new' paragraphs.

In such ways the 1819 octavo offered its new readers a more regular, 'open' and (in conventional terms) logical and explicit text. It is also a significant degree further removed from the manuscript—restored only in the case of one verbal emendation—and sometimes even seems distant from the spirit of the earliest printed editions. Its transferences to Scots (10 cases, with 3 vice versa) are noticeably spottier and more haphazard in application than those found in the second, third, and fourth editions.

In correspondence the 1822 octavo edition was referred to by its publishers as a 'new edition' of the 1819 set, and there is little reason to think that it represented anything other than a routine job. Shipment took place in January 1822, and publication was announced in the *Edinburgh Evening Courant* on 2 February. There are approximately 225 variants against the 1819 octavo, many being standard applications (for example, the removal of apostrophes in words such as 'gi'e'), and for the first time the movement to Scots is arrested (4 words to English, 2 to Scots). Most of the 30 verbal changes are localised attempts at improving grammar or clarifying sense.

The Duodecimo *Novels and Tales* (1821, 1825). The two duo-decimo ('foolscap octavo') 16-volume sets of *Novels and Tales* represent another dead end in the textual history of the *The Black Dwarf*. The 1821 duodecimo edition should not be confused with a 24-volumed set of *Novels and Tales*, with the same title-page date, manufactured by Constable out of old unsold single editions of novels.[62] 1500 copies of the new set were printed early in 1821, and the bulk taken by Hurst, Robinson & Co. in London in April 1821.[63] The set was announced in the *Edinburgh Evening Courant* on 31 March at £6 in boards. The 1825 edition appeared, largely unheralded, in Spring 1825.[64]

Together with the 'Introduction' to *Tales*, the *Dwarf* covers up to page 253 of Volume 9 in both editions. The 1821 version shows in the region of 190 variants against the 1819 octavo, of which about 35 are verbal. Eight of its 25 word changes, and one insertion (',Annaple,' between 'go' and 'and' at 50.27), match those in the 1822 octavo, perhaps reflecting the use of the same marked-up copy text in preparation. Punctuation is characterised by the usual influx of commas and a penchant for exclamation marks.

To this the 1825 duodecimo added 296 further variants: a figure swollen by a major overhaul of spelling, most pervasively in the case of Scots words ('mysel' to 'mysell' etc.). The 1825 version also shows a clear preponderance of anglicisations (7 words to English, only 2 to

Scots). Thirty or so verbal variants combine emendatory daring with an alarming capacity for error. In Jedidiah's 'Introduction', which early editions had left largely untouched, 'called' (7.9) is changed to 'termed', 'soul' (7.22) to 'spirit', and 'recruit' (7.26) to 'refresh'. More questionable transferences, in the story itself, include 'wood-cooks' for 'wood-cocks' (22.10), 'south' for 'sooth' (24.7), and 'aggressor' for 'engrosser' (38.40). Between them the duodecimo sets assembled 84 substantive changes (including transferences between English and Scots), only seven of which are paralleled by the Magnum.

The 18mo *Novels and Tales* (1823). A more elegant cul-de-sac is found in the 12-volume 18mo *Novels and Tales*, where the *Dwarf* occupies about one half of of Volume 7. Hurst, Robinson & Co. contracted for 5000 copies in August 1821, with Constable forecasting a new market for Scott's fiction. Unusual care went into the production of the set, for which Ballantyne was instructed to use a new type. Work in preparing the edition had begun by April 1822; printing was completed in mid-August 1823, and a last consignment went off to London on 5 September.[65] A new 'miniature edition' at £4. 4s (£4.20) was advertised in the *Edinburgh Evening Courant* on 20 September 1823.

The attention given to this edition is evident in the thoroughgoing nature of its emendations. 250 variants are found against the 1822 octavo, including nearly 60 verbal changes and 18 transferences between English and Scots (ten to Scots). A distinctive characteristic, in 36 local transferences, is a willingness to tackle apparent instabilities head-on: at 37.14, for example, 'flowers and butterflies' is changed to 'flowers and buds', regularising the pattern of seasonal development. The 18mo edition also inserts words or embellishes phrases on 14 occasions, adding 24 extra words in all. One insertion has a smack of Scott: 'as fast as I have seen the ash-keys fall ↑from the great Hanging-tree at Castleton↓ in a frosty morning in October' (49.35–36). It is also interesting to observe the addition of 8 dashes: a mark favoured by Scott in proofs, though alien to the practice of compositors. Quite possibly the special interest shown in the 18mo set led to a fuller co-operation between Scott and Ballantyne than was usual in the case of collected editions: two letters from Scott, dateable in March and September 1822, appear to concern proofs relating to this edition.[66] If some of the emendations *are* authorial, then they were consigned to relative obscurity: only three of the 18mo's verbal changes are paralleled by the Magnum.

The Interleaved Set and The Magnum. The first twelve volumes of the Interleaved Set (in which Scott made notes and alterations for a collected edition originally planned by Constable) are based on the 1822 octavo *Novels and Tales*, the text of *The Black Dwarf* occupying the first 260 pages of the seventh volume. Scott made 156 entries in the Interleaved Set, only five of which are directly punctuational. Most of his emendations are written on the interleaves (of which 64 remain in position), normally with a caret leading from the printed text, though some appear in the margins. Inking is not consistent, and changes could have been made at any point after the Interleaved Set was presented by Constable in 1823. Scott though was actively working on the text of the first series of *Tales* with the Magnum in view during November/December 1828.[67]

On 87 occasions Scott adds to the text by inserting words or embellishing established phrases. An outstanding feature is the insertion of 42 dialogic signposts, identifying speakers. Many are routine in character such as 'said Earnscliff'. Others provide more complicated formulations: '↑said the young Lady no way desirous of a tete-a-tete↓' after 'father' (37.35); or '↑said the stout borderer—"stand back or I'll strike ye through—"↓' after 'steer him' (116.21). A large majority of the remaining additions are short insertions, introducing a fresh detail or opening out a phrase more explicitly. Two at 105.43–106.1 are not untypical: 'He was placed under ↑medical↓ restraint ↑as a lunatic↓'. Though Scott can sometimes be seen grappling with instabilities which have their origin in the earliest formulation of the text, there is not the slighted hint of the manuscript being involved in any way. A rare echo of the MS state occurs at 43.10, where 'passd' is restored, though without the excision of 'clear' that had replaced it by the first edition: 'All ↑passd↓ clear away . . .'. Five of Scott's larger insertions, dovetailed into the conversation between Isabella and Ratcliffe in Chapter 15, are standard rhetorical amplifications. Only once does one sense a fully active re-engagement with the text. In the closing stages, having changed 'sincere' (123.43) to 'singular' in the margin, Scott uses the interleaf to spell out the true origin of the Westburnflat's epitaph: 'being epithets which the village sculptor had at command of any person who orderd a *tomb stone* of his manufacture'. This is one of 27 additions not taken up by the Magnum.

The Interleaved Set also makes 38 localised verbal alterations, 24 of which survived into the Magnum. The majority appear to aim for greater clarity or specificity, though the vitality of the original is sometimes lost. Characteristic exchanges are: 'conceits' for 'thinks' (18.17), 'figure' for 'object' (21.16), 'whisperd' for 'said' (22.3), 'sharp-featured' for 'thin' (42.33), 'neck' for 'head' (55.40), 'strangers' for 'men' (116.41), and 'subterranean cave' for 'soutterain' (120.12). Two changes have the effect of removing Scots: 'bluid' at 43.34 becomes 'bristles', and 'anither' at 49.7 is expanded to 'a new bride'. Elsewhere 'sae angry' (24.6) is changed to 'angry aneugh'. (There is no indication of any primary engagement on this level, however, and the Interleaved Set's tally of one Scots word gained, three lost, is largely coincidental.) Scott rearranges words more substantially on two occasions; he also prunes three words (as opposed to more than 300 added), and makes one simple transposition ('was probably' to 'probably was' at 105.6–7). As suggested, punctuational changes are rare: single words are italicised on two occasions; one new paragraph is created, two dashes and an exclamation mark added. Scott nevertheless shows the responses of a habitual proof-reader by correcting one flagrant typographical error.

In line with the Magnum's policy of providing annotation, the Interleaved Set contains 20 original notes. These vary from word glosses to full historical commentaries. One mystery in the textual history of the *Dwarf* is the omission of all but six from the Magnum. Difficulty in deciphering Scott's hand, especially proper names, might conceivably have played a part; and a whiff of senility about one or two of the more anecdotal interventions could also have acted as a deterrent. It is not impossible, too, that pressure of space—particularly the need to include a fair portion of the better-known *Old Mortality* in the same volume—led to a cutting back during the final stages of planning the Magnum. Certainly it is difficult to see a clear principle of selection at work, and three substantial historical notes in the grand Magnum manner were left out. All but two of those omitted were reinstated in volume six of the Centenary Edition of the Waverley Novels (1870), though one note is incomplete and others have been imperfectly transcribed.

Robert Cadell received 'the revised Black Dwarf and Old Mortality' from Scott on 22 December 1828. On 26 February 1829 he also wrote in his Diary that he had 'revised and wrote in Sir Walters Notes into Black Dwarf'.[68] Almost certainly Cadell used a copy of the 1819 octavo *Novels and Tales* to transcribe Scott's material. This accords with the wholesale loss of variants peculiar to the 1822 octavo, and helps explain the failure of at least one intervention to make its way to the Magnum. In working on the Interleaved Set, Scott had added 'and' to complete the 1822 octavo's imperfectly implemented substitution of 'exhausted' for 'exhausting' in the passage below:

> the supposed maniac ... roamed wildly around the great stone,
> ↑and↓ exhausted his voice in shrieks and imprecations, that
> thrilled wildly along the waste heath. (compare 22.32–34)

In the 1819 octavo, however, the change would have seemed superfluous, and the Magnum reverts to the earlier printed state. Later references to the *Dwarf* in Cadell's diary occur on 18 March ('wrote up and finished the Black Dwarf') and 26 March ('revised Notes of Black Dwarf'); and on 21 May 1829 Cadell recorded that he had 'completed the revision of Tales of My Landlord 1st Series for Press'.[69] The air of meticulous attention conveyed by Cadell's entries is not matched by the *Dwarf*'s later textual history. Only 96 of Scott's interventions survived into the Magnum, and more than 120 words of additional text (excluding Notes) were not included. Some might simply have been overlooked —a noticeably higher proportion of emendations in the margins are missing, indicating perhaps that these were less scrupulously scanned. Others could have met their fate at a later stage of transmission. Nevertheless there is an ominous ring to Cadell's use of the term 'revised' (a favourite of his); and it is quite possible that while failing to transfer Scott's revisions Cadell was busily making 'improvements' of his own.

Of 1400 variants accumulated by the Magnum, as measured against the first edition, about 500 can be isolated as its own creation. A large majority (if not all) are likely to have entered into the text during setting and proofing before publication on 1 February 1830. 150 spelling alterations are dominated by the imposition of preferred forms: 'yoursell' for 'yoursel' and 'connexion' for 'connection' are examples. Another 50 variants involve the suppression of apostrophes in colloquial Scots words ('gi'e' to 'gie', 'de'il' to 'deil', etc.). Four words are transferred to Scots forms; three revert to English. At least 20 words are conflated by the removal of hyphens, though in case of 'Heugh-foot' hyphens are added to achieve uniformity. 135 changes in punctuational marks (the figure excludes punctuation necessitated by the inclusion of material from the Interleaved Set) have an overall tightening effect: 58 commas are added; 21 commas are turned to semicolons; at least 12 exclamations replace softer marks. The Magnum also removes italics from one word, adds accents to two French phrases, and corrects Latin once. With the 1823 18mo it shares the distinction of having correctly numbered its chapters.

A majority of the Magnum's 100 or so verbal changes are categorisable as grammatical 'corrections' or attempts at improving clarity. This follows a pattern set by some earlier editions, though the application is more rigorous than before. The grammatical rule-book is unusually obtrusive, ironing out Jedidiah's 'antique' pedantry, the Dwarf's Timon-like misanthropy, Marischal's dramatic flourishes alike. A preference for the explicit and logically coherent is sometimes pushed to the point of banality. Hobbie's 'Hae I not fed thee, and bred thee' (65.40–66.1), addressed to his horse, is transposed to the more predictable 'bred thee . . . fed thee'; the 'steep glen', which shelters the traveller at the end of the tale, is likewise transformed into a 'deep glen'. Occasionally one senses a deliberate policy of updating language, perhaps with the new readership in mind. Pertinent exchanges are 'cultivate' for 'labour' (31.2) and 'misshapen' for 'mutilated' (45.35). Compared with the Interleaved Set, the Magnum by itself adds only a small amount of text (approximately 30 words in all, compared with 5 omitted). Insertions include three new dialogic signposts, all routine; and, more noticeably, the somewhat implausible addition of 'It's as clear as the sun.' at the end of the Borderer's speech at 52.9

The Magnum's claim to offer an improved, authorially sanctioned text is not matched by what is deducible about the closing stages in *The Black Dwarf*'s history. While there is evidence of Scott adding editorial material to *The Tale of Old Mortality*, and perhaps reading proofs, there is nothing to indicate any active re-engagement with the *Dwarf* after December 1828. General procedure suggests that Scott would have been asked to check the new Magnum Introduction, but his full parti-cipation in proof-reading the main text is not a foregone conclusion. Many of the Magnum's new variants are explainable as the work of Ballantyne's staff, given a new licence to regularise; others might pos-sibly betray the dead hand of Robert Cadell—almost twenty years younger than Scott, and with a long-term interest in the Magnum's suc-cess. The relative incapacity of Scott to control his own text is poignantly suggested by the fate of the only direct instruction relating to the *Dwarf* found in the Interleaved Set. Firmly altering 'knapsack' to 'knapscap' (53.20), Scott adds in parenthesis: 'pray dont let it be knapscap not knap *sack* to which it has been repeatedly been alterd'. The superfluous neg-ative can hardly have misled anyone close to the author or familiar with the ballad origins of the story. 'Gie me my sword and my fathers knapscap', Scott had written in the manuscript. Hobbie Elliot is asking for the steel bonnet which characterised the legendary Border reiver. The Magnum, in accordance with all printed editions before the pres-ent, reads 'knapsack'.

4. THE PRESENT TEXT OF *THE BLACK DWARF*

There are a number of compelling reasons for choosing the first edition, published early in December 1816, as the foundation (or 'base-text') for a modern edition of *The Black Dwarf*. While the manuscript is an interesting and vital document in its own right, it was clearly written with the intention that it would be transformed into print, and in several respects can be seen to incorporate codes and signals designed for that purpose. As the start of a new venture, involving a fresh authorial per-sona and new publishers, the work was of considerable importance when originally printed, and James Ballantyne is almost certain to have employed his best available staff in its production. This compares with the later history of the *Dwarf*, especially in the collected sets, when one senses the title had become something of a low priority, to be bundled out of the way before starting on *The Tale of Old Mortality*. When Scott returned to the story with the Interleaved Set, he was dealing with a text which had gone through six different printed states, accumulating inter-ventions by a succession of unknown intermediaries, and at some dis-tance himself from the initial creative process. As previously noted his influence on the Magnum text, apart from the new Introduction, appears to have been negligible. But in 1816 Scott was a dominant partner in the Ballantyne press, in receipt of proofs and (when desired) revises which often became the vehicle for further creativity, and in a position to countermand rules of procedure in the press had he wished.

Blackwood, potentially a 'hands-on' publisher, was kept at arm's length during the production procedure in August by a variety of strategies—and swiftly dispatched by Scott when attempting to intervene over the conclusion of the story early in October.

On the other hand, it would be misguided to treat the first edition as representing a 'finished' version of the text, or to place it in amber just because it is the first edition. Owing to the need to pacify Blackwood—whose withdrawal would have plunged Ballantyne and Scott into financial crisis—the text was prepared at breakneck speed, even by the usual standards of the Waverley Novels. Though forming the first volume in its set, the initial preparation of the *Dwarf* can be likened in some respects to the frenzied last-minute rush to complete final volumes of titles such as *Rob Roy* (1818) in order to to meet deadlines. At the heart of the process the pressure would have been especially intense as author and production staff juggled with old sheets, incoming and outgoing proofs, along with new areas of text. In the case of the final sheets there are indications that Scott might not have seen proofs, and it is not improbable that some of the final stages in the printing house were bypassed so as to get the required volume into Blackwood's hands.

The aim of the present edition is to provide a version of *The Black Dwarf* similar to what might have been produced if conditions in the printing house had been less pressurised and intermediaries working there had carried out all their different functions correctly. Frequently this has involved a process of looking in two directions: backwards to the evidence of the manuscript to identify areas where intermediaries misinterpreted Scott's intentions or exceeded standing orders which had his tacit approval; forwards to the early subsequent editions (up to and including the fourth) for aspects of that formal stability which would have been achieved earlier if the first edition had been prepared without mishap. This final section of the textual essay offers a condensed view of more than 900 emendations to the first edition base-text.

Punctuation and Orthography. The present text for the most part preserves the first edition's punctuation, which combines competence in implementing conventions of print then in operation with a fair measure of skill and sensitivity in interpreting key areas of the text. Certainly the first edition compares favourably in the last respect with later editions, where punctuation becomes progressively heavier and more standardly grammatical, with a noticeable levelling out of dialogue and narrative. Readers of the present edition will find a punctuation style mixing grammatical and rhetorical priorities, which in several ways leads us back to the rhythmic responses of Scott's earliest readers.

Nevertheless mistakes inevitably occurred as the text of the *Dwarf* sped through its various stages of production. An early problem facing intermediaries was how to unpick the syntactical structure of long areas of narrative business, unguided by any form of manuscript punctuation other than the opening and closing of sentences. An example of how mistakes were made is found in Jedidiah's Introduction at 6.39–40, which in the manuscript reads 'fowls black & grey partridges'. In punctuating this as 'fowls, black and grey partridges' the first edition erroneously created two types of partridge. The mistake was spotted by the 1819 octavo *Novels and Tales*, which re-punctuated as 'fowls black and grey, partridges'; though a perceptive eye might have inferred the same through the disposition of words in the manuscript itself, where an unbroken pen stroke joins 'fowls' and 'black', and the use of an ampersand implicitly forms a linkage between 'fowls black & grey'. In some cases failure to unravel Scott's meaning led to unnecessary verbal emendation. At the end of the present Chapter 17 the manuscript reads as follows:

> And it was a lucky chance he said that on the very day they had got notice that Westburnflat did not intend to keep his tryste at Castleton but to hold them at defiance. A considerable party had assembled at the Heugh-foot with the intention of paying a visit to the robbers tower on the ensuing morning and their course was easily directed to Ellieslaw Castle. (compare 118.17–22)

Failure to sense the integrity of the first sentence evidently led intermediaries to merge the passage into one, substituting 'that' for the first 'the' and adding a superfluous 'so that' (preceded by a semicolon) after 'defiance'. Reference to the present text will show how with only minor punctuational adjustment the full sense of the original wording can be restored. Occasionally Scott is found in the manuscript supplying single guiding marks in an effort to forestall misinterpretation. At 34.33–34 the intended sense is restored by following a rare manuscript comma, in preference to the first edition's alternative positioning after 'tomahawk', to create 'with my tomahawk at once, spoil': a rhetorically stronger statement in the Dwarf's mouth, if less grammatically and logically conventional.

Additionally on some 20 occasions the present edition omits commas added by the first edition, because they significantly impede rhetorical flow and/or deflect from the force of Scott's meaning. Allowance naturally needs to be made for a system of punctuation that is indicative rather than prescriptive, and where commas sometimes appear to have no larger function than to intimate a pause on behalf of the reader. But in the following cases, intermediaries seem to have sprinkled marks over-liberally or with scant regard to the larger rhythms of Scott's narrative: 'neighbours, from other motives' (32.15–16); 'offices, stocked with cattle' (50.42); 'Vere, not only alive but unwounded' (76.39); 'figure, and the living suppliant' (117.38); 'Derwentwater, and others' (123.18). Interestingly all the above commas were removed by early subsequent editions, against the general influx of new commas, indicating that later intermediaries considered their predecessors had acted too invasively. Similarly placed commas also have a disruptive effect in dialogue—as in the following cases, where the displayed comma has again been removed by the present edition: 'law pleas, and losses sinsyne' (compare 26.42); 'promises . . . made during your illness, forgotten?' (43.8–9); 'the king, or the laird I live under' (compare 83.4).

Another task falling to intermediaries was the interpretation of the multiple dashes which almost exclusively guide Scott's long sequences of dialogue in the manuscript. At first sight these can appear almost casual in use, but closer examination reveals a complex network of signals inviting different kinds of interpretation. Dashes with quotation marks are employed systematically as a means of denoting paragraph breaks at the end of utterances. In the earliest stages of the *Dwarf* there are signs that intermediaries were slow to enter into this system. Two new paragraphs, indicated by dashes in the manuscript, will be found in the present edition at 11.25 ('The hint was sufficient . . . ') and 11.30 ('"News?" said the farmer . . . '). Less frequently, intermediaries made the opposite mistake of creating unnecessary paragraphs. An interesting case is found in the *Dwarf* at 13.8, where the first edition apparently interpreted a slight dash between 'muckle need' and 'Odd' as signalling a new speech paragraph, thus separating what is unmistakably one utterance by the principal farmer. Scott later tangled with the resulting ambiguity about speakers by adding in the Interleaved Set 'he continued after a moments reflection' after 'Odd, Bauldie says very true' at the beginning of the 'second' speech; while another dialogic pointer, 'said another farmer', was less ingeniously added in the 1823 18mo *Novels and Tales*. Reference to the manuscript, where 'did' is underlined in the immediately following words ('short sheep *did* make short rents'), places the issue beyond doubt, and the present edition is able to reproduce the original farmer's full speech intact for the first time in print.

Dashes within utterances also occasionally gave rise to mistakes. There can be little doubt that Scott expected their reinterpretation into a more complex punctuational pattern involving commas, colons and semicolons, exclamation and question marks. At the same time the first edition retains a good number of the manuscript's dashes, often in conjunction with other marks so as to create a more visible scale of pauses. As a whole, the story's speech patterns survive the process surprisingly well and in some cases are actively enhanced by what is undoubtedly the most fluid punctuation to be found in any edition of the *Dwarf* printed in Scott's lifetime. Nevertheless on approximately 50 occasions the present edition intervenes in an effort to re-establish the original force of the manuscript's dashes, either by restoration, substitution, or adjustment of adjacent marks and subsequent initial letters. Emendations generally fall into one of the following categories:

a] dashes reflecting the tone or mood of the speaker, such as extreme passion, breathlessness, or peremptory command; b] dashes necessary to larger patterns of speech, some of which when restored obviate the need for verbal additions made by the first edition; c] dashes indicating significant pauses or moments of intensity, especially near or at the end of utterances. Care has been taken to ensure that restored or adjusted dashes correspond with surrounding marks, and in some cases the manuscript punctuation has been adjusted in line with contemporary conventions of print. For example, at 76.7 the manuscript's dash is restored before Vere's sudden last sentence, but without removing the first edition's full stop—the resulting combination matching the stand-ard printed way of signifying an abrupt change of subject or focus in speech. In a few other cases especially long dashes used for strategic effect have been reinstated (see Hobbie's startled ejaculation at the end of Chapter 2), and quotation marks and dashes transposed where the manuscript correctly distinguishes uncompleted from interrupted speech (see the breaking-off of Hobbie's speech at 52.26). In addition to dashes, a handful of other marks used in the manuscript, notably exclamation and question marks, have been restored in preference to the pointing used by the first edition.

A large number of other non-verbal changes made by the first edition, such as the raising and lowering of initial letters, the addition and removal of hyphens, and the insertion of apostrophes, have been accepted as broadly consistent with the process of transference into print. The manuscript form is nevertheless restored where the first edition is palpably in error or has the effect of distorting rhetoric and/or meaning. In the case of initial letters, for example, the first edition's habit of raising 'heaven' to 'Heaven', for the sake of propriety, or 'dwarf' to 'Dwarf', as a kind of nomenclature, has been generally accepted. In a few single instances, however, the present edition reverts to initial lower case letters, notably where the first edition has wrongly granted titular status to Scott's words. At 24.11 the manuscript's 'sheelling hill' denotes a functional location rather than established place name, making the first edition's upper case 's' misleading. On rather more occasions—approximately 20—the present edition restores initial upper case letters, largely where intermediaries failed to observe the special significance accorded to a term in context. Restorations from the manuscript include: 'Act of Security' (15.7, 26), a specific act of legislation; 'Chamberlain' (23.31) and 'Country-Keeper' (90.6), as individual functionaries; 'Baudrons' (60.37), the name of a pet; and 'Clerk of this Parish' (87.13), a distinct literary allusion. Certain words given prominence by their speakers are also reintroduced in their manuscript form: Marischal is thus allowed propose his toast, in full vigour, to 'The *Independence* of Scotland, and the *Health* of our lawful *Sovereign*' (88.35–36, my italics). The present edition also recognises a composite nickname in 'Canny Elshie', the predominant form in the manuscript, though on its first appearance Scott failed to raise the initial 'c'.

The first edition's orthography has likewise been largely accepted, even though this involves carrying over a number of inconsistencies in the spelling of individual words. The temptation to regularise 'ay'/'aye' is especially strong, not least since it offers a means of distinguishing *ay* as yes from *aye* as 'always' or 'still'. But idiosyncrasies of this kind are legion in printed books of the period, and, in comparison with the instantaneous results allowed by today's technology, were immensely difficult to eradicate once established. (Though the affirmative 'aye' had been largely transferred to 'ay' by the third edition, a residual 'aye' remained at 36.39, and it was not until the 1821 duodecimo *Novels and Tales* that the opening 'Aye, aye' at 12.3 was altered.) The diversity of forms accepted by the present edition (evident in the dual entries in the Glossary) reflects the surface tenor of an early edition of Scott's fiction. In a few cases, however, the manuscript is used as an authority where the first edition form is erroneous or contextually inappropriate. On this basis 'cousin-german' (24.8–9) replaces 'cousin-germain' as more suitable in Hobbie's mouth; 'stouthrief' (68.30), the correct legal spelling, replaces 'stouthrife'; and 'confidante' (relating to a female subject) replaces 'confidant' at 79.4. A number of other changes affecting place names and the rendering of Scots words are discussed under separate headings below.

Verbal Emendations from the Manuscript. Owing to the absence of proofs it is not possible to trace in any detail the path of 1200 or so verbal changes (including transferences between English and Scots) which took place between the manuscript and first edition versions of *The Black Dwarf*. Nevertheless, there is no reason to believe that the process of textual development differed substantially from that which is ascertainable in the case of novels where proofs have survived; so that, in its first edition form, the text of the *Dwarf* includes a mixture of verbal alterations and mistakes introduced by intermediaries at various stages of the production process alongside interventions made by Scott in proofs. Two additional factors however are worth bearing in mind. The first is the unusually heavy commitment of James Ballantyne to the project: not just as negotiator of the contract of *Tales*, but as the main vehicle of communication with Blackwood and, in the absence of his brother, John, throughout August,[70] Scott's sole literary adviser. Late proofs of *Quentin Durward* (1823) and *Woodstock* (1826) have shown that Ballantyne was capable of making substantive changes after Scott had returned proofs; and it not improbable that, due to his eagerness to impress Blackwood, his input into the *Dwarf* was more considerable than usual. The second factor is the strong likelihood that in the rush to complete the volume, and perhaps as a result of Scott having lost interest in the story, the last sheets were at best cursorily checked by the author. As a rule, only those verbal variants found in the first edition judged to be authorial in origin, or the product of intermediaries working according to standing orders, have been retained in the present text. Conversely, where deterioration appears to have taken place either through slippage or intermediaries exceeding standing orders, the manuscript reading has normally been restored, with adjustments as necessary to match the conventions of print. In a few other instances, where Scott was evidently forced into making changes at proof through a failure in textual transmission, the manuscript reading has again been restored.

More than 500 verbal changes ranging from single-word substitutions to substantial areas of textual rearrangement have been made from the manuscript (a figure that swells to 600 when transferences between English and Scots are included). While every effort has been made to establish how the rejected first edition readings took place, in some cases it has been difficult to settle on a single cause. One substitution near the beginning of the *Dwarf* proper will give an idea of the range of possibilities available. At 12.24 the manuscript's 'beard' was changed at some stage to 'head', to produce 'never fash your head'. The first edition thus offers perhaps the best-known form of an established Scottish idiomatic phrase, though the *Scottish National Dictionary* provides an antecedent for the manuscript version, which itself was later to feature in both the manuscript and first edition of *St Ronan's Well* (1824).[71] Possible reasons for the change include: a] misreading by the transcriber (the manuscript's 'be' could be taken for 'h', especially by someone feeling their way into Scott's writing); b] slippage from a 'hard' to a 'soft' word, in this case to the more familiar version of a phrase; c] an officious attempt to 'correct' a phrase to its normal form; d] a more literal concern that the Border shepherd addressed is not bearded! Elsewhere it has been possible to focus more sharply on specific causes, with the result that the majority of emendations can be justified in terms of one of the following categories of error made by intermediaries.

1] *Misreadings*. At this point in his career Scott was already packing text tightly into his leaves, with the result that words are sometimes compressed at the end of lines and trailing letters occasionally obscure words immediately below. In the case of the *Dwarf* the difficulties could have been compounded by the employment of a new transcriber—John Ballantyne had almost certainly been involved in earlier titles—and this is perhaps reflected in a high proportion of mistakes made near the beginning of the manuscript. Other errors are more pervasive, with up to 20 emendations being explainable by a failure to distinguish visually similar words such as 'in'/'on', 'these'/'those', and 'when'/'where'. Another difficulty lay in distinguishing words ending with or without an 's', especially when a genuine ambiguity exists as to whether Scott has finished with a flourish or an additional letter. Up to 30 misreadings potentially fall into this group, including deviations between 'forward'/'forwards' and 'toward'/'towards'. In the parallel case of 'farther'/'further' it has proved impossible to distinguish Scott's intention with certainty, so that the first edition's blanket use of 'farther' in the main story is followed by the present text.

Between 20 and 30 individual words also appear to have been misread, sometimes with a more disruptive effect on the text. The Dwarf wishes to 'inflame' not 'influence' his imagined enemy (35.13); Westburnflat's jacket is of an antique 'cut' not 'cast' (42.40); the inhabitants of Hobbie's 'dale' not 'dell' gather in his support (51.11); a less snobbish Marischal insists on respect for 'truth' not 'birth' (83.8); Ratcliffe can 'discern' rather than 'discover' the Dwarf's cottage (107.6); Vere is preoccupied by his daughter's 'income' not her 'increase' (121.3). Additionally, failure by the transcriber might have triggered more elaborate changes. One example is 'carman' (104.41), where a combination of Scott's uncharacteristically open letters and unfamiliarity with the term could have led the transcriber to guessing at 'common', leading to later expansion into 'common people'.

2] *Misunderstandings.* Scott's knowledge outmatched that of his associates in several crucial areas, and this rather than simple misreading is the most likely root cause of a number of failures in transmission. While intermediaries were practised in handling familiar vernacular Scots, some older or more obscure words evidently caused difficulty. To the failure to recognise 'knapscap' at 53.20 can be added the simplification of 'daffing' to 'joking' (24.6), 'pow' to 'head' (27.9), 'haffits' to 'face' (48.34), and 'con' to 'gi'e' (72.30). Scott's response in the Interleaved Set to the persistent reintroduction of 'knapsack' makes it unlikely that he would have bowed lightly to the suggestion that more recognisable terms were needed for English readers. Some 'English' terms with nuances relating to the story's temporal setting were also missed. The Dwarf's sardonic reference to the 'wanton curiosity' of sporting fishermen (see 33.21) echoes Izaac Walton's *Compleat Angler* ('this pleasant curiositie of Fish and Fishing'), but by the first edition has slipped into the more predictable 'wanton cruelty'. Scott was also ahead of the intermediaries in certain technical areas, notably in Scots law, where Hobbie in the manuscript is unusually precise in matters relating to conveyancing. At 73.29 'subscrive', the correct Scots term, slipped to 'subscribe' in the first edition; and elsewhere 'band', not simply a colloquialisation but a form found in classic Scottish legal books, is reduced to the more familiar 'bond'. Hobbie's knowledge of horses also seems to have outstripped that of the intermediaries: failure to recognise the term *mallenders* (a disease affecting the knees of horses), leading to a garbled version at proof, is the most obvious explanation for a wholesale rewriting of Hobbie's scathing assessment of Westburnflat's equine assets at

68.39–41 ('He has nae . . . to boot'). While missing the splendid piece of improvisation which appeared in the first edition (see Emendation List for a text), readers of the present text will find ample compensation in the restored version of the original manuscript reading.

3] *Wrong insertions*. In view of Scott's tendency to miss out words accidentally in the manuscript, it is not surprising that intermediaries sometimes imagined lacunae and syntactical lapses where none existed. In the case of the *Dwarf*, they appear to have inserted single words unnecessarily on approximately 80 occasions. A failure to recognise idiomatic expressions in colloquial dialogue is apparent in the following instances, where the first edition insertions (omitted from the present edition) are marked by arrows: 'in the fashion it is ↑at↓ this day' (12.22); 'see ↑an'↓ get the yauds fed' (13.12); 'and muckle ↑harm↓ they got by it' (27.3); 'the gear a' driven ↑away↓' (50.29–30); 'a peaceable ↑and↓ honest man' (62.31). Superfluous syntactical support was also added to some of the Dwarf's more stylised rhetorical outbursts: 'For this I ↑have↓ preserved thee!' (34.21); 'and perhaps ↑afford↓ happier prospects to thine' (38.23); 'defacing, destroying, ↑and↓ degrading her fairest works' (110.35–36). A similar movement is evident in the mouths of aristocratic speakers, with a consequent loss of period flavour: 'a fever that might have cost ↑him↓ his life' (34.3); 'I ↑am↓ weary of the subject' (75.40); 'You should say *you*, ↑and↓ not *we* . . .' (93.12). The rhythm of Scott's own narrative is also occasionally disturbed by unnecessary interventions, some of which appear to misjudge the original usage: 'caballing ↑themselves↓ against' (15.22-23); 'indicative of ↑a↓ partial insanity' (29.13–14); '↑composed↓ entirely of hammered iron' (61.22); 'Marischal shrugged ↑up↓ his shoulders' (114.43–115.1).

Insertions of groups of words are more likely to be authorial, and only a handful of cases have been emended in the present edition. Three involve unnecessary additions to dialogue. The insertion of 'Aweel, that *is* kind, I must say' at the beginning of Hobbie's speech at 23.18 is found to be redundant once the two-sentence structure of Earnscliff's preceding speech is recognised; and the exchange in its less encumbered form gives a much better sense of the almost instinctual responses of the two speakers. Similarly, the addition of 'Will ye do this?' at the end of Westburnflat's speech at 63.17 was probably occasioned by the alteration of 'And' to 'Will' at the beginning of the paragraph (though a desire to end with an explicit question may also have played a part). Another redundant, if grammatically proper, change is the addition of 'by him' at the end the Dwarf's rhetorical question at 111.2.

4] *Wrong omissions*. Words omitted by the first edition are brought back on about 90 occasions—two thirds of the restorations involving single words only. A number of accidental factors undoubtedly played a part in the single word omissions, though in roughly half the cases a more deliberate kind of pruning is ascertainable. The policy of excising 'very', for example, appears to have been applied over zealously in 'the ⟨very⟩ week before my bridal' (51.4), where emphasis is at stake, and 'out o' his ⟨very⟩ heart's blood' (65.11–12), with its ballad sound. Other omissions point to an inability to distinguish special idioms and literary allusions. A biblical resonance is muffled by the removal of 'much' in Jedidiah's 'delighted ⟨much⟩ in the collection of olden tales' (8.6), and a contemporary fashionable phrase loses some of its freshness through the disappearance of the first word in '⟨all⟩ the delicacies of the season' (87.7).

Amongst larger omissions, the most common factor appears to have been error by the transcriber. At 13.38–40 a complete sentence after the quotation from Allan Ramsay's *The Gentle Shepherd* failed to make its way to the first edition, presumably through a mistaken interpretation of underlining (used to distinguish Jedidiah's interpolations) as deletion. A failure to bring in insertions is particularly noticeable in the closing stages, where the obscuring of a caret can be enough to ensure the loss of a significant verso addition. One example is the disappearance of the specific circumstances of Isabella's return to Ellieslaw Castle at 111.43–112.1 ('in less than half an hour . . . so much had'). Other verso casualties include a typical philosophical modulation by Ratcliffe ('in the eye of sound reason' at 106.36) and a delightful embellishment to the account of Westburnflat's declining years: 'spoke much of the Duke of Marlborough and very little of Charlie Cheat-the-Woodie' (123.40–41). At 106.31 a complete line in the manuscript was missed from Ratcliffe's speech ('which distinguish . . . sound mind'). In all, the present text reinstates 230 words from the manuscript, with significant improvements to the later stages of the story.

5] *Wrong substitutions or alterations.* Over 200 single words are also restored to the present edition on the basis that they were unnecessarily or wrongly altered in the first edition. Intermediaries a] made changes in the pursuit of grammatical correctness, with a tendency to match up parts of speech and co-ordinate tenses which is especially inapposite in spontaneous Scots dialogue. At 47.5, for example, it seems fitting that Hobbie should defend Killbuck on the grounds that 'he *acts* [rather than *acted*] but according to his nature after a'' (my italics). The intermediaries also b] intervened fussily on 'logical' grounds. Under this category can be counted the transference of Marischal's 'her cheek is whiter than her white dress' to 'her cheeks are . . .' (114.35–36), and the alteration of Vere's 'in which I unwillingly acquiesced' (119.15–16) to '. . . willingly acquiesced'—which misses the point about the speaker's hypocrisy. From time to time intermediaries c] failed to recognise idiomatic expressions. Unnecessary normalisation is found in the alteration of '*this* last spring' to '*the* last spring' at 33.37; 'hear me *to* Carlisle' to 'hear me *at* Carlisle' (39.41); '*with* the bridle' to '*by* the bridle' (50.21); and '*by* the ingle-side' to '*at* the ingle-side' (72.40). On other occasions the intermediaries d] replaced words in favour of more familiar or conventional alternatives. A lack of awareness of the correctness of Scott's usage apparently underlies the replacement of the manuscript's 'remove' by 'move' (28.35), 'accounted' by 'considered' (50.5), 'remark' by 'observe' (104.14), and 'suppressing' by 'stifling' (107.15). The hand of intermediaries is also perceptible in e] over-mechanical elimination of repetition. A prominent example is the adjustment of the manuscript's emphatic 'it is not in my nature & it is not worth my while' (compare 117.16−17), as spoken by Marischal, to the more petulant-sounding 'It is not in my nature, and it is hardly worth my while'. To the above can be added f] interventions which show scant regard for context. At 117.9 it is quite fitting that Ratcliffe should be described as having '*re*-entered' the room; and it is natural Vere should refer to 'them' rather than 'him' when describing an offer made by Ratcliffe on Sir Edward Mauley's behalf (see 120.43; 121.2).

Alterations involving more than single words have been rejected on nearly 50 further occasions. In resisting a number of stylistic 'improvements' the present text has inherited something of a 'rougher' feel from the manuscript. At 31.42 'the wanderer' replaces the more orotund 'an occasional passenger'; the Dwarf is seen to 'arrange it in his own way' rather than 'place it according to his wish' (28.39); and Isabella refers to 'an unfortunate like myself' instead of 'one so unfortunate as myself' (107.21−22). In a few other instances, the manuscript reading is given where Scott was presumably drawn into making revisions through errors in the transmission of the text. The longest sequence in this grouping occurs near the beginning of Chapter 8, where the transcriber appears to have inserted the passage 'Ay . . . ye speak' (one of two verso additions) at the wrong point in the recto text. In spite of an element of unevenness, the restored version gives a fuller sense of the confusion Hobbie witnesses on facing his assembled clansmen, while obviating the need for an additional 'senior' spokesman (see Emendation List entry at 54.11 for parallel texts).

6] *Wrong rearrangements.* In approximately 40 cases words rearranged by the first edition have been restored to their original manuscript order. Nearly half are local transpositions in direct speech. In Scottish mouths the first edition form (as marked in italics below) sometimes has the effect of introducing an alien dramatic element: as in 'I dinna believe there's ane *now living* that kens the lawful mode' (51.40), or 'sure *am I*, that ae ill-deviser' (compare 70.8). While transposition is one of the activities known to have been carried out by Scott in proofs, it should be noted that almost half the instances found in the *Dwarf* occur in the final four sheets of the first edition, where he was arguably least involved. The last two interventions seem to misjudge the degree to which the Dwarf adopts a more measured tone after his identification as Sir

Edward Mauley. On this basis the present edition prefers 'Do not speak to me!' to 'Speak not to me!' at 118.3, and 'I will be dead to you' rather than 'To you I will be dead' at the start of the following sentence.

Also included under this heading are some 15 instances where the first edition endeavours to colloquialise speech through contraction (most commonly by changing 'I am' to 'I'm'). At first this might seem part of a more general process of Scotification, but there is little evidence in the manuscript and in comparable proofs of Scott participating in or inviting such a process. Far from adding fluency, the effect in the following passages is rather to disrupt the deliberate manner of speaking characteristic of Hobbie and his fellow Borders: 'his saul maun be in a puir way, ⟨I am⟩ ↑I'm↓ jealous' (22.4); 'The ⟨night is⟩ ↑night's↓ very dark' (70.38); 'And now ⟨I am⟩ ↑I'm↓ ganging awa'' (73.33); 'and that ⟨it is⟩ ↑it's↓ a' his doing' (122.37). In a further 8 cases, all in direct narrative, the structure of Scott's original sentences is restored on the grounds that their rearrangement by the first edition has been conducted on narrow grammatical grounds. One noticeable feature is a tendency in the printed version to flatten out passages where the narrative voice is offering a kind of reported speech, echoing the responses of others.

7] *Misguided corrections.* Faced with the difficulties of the manuscript intermediaries sometimes made plausible-seeming emendations, which once established became virtually impossible to dislodge. At 44.36 the manuscript reads 'the ingratitude with which I have repaid', which the first edition renders as 'the ingratitude which I have repaid'. The change makes good grammatical sense, yet reads awkwardly in context, since the Dwarf here is describing what he has suffered rather than avenged. A better solution is found through the insertion of 'been' between 'have' and 'repaid', a change made in the present edition. At 124.27 Scott's failure to add the final letter in 'to precipitate dow[n]' apparently invited the ponderous insertion of 'its weight' as a replacement for the last word. James Ballantyne's presence is perhaps felt in at least one attempted correction of factual 'error'. In Jedidiah's Introduction (8.12) the manuscript accurately identifies 'Thomas Carey [Carew]' as author of the 'Elegie upon the Death of Dr Donne', though in the first edition this is incorrectly altered to Robert Carey, whose *Memoirs* Scott had edited in 1808—and who was almost certainly better known to Ballantyne than his poetical namesake. All printed editions until the present have followed this wrong emendation, with one recent editor ingeniously commenting that 'this is more likely to be Jedediah's slip than Scott's'.[72]

8] *Problems with names.* Notwithstanding the extra care often taken by Scott when first writing out proper names, intermediaries were still prone to make errors when handling unfamiliar items. In the following cases the manuscript spelling (given first) proves to be the correct form, and has been restored in the present edition: 'St Boswells'/'St Boswell's' (13.15); 'Forster'/'Foster' (48.32); 'Dundrennan'/'Drundennan' (52.8); 'Græme's-gap'/'Græmes'-gap' (54.40–55.1); 'Wideopen'/'Widopen' (57.10); 'Beelzebub'/'Belzebub' (71.41). Invented place names could also slip from their manuscript form: 'Carla Cleugh' thus replaced the etymologically more interesting 'Caillie Cleugh' at 17.33; and 'Tinning Beck' dislodged 'Finning-beck' at 48.32. A more complex problem is posed by the first edition's preference for 'Mareschal' (of 'Mareschal-Wells') rather than 'Marischal'. In more than 60 occurrences the manuscript fails to provide one unequivocal 'Mareschal', though clear examples with a dotted 'i' are found at 81.3 and 84.29, and in the closing stages Scott still appears to be writing Marischal rather than Mareschal. The printed form is explainable in terms of misreading by an intermediary; a routine adoption of the more standard 'English' form; or a more conscious decision to obscure a connection with the last Earl Marischal of Scotland, perhaps with present descendants in mind. Scott's persistence in using the Scottish form, with its rich historical associations, argues strongly in favour of its reinstatement in the present text.

More genuine difficulties were faced by intermediaries when Scott himself proved to be inconsistent in naming characters and places. Some discrepancies were cleared up effectively, as in the standardisation of *Earnscliff* (though in some sequences Scott uses *Earnscliffe*, and an early *Earnscleuch* (17.33) is also found). On two important occasions, however, a clear preference appears to have been overridden. The present edition adopts *Meikle-stane-Moor* as a standard spelling throughout, largely because: a] Scott writes this form with particular care on its first two occurrences (16.3, 14), and again on its first use (69.34) in the next large batch of manuscript; b] *Meikle* is the preponderant spelling, while *stane* remains separate either by a hyphen or space on all but two occasions; c] the manuscript indicates that Scott only started writing *Mucklestane* having realised from proofs that this had become the standard printed form. (A further mistake occurred at 32.22 and 36.20, where intermediaries failed to recognise the Dwarf's nickname as 'the Wise Wight of Meikle-stane', in each case adding an unnecessary 'Moor'.) Also adopted as standard is *Heugh-foot*, again the common form in the manuscript, though an unhyphenated *Heughfoot* dominates in the first edition. Not only is it probable that Scott was 'hearing' the more emphatic and descriptive *Heugh-foot* when writing, but the form (especially when preceded by the definite article) is well suited to the Liddesdale and ballad elements in the story.

9] *Transferences between English and Scots.* To the lost antique Scots terms already discussed can be added the first edition's dilution of a number of idiomatic expressions, which might not have been understood by intermediaries: 'mair be token', for example, becomes 'mair by token' at 18.4; and 'by others' slackens into the more commonplace 'before others' (27.2). A reduction of the original force of meaning is also noticeable in the anglicisation of 'is ganging' (49.1) to 'is to be sent' and 'eneuch in the country' (50.17–18) to 'in the country besides'. The present edition similarly restores from the manuscript nearly 60 single Scots words, which either slipped accidentally or were more deliberately turned into English by the first edition. Of course, the possibility of an intervention by Scott (perhaps nudged by intermediaries) has to be kept in mind. For example, 'kintra' might have been felt too arcane for a general audience: yet its replacement by 'country' on its first two occurrences (17.43; 18.3) involves a loss of some of the pliability of the original; and the introduction of 'country folk' as a substitute at 18.37 is clumsily executed and unlikely to be Scott's unprompted work. Equally, the substitution of 'then' for 'than' could reflect a concern that readers might fail to recognise the Scots form. The transference, nevertheless, has the effect of flattening some of the more intense moments in the story, as when the Borderers look to the old ways in their eagerness to avenge Hobbie's loss: 'Let us follow him ⟨than⟩ ↑then↓ . . . and ⟨than⟩ ↑then↓ have at the Cumberland reivers—Take, burn, and slay' (51.26–28). (Once established in print, it would have been very difficult for Scott to spot these changes.) More generally, a restoration of the manuscript's original terms allows a fuller sense of how the density of Scots employed can vary according to mood and context. Hobbie's grandmother, for instance, ranges from almost pure liturgical 'English' to the darker, more brooding Scots which expresses her apprehension of a return by the Brown Man of the Moors: 'My father ⟨aften⟩ ↑often↓ tauld me he was seen in the year o' the ⟨bluidy⟩ ↑bloody↓ fight at Marston-Moor, and ⟨than⟩ ↑then↓ again in Montrose's troubles' (26.24–26).

Changes within Scots have usually been accepted as having no significant effect on pronunciation or meaning. An exception, however, is made on phonetic grounds in the case of the first edition's 'burnt', with the restoration of the manuscript's 'burnd' (as 'burned') in two instances (51.21, 70.12) where appearing in Scots speech. Similarly, in two single cases Scott's original spelling has been reinstated: 'clamjamfarie' replaces 'clanjamfrie' at 61.9, and at 72.22 'jookery-packery' is preferred to 'jookery-paukery'.[73] More substantive changes have been made in the case of Scott's usage of the negatives no, nae, and no, which is not always followed by the first edition, sometimes with a distortion of meaning and/or speech rhythms.

A large majority of words Scotified by the first edition have also been accepted, except in a few instances where intermediaries appear to have exceeded their brief or acted insensitively. As John Galt, the contemporary Scottish novelist, observed in the 'Postscript' to Ringan Gilhaize (1823): 'very good Scotch might be couched in the purest English terms, and without the employment of a single Scottish word'.[74] In this respect, an element of gilding the lily might be perceived in the following (rejected) alterations made by the first edition: 'the best goer ⟨in⟩ ↑about↓ the toun' (23.29); 'naething ⟨in⟩ ↑a'↓ the live-lang day' (26.6); 'If they had ony quarrel ⟨at⟩ ↑wi'↓ us' (68.21); 'seek for relief ⟨to⟩ ↑frae↓ them that deal wi' the Evil One!' (69.42). The present text also restores 'spake' for 'spak' and 'came' for 'cam', primarily on the grounds that neither 'Scots' form is in evidence at any point in the manuscript.

Later Editions. If Scott or the intermediaries subsequently felt that aspects of the first edition had been impaired by the rush to meet Blackwood's deadlines, then the early subsequent editions would have offered an open invitation to set matters right. Indeed, in the case of the *Dwarf* there are reasons for considering the initial creative process of preparing the printed text to have continued in several areas as far as the fourth edition. Nearly 80 emendations stemming from later editions have been introduced into the present text, all but 6 from the second, third, and fourth editions. These can be divided into three categories.

1] *Scotification.* Just as 90 per cent of the Scots dialogue found in the *Dwarf* is concentrated in the first ten chapters, so it is entirely within these pages that the second, third, and fourth editions made more than 60 changes from English to Scots. This compares with some 35 such alterations found in Volume 2 of *Tales of my Landlord*, 30 in Volume 3, and 25 in Volume 4. The difference cannot be fully explained in terms of a lower density of Scots in *The Tale of Old Mortality*; on the contrary, there are strong reasons for believing that the level of activity in the first volume is unusual, and possibly stems from a general directive to concentrate on this factor. In some respects, the continuing Scotification in the early editions of the *Dwarf* might be said to complete a process which had begun with the earliest preparation of Scott's manuscript for publication.

Nevertheless there are clear dangers in accepting Scots for its own sake. Emendations have generally only been made when transferences fall into at least one of the following areas: a] where activity of this kind has already taken place between manuscript and the first edition (at 12.17, for example, previous alterations of 'told' to 'tell'd' and 'master' to 'maister' lead naturally to the second edition's 'tell'd *ye*, maister' (my italics)); b] where the transition between English and Scots is matched by equivalent transferences in the manuscript or between the manuscript and first edition (only five words introduced from later editions fail to meet this criterion); c] where a change shows an element of sensitivity to the regional setting of the story (e.g. the second edition's 'yowes' (12.1), though foreign to the manuscript, has a good Border provenance);[75] and d] where a more than routine engagement with the text is evident. Prominent in the last category is the fourth edition's triple substitution of 'frighted' for 'frightened' (26.4, 8, 11), which enhances the air of (comic) expostulation in the interlude, while echoing Hobbie's earlier scathing dismissal of Willie of Winton as 'soon frighted for himself' (at 20.10–11, where 'frighted' stems from the manuscript).

Conversely, transferences falling into any one of the following areas have normally been rejected: a] where Scotification seems arbitrary, as in the case of a single word in a context where no previous activity has taken place; b] where there is no precedent for a change (i.e. where a word is not found at any point in the manuscript and/or is not matched by equivalent changes between the manuscript and first edition); c] where a transference is rhetorically inappropriate (at 26.12 the emphatic 'you' in Hobbie's 'you saw it as weel as I did' is preserved in preference to the second edition's 'ye'); or d] where a transference runs counter to pronunciation in the Border region. On this basis a handful of changes from 'make' to 'mak' and 'take' to 'tak' by the second and third editions have been rejected. No instances of these Scots forms are found in the first edition, and the manuscript offers only one possible 'mak' at 19.34. In *The Tale of Old Mortality*, on the other hand, 'mak' and 'tak' are evident in both manuscript and first edition. Scott's spelling in the *Dwarf* is also closer to the pronunciation of both words in the Southern counties of Scotland (as 'meake' and 'teake').

As a whole, the present edition has accepted 41 transferences to Scots made by later editions: 18 (out of 31) from the second edition, 16 (23) from the third, and 7 (11) from the fourth.

2] *Repetition.* The present edition accepts nine alterations made by the second edition to avoid repetition, and six more similarly introduced by the third. All but one (the second edition's omission of 'steep' from 'broad steep loaning' at 24.32) involve the substitution of single words. Several can be traced back to problems in the original preparation of the text. At 77.14 the first edition's 'he continued, as if noticing him for the first time', evidently added in proof, clashes awkwardly with 'continued Mr Vere' almost immediately above—a problem usefully dealt with by the second's introduction of 'proceeded' as an alternative. Two changes made by the third edition deal with repetitions at the end of Chapter 9, where the manuscript indicates Scott was coming to the end of a long phase of writing. One hardly thinks he would have quarrelled with the substitution of 'conducted' for 'conveyed' (65.20) and 'adopted' for 'taken' (65.26), even if a secondary effect is to add a slightly more 'elevated' air to the narrative. Noticeably the fourth edition makes no new interventions on the grounds of repetition.

3] *Correction of error.* The remaining 20 emendations from later editions divide equally into two groups. The first involve corrections of details of presentation, where obvious mistakes had been made by previous intermediaries: these range from the insertion of supplementary speech marks to the Magnum's addition of accents to Marischal's snatches of French. The remainder are concerned with tidying up epigraphs and mottoes. An interesting example is provided by the motto to the present Chapter 14, where in the first edition 'change' erroneously reads 'charge' and James Thomson's play is wrongly titled *Tancred and Sigismund*. Even here it took two stages for the corrections to be made: the second edition correcting *Sigismund* to *Sigismunda*, and the third clearing up the text. Both are changes Scott would have wished for, and in each instance an earlier edition anticipates an emendation which otherwise would have been made editorially on the grounds of egregious error. Some such errors remained undisturbed throughout Scott's lifetime: the passage at the head of Chapter 13 was wrongly attributed to the *second* part of Shakespeare's *Henry IV*—a mistake which remained until the present edition.

Preliminaries. The preliminaries to *Tales of my Landlord*, consisting of title-page, epigraph and Dedication, are the first to confront a reader of *The Black Dwarf*; but in the case of the first edition these were almost certainly among the last parts of the *Tales* to be printed. Writing to James Ballantyne on 27 October 1816 Scott urged pushing on this routine work during a delay in preparing *The Tale of Old Mortality*: 'I intreat title pages and all the dragwork may be got forward'. But Blackwood's letter to Murray on 20 November indicates that it was not undertaken until the final stages of printing: 'Ballantyne has been with me & informs me that the last sheet and titles of the Tales will go to press tomorrow'.[76] One reason for setting the title-pages together would have been to save paper, by printing them all on the same last sheet. This time gap best explains a number of discrepancies between the wording on the title-pages of the first edition of *Tales* and the heading relayed to Murray by Blackwood on 22/23 August 1816: 'The title is "Tales of My Landlord;" collected and reported by Jedidiah Cleis[h]botham, Parish-Clerk and Schoolmaster of Gandercleugh'. Blackwood's 'title' is virtually identical to the heading printed immediately above Jedidiah's Introduction in the first edition. Yet it differs in three respects from the title-page, where: a] 'collected and reported' appears as 'collected and arranged'; b] Jedidiah is spelt as Jedediah; c] 'Parish-Clerk and Schoolmaster' is transposed to 'Schoolmaster and Parish-Clerk'. The version seen by Blackwood is also found at the head of Jedidiah's Introduction in the manuscript, though in a thicker stroke which suggests it might have been added at a later stage.

While in all probability the 'title' transcribed by Blackwood was also seen by the author in second proofs, it is unlikely Scott composed or even vetted the final wording rushed through the press late in November. In fact, all three variants can be attributed to intermediaries.[77] The replacement of 'reported'—a suitably Latinate word for Jedidiah, accurately conveying his assumed position with regard to Peter Pattieson's narratives—probably took place between 21 and 27 November, when newspaper advertisements switched from the old to new formula.[78] Why the change occurred is uncertain, but it quite possibly originated in a slip made by compositors, or a conscious decision to promote the work with a more explicit wording. Reference to the Introduction however suggests that 'arranged' is inapposite as a term, as well as unlikely to be authorial, since it is Pattieson who is represented there as 'arranging' his materials for the press (see 8.40–41). Similar factors could underlie the transposition of 'Parish-Clerk and Schoolmaster' to a more 'normal' order, reflecting Jedidiah's main occupation, though the preamble itself indicates that Jedidiah would have placed his ecclesiatical function first.

The spelling of Jedi/ediah is a more complex issue, though the weight of evidence again suggests that the form reproduced by Blackwood in August matches Scott's true preference. Jedidiah is the correct spelling of the biblical name, given by David to Solomon. In the manuscript, Scott clearly wrote Jedidiah in his opening Dedication, before adding Cleishbotham at a later point. Apart from the title-page and Dedication, Jedidiah is the form used throughout the first edition of *Tales of my Landlord* until the 'Peroration' in the last sheet of Volume 4, which is signed 'Jedediah Cleishbotham' (though the manuscript here reads Jedidiah). Scott also continued to write Jedidiah in the manuscript of his review of *Tales* for the *Quarterly Review*; and the form is evident again in the manuscript of the second series of *Tales* (*The Heart of Mid-Lothian*), both in the heading and concluding 'L'Envoy'. Writing to James Ballantyne on 16 April 1817, Scott likewise persisted in referring to negotiations for 'the new Jedidiah'.[79] On the other hand, there is reason to believe that Ballantyne preferred the form Jedediah (his letter to Blackwood on 1 September, dictated to his mother, refers clearly to 'Our friend Jedediah');[80] and it was most probably Ballantyne who constructed the advertisement that went into the *Edinburgh Evening Courant* on 31 August 1816, whereby the *Tales* were first made public.

In introducing his first work of fiction in 1814, Scott had implicitly announced a turning-point both for the author and the novel as a form: 'I have . . . , like a maiden knight with his white shield, assumed for my hero, WAVERLEY, an uncontaminated name'. The title-page of the present edition, which incorporates all three elements lost in the original preparation of *Tales of my Landlord*, allows a sharper first glimpse of the bearings worn by his next major literary persona than has previously been possible.

All manuscripts referred to are in the National Library of Scotland (NLS) unless otherwise stated.

1   Samuel Smiles, *A Publisher and His Friends. Memoir and Correspondence of the late John Murray*, 2 vols (London, 1891), 1.458.

2   MS 4001, f. 216r.

3   Murray Archives (Blackwood to Murray, 20 April 1816).

4   *The Letters of Sir Walter Scott*, ed. H. J. C. Grierson and others, 12 vols (London, 1932–37), 1.497–98.

5   MS 4001, f. 219v.

6   Murray Archives (Blackwood to Murray, 1 May 1816).

7   Smiles, 1.458; Murray Archives (Blackwood to Murray, 15 April 1816).

8   Murray Archives (James Ballantyne to Murray, 1 May 1816).

9   Smiles, 1.461.

10 Smiles, 1.464 (with corrections and additions from the original letter to John Murray in Murray Archives).

11 Mrs Oliphant, *William Blackwood and His Sons*, 2 vols (London, 1897), 1.62–63. (A copy of Blackwood's letter to James Ballantyne of 24 June 1816 is in NLS Acc. 1424 A, Box 1.)

12 Oliphant, 1.63.

13 Oliphant, 1.64, 66.

14 MS 4001, f. 235r.

15 MS 4001, f. 236r.

16 MS 4001, f. 237r.

17 Oliphant, 1.66.

18 MS 4001, f. 262r (headed 'Thursday ½ past 6'). Compare Ballantyne's letter earlier on 22 August in Oliphant, 1.67–68.

19 Quotations are from the original letter in Murray Archives (headed 'Thursday Night 12 Oclock': postmark Aug 23 1816). Printed extracts are given in Oliphant, 1.68 and Smiles, 1.466.

20 *Letters*, 1.497.

21 MS 3277, pp. 22–23.

22 J. G. Lockhart, *Memoirs of the Life of Sir Walter Scott, Bart.*, 7 vols (Edinburgh, 1837–38), 4.37.

23 MS 3887, ff. 43–44v. In an earlier letter of 12 February 1816, Train had informed Scott of his plans for a 'Brief Sketch of the Rise and Extent of Illicit Distillation in Scotland' (MS 3887, ff. 9–10): this is perhaps echoed in the references to illicit distilling in Jedidiah's Introduction.

24 MS 8993, ff. 96–98.

25 *Letters*, 4.216, 219.

26 *Letters*, 4.210–11.

27 MS 8993, ff. 99, 101. For an account of Scott's excursions with Shortreed and the ballads found in Liddesdale, see Michael J. H. Robson, *The Ballads of Liddesdale* (Newcastleton, 1986), passim.

28 *Quarterly Review*, 16 (January 1817), 443.

29 *Waverley Novels* (hereafter 'Magnum'), 48 vols (Edinburgh, 1829–33), 9.xxvii; *Letters*, 1.58.

30 *Chambers' Edinburgh Journal*, no. 65 (Saturday, 27 April 1833), 99.

31 *Letters*, 4.196.

32 *Letters*, 11.487.

33   *Edinburgh Magazine*, 1 (October 1817), 210, 209.

34   MS 3912, f. 109r. Scott had attributed the article to Robert Chambers in Magnum, 9.xx.

35   MS 3888, ff. 150–51.

36   *Edinburgh Magazine*, 1.211–12, 212n. The passage quoted in the article bears little relation to *An Elegy on David Ritchie, Peebles-shire* (Edinburgh, 1812), written in a naif style; the next full publication on Ritchie is William Chambers's *The Life and Anecdotes of the Black Dwarf, or David Ritchie* (Edinburgh, 1820).

37   *Letters*, 4.293.

38   Murray Archives (Blackwood to Murray, 28 August 1816); MS 4001, f. 244r (James Ballantyne to Blackwood, 26 August 1816).

39   MS 4001, ff. 246r, 248r.

40   *Letters*, 4.276.

41   Murray Archives (Blackwood to Murray, 13, 20 November 1816).

42   Oliphant, 1.76.

43   MS 4001, ff. 254–5v.

44   NLS Acc 1424 A, Box 1 (Blackwood's clerk to Murray, 25 November 1816, with an additional note by James Ballantyne); MS 4001, f. 277r (Murray's clerk to Blackwood, 29 November 1816).

45   The manuscript consists of 110 quarto-type leaves, measuring approximately 27 cm high and 21 cm wide at maximum (down to 26 and 20.5 cm respectively in their smallest form). Two watermarks are found throughout: a] a crown and horn device and b] the countermark 'J WHATMAN 1811'. In these respects, the paper bears a close resemblance to Item 2755 in Edward Heawood's *Watermarks, Mainly of the 17th and 18th Centuries* (Hilversum, Holland, 1950). The chain lines are approximately 2.65 cm apart. It is reasonable to assume that the paper used originally formed part of larger demy sheets, incorporating both devices.

46   MS 4001, f. 262r.

47   *Tales of my Landlord*, press mark res PR.5316.T2.

48   MS 4001, f. 240r; 'imposed' is misread as 'composed' in Oliphant, 1.67.

49   See *Letters*, 1.508.

50   Murray Archives (Blackwood to Murray, 13 November, 20 December 1816); MS 4002, ff. 25–26 (James Ballantyne to Blackwood, 1 January 1816 [1817]).

51   Murray Archives (Blackwood to Murray, 10 February 1817); MS 4002, f. 23r (James Ballantyne to Blackwood, 12 February 1817).

52   See Oliphant, 1.81.

53   Oliphant, 1.79–80.

54   Murray Archives (Blackwood to Murray, 10 February, 29 March 1817). Ballantyne was asked to delay, and only after pressure from Scott was the edition accepted (see Oliphant, 1.81–82). Ballantyne's statement was sent on 21 April 1817 (MS 4002, f. 33r). Murray and Blackwood's haggling was a major factor in Scott's decision to hand the second series of *Tales* to Constable (see *Letters*, 4.431, 507).

55   Oliphant, 1.81.

56   MS 21001, f. 257r.

57   For an account of negotiations between Scott, Cadell, and the Ballantynes

see MS 790, pp. 486–88 (Cadell to James Ballantyne, 11 May 1819).
Compare MS 790, pp. 299–300 (Cadell to John and James Ballantyne, 23 November 1818).

58   Trinity College Library, Cambridge, press mark H.23.12–15. Another copy, with similar press figures, is held by the University of South Carolina.

59   As quoted in MS 790, p. 487.

60   *Letters*, 5.367. The size of the impression is given as 1500 in MS 319, ff. 300r, 302r; but 2000 is cited in a later memorandum dated 26 February 1822 (MS 23232, f. 60r).

61   MS 790, pp. 649, 692.

62   The disdain of J. O. Robinson (Constable's new associate in London) for these old '*Tea paper* books' was a direct factor in the planning of the new composite set with its vignette title-pages (see MS 323, f. 100v).

63   MS 23232, f. 60r; MS 323, f. 194r.

64   1000 copies were accepted by Hurst, Robinson & Co. on 29 March 1825 (MS 323, f. 524r).

65   MS 326, f. 42r; MS 323, ff. 238r, 245v; MS 792, p. 138; MS 320, f. 160.

66   *Letters*, 7.170, 245.

67   *Letters*, 11.36, 74.

68   MS 21018, f. 54v; MS 21019, f. 11r.

69   MS 21019, f. 13v, 15r, 23r.

70   John Ballantyne's departure from Edinburgh, for London and then the Continent, is noted in a letter of Scott's on 18 June 1816 (*Letters*, 4.258); for his return in mid-September, see *Letters*, 1.500n).

71   The manuscript reading in *St Ronan's Well* ('Never fash your beard about that Mr Winterblossom' (f. 66r)) is reproduced at 1.290.18–19 in the first edition. The example given by the *Scottish National Dictionary* is from Allan Ramsay, *The Gentle Shepherd* (1725), 3.2.132 ('Howe'er I get them, never Fash your Beard').

72   Angus Calder, in his Penguin edition of *Old Mortality* (Harmondsworth, 1975), 524.

73   Compare 'joockery-packery' and 'clamjamfry', the forms given in George Watson, *The Roxburghshire Word-Book* (Cambridge, 1923), 9, 86.

74   John Galt, *Ringan Gilhaize*, ed. Patricia J. Wilson (Edinburgh, 1984), 323.

75   The appearance of *yowis* ('ewes') and *gaitt* ('goat') in Records of the Jedburgh Circuit belonging to the seventeenth century is noted by James A. H. Murray, *The Dialect of the Southern Counties of Scotland* (London, 1873), 161.

76   *Letters*, 1.508; Murray Archives (Blackwood to Murray, 20 November 1816).

77   For the practice of leaving the layout of title-pages to compositors, see Philip Gaskell, *A New Introduction to Bibliography* (Oxford, 1974), 52.

78   The *Edinburgh Evening Courant* resumed advertising *Tales of my Landlord* on 21 November 1816 with 'collected and reported', but this changed to 'collected and arranged' on 28 November. An advertisement in the *Edinburgh Weekly Journal* on 27 November reads 'arranged' rather than 'collected'.

79   MS 2525, f. 72r.

80   MS 4001, f. 246r.

EMENDATION LIST

The base-text for this edition of *The Black Dwarf* is a specific copy of Volume one of the first edition of *Tales of my Landlord* (1816), owned by the Edinburgh Edition of the Waverley Novels. All emendations to this base-text, whether verbal, orthographical, or punctuational, are listed below, with the exception of certain general categories of emendation described in the next paragraph, and of those errors which result from accidents of printing such as a letter dropping out, provided always that the evidence for the 'correct' reading has been found in at least one other copy of the first edition.

The following proper names have been standardised throughout on the authority of Scott's preferred usage as deduced from the manuscript: Heugh-foot, Marischal, and Meikle-stane-Moor (see 'Essay on the Text', 169). The typographic presentation of mottoes, chapter headings, letters, inset quotations, and the opening words of chapters has been standardised. Chapter numbers have also been altered as necessary to run consecutively. Ambiguous end-of-line hyphens in the base-text have been interpreted in accordance with the following authorities (in descending order of priority): predominant first edition usage; second, third and fourth editions (which usually follow first-edition lineation); octavo *Novels and Tales* (1819); Magnum; MS.

Each entry in the list below is keyed to the text by page and line number; the reference is followed by the new, EEWN reading, then in brackets the reason for the emendation, and, after the slash, the base-text reading that has been replaced.

A large majority of emendations are derived from the manuscript. Most merely involve the replacement of one reading by another, and these are listed with the simple explanation '(MS)'. Where the manuscript reading adopted by the EEWN has required editorial intervention to normalise spelling or punctuation, the exact manuscript reading is given in the form: '(MS actual reading)'. Where the new reading has required editorial interpretation of the manuscript, the explanation is given in the form '(MS derived: actual reading)'. Occasionally, some explanation of the editorial thinking behind an emendation is required, and this is provided in a brief note.

The following conventions are used in transcriptions from Scott's manuscript: deletions are enclosed ⟨thus⟩ and insertions ↑thus↓; an insertion within an insertion is indicated by double arrows ↑↑thus↓↓; superscript letters are lowered without comment. A question mark as in 'MS?' denotes an element of doubt about a reading, whereas '⟨?⟩' used within transcriptions normally indicates a deleted word which is indecipherable.

Readings from early subsequent editions are indicated by '(Ed2)', etc.; the 1819 and 1822 octavo *Novels and Tales* appear as '8vo 1819' and '8vo 1822'; while the Magnum Opus edition appears as 'Magnum'. Emendations which have not been anticipated by a contemporaneous edition are indicated by '(Editorial)'.

title-page	Reported (Editorial) / Arranged
	This and the following two emendations are discussed in 'Essay on the Text', 173–74.
title-page	Jedidiah / Jedediah
title-page	Parish-Clerk and Schoolmaster / Schoolmaster and Parish-Clerk
epigraph	Parte (Ed4) / Part
Dedication	Jedidiah (MS) / Jedediah
5.21	*dicere* (Magnum) / *diceri*
	In the manuscript the last letter has been altered, apparently at a later stage, though whether from 'e' to 'i' or vice versa is unclear.
5.23	toward (MS) / towards
5.23	metropolis of commerce and (MS Metropolis of commerce and) / metropolis and
6.8	twice, the (MS) / twice, and the
6.14	Again—and thirdly—If (MS) / Again—and, thirdly, If
6.18	those (MS) / these
6.22	vipers ((MS) / critics
6.28	in spurning (MS) / by spurning
6.33	compelleth (MS) / compelled
6.39	fowls black and grey, partridges (MS fowls black & grey partridges) / fowls, black and grey partridges
6.40	birds and (MS) / birds, and
6.41	hath (MS) / have
7.4	for those which resembled (MS derived: for which resembled) / for what resembled
7.18	Landlord's (MS landlords) / Landlord
7.38	pleasant (MS) / pleased
8.6	delighted much in (MS) / delighted in
8.12	Thomas (MS) / Robert
8.12	vaticination (MS) / Vaticination
8.13	death (MS) / Death
8.13	celestial (MS) / Celestial
8.20	notwithstanding symptoms (MS) / notwithstanding these symptoms
8.32	if it is at (MS derived: if it at) / if at
8.37	through which (MS thro which) / the which
8.41	legends (MS) / Tales
8.42	narration (MS) / narrative
8.43	plot (MS) / plots
9.2	manuscripts (MS) / manuscript
9.9	produce. And (MS) / produce; and
11.15	over (MS) / on
11.24	lambs!" [new paragraph] The (MS lambs"—The) / lambs!" The
11.26	rein (MS)/ reins
11.29	from the south hie-lands? [new paragraph] "News?" (MS derived: ↑from the south hie-lands↓—"News") / ... hie-lands?—"News?"
12.1	yowes (Ed2) / ewes
12.5	Dwarf!" (Ed2) / Dwarf?"
	No mark is provided by the MS, but Ed2 is closer to the implied rhetoric of the passage at this point.

12.7   Canny (8vo 1819) / canny
12.8   tell (MS) / tells
12.15   came (MS) / cam
12.17   ye (Ed2) / you
12.18   doun (MS? and Ed3) / down
          The MS is ambiguous here, but very possibly reads 'doun'.
12.20   doun (MS? and Ed2) / down
12.22   is this (MS) / is at this
12.24   beard (MS) / head
12.32   wark (Ed2) / work
12.39   * Note by the publisher.—We (MS derived: * Note by the publisher
          [new line] We) / * We
12.42   appear (MS) / seem
12.42   when (MS) / where
13.3   horse (MS) / hoarse
13.4   on that of (MS) / on the part of
13.8   need. Odd (MS derived: need—Odd) / need." [new paragraph] "Odd
          This emendation is discussed in 'Essay on the Text', 160.
13.9   *did* (MS) / did
13.10   punds (MS) / pounds
13.10   hunder (Ed3) / hundred
13.11   haenna (MS) / hae nae
13.12   see get (MS) / see an' get
13.13   doun (Ed3) / down
13.15   sax (Ed2) / six
13.15   St Boswells (MS St. Boswells) / St Boswell's
13.18   patron (MS and Ed2) / *patron*
          The MS's underlining ends immediately before 'patron', though
          brackets apparently used at a previous stage to denote Jedidiah's inter-
          polations enclose this word; Ed2 correctly places it in roman.
13.19   will back here again to (MS will back here ↑again↓ to) / will be back
          here to
13.22   gie ye a (MS gie ↑ye↓ a) / gie a
13.28   *known only to* (MS) / *known to*
13.36   enough (MS) / eneugh
13.37   keep. [new line] *It . . . merit.* [new paragraph] In (MS keep. [new line] *It
          hath indeed been observed of my learnd & worthy patron that he can never
          recite these verses especially in the evening without evincing in some such way
          ↑his↓ ⟨the⟩ overpowering sense of their merit.* [new paragraph] In) /
          keep. [new paragraph] In
          This emendation is discussed in 'Essay on the Text', 166.
13.41   was not (MS) / had not been
14.22   those (MS) / these
14.25   Still (MS) / But
14.25   many of the youth (MS) / many youth
14.40   *raids* and *forays* (MS) / raids and forays
15.2   these (MS) / those
15.7   Act of Security (MS) / act of security
15.21   present (MS) / presented
15.22   caballing against (MS) / caballing themselves against
15.23   same (MS) / English
15.24   universal (Ed2) / general
15.26   Act of Security (MS) / act of security
15.42   effort (MS) / efforts
16.43   fause thief—lang (MS) / false thief, lang

17.3   and of geese (MS) / and geese
17.22   speedily (MS) / quickly
17.29   dispositions. [new paragraph] "Wow! (MS derived: ↑... disposi-
        tions.↓—"Wow!) / dispositions.—"Now,
        Perhaps the paragraph break, signalled by dash and speech marks, was
        overlooked owing to the preceding verso insertion.
17.33   Caillie (MS) / Carla
17.43   kintra (MS) / country
18.3   kintra (MS) / country
18.4   be (MS) / by
18.6   ye (Ed2) / you
18.15   should. (MS) / should?
18.21   nae (MS) / na
18.22   gude-dame's (Ed2) / gude dame's
18.22   clavers aye about (MS) / clavers about
18.27   But (MS) / but
18.28   ye lairds (MS) / you lairds
18.37   kintra (MS) / country folk
19.1   na (MS) / nae
19.15   doings o' (Ed2) / doings of
19.29   o' (Ed3) / of
19.36   nae (MS) / na
19.42   lang-nebbit (MS? and Ed2) / lang-nebbed
20.1   I am, though I say it mysel, (MS I am though I say it mysell) / Though I
        sae it mysel, I am
20.8   than (MS) / then
20.8   puir (Ed3) / poor
20.10   puir (Ed3) / poor
20.17   mair——But (MS derived: mair——but) / mair—but
20.18   be?"—— (MS) / be!"
20.39   Ailie hersel (MS Ailie hersell) / Ailie, hersel
21.4   "Distracted yoursel (MS "Distracted yoursell) / "You're distracted
        yoursel
21.4   sae (MS) / so
21.10   (...) (Editorial) / [...]
        The parenthesised passage is a verso addition in the MS, where no
        punctuational guidance is supplied; but round brackets are used for
        similar narrative asides in both MS and Ed1.
21.17   appeared (Ed3) / seemed
21.26   you do here (MS) / you here
21.41   a thought bigger (MS) / na that awfu' big
22.4   I am (MS) / I'm
22.17   in it (MS) / in't
22.20   meditated laying (MS) / meditating to lay
22.22   garment (MS) / garments
22.31   often (MS) / after
23.9   God, Earnscliff, I'se (MS God Earnscliff Ise) / God, I'se
23.11   mile (Ed2) / miles
23.11   mile. Hadna (MS miles. Had na) / miles,—hadna
        For the emendation to 'mile', see previous entry.
23.12   powney (MS) / poney
23.15   And I (MS) / And as I
23.16   absence. I'll (MS derived: absence I'll) / absence, I'll
        No stop is apparent in the MS, but spacing and syntax indicate a sen-
        tence break.

23.18 propose." [new paragraph] "And (MS propose"—"And) / propose."
       [new paragraph] "Aweel, that *is* kind, I must say. And
       This emendation is discussed in 'Essay on the Text', 165.
23.18 Heugh-foot. (MS Heughfoot.) / Heugh-foot?
23.25 whiddin' (Ed2) / whidding
23.25 forrit (Ed2) / forward
23.29 action—is (MS) / action, and is
23.29 in the toun—now (MS) / about the toun, now
23.31 Chamberlain (MS) / chamberlain
23.35 grace (Editorial) (MS Grace) / Grace
       While a pun on Grace Armstrong's name is no doubt intended, the
       reference here appears to be primarily to the quality of grace.
23.36 Earnscliff, that (MS Earnscliff that) / Earnscliff, you that
23.40 spake (MS) / spak
24.6   Hout awa (MS) / Hout, awa
24.6   daffing (MS) / joking
24.8   cousin-german (MS cousin german) / cousin-germain
24.11 we are (MS) / we're
24.11 sheeling-hill (MS sheelling hill) / Sheeling-hill
24.14 a number (MS) / the number
24.19 puir (Ed3) / poor
24.19 tykes (MS) / beasts
24.26 things come (MS) / things may come
24.31 willing to leave his meaning in (MS) / willing his meaning should be in
24.32 broad loaning (Ed2) / broad steep loaning
24.43 for brother Hobbie. [new paragraph] Hobbie (MS derived: for brother
       Hobbie. Hobbie) / for their brother. Hobbie
       The creation of a new paragraph (though not openly signalled by the
       MS) copes more effectively with the problem of repetition than Ed1's
       emendation. Scott gave instructions for a new paragraph here in the
       Interleaved Set.
25.14 farm house-wife, as (MS) / farmer's-wife, while
25.20 grandame (MS Grandame) / grand-dame
26.1   has nae (MS) / hasna
26.4   frighted (Ed4) / frightened
26.6   naething in (MS) / naething a'
26.8   Frighted (Ed4) / Frightened
26.11 frighted (Ed4) / frightened
26.13 did." (MS derived: did"—) / did?"
26.23 luve (MS) / love
26.24 aften (MS) / often
26.25 bluidy (MS) / bloody
26.25 than (MS) / then
26.27 Bothwell-Brigg (MS) / Bothwel-Brigg
26.29 canna (MS) / cannot
26.42 law-pleas and losses sinsyne—and (MS law-pleas & losses sinsyne—
       and) / law pleas, and losses sinsyne;—and
27.2   —and you by others are (MS) / —you, before others, are
27.2   on (MS) / upon
27.2   ventures (MS) / adventures
27.3   yours (MS) / your's
27.3   muckle they (MS) /muckle harm they
27.6   haud (Ed3) / had
27.8   suld (MS derived: shuld) / should
27.9   pow (MS) / head

27.35   maunna (MS) / manna
28.10   nae (MS) / no
28.23   wee-bit (MS) / bit
28.33   some (MS) / most
28.34   which already formed the (MS which already formd the) / which he had already arranged for the
28.35   remove (MS) / move
28.37   until (MS untill) / till
28.39   arrange it in his own way (MS) / place it according to his wish
28.40   seemed inconsistent (MS seemd inconsistent) / seemed utterly inconsistent
29.2   he had exerted (MS) / he exerted
29.5   my (MS) / a
29.7   gude (MS) / good
29.10   immense (MS) / uncommon
29.11   shaggy black hair (MS) / shaggy hair
29.13   of partial (MS) / of a partial
29.18   round (MS) / square
29.25   afterward (MS) / afterwards
29.39   petted (MS) / peevish
29.41   third—to (MS) / third, to
30.2   had yet moved (MS) / had moved
30.4   thae (Ed4) / these
30.7   them!—take (MS them—take) / them! Take
30.12   I ken (MS derived: I know) / we ken
         The transference of 'know' to 'ken' is in accordance with standing orders; the plural 'we', on the other hand, is more arbitrary and arguably flattens the directness of Hobbie's statement.
30.21   placing (MS) / having placed
30.22   distance, left (MS derived: distance and left) / distance, he left
30.28   exhibited (Ed2) / assumed
30.38   dexterity. As (MS) / dexterity. [new paragraph] As
         The MS gives no support for a new paragraph; in fact, the transference between sentences occurs within a verso addition.
30.39   seemed so averse (MS derived: seem so averse) / seemed averse
31.9   unfitted by nature for (MS) / unfitted, at first sight, for
31.10   without aiding him (MS) / without stopping a few minutes to aid him
31.11   with the help (MS derived: with help) / with the degree of help
         Ed1 intervenes fussily, though the addition of the definite article is helpful.
31.14   cottage and its garden, formed (MS cottage ↑& its garden↓ formd) / cottage, formed
31.14   space and (MS space &) / space, and
31.15   being, the (MS) / being, and the
31.21   insisted, that, though (MS insisted that though) / insisted, though
31.22   phrase, he (MS ↑ . . . phrase↓ he) / phrase, that he
31.25   desert, but who (MS desert but who) / desert, who
31.26   also said to have been occasionally (MS) / also occasionally
31.28   on the moor (MS) / in the moor
31.28   fetching the water (MS) / fetching water
31.30   shadow. [new paragraph] "De'il (MS derived: shadow—"Deil) / shadow.—"De'il
31.34   came (MS) / cam
31.38   would (MS) / might
31.42   the wanderer (MS) / an occasional passenger

32.2   bolder (MS) / boldest
32.3   apologized for (MS) /and to apologize for it
32.6   Solitary (MS solitary) / solitary inmate
        The MS's lower case 's' obscures Scott's first use of 'the Solitary' as an
        alternative name for the Dwarf, leading to the unnecessary addition of
        'inmate'.
32.8   No efforts could (MS) / It was impossible to
32.10   whatsoever (MS derived: whatsoeve[?]) / whatever
        Scott's failure to complete his word fully appears to have misled the
        transcriber into seeing 'whatever'.
32.14   much was (MS) / much more was
32.15   neighbours from (MS) / neighbours, from
32.17   consulted on (MS) / consulted (as at length he slowly was) on
32.19   are (MS) / were
32.22   Meikle-stane (MS M[ei/ic]kle-stane) / Muckle-stane-Moor
        The letters between 'M' and 'k' are obscured by the gutter in the MS in
        its present form.
32.32   syllable (Ed2) / word
32.34   these (MS) / those
32.35   she-goats (MS) /she goats
32.36   moor, near his dwelling, and (MS moor near his dwelling and) / moor,
        and
32.42   Morai. Apparently (MS) / Morai;—apparently
33.5   basket with his trouts at (MS) / basket, with his trouts, at
33.21   better exercise (MS better exercize) / better to exercise
33.21   curiosity (MS) / cruelty
33.26   lie (MS) / be
33.30   assist (MS) / labour
33.30   that (MS) / whom
33.37   this (MS) / the
33.39   Reiver (MS) / Riever
33.39   lay (MS) / was deemed to be
33.41   sleep (MS) / bed
33.43   True (MS) / I own
34.3   cost his (MS) / cost him his
34.17   hay-stack (MS derived: hay-stack ↑above↓)/ abode
        Ed1's 'abode' probably derives from Scott's instruction in the MS to run
        in the passage 'above'.
34.18   boy?" (Earnscliff ... (MS derived: boy (Earnscliffe ...) / boy?"—
        Earnscliff ...
34.20   proceeded.) "And the trumpet (MS derived: ↑... proceeded) the
        trumpet &c↓ And the trumpet) / proceeded,—"The trumpet
        Repetition in the MS stems from the dovetailing of one inserted passage
        into another; in this case, the transcriber appears to have copied the
        catch-word in preference to the primary text.
34.21   shall (MS) / *will*
34.21   I preserved (MS) / I have preserved
34.33   tomahawk at once, spoil (MS) / tomahawk, at once spoil
35.2   perish—But (MS) / perish; but
35.6   that were (MS) / that, were
35.12   composedly (MS) / composed
35.13   inflame (MS) / influence
35.15   should itself (MS) / itself should
35.19   childless (MS child less) / friendless
35.26   such a miserable state (MS) / so miserable a state

35.31　about (MS) / respecting
35.35　Enemy of Mankind (MS) / enemy of mankind
36.16　Solitary (MS) / Recluse
36.20　Meikle-stane (MS) / Mucklestane-Moor
36.25　best-looked (MS best-lookd) / best-looking
36.29　we turned this way"——— (MS we turnd this this way"———) / we have turned this way to"———
36.31　conscience (MS) / consciousness
36.34　but how (MS) / but O how
37.10　and which, when caught, are successively (MS & ↑which↓ when caught ↑are successively↓) / and, when caught, successively
37.12　her (MS) / his
37.13　lovers and dupes (MS) / love and its absurdities
37.21　you not ask (MS) / you ask
37.34　accomplishment (MS) / accomplishments
37.43　father," said Miss Vere, "let (MS father" said Miss Vere "let) / father, let
38.16　tear—the first tear which (MS) / tear, the first which
38.17　eye-lid (MS) / eye-lids
38.17　year—for (MS) / year; for
38.20　and if thy hope be (MS and if ⟨it be⟩ thy hope be) / or but one leaf of it, were it
38.21　wildest and fiercest (MS) / fiercest and wildest
38.23　perhaps happier (MS) / perhaps afford happier
39.26　Gorgon's head (MS Gorgons head) / Gorgon head
39.40　no, *no*, NO (MS derived: no—*no*—NO) / *No, no, no*
　　　In the MS the second 'no' is underlined, and the third underlined twice.
39.41　to Carlisle (MS) / at Carlisle
40.4　say, Thus do—*or*———" (MS derived: say thus do—*or*———") / say,—Thus do, *or*"———
40.6　were the (MS) / were he the
40.7　romance to (MS) / romance, to
40.12　has cantered on (MS has canterd on) / is out of hearing
40.15　man—a . . . state—infamous . . . severity—a bad son—a bad brother—unkind (MS) / man; a . . . state; infamous . . . severity; a bad son, a bad brother, unkind
40.24　was (MS) / were
40.34　seems (MS) / seem
40.38　there's (MS theres) / there is
40.39　councils (MS) / counsel
40.43　Elliot (MS) / Renault
41.1　Jaffeir (MS) / Jaffier
41.1　or a Pierre (MS) / or Pierre
41.8　Jaffeirs (MS) / Jaffiers
42.13　the day (MS) / that day
42.17　that broad (MS) / the broad
42.19　towered (MS towerd) / lowered
42.40　cut (MS) / cast
43.4　"So———" (MS) / "So,"
　　　In the MS another set of end quotation marks, positioned closer to 'So', are deleted.
43.8　All (MS) / And all
43.9　illness forgotten (MS) / illness, forgotten
43.10　passed (MS passd) / clear
43.12　wi' (Ed2) / with

43.12 that (MS) / the
43.18 What (MS) / Why, what
43.18 me do (MS) / me to do
43.20 livers (MS) / reivers
43.24 leapt (MS) / leaped
43.29 it?—eh (MS) / it, eh
43.38 No! (MS) / No;
43.40 burrows-town (MS Burrows-town) / burrow-town
44.16 spurs and whip without (MS) / spurs without
44.20 but most furious (MS) / but furious
44.23 The villain . . . the cool-blooded . . . the wretch (MS) / That villain . . . that cool-blooded . . . that wretch
44.25 crimes, has (MS derived: crimes has) / crimes,—has
44.34 who account (MS) / which account
44.36 with which I have been repaid (MS derived: with which I have repaid) / which I have repaid
This emendation is discussed in 'Essay on the Text', 168.
44.37 imprisonment—my stripes—my chains—I (MS) / imprisonment, my stripes, my chains, I
44.38 humanity. I (MS derived: humanity [new line] I) / humanity—I
The absence of guiding punctuation in the MS is perhaps explained by the break at this point between lines.
45.1 the dwarf—the wizard—the hunch-back might (MS the dwarf—the wizzard—the hunchback might) / the Dwarf, the Wizard, the Hunch-back, may
45.24 its serene influence (MS) / the serene influence of the sky
45.38 chair—the (MS) / chair; the
46.1 restraint, for (MS restraint for) / restraint—for
46.2 humanity—Hubert (MS) / humanity.—Hubert
46.3 all of a piece—one (MS) / all are of a piece, one
46.5 such is their hardness (MS) / of such hardness
46.5 not even, without hypocrisy, thank (MS not even without hypocricy thank) / not, without hypocrisy, even thank
46.11 alang (MS allang) / along
46.11 you. [new line] At (MS) / you. [new paragraph] At
46.42 na (MS) / no
47.1 was a vexing thing (MS) / is as vexing to me as
47.3 gaits (Editorial) / goats
In a facing verso insertion, evidently added at a later stage, the 'gait' form is consistently used rather than 'goat'. At a later point in the recto (50.17) 'goats' is replaced by 'gaits'. This (and the following) emendation is made on the grounds that 'gait' represents Scott's final preferred reading.
47.5 gait's (Editorial) / goat's
47.5 acts (MS) / acted
47.7 gaits (MS) / goats
47.11 Dear! Elshie (MS) / Dear, Elshie
47.11 ye (Ed3) / you
47.11 I am (MS) / I'm
47.12 gaits (MS) / goats
47.13 I am (MS) / I'm
47.14 I am e'en (MS I am een) / I'm e'en
47.25 yet it is (MS derived: yet is is) / yes! it is
47.27 happy—those (MS) / happy (those
47.28 happy insult (MS) / happy) insult

47.32 comfort—go (MS) / comfort. Go
48.3   sent (MS) / brought
48.26 Aye, aye! (MS Aye aye!) / Aye, aye,
48.32 Forster (MS) / Foster
48.32 Finning-beck (MS Finning ⟨Cleugh⟩ ↑Beck↓) / Tinning Beck
       'Finning-beck' matches the MS form at 49.23, which is uncomplicated
       by alteration.
48.34 haffits (MS) / face
48.37 came (MS) / come
48.39 no—no—That (MS) / no, no; that
49.1   ladye (MS) / lady
49.1   be a better (MS derived: be ↑a↓ the better) / be a' the better
       Scott apparently failed to delete 'the' when inserting 'a' as its replace-
       ment in the MS.
49.1   is ganging (MS) / is to be sent
49.2   no—Now (MS) / no; now
49.3   lass—Hobbie (MS) / lassie. Hobbie
49.17 But hear me—let (MS but hear me—let)/ But, hear me, let
49.17 uninjured—return (MS uninjurd—return) / uninjured; return
49.18 friends—let (MS freinds—let) / friends, and let
49.23 Finning-beck (MS) / Tinning-Beck
49.33 ye (MS) / you
49.39 Elliot, in the meanwhile, had pursued (MS Elliot in the mean while had
       pursued) / Elliot had, in the meanwhile, pursued
49.40 right at home, which (MS right at home which) / right, which
50.2   nurse—a person then of (MS) / nurse, a person, then, of
50.5   accounted (MS) / considered
50.7   foster-son (MS) / foster son
50.17 gaits (MS) / goats
50.17 eneuch in the country (MS) / in the country besides
50.21 with the (MS) / by the
50.25 astounded (MS) / astonished
50.30 driven. (MS driven) / driven away.
50.31 een hae (MS) / e'en has
50.42 offices stocked (MS offices stockd) / offices, stocked
51.2   ruined now— (MS ruind now—) / ruined—
51.3   no (MS) / not
51.4   the very week (MS) / the week
51.4   doun (MS) / down
51.6   wi' Buccleuch (MS) / wi' auld Buccleuch
51.11 dale (MS) / dell
51.21 burned (MS burnd) / burnt
51.26 than (MS) / then
51.27 than (MS) / then
51.31 peacefu' (MS) /pacificated
51.40 living now (MS) / now living
52.5   than (MS) / then
52.5   it is (MS it ↑is↓) / it's
52.8   Dundrennan (MS) / Drundennan
52.26 are——" He (MS) / are"——He
52.27 kinsman (MS) / kinsmen
52.33 o' (Ed2) / of
53.1   around (MS) / about
53.3   (he hesitated . . . effort,) (Ed2) / he hesitated . . . effort,—
       The insertion of this passage, which is absent in MS and was probably

added by Scott at proof stage, appears to have been clumsily handled.
Parentheses surround similar narrative asides in Ed1, and Ed2 evaluates
the situation correctly.

53.6   "O our poor (MS) / "Our poor

53.8   extricating him (MS derived: extricating ⟨himsel⟩ her son) / disengag-
        ing him

53.9   piety (MS) / pity

53.16   and have carried (MS) / and carried

53.20   knapscap (MS) / knapsack

53.23   He (Ed2) / he

53.27   Earnscliff—his father's son—a (MS Earnscliffe—his father's son—a) /
        Earnscliff—he's his father's true son—a

53.29   "let us on (MS derived: "Lets' us on) / "let's on

53.31   His (MS) / HIS

54.4   Telfer's (Ed2) / Tellfer's
        This motto does not appear in the MS; Ed2 supplies the orthodox
        printed spelling.

54.11   "Hae ye ony tidings?...wrang'd ye?" (MS derived: Have ye ony tidings
        —hae ye ony speerings Hobbie—↑said old Dick of the Dingle↓ O
        callans dinna be ower hasty—" ↑ "Aye Aye" exclaimd Simon of ⟨Wh⟩
        Hackburn "thats the gate to take it Hobbie—let women sit and greet at
        hame—men must do as they have been done by ↑↑its the scripture
        say'st↓↓"—Haud your tongue Sir said ⟨?⟩ ↑↑the ↓↓ Senior "ye⟨t⟩
        dinna ken what ye speak↓ "What signifies preaching to us ⟨eno⟩
        e'enow said Simon—if ye canna make help yoursell dinna keep them at
        hame that can"—"Whisht Sir! what do ye ken wha's wrang'd ye—") /
        "Ay, ay!" exclaimed Simon of Hackburn, "that's the gate to take it,
        Hobbie. Let women sit and greet at hame, men must do as they have
        been done by; its the Scripture says't." [new paragraph] "Haud your
        tongue, sir," said one of the seniors, sternly; "dinna abuse the Word
        that gate, ye dinna ken what ye speak about." [new paragraph] "Hae ye
        ony tidings?—Hae ye ony speerings, Hobbie?—O, callants, dinna be
        ower hasty," said old Dick of the Dingle. [new paragraph] "What sig-
        nifies preaching to us e'enow," said Simon; "if ye canna make help
        yoursel, dinna keep them back that can." [new paragraph] "Whisht, sir;
        wad ye take vengeance or ye ken wha has wrang'd ye?"
        This emendation is discussed in 'Essay on the Text', 167.

54.23   we'se (MS) / we'll

54.32   which, roving...habitation, were filling (MS derived: which ↑were↓
        roving...habitation were filling) / which were roving...habitation, and
        filling
        Scott's insertion of 'were', evidently at a later stage, appears to be
        superfluous.

54.36   ill-fa'ard (Ed2) / ill fa'ard
        The MS form, 'ill-favourd', is also hyphenated.

54.36   spake (MS) / spak

54.40   Græme's-gap (MS) / Græmes'-gap

55.8   Canny (MS) / canny

55.8   whate'er (MS) / whatever

55.10   shall tell (MS) / *shall* tell

55.22   wood of copse, (MS wood of copse) / wood,

55.25   consider more maturely (MS) / consider maturely

55.38   doun (MS derived: doon) / down

56.3   doun (Ed3) / down

56.7   Canny (MS) / canny

56.9 carcase (MS) / cascase
56.18 alive (MS) / living
56.27 is but as (MS) / is as
56.40 long (Ed3) / deep
57.4 willingly (MS) / readily
57.7 Heaven (MS heaven) / Heavens
57.9 ye (MS) / you
57.9 band (MS) / bond
57.10 Wideopen (MS) / Widopen
57.17 ye (MS) / you
57.20 gang,—if I could but hear—if ye (MS gang—if I could but hear—if you) / gang,—if ye
57.25 partner. Seek (MS) / partner, seek
57.29 shutter (MS) / shutters
57.36 answer—It (MS answer—it) / answer?—It
57.38 there is (MS) / there's
57.38 o' (Ed4) / of
57.40 downa (MS) / dounna
57.41 trysting place (MS) / Trysting-place
58.27 to young (MS) / for young
58.36 morassy (MS) / marshy
58.36 expanding (MS) / expanded
59.1 for about (MS) / for the space of about
59.2 immediately around the foundations (MS) / itself in the immediate neighbourhood
59.3 that space (MS) / which
59.5 intimates (MS) / inmates
59.6 that (Ed3) / which
59.7 who (MS) / which
59.11 property prevented (MS) / property, prevented
59.19 awaked (MS) / awakened
59.21 but because (MS) / as that
60.13 There's (MS Theres) / There is
60.22 woman. [new paragraph] "That's (MS derived: woman—"thats) / woman.—"That's
60.37 Baudrons (MS) / baudrons
60.39 and am in (MS) / and in
61.9 clam-jamfarie (MS) / clanjamfrie
61.12 gi'e (Ed3) / give
61.15 skeel on it (MS) / skill on't
61.19 had (MS ⟨held⟩ ↑had↓) / held
61.20 might even, for a time, have (MS might even for a time have) / might, for a time, have even
61.22 door, entirely (MS door entirely) / door, composed entirely
61.23 they could bring (MS) / that could be brought
61.24 upon it (MS) / upon't
61.25 batter it (MS) / batter at it
61.29 breadth (MS) / brea th
61.34 intimate (MS) / indicate
61.35 direction. This was doubted . . . southern direction. [new paragraph] (MS direction ↑This was doubted by others who pretended to trace the same ⟨foot-⟩ hoof-marks out of the morass & receding from the tower in a Southern direction.↓ [new paragraph]) / direction. [new paragraph]
61.38 slender means of (MS) / want of means for

61.41   bars—scaling (MS) / bars. Scaling
61.41   question. Mining (MS) / question; mining
61.42   gunpowder. Neither (MS) / gunpowder; neither
62.5   But (MS) / And
62.13   dry (MS) / dried
62.31   peaceable honest (MS) / peaceable and honest
62.35   But (MS) / And
63.4   cloot o' (Ed4) / cloot of
63.8   wrang that he (MS) / wrang he
63.10   Lord's sake (MS Lords sake) / Lordsake
63.11   puir (Ed3) / poor
63.11   hellicat's (MS hellicats') / Hellicat's
63.13   And (MS) / Will
63.15   wi' (MS) / with
63.16   and draw (MS) / and to draw
63.17   sairly." (MS: sairly—") / sairly. Will ye do this?"
        This emendation is discussed in 'Essay on the Text', 165.
63.22   secure (MS) / sure
63.40   quickened (MS quickend) / hastened
64.4   ye sall (MS) / you shall
64.8   Haud a care (MS) / Haud a' care
64.8   word wi' (MS) / faith with
64.12   keepit (MS derived: keepd) / kept
64.12   he said, "sirs! (MS he said "Sirs!) / sirs!" he said,
64.13   na (MS) / no
64.26   Nae man (MS) / Nae single man
64.40   God's sake (MS Gods sake) / God sake
65.8   gude care (MS) / the better care
65.12   his very heart's (MS his very hearts) / his heart's
65.20   conducted (Ed3) / conveyed
65.26   adopted (Ed3) / taken
65.35   *Ballad* (Ed2) / *Play*
65.40   o' (Ed4) / of
66.1   ain (Ed2) / own
66.2   wouldst snapper (MS) / wouldst thou snapper
66.6   ain (MS) / own
66.7   in the Heugh-foot (MS in the Heugh foot) / in Heughfoot
66.12   towards (MS) / toward
66.17   heart (MS) / hearts
66.27   aff (MS) / off
66.34   of good-humoured (MS ⟨between a⟩ ↑of↓ goodhumourd) / of a
        good-humoured
66.42   sisters' (MS) / sister's
67.9   upon (MS) / on
67.10   this (MS) / the
67.16   might soon hae (MS) / might hae
67.23   devotions (MS) / devotion
67.27   enquiry was (MS) / enquiries were
67.30   offered (MS offerd) / made
67.32   in the scuffle having seen (MS in the scufle ⟨she saw⟩ ↑having seen↓)
        / having seen, in the scuffle,
67.33   off, she imprudently (MS off ⟨?⟩ ↑she↓ imprudently) / off, imprud-
        ently
68.12   in (MS) / on
68.12   hills. But (MS hills But) / hills, but

68.13 see; and (MS derived: see and) / see! And
68.13 it—And (MS) / it; and
68.17 puir (Ed3) / poor
68.21 at (MS) / wi'
68.24 its (MS) / it's
68.25 him yet, is (MS him yet—is) / him, is
68.30 stouthrief (MS) / stouthrife
68.32 but the (MS) / but——the
68.39 He has nae . . . to boot. (MS He has nae a four-fitted thing but the bay naig he rides on & thats but a washy beast & has the mallenders to boot —) / He hasna a four-footed creature but the vicious blood thing he rides on, and that's sair trash'd wi' his night-wark. This emendation is discussed in 'Essay on the Text', 164–65.
69.10 o' (Ed2) / of
69.10 o' (Ed2) / of
69.19 good-humoured (MS good humourd) / good-natured
69.20 themsels.—But (MS derived: themselves—But) / themsels. But
69.26 gude (MS) / good
69.39 suld (MS) / should
69.39 Canny (8vo 1819) / canny
69.42 to them (MS) / frae them
70.1 kens that that body (MS) / kens that body
70.8 sure I am that (MS) / sure am I, that
70.12 Fastern's (MS) / Fastren's
70.12 burned (MS burnd) / burnt
70.17 died o' (Ed3) / died of
70.19 out o' (Ed3) / out of
70.20 hear (MS) / have heard
70.21 that it's (MS that its) / that's
70.27 ower (Ed3) / down
70.32 naig (MS) / nag
70.35 on ye (Ed2) / on you
70.36 twenty-four (MS twenty four) / four-and-twenty
70.38 night is (MS) / night's
71.12 na (MS) / no
71.15 will maybe hae been (MS will ↑may↓ be ↑hae been↓) / will hae been
71.30 to mortal (MS) / to a mortal
71.31 under the full (MS) / under full
71.41 Beelzebub (MS) / Belzebub
72.4 hand! Lord (MS hand! lord)/ hand—Lord
72.5 word—It (MS) / word!—It
72.5 I am (MS) / I'm
72.8 its (MS) / it's
72.9 I am (MS) / I'm
72.13 siller that he (MS) / siller he
72.13 o' window (MS) / o' the window
72.15 me." [new paragraph] He (MS derived: me"— He) / me." He
72.22 jookery-packery (MS) / jookery-paukery
72.23 gude (MS) / good
72.29 came ower (MS) / cam o'er
72.30 con (MS) / gi'e
72.32 suffered (MS sufferd) / happened
72.32 sowthered (MS sowtherd) / suffered
72.39 than there's my (MS than theres my) / then my
72.40 by (MS) / at

72.42   gude (Ed2) / good
73.16   she's liferenter and (MS) / she's a life-renter, and
73.16   lands o' (Ed2) / lands of
73.17   band (MS) / bond
73.18   band (MS) / bond
73.28   missive, as they ca't at Jeddart, in (MS ↑ . . . missive ↑↑ as they ca't it at
        Jeddart↓↓ ↓in) / missive, in
        The restored passage is on the facing verso in the MS, and is an addition
        to an insertion in the recto text.
73.29   subscrive (MS) / subscribe
73.30   pit (MS) / put
73.32   be only (MS) / only be
73.33   I am ganging (MS) / I'm ganging
73.35   see ye (MS) / see you
74.33   step and turning. (MS derived: step & turning with an account of the
        walks he intended to open ⟨?⟩ ↑for↓ the purpose of giving a more free
        access to his beauties.) / step.
        Apart from its first three words, the MS version resists satisfactory
        integration.
75.9   sir? (MS Sir?) / sir!
75.9   in (MS) / on
75.25   humbler (MS) / humble
75.28   offend you, sir (MS offend you Sir) / offend, sir
75.36   profess (MS) / confess
75.40   I weary (MS) / I am weary
76.1   persecutions (MS) / persecution
76.6   will (MS) / shall
76.7   topic.—You (MS derived: ↑ . . . topic—↓ —You) / topic. You
76.14   mounted at the same time, and, placing (Ed2) / mounted, at the same
        time, and placing
        The narrative sequence suffers from imperfectly integrated revision in
        the MS, which at this point offers no guiding punctuation: Ed2's solu-
        tion is imperfect, but preferable to Ed1.
76.39   Vere not (MS) / Vere, not
77.6   child—an (MS) / child, an
77.9   here instantly—Let (MS here instantly—let) / here—Let
77.14   proceeded (Ed2) / continued
77.28   awanting (MS) / wanting
78.11   relief; (MS derived: relief,) / relief,
        A rare MS comma indicates a heavier pause here than is provided by
        Ed1's punctuation.
78.21   seemed to observe (MS seemd to observe) / indicated any observations
        of
78.24   indignantly, sometimes (MS indignantly sometimes) / indignantly, and
        sometimes
78.27   world, and it (MS world and it) / world; and that it
79.4   confidante (MS) / confidant
79.17   any one (MS) / you
79.20   others (MS) / there
79.20   out, to (MS out to) / out persons to
79.21   had (MS) / have
79.31   stand (MS) / be standing
80.1   lamented, recollection (MS lamented recollection) / lamented, the
        recollection
80.5   them were staunch (MS) / them staunch

80.8   disaffection (MS) / dissaffection
80.11   apartments (MS) / apartment
80.12   by (MS) / in
80.17   in so strange a manner (MS) / the strange manner in which it had
         happened
80.21   precede (MS) / preceded
80.28   on (MS) / in
80.38   morasses at Westburnflat." (MS morasses at Westburn-flat"—) /
         morasses."
81.1   Vere and Sir Frederick can (MS) / Vere can
81.3   it at them instantly (MS) / it instantly
81.4   not yet examined (MS) / not examined
81.12   driven, because (MS driven because) / driven away, because
81.18   in (MS) / on
81.18   otherwise (MS) / otherways
81.23   was heard . . . were perceived (MS) / were heard . . . was perceived
         The MS word order is also found in some copies of Ed1 (see 'Essay on
         the Text', 146).
81.34   said young Marischal-Wells (MS) / said Mareschal-Wells
81.36   affair—if (MS) / affair. If
81.37   be the first (MS) / be first
81.37   her—but (MS) / her; but
82.18   the lady (MS) / this lady
83.2   quarrel (MS quarrell) / quarrels
83.3   I'se a (MS) / I'se be a
83.3   I'll (MS) / I'se
83.4   King or the Laird (MS) / king, or the laird
83.8   truth (MS) / birth
83.37   where (MS) / when
84.1   are not (MS) / were not
84.5   presses (MS) / passes
84.9   friends)—Do (MS) / friends.) Do
84.14   discontented (MS) / disconcerted
84.21   downfall (MS) / downfal
84.29   that, who (MS that who) / that you, who
85.10   old end of the ballad (MS) / end of the old ballad
85.17   vindication of (MS) / way of vindicating
85.31   Part I (Editorial) / Part II
85.39   substance (MS) / subtance
86.8   men (MS) / persons
86.13   Luck-in-a-Bag (MS) / Luck-in-a-bag
86.16   party in other (MS) / party, in the other
86.16   kingdom consisted of more (MS) / kingdom, consisted of much more
86.17   as more (MS) / as much more
87.7   of all the (MS) / of the
87.13   Clerk of this Parish (MS) / clerk of the parish
87.13   himself as impressed (MS himself as impress'd) / himself oppressed
87.22   at (MS) / of
87.27   emotion (Ed2) / sensation
87.32   at (MS) / of
87.32   placed (MS) / designed
87.37   looked moody and (MS derived: ↑seemd↓ ⟨lookd⟩ absent moody
         and) / was absent, moody, and
         In the MS 'seemd' appears in the left margin next to the deleted 'lookd',
         but in a lighter pen stroke than that apparently used for the deletion.

The edited version is based on the conjecture that Scott at an earlier stage erroneously crossed out 'lookd' instead of the repetitious 'absent'.

88.19   [inset verse] (MS) / [new paragraph]
        This line is clearly the first of two inset passages of verse in the MS.
88.19   some (MS) / more
88.19   England?" (Editorial) / England,"
        Though no MS punctuation is supplied, syntax and setting imply a question.
88.34   Here (MS) / Then
88.34   Independence (MS) / independence
88.35   Health (MS) / health
88.35   Sovereign (MS) / sovereign
89.24   on (MS) / in
89.26   on (MS) / in
89.31   for protection (MS) / for the protection
90.2   press, presbytery and (MS) / press, and presbytery, and
90.6   Country-Keeper (MS) / country-keeper
90.7   ere (MS) / before
90.14   as far (MS) / so far
90.17   seemed (MS seemd) / seem
90.35   circumstances (MS) / circumstance
91.11   power (MS) / powers
91.31   *galère* (Magnum) / *galere*
91.36   seen, (MS seen) / seen before,
91.37   hands (MS) / hand
92.8   the needful (MS) / what is needful
92.14   King (MS) / king
92.22   you our (MS) / you that our
92.32   should (MS) / shall
92.33   I—it (MS) / I; it
92.33   plunging—you (MS) / plunging. You
92.40   the knight (MS) / Sir Frederick
92.42   them I suppose by (MS) / them by
93.12   *you*, not (MS *you* not) / *you*, and not
93.12   priority (MS) / priorities
94.7   me now when (MS) / me when
94.10   I am (MS) / am I
95.3   change (Ed3) / charge
95.4   *Sigismunda* (Ed2) / *Sigismund*
95.34   of obedience (MS) / of her obedience
96.2   recollection (MS) / recollections
96.4   was quite (MS) / were quite
96.12   father?—" (MS) / father!"
96.17   Sir?—Offence to me?—Take leave for ever?—What (MS Sir?—offence to me?—take leave for ever?—What) / Sir? Offence to me? Take leave for ever? What
96.42   would (MS) / wished
96.43   insurmountable, have (MS insurmountable have) / insurmountable, to have
97.12   pursues (MS) / pursued
97.25   fate.—On (MS fate—On) / fate—on
97.33   I (MS) / he
98.7   die? (MS) / die,
98.7   him? (MS) / him!
99.7   *à très* (Magnum) / *a tres*

99.25   bid Mr Ratcliffe (MS) / bid Ratcliffe
99.28   lips together with (MS) / lips with
99.29   internal (MS) / external
100.5   bless with (MS) / bless thee with
100.9   must—and where I must—but (MS) / must, and where I must, but
100.22 me—if (MS) / me; if
101.6   forwards (MS) / forward
101.7   the very servants (MS) / the servants
101.8   heard directions (MS) / heard the directions
101.13 be so, (MS be so) / be,
101.22 Start (MS) / Stare
102.1   almost an (MS) / an almost
102.10 will catch (MS) / will always catch
102.18 to the (MS) / into the
102.20 it. They spoke . . . commiseration. [new paragraph] "Married (MS it
        They spoke in a tone of commiseration—"Married) / it. [new para-
        graph] "Married
102.27 towards (MS) / toward
102.37 world—I (MS world I) / world; but I
        In the MS 'I' begins a new line; Ed1's punctuation lends an inappropri-
        ate logic to Isabella's breathless speech.
102.42 crediting such (MS derived: believing in such) / crediting in such
        Ed1's reading probably derives from an imperfectly implemented
        change in proof.
103.4   pledged (Ed2) / solemn
103.19 lady," replied Ratcliffe gravely, "was (MS lady" replied Ratcliffe gravely
        "was) / lady, was
103.20 men (MS) / those
103.31 of whom I speak (MS) / whom I speak of
103.41 cradle, according to the wise law of the ancient Spartans, than (MS
        cradle ↑according to the wise law of the ancient Spartans↓ than) /
        cradle than
        The passage omitted by Ed1 is an addition on the facing verso
        in the MS.
104.5   best (MS) / least
104.14 remark (MS) / observe
104.14 animals (MS derived: ↑animals↓ tribes) / animal tribes
        Scott appears to have forgotten to delete 'tribes' when inserting
        'animals' in the MS.
104.15 most (MS) / more
104.15 caricature?'" (Ed3) / caricature?"
104.28 scarce (MS) / scarcely
104.35 No—by no means—I—I (MS) / No; by no means, I—I
104.40 registered (MS registerd) / regarded
104.41 carman (MS) / common people
104.41 in (MS) / on
104.42 girl of quality to (MS) / girl to
105.8   now are (MS) / are now
105.28 pardon—the (MS) / pardon. The
105.31 having willingly incurred (MS having willingly incurd)) / having
        incurred
105.31 sustaining (MS) / restraining
105.35 would (MS) / could
105.37 deceived. Before (MS deceived—Before) / deceived; before
105.39 effect (MS) / effects

105.39 temperament, and a (MS temperament and a) / temperament, a
105.40 remorse and (MS) / remorse, and
105.43 to the (MS) / to all the
106.16 of alternately (MS) / alternately of
106.20 his most vile (MS) / his vile
106.23 kindliness (MS) / kindness
106.26 Ratcliffe. "That (Ed2) / Ratcliffe; "that
        Though the MS offers no guiding punctuation, Ed2 correctly senses a
        fresh sentence at this point.
106.27 dispute; and I (MS dispute ↑and I . . . ↓) / dispute; I
106.28 broke (MS) / broken
106.30 shades which distinguish the maniac from the man of a sound mind are
        (MS) / shades are
106.36 all in the eye of sound reason marked (MS all ↑in the eye of sound
        reason↓ markd) / all marked
107.6   discern (MS) / discover
107.15 suppressing (MS) / stifling
107.15 Recollect (MS) / Remember
107.19 what (MS) / the evil
107.21 an unfortunate like (MS) / one so unfortunate as
108.13 me; alas, it (MS me—alas it) / me; it
108.18 shall (MS) / *shall*
108.27 She entered; and, with a precaution which increased her trepidation,
        the (8vo 1822) / She entered, and with a precaution which increased
        her trepidation. The
        The punctuation supplied in Ed1 misinterprets the sense of the manu-
        script, which provides no punctuation; the 1822 8vo *Novels and Tales*
        offers a plausible solution without disturbing the wording.
109.6   drooping (MS) / dropping
109.11 streamers of a vessel droop (MS streamers of a ⟨stranded⟩ vessell
        droop) / streamers droop
109.12 away and (MS) / away, and
109.12 her (MS) / the vessel
109.22 fair suppliants (MS) / a fair suppliant
109.24 could (MS) / would
109.26 rising, interposing (MS rising interposing) / rising and interposing
109.31 decrepid outcast on (MS decrepid ⟨of⟩ ↑outcast on↓) / decrepid on
109.38 strongest and fairest (MS) / fairest and strongest
110.5   what is then (MS) / what, then, is
110.14 other. From (MS other ↑From) / other.—From
        Ed1 incorrectly retains a dash from the MS, originally indicating a
        speech end, but superseded there by a caret leading to a long verso
        addition.
110.30 the courage (MS) / the affected courage
110.35 destroying, degrading (MS destroying degrading) /destroying, and
        degrading
110.43 Revenge is like the (MS) / revenge is the
111.2   listened to?" (MS listend to"—) / listened to by him?"
111.6   need—you (MS) / need. You
111.24 act!" (Ed 2) / act!
111.43 castle . . . mettle (MS castle ↑in less than half an hour after she parted
        with Ratcliffe though the distance was five long miles so much had↓
        the mettle) / castle, the mettle
112.3   combined (MS) / combining
112.11 which (MS) / that

112.19   seem (MS) / be
112.25   *Ado* (Ed2) / *ado*
112.36   within (MS) / in
113.2   effect (Ed2) / glare
113.18   was dependent (MS) / were dependent
113.38   moody, thoughtful (MS moody thoughtful) / moody, and thoughtful
113.42   brows (MS) / brow
114.9   event just when (MS) / event when
114.12   comes (MS) / come
114.17   indicated his (MS) / indicated that his
114.22   a much lower (MS) / a lower
114.26   free and (MS) / free will and
114.28   a tenth (MS) / the tenth
114.33   own free choice (MS) / own choice
114.35   cheek is (MS) / cheeks are
114.43   shrugged his (MS shrugd his) / shrugged up his
115.7   wakened (MS wakend) / awakened
115.10   remote (Ed2) / distant
115.15   allowance (MS) / allowances
115.23   such time, place, and (MS such time place and) / such place and
115.28   what can (MS) / and what does
115.41   life!—Ay (MS life ⟨in famine⟩—Ay) / life! Ay
116.2   benefits that I (MS) / benefits I
116.7   for him (MS) / to him
116.12   use (Ed3) / assume
116.31   Canny (MS) / canny
116.38   peascods (MS) / pea-cods
116.43   hear me—hear me a bit—we (MS) / hear me a bit, hear me a bit. We
117.3   neighbour-war (MS) / neighbour war
117.3   Kirk. But (MS Kirk—But) / Kirk; but
         The MS's upper case 'B' and dash indicate a significant break; a new
         sentence is most appropriate in view of surrounding marks.
117.7   howsomever (MS) / however
117.9   re-entered (MS re-enterd) / entered
117.16   not worth (MS) / hardly worth
117.38   figure and (MS) / figure, and
118.3   Do not speak to me! do not thwart (MS Do not speak to me do not
         thwart) / Speak not to me! attempt not to thwart
118.4   I will be dead to you (MS) / To you I will be dead
118.6   as a (MS) / as of a
118.17   that, on the very day, they (MS that on the very ↑day↓ they) / that on
         that very day they
         This and the following emendation are discussed in 'Essay on the
         Text', 159. (A number of deleted words, some of which are indecipher-
         able, have been omitted from the MS transcription.)
118.19   defiance. A (MS) / defiance; so that a
118.26   *You Like* (8vo 1819) / *you like*
118.31   years (MS) / time
119.15   unwillingly (MS) / willingly
119.42   the poor man (MS) / he
120.16   of (MS) / at
120.23   forwards (MS) / forward
120.33   the (MS) / that
120.43   them (MS) / him
121.2   them (MS) / him

121.3   income (MS) / increase
121.9   and the mains (MS and the Mains) / and mains
121.23   he probably had (MS) / he had
121.39   hour (MS) / time
121.41   extinguished, the (MS extinguishd, the) / extinguished, and the
121.41   hut left (MS) / hut was left
122.4   hae (MS) / ha'e
122.4   Canny (8vo 1819) / canny
122.12   drew (MS) / brought
122.18   they would (MS) / would they
122.22   sair (MS) / light
122.24   sall (MS) / shall
122.27   day, and (MS day &) / day's time, and
122.37   it is (MS) / it's
123.1   Mr Vere (MS) / Ellieslaw
123.18   Derwentwater and (MS Derwentwater &) / Derwentwater, and
123.20   furnished (MS furnishd) / supplied
123.30   the native (MS) / his native
123.39   plundered—spoke . . . Cheat-the-Woodie—died (MS plunderd
         ↑spoke much of the Duke of Marlborough and very little of Charlie
         Cheat-the-Woodie↓ died) / plundered—died
124.11   uttering (MS) / naming
124.13   him secrecy (MS) / him strict secrecy
124.24   grandson (MS Grandson Js.) / grandsons
         This emendation is discussed in 'Essay on the Text', 140.
124.27   down (MS derived: dow) / its weight
         This emendation is discussed in 'Essay on the Text', 168.

END-OF-LINE HYPHENS

All end-of-line hyphens in the present text are soft unless included in the list below. The hyphens listed are hard and should be retained when quoting.

7.10	gauging-stick	60.42	steel-caps
18.19	to-morrow	65.39	over-fatigued
23.36	high-school	66.34	good-humoured
24.8	cousin-german	67.7	half-laughed
26.15	Meikle-stane	76.42	whin-stane
29.14	rough-hewn	81.34	Marischal-Wells
31.4	garden-ground	83.38	court-yard
43.6	leech-craft	85.6	to-morrow
44.33	ill-suppressed	89.22	Marischal-Wells
45.24	good-humour	90.6	re-echoed
45.29	she-goats	93.2	Ellieslaw-Castle
50.4	foster-children	104.4	cold-blooded
50.37	heart-breaking	109.42	self-sufficing
54.38	mis-shapen	110.17	fellow-mortals
54.40	Græme's-gap	115.32	Mauley-Hall
60.9	loop-hole		

HISTORICAL NOTE

Sources. *The Black Dwarf* is set on the Scottish Border in the immediate wake of the Union between England and Scotland in 1707, when the two nations merged as political bodies. In choosing such a setting, temporal and geographical, Scott was able to feed on two of his richest historical sources: his intimate knowledge of Border ballad and legend, which stemmed back to his childhood, and the large store of information he had collected about Scottish history in the years surrounding the Union, particularly in relation to a series of Jacobite attempts to restore the Stuart monarchy in Scotland.

The political action in *The Black Dwarf* is centred on the first uprising to be attempted by the Jacobites after the Union. On 6 March 1708 a fleet of thirty French vessels, carrying 6000 troops and commanded by the Comte de Forbin, sailed from Dunkirk with the exiled James VIII of Scotland on board. All the signs indicated that the situation in Scotland was ripe for insurrection. Large parts of the population were hostile to the Union, which had been finalised on 1 May 1707, and agents reported back widespread disaffection amongst the nobility and gentry, especially those who were Episcopalian or Catholic in religion, and the prospect too of an uprising amongst the Presbyterians (spearheaded by the zealous Cameronians) in the south-west. With large sections of the British army on the Continent, Scotland was almost denuded of troops: in the event of invasion, the Governor of Edinburgh Castle had contingency plans for a retreat to Berwick in England. The main French fleet approached the mouth of the Firth of Forth on the evening of 12 March. No clear signals were received from the shore, however, and the sight on the following day of a larger English fleet, commanded by Admiral Byng, resulted in Forbin manoeuvring his way into open sea (with the loss of one ship) to avoid being trapped in the Forth. James VIII is said to have begged to be put ashore with only his Scottish supporters; but, after an abortive attempt to land further north in the Moray Firth, the fleet returned to Dunkirk in some disarray.

The meeting of Jacobites at Ellieslaw Castle in the story, culminating in an open declaration of insurrection (Ch. 13), occurs at this crisis point in Scotland's history. At least one modern historian has suggested that it presented a better opportunity for a restoration of the Stuarts than the more extensive and better-known uprisings of 1715 and 1745.[1] A similar analysis was given shortly after the event by the anti-Unionist George Lockhart of Carnwath (1673–1731), whose *Memoirs Concerning the Affairs of Scotland . . . With an Account of the Origine and Progress of the Design'd Invasion from France, in March, 1708* (London, 1714) was well-known to Scott. Elements of his account are found almost verbatim in Scott's text, especially in the mouth of the committed and relatively idealistic figure of Marischal of Marischal-Wells. Lockhart also relates the fortunes of five Stirlingshire lairds, who 'having, as they thought, receiv'd certain Intelligence, that the King was Landed, mounted their Horses, and advanced in a good body towards *Edinburgh* . . ., but being quickly inform'd of the bad News, returned home again' (380). Scott in the Interleaved Set later offered this as a parallel to the inconclusive events at Ellieslaw. Nevertheless the range of incident available from an uprising which never happened was necessarily limited. To fill the gap the story appropriates materials from the better-documented uprising of 1715, particularly those relating to a subsidiary uprising of Jacobite gentry in the south-west Borders of Scotland, headed by the Earl of Kenmure and Lord Nithsdale, which eventually merged with a similar revolt by the Earl of Derwentwater in Northumberland. A fertile source here was Robert Patten's *The History of the Late Rebellion: with Original Papers, and the Characters of the Principal Nobleman and Gentlemen Concern'd in it* (London, 1717), an eye-witness record. Patten (an Anglican clergyman, who later turned king's evidence) describes the ineffectual progress of the insurgent army through the main Border towns of Langholm, Hawick, and Jedburgh. At Kelso, where a sermon was preached by a Scottish non-juring clergyman, the crowd received the rebel manifesto with acclamation, shouting '*NO Union! NO Malt, NO Salt-TAX!*' (2nd edn, 1717, 48). These cries are perhaps echoed in the patently self-interested objections of Scott's fictional anti-unionists. Patten's caustic observations on a troop of horse commanded by Robert Douglas, allegedly containing at least one notorious Border horse-thief, are more directly alluded to by Scott, and no doubt appealed to him as a means of linking his Jacobite and Border themes.

For the Border elements in the story Scott was most deeply indebted to the ballads he had collected and annotated for *Minstrelsy of the Scottish Border* (1802–03), at the start of his literary career. Above all, one senses an affinity with the 'reiving' ballads garnered on Scott's excursions into Liddesdale in the 1790s (see 'Essay on the Text', 131). In some respects, the fortunes of Hobbie Elliot—the pillage of Heughfoot, his appeal to the Black Dwarf for help, the gathering of forces and 'siege' of Westburnflat—parallel the events in one of Scott's favourite ballads, 'Jamie Telfer of the fair Dodhead'. In the version printed in the *Minstrelsy*, Telfer searches in vain for help in retrieving his stolen cattle until appealing to Scott of Buccleuch, who leads a devastating counter raid into England. Another version of the ballad, whose existence was recognised by Scott, has Martin Elliot of Pricken haugh (Prickinghaugh) in place of Buccleuch and describes what is effectively a raising of the Elliot clan. It has been demonstrated[2] that the place names in the ballad, especially when seen in the Elliot version, closely match the topography of Liddesdale, with a general movement from Teviotdale to the northern Hermitage area, from there to Martin Elliot's headquarters near Larriston, then down Liddel Water to the Border at Kershopefoot, ending at Stonegarthside in England. The gathering of Elliots after the burning of Heugh-foot (Chs 7, 8) also contains distinct echoes of

the uncompromisingly bleak and choric 'The Fray of Suport', with its
lament and call to arms, which Scott had heard from recitation in Liddesdale.[3] In the Explanatory Notes other instances are pointed out
where Scott seems significantly close to the ballads he had heard in
Liddesdale, including 'Hobbie Noble', 'Jock o' the Side' and 'Dick o'
the Cow'.

At the same time, Scott drew more broadly on materials which had
made the *Minstrelsy* as much a Border history as a ballad collection. The
Borderers' concern not to break faith with Westburnflat (Ch. 9), galling
to Hobbie's wishes, reflects rules for truce-making and the safe-keeping
of prisoners which had preoccupied Border Wardens from medieval
times—and which are still faintly remembered in Hobbie's world.
Willie of Westburnflat's own exploit in kidnapping Isabel Vere recalls
the historical fact that in 1642, at the instigation of the royalist Lord
Traquair, William Armstrong of Gilnockie kidnapped the respected
judge Lord Durie, incarcerating him for several months in the remote
tower of Graham near Moffat, in Dumfriesshire, to prevent him presid-
ing over a case where his opinion was likely to be hostile to Traquair.
The incident formed the basis for Scott's imitation in the ballad style,
'Christie's Will', where again it is possible to find echoes of the *Dwarf*.
In his Introduction to the ballad in the *Minstrelsy*, Scott described
William Armstrong as 'a lineal descendant of the famous John Armstrong' (hero of the famous ballad 'Johnie Armstrang') and as 'the very
last Border freebooter of any note'.[4] While the *Minstrelsy* was indelibly
impressed on Scott's mind, there is reason to believe that his sense of
Border history was sharpened in the years immediately surrounding the
Dwarf by the production of *The Border Antiquities of England and Scotland* (1814–17), which incorporated new materials from Scott, and
the Introduction to which he finally completed in 1817.[5]

Topography. In a letter to James Skene in 1829 Scott stressed that
much of the landscape in the story was imaginary: 'Of the places in
the Black Dwarf Meikle stane Moor Ellisla[w] Earnscliff are all & each
vox et praeterea Nihil [a voice and nothing more]'.[6] Only Westburnflat
was 'a real spot', and that a poor one for the pencil. The response,
partly conditioned by Skene's preoccupation with scenic illustration,
is not matched by Scott's *Quarterly* review of *Tales of my Landlord*,
which pictures Hobbie Elliot and Earnscliff (in Ch. 2) 'returning by
night from their sports on the hills of Liddesdale'.[7] It is interesting to
note that in the manuscript Hobbie is first described as returning from
'Tudhope-fit [foot]' (this was changed in the course of writing to
Inger-fell-foot), and that Hobbie's main home was originally Mossphadraig (a more complicated changeover led to its replacement by
Heugh-foot). Tudhope Hill is on the north-east border of Dumfriesshire, overlooking the upper Hermitage Water part of Liddesdale,
some 8 km NW of of Hermitage Castle. Mossphadraig is probably
based on Mosspatrickhope, an ancient farm, roughly midway between
Tudhope Hill and Hermitage Castle, close to the larger farm of Braidlie.
Both were within striking distance of Milburnholm, where Scott stayed
on the first of his Liddesdale 'raids', and there is a strong likelihood

that he had travelled in that direction himself. The manuscript in this respect offers an unique insight into the process whereby known localities in Liddesdale, usually those with ballad associations, are transposed into the larger imaginative landscape which provides the setting for Scott's Border story. In the Explanatory Notes references will be found to other localities that have survived by name: Westburnflat, at the junction of Liddel and Hermitage waters, the nearby old town of Castleton, once an important settlement, Turner's-holm, near Kershopefoot, at the Border line between England and Scotland. The participants in the story also look out to broader horizons: from the 'Hie Te'iot' (Upper Teviotdale) in the North to Brough-under-Stanmore over the Border to the South; from Tarras Water in the West (where Hobbie wishes he were drowned) to Jedburgh in the East (to which he looks for Law). Ingredients from other areas known to Scott, including Durham and Northumberland, are also assimilated in the form of place names and surnames, constructing a landscape which is at once specific and ideal. Surprisingly little, however, appears to have been contributed by the Manor Valley, in Peeblesshire, the home of the Dwarf's most obvious prototype, David Ritchie.

Principal characters. The importance of David Ritchie as a model for the character of the Black Dwarf has already been discussed (see 'Essay on the Text', 132). Scott's Introduction (1830) in the Magnum Opus edition acknowledged the debt in some detail, while arguably obscuring an equally influential source from Border folklore. Hobbie Elliot's grandmother is convinced that the Dwarf is the 'Brown Man of the Moors' (Ch. 3). In John Leyden's ballad 'The Cout of Keeldar' (1802), first published in the *Minstrelsy*, the 'Brown Man of the Muirs' appears as a malignant supernatural being who shadows the hero to his death. Details of another moorland confrontation involving a 'Brown Dwarf', with near fatal consequences, were also sent to Scott by the Durham antiquary, Robert Surtees, in a letter of 9 November 1809.[8] Surtees's communication—which coincided with the release of other relevant materials—was undoubtedly an important catalyst in the creation of the story. Almost certainly too the 'Brown Man' linked in Scott's mind with the more familiar figure of the Brownie, a rich source of Border legend. One of the more substantiated appearances by a Brownie had come to Scott's attention via Lady Dalkeith, who late in 1802 had received information on the history of 'Gilpin Horner' from Thomas Beattie of Meikledale (near Langholm). Rather like the Dwarf in the story, Gilpin Horner had attached himself as a familiar on a farm at Todshawhill in Eskdalemuir (Dumfriesshire), before eventually disappearing in mysterious fashion at the call of his name. Lady Dalkeith's suggestion that Scott write a ballad on the subject finally resulted in Horner's transformation into the Goblin Page in *The Lay of the Last Minstrel* (1805).[9] In some respects, the Dwarf might be seen as an attempt to recast the same materials in prose. Other elements, though, went to make up the figure who is finally discovered to be a covert Laird. Much of his rhetoric derives from the Old Testament and Shakespearean drama, and an interesting correlation could be traced with the plot of *Timon of Athens*.

It is not impossible that Scott also had (the club-footed) Lord Byron
somewhere in mind. Writing to Blackwood on 22 February 1817, John
Murray noticed 'the most extraordinary coincidences' in the character
of the Dwarf; and Scott's letters in 1816 show his concern for what he
considered to be the anti-social behaviour of his fellow poet.[10]

The remaining characters in the *Dwarf* are broadly divisible into two
groups: Border folk and Jacobite conspirators. The leading Border
figures bring into play three of the most prominent clan names in Liddesdale and on the West Border. Hobbie Elliot, as 'something between
a freebooter and a peaceable though rough mountaineer of our own
times',[11] stands temporally between his ancestor Martin Elliot and the
Elliots of Milburnholm in the 1790s. Grace Armstrong's *sur*name
places her with the Armstrongs who occupied the lower part of Liddesdale, and brings to mind a line of celebrated reivers. Willie of Westburnflat is represented as one of the Grahams: long-standing occupants of
the Debateable Land on the West Border, who by the seventeenth
century had gained the reputation of being the most disorderly clan.
The character is apparently based on a real 'Willie of Westburnflat',
who was condemned for cattle-thieving *circa* 1650, though in the *Minstrelsy* this person is identified as an Armstrong and not a Graham. In his
review of *Tales* Scott acknowledged that, as 'a thorough-paced border
robber', he was 'perhaps placed somewhat too late in the story'.[12] None
of the Jacobite conspirators depict actual historical personages, though
Scott would seem to have drawn heavily for his characters on the set-
piece portraits in Lockhart's *Memoirs*.

Notwithstanding Scott's efforts at linkage, *The Black Dwarf* remains
for the most part a tale of two sources. Thematically, however, it is
possible to claim one area of overlap. By choosing 1708 as a temporal
setting Scott focused the first of his new *Tales* on a major transitional
point in Scotland's history. Both the Borderers and the Jacobite rebels
stand at comparable turning-points: Hobbie can either revert to the old
Border ways or move forward to a new domestic prosperity; the Jacobites attempt to turn back the clock of history, in an effort to restore the
feudalism of independent Scotland. In this way, *The Black Dwarf* raises
issues of national destiny and identity which continued to preoccupy
Scott in his subsequent *Tales of my Landlord*.

NOTES

1   John S. Gibson, *Playing the Scottish Card. The Franco-Jacobite Invasion of
    1708* (Edinburgh, 1988), passim. Compare Bruce Lenman, *The Jacobite
    Risings in Britain 1689–1746* (London, 1980), 89.
2   See Michael Robson, 'Sir Walter Scott's Collecting of Ballads in the
    Borders', *Transactions of the Hawick Archaeological Society* (1974), 30–33.
    The Elliot version of the ballad is printed in Francis James Child, *The
    English and Scottish Popular Ballads*, 5 vols (Boston and New York,
    1882–98), 5.249–51. For Scott's version, see *Minstrelsy of the Scottish
    Border*, ed. T. F. Henderson, 4 vols (Edinburgh, 1902), 2.1–17.
3   *Minstrelsy*, 2.159–168. Scott heard the ballad performed by the octogen-
    arian Jonathan Graham ('the Lang Quaker') at Dr John Elliot's house (see
    MS 8993, f. 99).

4 *Minstrelsy*, 4.61, 66.
5 For Scott collecting materials that later formed appendices in *Border Antiquities*, see *The Letters of Sir Walter Scott*, ed. H. J. C. Grierson, 12 vols (Edinburgh, 1932-37), 4.159. His part in the work is discussed by James C. Corson in *The Bibliotheck* 1 :1 (Autumn 1956), 23 – 26; 3 :1 (1960), 15 – 23.
6 *Letters*, 11.223; corrected from the original in MS 965, f. 203v.
7 *Quarterly Review*, 16 (January 1817), 442.
8 MS 870, ff. 29 – 30 (a paraphrase of Surtees's account appeared in a note to the Magnum Opus edition (9.6n – 7n)). For Leyden's ballad, see *Minstrelsy*, 4.259 – 276.
9 *Letters*, 1.242. See also Michael Robson, 'The Story of Gilpin Horner', *Transactions of the Hawick Archaeological Society* (1973), 12 – 19.
10 The letter is in the Murray Archives (Blackwood Correspondence). Murray extends the comparison to Claverhouse in *The Tale of Old Mortality*. For apposite comments by Scott on Byron, see *Letters*, 4.203, 234.
11 This observation, which is found at f. 21r in the holograph manuscript of Scott's review of *Tales of my Landlord* (Murray Archives), did not appear in the printed version.
12 *Quarterly Review*, 16 (January 1817), 444.

EXPLANATORY NOTES

In these notes a comprehensive attempt is made to identify Scott's sources, and all quotations, references, historical events, and historical personages; to explain proverbs; and to translate difficult or obscure language as well as Scots idioms that are likely to be unfamiliar. (Phrases are explained in the notes while single words are treated in the glossary.) The notes are designed to offer information rather than critical comment or exposition. When a quotation or allusion has not been recognised this is stated; any new information from readers will be welcomed. Proverbs are identified by reference to the third edition of Ray's *A Compleat Collection of English Proverbs*, to Ramsay's *A Collection of Scots Proverbs*, and to *The Oxford Dictionary of English Proverbs*. When quotations reproduce their sources accurately, the reference is given without comment. Biblical references are to the Authorised Version. Plays by Shakespeare are cited without authorial ascription, and references are to *William Shakespeare: The Complete Works*, edited by Peter Alexander (London and Glasgow, 1951, frequently reprinted).

The following items are distinguished by abbreviations in the notes and essays.

Border Elliots   Hon. George F. S. Elliot, *The Border Elliots and the Family of Minto* (Edinburgh, 1897).
ISet   The Interleaved Set, *Novels and Tales of the Author of Waverley*, 12 vols (Edinburgh, 1822): Vol. 7, MS 23007.
Letters   *The Letters of Sir Walter Scott*, ed. H. J. C. Grierson and others, 12 vols (London, 1932–37).
Minstrelsy   *Minstrelsy of the Scottish Border*, ed. T. F. Henderson, 4 vols (Edinburgh, 1902).
ODEP   *The Oxford Dictionary of English Proverbs*, 3rd edn, rev. F. P. Wilson (Oxford, 1970; reprinted 1989).
Poetical Works   *The Poetical Works of Sir Walter Scott, Bart.*, ed. J. G. Lockhart, 12 vols (Edinburgh, 1833–34).
Prose Works   *The Prose Works of Sir Walter Scott, Bart.*, 28 vols (Edinburgh, 1834–36).
Ramsay   Allan Ramsay, *A Collection of Scots Proverbs* (1737), in *The Works of Allan Ramsay*, ed. Alexander M. Kinghorn and Alexander Law, 5 (Edinburgh and London: Scottish Text Society, 1972), 59–133.
Ray   J[ohn] Ray, *A Compleat Collection of English Proverbs*, 3rd edn (London, 1737).

All manuscripts referred to in the notes are in the National Library of Scotland, unless otherwise stated. Information derived from the notes of the late Dr J. C. Corson is indicated by '(Corson)'. For legal matters the notes by Lord Normand (MS 23074) have been useful.

title-page   Jedidiah Cleishbotham   Jedidiah ('beloved of the Lord') is the name given to Solomon in 2 Samuel 12.25. 'Clashbottom' was a facetious name used by one of Joseph Train's corresponding 'Parish Clerks and Schoolmasters of Galloway', 'derived . . . from his using the Birch' (MS 3277, pp. 22–23); *clash* in Scots means 'strike' or 'flog'. For further discussion of the name and its origins, see 'Essay on the Text', 129–30.

title-page Gandercleugh in Scots, *cleugh* is a gorge or ravine; hence, most obviously, 'goose-hollow'.

title-page Hear, Land o' Cakes ... prent it Robert Burns, 'On the Late Captain Grose's Peregrinations thro' Scotland, collecting the Antiquities of that Kingdom' (1789), lines 1–6.

epigraph for the translated passage, see *The Life and Exploits of the ingenious gentleman Don Quixote De La Mancha Translated from the original Spanish of ... Cervantes ... by Charles Jarvis, Esq.*, 2 vols (London, 1742), 1.204. The incident occurs in Part 1, Bk 4, Ch. 5 ('Which treats of what befel *Don Quixote*'s whole company in the inn'). Jarvis's translation of Don Quixote was frequently reprinted in the 18th and early 19th centuries.

5.10 candle to the day-light matches the action of the Greek philosopher, Diogenes of Sinope (*c.* 400–*c.* 325 BC), principal representative of the Cynic school of philosophy. 'He lit a lamp in broad daylight and said, as he went about, "I am looking for a man"' (Diogenes Laertius 6.41).

5.19 threefold reflecting the divisions of presbyterian sermons; a fairly low number for a sermon, for evangelical ministers would have used more.

5.20–21 si fas sit dicere *Latin* if it is lawful to say so.

5.28 Wallace Inn named after the Scottish national hero, Sir William Wallace (*c.* 1270–1305).

5.31–32 tollman ... Wellbrae-head some 350 Acts for establishing turn-pike roads in Scotland were passed between 1750 and 1844. The right of collecting tolls was let annually; toll-houses frequently sold alcohol, sometimes without licences. See Anne Gordon, *To Move with the Times. The Story of Transport and Travel in Scotland* (Aberdeen, 1988), 36–49. Wellbrae-head is apparently a fictional name.

6.3 more kicks than halfpence i.e. more harshness than kindness; tradi-tionally known as the 'monkey's allowance' (see Francis Grose, *A Classical Dictionary of the Vulgar Tongue*, 3rd edn (London, 1796), under *Monkey*).

6.4–5 Ithacus, the most wise of the Greeks Ithacus is another name for Odysseus, the central figure of Homer's *Odyssey*. 'Wise' represents one of the standard Homeric epithets of Odysseus, which is normally used in Greek in a slightly pejorative sense ('wily' or 'cunning').

6.5 Roman poet Horace (65–8 BC). For the view of Odysseus attributed to him, see *Ars Poetica* 141–42 and *Epistles* 1.2.17–20. Both passages make broad allusion to the beginning of the *Odyssey* ('Many were those whose cities he viewed and whose minds he came to know').

6.6 Zoilus of Amphipolis (4th century BC), notorious for his censorious criticism, especially of Homer.

6.9–10 General Assembly the ultimate governing body and court of the Church of Scotland. Jedidiah's attendance as an *auditor* (a non-technical term) indicates no more than that he has listened to the debate from a public gallery.

6.11 law of patronage the Patronage Act of 1712 restored the right of lay patrons in Scotland to appoint incumbents to parishes, a source of frequent controversy in the Church of Scotland in the 18th century, leading to a number of secessions, and eventually to the great Disruption of 1843.

6.22 ye generation of vipers Matthew 23.33.

6.23 brazen serpents see Numbers 21.9.

6.25–26 ye are caught ... yawned for you see Psalm 57.6.

6.39–41 destruction of hares ... unlawful seasons legislation for the preservation of game in Scotland dates from the 15th century. The Act of 1773 (13 Geo. III c. 54), in force in Scott's time, determined the close season for muir fowl (10 Dec.–12 Aug.), heath fowl (10 Dec.–20 Aug.), partridge (1 Feb.–1 Sept.) and pheasant (1 Feb.–1 Oct.). Section 3 of the same act fixed penalties for 'every Person whatsoever ... who shall have in his or her Custody ... any

Hares, Partidges, Pheasants, Muir Fowl, Tarmagans, Heath Fowl, Snipes, or Quails, without the Leave or Order of a Person qualified to kill Game in *Scotland*'. Rabbits, though included in Jedidiah's list, were not treated as game.

6.42   great of the earth   the right to hunt was a property right: a proprietor could hunt on his own land, and on the land of another if he had a right (called a *servitude*) to do so.

7.3–4   deceptio visus   *Latin* deception of sight; a mistake of the eye.

7.6   eo nomine   *Latin* by that name.

7.8–9   distillation . . . licence   the earliest record of a spirit being distilled from barley in Scotland dates from the late 15th century. In the 18th century, the manufacture of spirits increasingly attracted the attention of tax-hungry governments, with the prohibition of small private stills in 1781 and drastic increases in duty from 1793 as a means of funding the war with France. One effect was to encourage the growth of illicit distilling and smuggling. The Act 54 Geo. III. c. 172 (1814) shifted the charging of duty on spirits from still capacity to volume produced, with substantial increases overall, and set a fee of £10 for a licence to distil in Scotland. Similar legislation, designed to protect the London distillers, depressed Scottish production; the situation was exacerbated by the Corn laws and failures in the harvest, and many legal distilleries in the Highlands and Lowlands were closed. In April 1816, Lowland distillers petitioned the Chancellor of Exchequer, claiming that legislation encouraged illicit distillation. The Act 55 Geo. III c. 106, which received the royal assent in July, harmonised the system in Scotland by abolishing distinctions between the Highlands and Lowlands; it also allowed the granting of permission to use smaller stills and permitted weaker washes, with beneficial results throughout the industry. Jedidiah's references to moonshining could hardly have come at a more topical moment.

7.10–11   gauging-stick   implement used for calculating the contents of a cask or other vessel. Excisemen (*gaugers*) collected duties at local level, and were popularly disliked; they were specially rewarded by the authorities for detecting illicit stills.

7.12   aqua vitæ   *Latin literally* water of life; commonly used to describe alcohol in a number of forms, but once applying in Scotland to plain malt spirit as opposed to compounded cordials. Exemptions on 'spirits made from malt, and retailed, and consumed in *Scotland*, and commonly called and known there by the name of *aquavitae*' are noted in Henry Mackay, *An Abridgement of the Excise-Laws . . .* (Edinburgh, 1779), 337. The exemption had been repealed by Jedidiah's time, so perhaps he is using the term in a somewhat wistful, nostalgic way.

7.32   quarter-day   when payment of rent and other quarterly charges customarily fell due.

8.4   Peter, or Patrick, Pattieson   it was not uncommon for Patrick, a Gaelic name, to be 'anglicised' as Peter in the Lowlands of Scotland. Pattieson's full name perhaps hints at a Highland ancestry, linking him with an ancient bardic tradition. 'Patie' is a diminutive of Patrick; while *paiter* in Scots means to 'patter', or 'chatter on endlessly'.

8.12–17   Mr Thomas Carey . . . ballad rhime   Thomas Carew (1594/5–1640), pronounced 'Carey', whose 'An Elegie upon the Death of the Deane of Pauls, Dr. John Donne' (1633), lines 61–2, 68–9, is quoted. In Donne's *Poems, 1633*, where the elegy was published, the author is given as 'Mr Tho: Carie'.

8.26   one cunning in the trade . . . of bookselling   a compliment to John Ballantyne (1774–1821), Scott's friend and literary agent. Ballantyne's career as a commissioning bookseller (in the then synonymous sense of publisher) was brought to a close in 1816 by the formal dissolution of John Ballantyne & Co., though the firm (where Scott was a partner) had virtually ceased trading as an independent house after a financial crisis in 1813.

8.34–37   the Dean of St Patrick's … sine qua non   Jonathan Swift was appointed Dean of St Patrick's Cathedral, Dublin, in 1713. The extract that follows is from 'Dr. Sw— to Mr. P–e, while he was writing the *Dunciad*' (1732), lines 19–20, in which Swift claims that his deafness (by preventing conversation) has been a contributory factor in the writing of *The Dunciad*. Literally translated, the Latin *causa sine qua non* is 'a cause without which not': in other words, a necessary cause. Jedidiah is saying that without him the *Tales* would never have seen the light of day in their present form.

11.4   motto   *As You Like It*, 3.2.21.

11.11   dreadnought overalls   outer garment made of a stout woollen cloth with thick long pile.

11.17–18   stained with tar   tar was used for marking (*buisting*) and smearing sheep, more especially the latter. Smearing was a means of protection against vermin and the weather in pre-dip days.

11.29   the south hie-lands   the Border hill country.

12.7   Canny Elshie   *canny* in Scots normally indicates skilfulness and shrewdness, but in this kind of combination (e.g. 'canny man') can intimate that a person deals in the supernatural. On the Borders it also signified a good, kind, or likeable sort of person. In Elshie's case the epithet forms part of a complete nickname, apparently combining elements from all these meanings.

12.13   Bauldie   an abbreviation of Archibald.

12.13–15   blackfaces … lang sheep   while still common in large parts of southern Scotland in 1800, the 'blackface' breed of sheep was being replaced in several areas by 'Cheviot' sheep, notably from the eastern Borders. The Cheviots were polled, smooth faced, and had unmixed white fleeces. The body and especially the tail were long: the most obvious derivation of the descriptive phrases 'long sheep' (Cheviots) and 'short sheep' (blackfaces), used to distinguish the two breeds. For a fuller account, see Michael J. H. Robson, *Sheep of the Borders* (Newcastleton, 1988).

12.18   pu'd doun to make park dykes   pulled down to make field walls, a not improbable fate for many of the peel-houses (fortified towers) that fell into neglect after the pacification of the Borders. The process continued into Scott's time: William Laidlaw's reminiscences of Scott record how he and Scott were disturbed by a proposal of Robert Ballantyne in Dryhope, Yarrow, to dismantle the tower there for dyke-building—'a Conclusion that was, and had been, only too Common and likely to happen' (Edinburgh University Laing MSS II 281/2, f. 17).

12.19   the bonny broomy knowe   the 'broomy knowe [knoll]' is reminiscent of the traditional song, 'The Broom of Cowdenknows' (see *Minstrelsy*, 3.43–50). A similar motif featured in *An Elegy on David Ritchie* (Edinburgh, 1812), the first known publication on Ritchie: 'On yon green know, wi' planting drest,/ His frail remains he wish'd to rest' (stanza 16).

12.22   riven out wi' the pleugh   the ploughing of new arable land is characteristic of the agricultural revolution in the later 18th century, when turnips were increasingly grown as winter food for livestock. High prices and the Corn Laws in the early 19th century led to a renewed breaking up of pasture ground.

12.36–37   short sheep had short rents   while sometimes gaining the security of longer tenure, tenant farmers in southern Scotland faced escalating rents in the period 1780 to 1815. Buccleuch estate farms rents were greatly increased around 1790–92, when Cheviot (long) sheep were replacing blackfaces and when wool prices were rising; but there was no lengthening of tenancies, which, after a period (in the 1790s) of reverting to one year, eventually settled at nine years after 1800. For 'short sheep' see note to 12.13–15.

13.4   It's the woo'   a similar incident, involving Scott as the questioner, occurred during an evening (probably in July 1802) at Ramseycleuch, Ettrick, when James Hogg and William Laidlaw were present. The earliest account is in Robert Chambers, *Illustrations of the Author of Waverley*, 2nd edn (Edinburgh, 1825), 93. Hogg's own version appeared in 'My First Interview with Sir Walter Scott', *Edinburgh Literary Journal*, 2 (1829), 51–52; see also his *Memoir of the Author's Life and Familiar Anecdotes of Sir Walter Scott*, ed. Douglas S. Mack (Edinburgh and London, 1972), 61–63, 136–38.

13.10–11   plack and bawbee   to the last penny, to the full. Based on two Scots coins of low value: *plack* (usually valued at four pennies Scots) and *bawbee* (six pennies Scots, equivalent to a halfpenny sterling).

13.14   luckpenny   small sum of money given as a symbol of a bargain. In Scots law, it merely constitutes evidence that a contract has been completed. According to Robert Chambers, the dispute with Christy Wilson had 'its origin in a process once before the Court of Session, respecting what is termed a *luck-penny* on a bargain' (*Illustrations of the Author of Waverley*, 2nd edn (Edinburgh, 1825), 94).

13.15   St Boswells fair   held on 18 July at St Boswells, near Melrose, Roxburghshire; in Scott's time, one of the largest in Scotland for livestock, wool, and general business.

13.20   against ane o'clock   towards (or near) one o'clock.

13.22   crack . . . like a pen-gun   keep up a continual flow of conversation. A *pen-gun* is a kind of pop-gun made from a bird's quill; the expression involves an element of punning on *crack* (*Scots* 'to gossip').

13.26   gentlemen of the long robe   lawyers; more specifically, in this case, the judges of the Court of Session (the Supreme Court in Scotland for civil matters).

13.36–37   He that . . . to keep   see Allan Ramsay, *The Gentle Shepherd* (1725), 1.1.47–48.

14.14   motto   *The Merry Wives of Windsor*, 5.5.102.

14.18–19   Halbert, or Hobbie Elliot   Scott's suggestion that Hobbie represents a form of Halbert (compare *Minstrelsy*, 1.365n) overlooks the more obvious origin of Hob as a diminutive of Robert (see *Border Elliots*, 559). See also note to 15.41–42.

14.19–20   old Martin Elliot of the Preakin-tower   Martin Elliot of Braidlie (fl. 1560–95), a leading member of the Elliot clan in Liddesdale (*Border Elliots*, 77, 129, 161), whose activities occasionally touched on national events (see *Minstrelsy*, 2.94). Elliot moved to a tower at Prickinghaugh, near Larriston, in about 1584. 'Martin Elliot of the Preakin Tower' is acknowledged as an alternative hero to 'auld Buccleuch' in Scott's Introduction to 'Jamie Telfer of the Fair Dodhead' in *Minstrelsy*, 2.1.

14.28   union of the crowns   brought about by the accession of James VI of Scotland to the throne of England in 1603. This encouraged a sometimes ruthless process of 'pacification' on the Borders, leading to a widespread dispersal of the old 'reiving' clans.

14.34   black cattle   beef-cattle, which traditionally dominated the agriculture of the Highlands and south-west Scotland. Compare Scott's letter on 'depopulation' to Lord Dalkeith in 1806: 'It must also be considered that during the 17th Century there was comparatively little of our Border country occupied by sheepwalks. Black cattle were in high estimation & the number of hands necessary to to attend this kind of stock is much more numerous than that requisite for sheep' (*Letters*, 1.332).

15.7   Scottish Act of Security   passed by the Scottish Parliament in 1703. According to its provisions, in the event of Queen Anne's death without issue, the Scottish Parliament would be vested with the right of choosing a Protestant successor of the royal line to the Scottish throne.

15.10 Godolphin Sidney Godolphin, first Earl of Godolphin (1645–1712), Lord High Treasurer under Queen Anne; generally acknowledged as the leading English promoter of the Union of 1707.

15.12–13 an incorporating union a full integration of the parliaments of the two kingdoms, combining the two nations under one government. A body of opinion in Scotland had argued instead for a federal union.

15.19–20 Cameronians . . . house of Stuart the Cameronians, extreme Presbyterians so named after their leader Richard Cameron (d. 1680), were persecuted during the later Stuart period (1660–88) for their refusal to accept the authority of the King in spiritual matters. In 1706, at a time of widespread Jacobite conspiracy in Scotland, armed Cameronians marched into Dumfries and burned the Articles of Union at the Market Cross. According to Scott in *Tales of a Grandfather* (Ch. 60: *Prose Works*, 25.81–84), plans had existed to co-ordinate a fuller uprising in the West with another in the Highlands.

15.25–26 trained to arms the Act of Security (see note to 15.7) ended with an order that heritors (landed proprietors) and burghs provide themselves with arms for all the Protestant fencible (able-bodied, between 16 and 60) men in the country, and train them in their use at least once a month.

15.40 the Heugh-foot *heugh* (a crag, or steep bank) is common in Scottish place names. Hobbie's farm, while apparently fictional, has strong Liddesdale associations. 'Hobbe Ellot of the Hewghus' was listed as one of 'The Ellottes of Lyddisdall' in 1583 (*The Border Papers*, ed. Joseph Bain, 2 vols (Edinburgh, 1894–96), 1.121); 'doughty Cuddy in the Heugh-head' appears in 'The Fray of Suport', *Minstrelsy*, 2.162. The definite article ('*the* Heugh-foot') is still used in the district when describing farming establishments.

15.41–42 Elliots . . . christian name Hob [Robert] Elliot was an especially common combination: the index to volume one (1894) of Bain's *Border Papers* (see previous note), covering the period 1560–94, includes more than twenty Hob Ell(i)ots with various nicknames based on place, paternity, or personal attributes. The form 'Hobb*ie*' is not found in contemporary records.

16.3 Meikle-stane-Moor *literally* big stone moor. Later said by Scott to be imaginary (*Letters*, 11.223), though the name invites comparison with a number of localities. 'Meikle Land Rig' is found on John Thomson's map of southern Roxburghshire (1822) 5 km NW of Hermitage Castle; Meikledale, in Dumfriesshire, 8 km N of Langholm, had long been associated with the Elliot clan and was the home of Thomas Beattie, Scott's informant about Gilpin Horner (see 'Historical Note', 203). There is also a Mickleton Moor 12 km NW of Barnard Castle, Durham.

16.13–14 Grey Geese the legend follows the pattern of numerous traditional stories involving transformation into stone (see Motif A 977.4, 'The devil turns object or animal to stone which is still seen', in Stith Thompson, *Motif-Index of Folk-Literature*, 6 vols (Copenhagen, 1955–58), 1.180). Stories of petrification relate to a number of stone circles in Britain: notably, the Rollright Stones (a king and his army) in Oxfordshire; the 'Bride and her Maidens' (victims of transgression at a wedding party), at Stanton Drew, Avon; Long Meg and Her Daughters, Hunsonby, Cumbria (witches turned to stone). Similar legends are connected with stone formations in the Borders, such as the Hownam Shearers, Brethren Stanes, and Nine Stane Rig, all in Roxburghshire.

More particular similarities can be found in a legend about a stone formation at Adlestrop, Gloucestershire, which formed the basis of a poem communicated to the *Gentleman's Magazine* for April 1808: 'It is . . . pretended that as an old woman was driving her geese to pasture upon Addlestrop hill, she was met by one of the Weird Sisters, who demanded alms, and upon being refused, converted the whole flock into so many stones, which have ever since retained the name of the Grey Geese of Addlestrop Hill'. (Corson) According to the correspondent, these stones had been dismantled by Warren Hastings to help build a cascade on his grounds at Daylesford (*Gentleman's Magazine*, 78, 341).

16.19–20 rings…calcined 'fairy rings' caused by fungus; the grass sometimes looks brown as if scorched.

16.38 Ovid Roman poet (43 BC–AD 18), author of *Metamorphoses*. Several of his characters are turned to stone—Battus and Aglauros in Bk 2, those affected by the Gorgon's head in Bk 5, and Niobe in Bk 6—though the comparison here seems to be more general than specific.

16.39 the angel whom she served see Macbeth, 5.8.14.

17.4 praisers of the past 'laudator temporis acti' (Horace, *Ars Poetica*, 173).

17.9 kelpies, spunkies kelpies are water spirits, normally in the form of horses; spunkies are 'will o' the wisps', mischievous rather than evil (like Puck).

17.17 like the clown in Hallowe'en see Robert Burns, 'Halloween' (1784), lines 163–64. Burns's rustic ('fechtan [fighting] *Jamie Fleck*') whistles '*lord Lenox' march*' to keep up his courage during a Halloween night dare.

17.18 Jock of the Side one of the raiding Border ballads (*Minstrelsy*, 2.93–109), in which a rescue attempt on Newcastle gaol is successfully mounted by Hobbie Noble and others. Scott obtained the tune of the ballad from John Elliot of Whithaugh on one of his early visits to Liddesdale. Robert Shortreed recalled having woken Scott at Whithaugh with the same song: 'He sprang ow'r the bed & cam to the door saying such a wakening was worth the whole journey—He was vera wild abt. Jock o' the Side then—We had just gotten the Ballad & the air a bittie before' (Shortreed Papers, MS 8993, f. 106).

17.24 of that ilk of the place of the same name (i.e. 'Earnscliff of Earnscliff'), a form often used in the designations of landed proprietors in Scotland.

17.33 Caillie Cleugh probably fictional. A *cleugh* is a gorge or ravine; 'Caillie' perhaps derives from *coille*, the Gaelic for 'wood': as in *capercailzie* ('wood-grouse') and the place name Kailzie, 3 km SE of Peebles. For Scott on the *capercailzie*, see *Letters*, 2.318.

17.35 De'il a fear no fear. *De'il* (devil), when used in such phrases in Scots, expresses strong negation.

17.37 Inger-fell-foot probably fictional. For a possible origin, see 'Historical Note', 202.

18.4 mair be token especially, in particular.

19.29 Davie o' the Stenhouse *Stenhouse* ('stone house') is a common place-name in Scotland, and in the Borders would probably have signified a peel-tower.

19.36 Loudon folk people of the Lothians (the region in central Scotland round Edinburgh).

20.6 Jeddart variant form of Jedburgh, royal burgh and county town of Roxburghshire.

20.7 Rood-day in Roxburghshire, 25 September, the date of the Jedburgh Rood-fair. In a note to *The Lay of the Last Minstrel* (1805) Scott quotes from the Scottish air, 'Rattling Roaring Willie': 'Now Willie's gane to Jeddart,/ And he's for the *rood-day*' (*Poetical Works*, 6.279).

20.20–23 motto John Leyden, 'The Cout of Keeldar' (1802), stanza 18.

20.28 wading moving through cloud or mist. The picture given is that of the moon being shrunk and watered-down by a veil of cloud. Some shepherds would say that it was a 'bad sign'.

21.9–10 hirples like a hen on a het girdle hobbles like a hen on a hot griddle (flat iron pan for baking); proverbial (see *ODEP*, 369), usually indicating restlessness or anxiety. Compare William Tennant, *Anster Fair* (1812), 6.54: 'As would a hen leap on a fire-hot griddle,/ So leap'd the mustard-pot toward the table's middle' (*The Comic Poems of William Tennant*, ed. Alexander Scott and Maurice Lindsay (Edinburgh, 1989), 93).

21.12   better a saft road as bad company   found in proverb books only after Scott, and perhaps his creation. *Saft* is used in the Scots sense of wet or damp.

21.33   Tarras-flow   i.e. Tarras marsh. Tarras Water, Dumfriesshire, rises on Hartsgarth Fell and flows into the Esk, 4 km SE of Langholm. It was surrounded by tracts of marsh, which formed part of the Debateable Land and provided refuge for the Armstrongs and other Borderers. 'The morass itself is so deep, that, according to an old historian, two spears tied together would not reach the bottom' (*Minstrelsy*, 1.331).

21.39–40   Humphrey Ettercap, the tinkler   an *ettercap* in Scots is a spider, but can also signify a spiteful or quarrelsome person. A *tinkler* (tinker) was an itinerant tinsmith or pedlar, though the term is also used derogatively for any kind of coarse, foul-mouthed or abusive person.

21.41–42   a thought bigger in the bouk   somewhat bigger in the body.

22.9–10   noose for woodcocks   compare *Hamlet*, 1.3.115 ('springes to catch woodcocks').

23.31   the Chamberlain   a *chamberlain* supervised the management of country estates in Scotland. In the early 18th century tenancies of farms belonging to the Duke of Buccleuch in Liddesdale were administered by a local chamberlain, though at a later date (c. 1768) the Buccleuch Estates came under the control of one central chamberlain. The Liddesdale chamberlain resided at Roan, 2 km N of Newcastleton.

23.31   Mossphadraig   probably based on Mosspatrickhope, site of an ancient farm about 3 km NW of Hermitage Castle. It was subsumed c. 1640 into the nearby Braidlie farm, and might at one point have been its 'led farm' (see next note). Scott's gaelicised form (*Pàdraig* is Gaelic for Patrick) brings out Celtic origins in the name.

23.32   led farm   a smaller or outlying farm on which the tenant does not reside. According to the minister of Castleton in 1795: 'Farms are styled *led*, when one tenant possesses two or more, and does not reside on them' (*Statistical Account of Scotland*, ed. Sir John Sinclair, 21 vols (Edinburgh, 1791–99), 16.69n).

23.36–37   high-school of Edinburgh   the Edinburgh High School, a medieval foundation, which occupied the same building on the south side of the Cowgate in Edinburgh from 1578 until rebuilding in 1777; Scott was a pupil from 1779 before attending Edinburgh College (University) in 1783.

24.4   Levitical law   the degrees of consanguinity within which marriage is forbidden in Leviticus 18.6–18. In Scotland the Marriage Act 1567, c. 16, permitted marriage to first cousins; the Incest Act 1567, c. 15, passed by the Scottish Parliament on the same day, defined incest by reference to Leviticus 18. At the time Scott wrote, the two Acts were generally construed together to make the prohibited degrees of relationship for marriage and the criminal law prohibiting incest the same. The prohibitions on marriage according to the Canon Law of the Roman Catholic Church were considerably more extended.

24.20   Love me, love my dog   proverbial (Ramsay, 98; Ray, 98; *ODEP*, 492).

25.12   coif and pinners   a close-fitting cap, with two flaps pinned on and hanging down, sometimes fastened at the front; worn by women, especially of rank, in the 17th and 18th centuries.

25.25   the gathering peat   a large piece of peat or turf laid on the embers to keep a fire alive over a long period.

25.29–30   buck's horn to blaw on   proverbial (see *ODEP*, 70).

25.38   cadger carrying calves   *cadgers* ('travelling hawkers') often worked from single horses in country districts; in the Borders they collected sheepskins from farms, and there is no reason why they should not have picked up and carried dead calves in the way indicated. Compare 'Jock o' the Side', stanza 8: 'Like gentlemen ye mauna seem,/ But look like corn-caugers ga'en the road' (*Minstrelsy*, 2.100).

26.1   has nae every dog his day   proverbial: 'Every dog has his day' (Ramsay, 76; Ray, 98; *ODEP*, 195).

26.6–7   whirling a bit stick . . . boring at a clout   the actions of spinning and sewing.

26.17   the Enemy himsel   i.e. the Devil.

26.18   Peghts   Pics, inhabitants of ancient Scotland. 'Castles, remarkable for size, strength, and antiquity, are, by the common people, commonly attributed to the Picts, or Pechs' (*Minstrelsy*, 4.275).

26.20–21   Brown Man of the Moors   a supernatural being: similar in several respects to the Brownie (commonly associated with the Borders), but more malevolent in character. For fuller discussion of one of Scott's more important sources, see 'Historical Note', 203.

26.21   weary fa'   a curse upon, woe betide. A similar use of *weary* is found in 'weary on' at 26.23.

26.23   living in luve and law   *love* (standing for agreement and peace) and *law* (the application of rules) were common oppositions in medieval times, and *lovedays* were days on which disputes were settled. In this sense, 'living in luve and law' would mean living in peace and under settled government. See Michael Clanchy, 'Law and Love in the Middle Ages', in *Disputes and Settlements. Law and Human Relations in the West*, ed. John Bossy (Cambridge, 1983), 47–67.

26.25–27   Marston-Moor . . . Bothwell-Brigg   alluding to a sequence of military actions, each of which had devastating effects on the losers. At Marston Moor, fought on a plain near York in 1644, the forces of Charles I suffered a crushing blow in the Civil War; royalist hopes in Scotland were dashed by the defeat of the Marquis of Montrose (1612–50) in 1645 at Philiphaugh, near Selkirk, which was followed by a massacre of prisoners; at Dunbar, in 1650, the Scottish army was overwhelmed by Cromwell's forces, leaving the country open to occupation; the battle of Bothwell Bridge, fought in 1679, ended in carnage as the defeated Covenanters fled into wild country. Another linking factor is that each battle was fought on or near open moorland and/or close to the Border country.

26.28   second-sighted Laird of Benarbuck   apparently fictional. Similar sounding names appear in Robert Law's *Memorialls*, ed. Charles Kirkpatrick Sharpe (Edinburgh, 1818): e.g. 'the Laird of Bardowie, in Badernock parish' (109) and 'the Laird of Barbigno in Stirling' (162). The gift of 'second sight', allowing the foretelling of events, is most commonly associated with Gaelic prophets.

26.29   Argyle's landing   on the coast of Kintyre, at the start of an abortive rebellion in Scotland. Archibald Campbell, ninth Earl of Argyll, was subsequently beheaded in Edinburgh on 30 June 1685.

26.31–32   the day of trouble   see Psalms 20.1, 50.15.

27.2   by others   more than others.

27.23–25   motto   *Timon of Athens*, 4.3.52–54.

27.32   feind o' me will   I certainly won't (*feind* means literally 'the devil').

28.9   suldna ca' them fairies   stemming from a taboo against using the proper name for any spirit or dangerous creature (circumlocutions such as 'good neighbours' or 'little people' still survive).

28.12–14   heard ane whistle . . . drink   many such accounts survive in folklore, and the association with drink is common. See e.g. James Hogg's account of an encounter between the fairies and his grandfather, Will Laidlaw of

Phaup, in *Blackwood's Edinburgh Magazine*, 21:124 (April 1827), 442–43.

28.26 dry-stane dyke stone wall built without mortar.

29.5 rood...march-dyke building walls by the rood (usually 18 feet: 5.4 metres) was a common activity in the 18th century; a *march-dyke* provided a boundary line between farms.

29.6 Cringlehope and the Shaws Cringlehope is probably imaginary. A farm called the Shaws has long existed in Liddesdale: 'Hab of the Schawis' is named in Maitland's 'Complaynt aganis the Thievis of Liddisdail' (*Minstrelsy*, 1.189) and in other papers in the 16th century (see *Border Elliots*, 81). In 1708 it was a small place, prior to the merging of other holdings to form the present Shaws farm. 'The Shaws' (signifying wooded ground) is also a common name used for farms in Scotland.

31.22–23 philosopher's application . . . alone see Cicero, *De Officiis* (44 BC), 3.1, recounting a story about Publius Scipio Africanus ('that Scipio used to say that he was never less idle than when he had nothing to do and never less lonely than when he was alone').

31.32–33 Auld Ane...shadow 'Auld Ane' is another name for the devil. Spirits are believed to cast no shadow.

32.20 Elshender a version of Alexander.

32.22 Wise Wight wise man, a variation of the more common term 'wise wife'. Compare Scott's account of 'Agnes Sampson, or Samson, the Wise Wife of Keith': 'This grave dame . . . seems to have been a kind of white witch, affecting to cure diseases by words and charms,—a dangerous profession, considering the times [late 16th century] in which she lived' (*Letters on Demonology and Witchcraft*, 2nd edn (London, 1831), 300).

32.42 Morai name given to temples constructed from stone in the shape of a pyramid. Their use as burial grounds and as places of worship was observed on Captain Cook's visit to Otaheite (Tahiti) in 1769 (see *An Account of the Voyages . . . for making Discoveries in the Southern Hemisphere, drawn up . . . by John Hawkesworth*, 3 vols (London, 1773), 2.166–68). Scott's interest in Tahiti was perhaps aroused by John Ballantyne, who at this time encouraged James Hogg to write a story or poem on the 'innocent Otaheitans' (see MS 2245, f. 11).

33.21 curiosity on mute fishes compare Izaac Walton on 'this pleasant curiositie of Fish and Fishing' (Epistle Dedicatory to *The Compleat Angler*, 1653).

33.24 Behemoth biblical animal, thought by some to be the hippopotamus. See Job 40.15–24. Compare *Letters*, 2.318.

33.37 young Ruthwin the name invites comparison with Alexander Ruthven, the younger of two brothers stabbed to death in the Gowrie Conspiracy, an alleged assassination attempt on James VI in 1600. A broadside ballad, 'The Young Ruthven', subsequently claimed the true cause of the slaying of Ruthven lay in the king's jealousy.

33.38 beneath the tower the bottom storey in peel-towers was used as a store room, the floors above being reached by a narrow staircase; in times of danger cattle were also housed on the ground floor.

33.39 the Red Reiver of Westburnflat 'one of the last Border robbers', according to Scott's note in the Interleaved Set. 'He is probably placed about forty or fifty years too late by introducing him in the beginning of the Eighteenth Century. He is said to have [been] condemnd to death at the last circuit Court of Justiciary which was held in the town of Selkirk When the Judge was about to pronounce sentence the prisoner arose and being a man of great strength broke asunder one of the benches and seizing on a fragment was about to fight his way out of the Court House. But his companions in misfortune for several persons had been convicted along with him held his hands and implored him to permit them to die the death of Christians & both he and they agreeable to their decorous desire had full honours of Rope and Gallows.' (ISet, 91)

Similar details are given in Scott's Introduction to 'Johnie Armstrang', in *Minstrelsy*, 1.338–39, where '*Willie of Westburnflat*' is said to have been arrested with nine friends and condemned 'at the last Circuit Court held at Selkirk'. The last Justiciary Court at Selkirk, according to Thomas Craig-Brown's *The History of Selkirkshire* (2 vols, Edinburgh 1886), was held on 10 July 1649. Craig-Brown adds: 'A tradition concerning the execution of ten men at a time in Selkirk is supposed to refer to a "vindication of the law" after this court' (2.62). This would seem to corroborate Scott's statements that his character is based on a historical figure. The title of 'Red Reiver', however, is almost certainly a fictional embellishment.

For similarities between the fictional Westburnflat and William Armstrong of Gilnockie, hero of Scott's 'Christie's Will', see 'Historical Note', 202. West-burnflat as a location is discussed in note to 58.41–42.

33.40   my skill recovered him   *skill* here denotes medical skill specifically.

33.42   sleuth-hound   a bloodhound. 'Our ancient statutes inform us, that the bloodhound, or sluith-hound (so called from its quality of tracing the slot, or track, of men and animals), was early used in the pursuit and detection of marauders' (*Minstrelsy*, 2.128–29). Their use as watch-dogs is documented in the notes to 'The Fray of Suport' (*Minstrelsy*, 2.166–67).

35.1–2   the beasts that perish   Psalm 49.12, 20.

35.7   mammocks   shreds, broken or torn pieces: a term found in Jacobean and Restoration drama (see e.g. *Coriolanus*, 1.3.65; William Wycherley, *The Plain-Dealer* (1677), 4.1).

35.9   pot-sherd   *literally* a fragment of a broken earthenware pot. There are a number of biblical references to God as a potter (creator), with divine retribution being likened to a breaking of the pot in pieces. See Isaiah 30.14, Psalm 2.9.

35.35   Enemy of Mankind   the Devil.

36.2–7   motto   not identified: probably by Scott.

37.9–16   an endless chase . . . flung aside   compare Alexander Pope, *Moral Essays*, Epistle 2, 'Of the Characters of Women' (1735), lines 231–48.

37.13   spadille and basto   the ace of spades and clubs in ombre and quadrille, fashionable card games in the early 18th century. See also Alexander Pope, *The Rape of the Lock* (1714), 3.49-54.

39.9–10   Japan cabinet   a cabinet that has been *japanned* ('lacquered'). Considerable quantities of furniture decorated in this way were imported in the late 17th and early 18th centuries; the best came from Japan, and ornate cabinets (usually incorporating oriental designs in bright colours) were the most highly prized.

39.12   Canton and Pekin   Canton, the leading port for sending Chinese porcelain to Europe, also developed in the 18th century as a centre for painting and enamelling. Pekin(g) or Beijing, the imperial capital of China from 1421, was not noted for the *manufacture* of porcelain; 'Pekin ware', famous in Scott's time, probably derived its name from the Emperor's collection. Monsters and fabulous animals, such as dragons, are commonly found in Chinese porcelain, sometimes modelled as statuettes.

39.23   magic natural   once regarded as a legitimate science, as opposed to 'black magic' or 'necromancy'. See Geoffrey Chaucer, *The Canterbury Tales*, 'General Prologue', lines 415–16.

39.26–27   Gorgon's head   the head of Medusa, one of three Gorgon sisters, which in classical legend retained its petrifying power even after her slaying by Perseus.

39.42–43   nineteen nay-says are half a grant   proverbial (see Ramsay, 103; *ODEP*, 567).

40.43–41.1 Elliot..Jaffeir...Pierre characters from *Venice Preserv'd; or, a Plot Discover'd* (1682), by Thomas Otway. Otway's play remained popular throughout the 18th century: performances included its staging at Drury Lane on 9 May 1707 (a few days after the conclusion of the Act of Union) and a revival at Covent Garden in 1811, with Charles Kemble and Mrs Siddons amongst the cast. In the story, Jaffeir's friendship with Pierre surmounts his exposure of a planned coup d'état to which he had been introduced by Pierre; at the end, Jaffeir stabs Pierre (then himself) to avoid the indignity of his friend's public execution. Eliot, an Englishman, is one of the minor conspirators.

41.4 an eagle and a rock *earn* is Scots for an eagle: hence 'Earnscliff'.

41.10 Renaults and Bedamars Bedamar leads the conspiracy in Otway's *Venice Preserv'd* (see note to 40.43–41.1); Renault, another prominent conspirator, is notable for his lechery and bloodthirstiness.

41.25–26 slashed doublets and trunk-hose articles of male dress, fashionable in the early 17th century. A *doublet* was a close-fitting jacket; when 'slashed' it had vertical slits to show a contrasting lining. *Trunk-hose* were bag-like breeches, sometimes stuffed with wool or other materials.

41.41 as lief touch a toad compare *Romeo and Juliet*, 2.4.196–97 ('but she, good soul, had as lief see a toad, a very toad, as see him').

42.9–11 motto *1 Henry IV*, 1.2.22–25.

42.40 buff jacket leather coats, called 'jaks', were worn by the Border reivers (see Robert Bruce Armstrong, *The History of Liddesdale* (Edinburgh, 1883), 79–80).

43.13–14 When the devil...monk was he proverbial (see Ramsay, 110; Ray, 231; *ODEP*, 184). An early example in its English verse form is found in Peter le Motteux's translation (1694) of Rabelais (*Gargantua and Patangruel*, Bk 4, Ch. 24).

43.40 burrows-town *Scots* a borough; here, in effect, Edinburgh.

43.42 Auld Reekie nickname for Edinburgh ('Old Smokey').

44.5 Ba'-spiel on Fastern's E'en football (more like rugby than soccer) was traditionally played in Border towns and villages in early spring, from Candlemas to Fastern's E'en (Shrove Tuesday). For an account of the game played on Fastern's E'en between the villages of Kirk Yetholm and Town Yetholm, 'the toughest foot-ball match now played in the south of Scotland', see 'Notices Concerning the Scottish Gypsies' [partly by Scott], *Edinburgh Monthly [Blackwood's] Magazine*, 1:2 (May 1817), 155.

44.6 Country Keeper a kind of early police officer, appointed by magistrates in Northumberland and Cumberland; for an annual fee they undertook to protect their districts against theft and make good losses at their own expense. In Cumberland the office came into being as a result of legislation against Border moss-troopers in 1662, and died out in the 1750s. For an account of activities in Northumberland, see Scott's *Border Antiquities of England and Scotland*, 2 vols (London, 1814–17), Vol. 2, Appendix 13, xciii. The activities of Country Keepers in Northumberland are also mentioned in Robert Surtees's letter to Scott on 9 November 1809 (MS 870, f. 30v).

44.19 part of the horse which he bestrode like the 'gentleman of Normandy' in *Hamlet*, 4.7.85–88.

45.15–19 motto Thomas Campbell (1777–1844), 'Lochiel's Warning' (1801), lines 24, 38–40. In the poem, a Highland seer warns of impending disaster as Cameron of Lochiel prepares to support Prince Charles Edward in the 1745 rebellion.

46.10–11 Canny Hobbie Elliot...alang wi' you in the ballad style, evidently Scott's invention.

46.14–16 scent of the goat...fly upon them a similar incident, according to James Skene, was witnessed by Scott when riding to Blackhouse, near St

Mary's Loch, Selkirkshire (*c.* 1805): 'After all, the dogs were not so much to blame for mistaking the game flavour of the luckless capricorn for legitimate sport, as the fog effectually hid the object of pursuit from their sight as well as from ours' (*Memories of Sir Walter Scott*, ed. Basil Thompson (London, 1909), 35–36).

46.26   Let a be   let alone. See also *ODEP*, 456.

46.27   Killbuck   an old name for a hunting dog. 'Kilbuck' is mentioned as an otter hunter in Izaac Walton's *Compleat Angler* (1653) (Ch. 2); 'Kilbucke' also appears in George Chapman's *The Gentleman Usher* (1606), 1.1. A greyhound belonging to Scott's father, called 'Kill-buck', is referred to in a note to *The Abbot* (Magnum, 20.172).

47.17   on a sled   i.e. a sledge, capable of being pulled along rough tracks. Scott is supposed to have taken the first wheeled carriage into Liddesdale (see J. G. Lockhart, *Memoirs of the Life of Sir Walter Scott, Bart.*, 7 vols (Edinburgh, 1837–38), 1.195).

47.18   Riders' Slack   *slack*, indicating a pass, is common in Scottish place names.

47.18–19   Dallom-lea, as the sang says   'Dallom-lea' is perhaps related to Day-holm, on the Scottish side of the river Kershope, a traditional meeting-place for the Border wardens. No song has been identified.

47.36   a hundred strapping Elliots   it has been calculated that between 350 and 450 men belonging to the Elliot clan inhabited Liddesdale in the late 16th century (see *Border Elliots*, 50)

47.36   ride the brouze   'The Brouze a fashion not yet out of date at Country bridals. The best mounted gallants present gallop as first [*sic*] as they can from the Church to the Brides door and the first who arrives gets a silk handkerchief or some such token. The name seems to be taken from the dish of *brose* with which he who won the race was anciently regaled.' (ISet note, interleaf facing 97).
The custom was common on the Borders and in other parts of Scotland, though the prize could be whisky or ale; Scott's derivation of *brouze* from *brose* (a kind of soup made from meal) apparently confuses two distinct terms.

47.40   common herd   see Horace, *Epistles*, 1.19.19: 'o imitatores, servum pecus' ('you mimics, you slavish herd').

48.15   scouther . . . tar-barrel   Hobbie has in mind burning, rather than simply daubing, with tar. *Scouther* (*Scots* a scorching) is glossed in ISet as a 'singing [*sic*] bout' (interleaf facing 98). Compare Scott's ballad 'Christie's Will': 'I have tar-barrell'd mony a witch' (*Minstrelsy*, 4.72).

48.15–16   five parishes   not identified. The parish of Castleton in Scott's time embraced virtually the whole of the Liddesdale area. In 1793, however, its minister reported that there had been 'no less than 5 chapels or churches in the parish, besides the parish church' (*Statistical Account of Scotland*, ed. Sir John Sinclair, 21 vols (Edinburgh 1791–99), 16.71). A more obvious grouping of five parishes (Westerker, Eskdalemuir, Staplegorton, Wauchope and Ewes) existed in Eskdale, in the area of Langholm.

48.22   Banquo's murderer   see *Macbeth*, 3.4.12.

48.28   a toom byre and a wide   an empty and wide-open cowhouse. The same words are found in 'The Fray of Suport', stanza 1 ('Nought left me . . ./ But a toom byre and a wide' (*Minstrelsy*, 2.161)).

48.31–32   Charlie Cheat-the-Woodie . . . Charlie Forster of Finning-beck   apparently Scott's invention. The nickname signifies an ability to avoid the gallows (*woodie* in Scots means the gallows rope). Forster was a common surname just south of the Border, in north Cumberland; *beck* is the Cumbrian word for a 'brook', and *finning* perhaps indicates the pursuit of fishing.

48.40   away to the plantations   many 17th and 18th-century emigrants to

America and the West Indies plantations got their passages free from ship's captains, who received payment by selling them as indentured servants on arrival. Some captains extended this to kidnapped youths and others unlikely to be missed, and burgh authorities at times used the trade to dispose of of poor children who might prove a financial burden or a threat to law and order.

49.6 Castle-hill at Jeddart at the head of Castlegate, in Jedburgh. It was the site of Jedburgh Castle and is now the location of the Castle Jail, built *c.* 1823. John Ainslie's plan of Jedburgh (*c.* 1780) names Castle Hill and marks on it 'Galows'. Wholesale executions took place in Jedburgh during the 'pacification' of the Borders. For Jeddart, see note to 20.6.

50.12 for ordinar normally, as a rule.

50.20 like a tragic volume see *2 Henry IV*, 1.1.60–61.

51.6–7 wars in Flanders ... wi' Buccleuch two expeditions to Flanders were undertaken by the Buccleuchs in the 17th century. In 1604 Sir Walter Scott of Buccleuch took a body of 200 men to the Netherlands to aid the States-General against Spain, an expedition which lasted until 1608. Walter, second Lord Scott of Buccleuch (succeeded 1611, created Earl of Buccleuch in 1619), embarked on a similar campaign in 1627, an event recalled from memory in Walter Scott of Satchells's *A true History of ... the .. Name of Scot* (1688), lines 29–39. In a note in ISet (interleaf facing 104), Scott mentions only the departure of the first Lord of Buccleuch ('auld Buccleuch' of the ballads) with a 'legion of Borderers'. On the other hand, Scott's most obvious source is Satchells; and when originally writing he may have had in mind the second engagement (itself closer to the likely lifespan of Hobbie's 'gude-sire'). In the MS Scott wrote 'wi' Buccleuch'; this appeared as 'wi' auld Buccleuch' in the first edition. The change implies some misunderstanding of the reference and the chronology, and was possibly not made by Scott.

51.26 make mair help take on more support.

51.40 lawful mode of following a fray alluding to the 'Border Laws', developed over the years by the wardens of each kingdom, particularly those relating to 'hot trod' (literally, a 'warm footprint'). Under the rules of 'hot trod' offended parties could make fresh pursuit of stolen goods over the Border, subject to various conditions.

51.41 Tam o' Whittram presumably an imaginary descendant of 'old Sim of Whittram', identified by Robert Carey in the late 16th century as chief of the outlawed Armstrongs (see *Memoirs of Robert Carey ...*, ed. Scott (Edinburgh, 1808), 101). 'Whittram' is a corruption of Whithaugh, 0.5 km N of Newcastleton, once the main seat of the Armstrongs in Liddesdale.

51.41–42 the hard winter the 'ill winter' of 1673–74 laid waste ground in Liddesdale for up to three years; lost sheep led to widespread bankruptcies amongst Border farmers.

51.43–52.1 great gathering ... Thirlwall ... Philiphaugh not identified as an event. Thirlwall Castle is a ruined fortress near Hadrian's Wall, some 25 km SE into England from Liddesdale. Protests against depredations on the Borders were made on several occasions in the Civil War years: e.g. in 1645 the Scottish Parliament registered complaints from the county of Northumberland concerning 'the moss Troupere or brokine men in the borderes' (*The Acts of the Parliament of Scotland*, Vol. 6, Pt 1 (1870), 401). For the battle of Philiphaugh, fought in 1645, see note to 26.25–27.

52.8 Dundrennan ... Black Douglas Dundrennan Abbey, founded in 1142, is on the Solway Firth about 6km SE of of Kirkcudbright. Here it is apparently a mistake for Lincluden, 2 km N of Dumfries, transformed in the late 14th century from a Benedictine nunnery into a collegiate church, on the petition of Archibald de Douglas, lord of Galloway. The idea of 'the Black Douglas' as a Border law-giver largely derives from the ancient record of a meeting held at

Lincluden in 1448 to establish 'The statutis and use of merchis in tym of were':
According to its preamble: 'Erl Williame of Douglas assemblit the haill lordis,
frehaldiris, eldest bordouraris that best knawlege had at the college of Lynclow-
den. And thair he gert thai lordis and bordouraris be bodily suorne the haly
awangelis tuichit that thai lelely and trewly efter thair connyng and knawlege
suld decret, decern, deliuer, and put in wryt the statutis, ordinancis, and use of
merchis that was ordanit to be kepit in blak Archibald of Douglas dais and
Achibald his sonnis dayis in tyme of weifar' (*The Acts of the Parliament of
Scotland*, 1 (1844), 350). Black Archibald of Douglas, also called Archibald the
Grim, is identifiable as Sir Archibald Douglas (d. 1400), lord of Galloway,
Warden of the West Marches, and third Earl of Douglas (for his patronage of
Lincluden, see above).

Other members of the family have also been called the 'black Douglas'. In
Hume of Godscroft the title is given to William Lord of Nithsdale (d. 1392?),
'sonne naturall to *Archbald* Lord of Galloway', and 'of a blacke and swart com-
plexion': 'his name was terrible to the English, especially of the common sort,
who did ordinarily affright and skare their children, when they would not be
quiet, by saying, The blacke *Douglas* comes, the blacke *Douglas* will get thee'
(*History of the Houses of Douglas and Angus* (Edinburgh, 1644), 108). In *Tales of
a Grandfather* (Ch. 11: *Prose Works*, 22.174), Scott associates the name with
Robert Bruce's renowned follower, Sir James Douglas (1286?–1330). The
title is also sometimes used generically to distinguish the Black from the Red
Douglases (the Angus line). Perhaps one should not expect too much precision
in defining an almost legendary name.

52.11   Cuddy the muckle tasker   'muckle tasker' would normally indicate
an agricultural piece-worker or labourer of large build. The phrase echoes
Alexander Pennecuik (d. 1730): 'The meikle tasker, Davie Dallas . . .' (*A
Collection of Scots Poems on Several Occasions* (Edinburgh, 1769), 7; quoted in
Minstrelsy, 1.164).

53.15   moss-troopers   a term used in the 17th century to describe lawless
men on the Borders; it derives from their frequenting the moss country of the
wastes, through which troops of them passed on secretive expeditions for plunder. See also note to 51.43–52.1.

53.20   knapscap   a skullcap, metal headpiece. Originally shaped like a metal
bowl, in Elizabethan times it was being replaced by more elaborate helmets.
Compare 'Jamie Telfer of the Fair Dodhead', stanza 35: 'But Willie was
stricken ower the head,/ And thro' the knapscap the sword has gane' (*Minstrelsy*,
2.10).

54.2–5   motto   the last two lines of verse match stanza 25 of 'Jamie Telfer of
the Fair Dodhead' (see *Minstrelsy*, 2.8). The first two have no connection with
the ballad, and are apparently Scott's invention. 'Horse and Hattock' in folklore
are words used by witches and fairies before flying. An account of the trans-
portation to France of an ancestor of Lord Duffus, through their agency, is
cited from John Aubrey's *Miscellanies* (1696) in *Minstrelsy*, 2.366–68. Another
source known to Scott was the confessions (1662) of the Scottish witch, Isobel
Gowdie: 'The witches bestrode either corn straws, bean stalks, or rushes, and
calling "Horse and Hattock, in the Devil's name!" which is the elfin signal for
mounting, they flew wherever they listed' (*Letters on Demonology and Witchcraft*,
2nd edn (London, 1831), 158). For another instance of Scott improvising on
'Jamie Telfer', see *Letters*, 4.125.

54.28   Ringleburn   not identified; probably a variation of Rankleburn, in
Ettrick, one of the oldest possessions of the Scotts of Buccleuch. See *The Lay of
the Last Minstrel* (1805), Canto 4, stanza 14 (*Poetical Works*, 6.135), where it
appears as 'Rangleburn'.

54.40–55.1   Græme's-gap   'Fargy Grame's gap' is mentioned in stanza 9 of 'The Fray of Suport' (*Minstrelsy*, 2.164).

55.3   the Trysting-pool   a trysting place was a location, usually a well-known landmark, employed as a rendezvous. No specific site has been identified in this case, but see note to 63.24.

57.9   a band for some o' the siller   a *band* ('bond'), as used here, was a written undertaking to pay. The form *band* is common in older Scots law books (e.g., in Sir George Mackenzie's *The Institutions of the Law of Scotland*, 2nd edn (Edinburgh, 1688)). As on other occasions, *siller* is used to signify money generally.

57.10   wadset   a conveyance of land by a debtor to his creditor as a security for the repayment of the debt. The debtor had power to compel the reconveyance to him of the land on payment of the debt.

57.10   Wideopen   among several instances of this name in the Border region, there is an ancient farmstead 4 km S of Hownam, in SE Roxburghshire.

57.12   sclate-stanes   pieces of slate or slate-like stones: a term frequently used in proverbs and similes alluding to money. According to popular superstition, money given by the the devil as a reward for service, though having the appearance of good coin, would turn into slate the following day.

57.19   the Cat-rail   'A strange boundary ditch seemingly design'd to defend the Celtic or Gaelick portion of the south against the invasions of the Saxons.' (ISet note, interleaf facing 117) The Cat-rail runs for about 20 km in a north-westerly direction, with some breaks, from a southern point approximately 8 km NE of Hermitage Castle. Scott's view that it served as a boundary between the Strathclyde Britons and Saxon colonists from the north is echoed by some later commentators, though the question of origins is still a matter of debate. Geographically, it might be said to divide the West Border hill country from the fringes of the main Lowland area of Scotland.

57.32   Jock o' the Tod-holes   i.e. of the fox-holes. Probably Scott's invention, though the Canonbie district, immediately SW of Liddesdale, had a 'Todholewood' (now Todhillwood) and a 'Todcleugh', both farm holdings in the 17th century. There is also a Todhills in Cumbria, 8 km NW of Carlisle.

58.24   James VIII   James Francis Edward Stuart (1688–1766), son of the exiled James VII of Scotland and II of England, recognised by France as King of England, Scotland and Ireland in 1701.

58.41–42   the Tower of Westburnflat   Westburnflat, a small tract of grassland on the south bank of Liddel Water near its junction with Hermitage Water, is now unoccupied. Old Ordnance Survey maps (almost certainly as a result of Scott's influence) record the site of a tower at Westburnflat; but no other evidence of a peel-tower having stood there has survived. Scott's description, however, invites comparison with the remains of Liddel Castle, at Castleton, and the old Whithaugh Tower, situated 1.5 km downstream from Westburnflat on the same bank of Liddel Water.

59.31–36   motto   not identified; probably by Scott.

60.13–14   the Lowdens   the Lothians, the region in central Scotland around Edinburgh.

60.28   Græme   another prominent Border name, albeit contradicting Scott's account of Westburnflat as an Armstrong in *Minstrelsy*, 1.338. The Grahams lived on both sides of the West Border, but normally not in Liddesdale, and were notorious for their dual allegiances. They were savagely persecuted during the reign of James VI and I.

60.37   Baudrons   familiar name for a cat (similar to the English *puss*). Compare Scott's ballad 'Christie's Will': 'And whiles a voice on *Baudrons* cried' (*Minstrelsy*, 4.71).

61.11   the king's keys   'The Kings keys for searching lock-fast places if peaceful entrance be refused are the broad axe and crow-bar. Entrance in a word is forced.' (ISet note, interleaf facing 125).

61.14   Threatened folks live lang   proverbial (Ray, 162; *ODEP*, 815).

63.7   the Castleton   the settlement of (old) Castleton, 3.5 km NE of New-castleton, was virtually unoccupied by Scott's day. Consisting of a castle, church, customs house and an inn, it was once an important focal point in Liddesdale.

63.24   Turner's-holm   located by Scott in a Magnum note at the junction of Liddel Water and the river Crissop (Kershope); i.e. on the other side of the Liddel from Kershopefoot, Cumbria. 'It is said to have derived its name as being a place frequently assigned for tourneys, during the ancient Border times' (Magnum, 9.101n). The location also features in the ballad 'Hobbie Noble': 'At Kershope foot the tryst was set,/ Kershope of the lilye lee' (see *Minstrelsy*, 2.116, 119).

63.27   white feather in his wing   proverbial (see *ODEP*, 885), indicating cowardice. According to Francis Grose, 'an allusion to a game cock, where having a white feather is a proof he is not of the true game breed' (*A Classical Dictionary of the Vulgar Tongue*, 3rd edn (London, 1796), under *White Feather*).

64.8   Haud a care   take care, beware.

64.26–27   A' the men o' the Mearns ... than they dow   a popular saying in Scotland, according to Robert Chambers, who quotes as from Aberdeen-shire: 'I can dae fat I dow [do what I can]: the men o' the Mearns can dae nae mair' (*Popular Rhymes of Scotland*, 3rd edn (Edinburgh, 1858), 70). The Mearns is an area of Kincardineshire, south of Aberdeen.

65.10   slaughter under trust   the murder of one 'under the traiste [trust] credite assurance and power of ye slayer' (Act 1587, c. 34): treated as treason in Scots law until 1708.

65.31–34   motto   probably by Scott, though the theme is traditional. It is found in *Rokeby* (1813), Canto 3, after stanza 28: 'This morn is merry June, I trow,/ The rose is budding fain;/ But she shall bloom in winter snow,/ Ere we two meet again' (*Poetical Works*, 9.156). Compare David Herd, *Ancient and Modern Scottish Songs*, 2 vols (Edinburgh, 1776), 2.6: 'False luve! and hae ze played me this,/ In the simmer, 'mid the flowers?/ I sall repay ze back again,/ In the winter 'mid the showers'. The latter is quoted in *Waverley* (1814), 1.118.15–18.

66.22   deepest pool o' Tarras   see note to 21.33.

68.41   stoop and roop   completely, entirely; 'lock, stock, and barrel'.

69.2–3   Sir Thomas Kittleloof   burlesque name, indicating a willingness to take bribes; *Kittleloof* in Scots means 'tickle palm'.

69.5   commisioners at the Union   thirty-one Scottish commissioners were appointed to negotiate terms with their English counterparts in London. Only three of the thirty-one subsequently voted against the Treaty of Union when debated in the Scottish Parliament. Accusations of bribery and corruption were widespread in Scotland.

69.10   Laird o' Dunder   a fictitious name, perhaps suggested by Sir David and Lady Dunder of Dunder Hall, characters in George Colman the younger's play, *Ways and Means; or, A Trip to Dover* (1788) (see *Letters*, 6.201). (Corson)

69.10–11   Tiviotdale   Teviotdale, in Roxburghshire.

69.12   tolbooth ... heart of Mid-Lowden   a reference to the old Edin-burgh prison, demolished in 1817, ironically known as 'the Heart of Mid-Lothian'.

69.13   Saunders Wyliecoat   in Scots a 'wyliecoat' is an under-garment, usually of flannel, worn by men for extra warmth.

69.42   broken cisterns   Jeremiah 2.13.

70.3–4   suldna be suffered to live   see Exodus 22.18: 'Thou shalt not suffer a witch to live'.

70.4   wizard and the witch   the law on witchcraft in Scotland was regulated by the Act 1563 c. 9, which provided for the penalty of death for those practising witchcraft, sorcery, and necromancy and for those who consulted them. It was not repealed until 1735. Wizards are listed with witches as an 'abomination unto the Lord' in Deuteronomy 18.10–12.

70.12   Fastern's E'en   Shrove Tuesday: unlike Hallowe'en, not normally associated with witches' revels.

70.15   Brough under Stanmore   in Westmorland (now part of Cumbria), 10 km SE of Appleby. Brough is mentioned in the last stanza of the ballad 'Dick o' the Cow': 'And at Burgh under Stanmuir there dwells he' (*Minstrelsy*, 2.89).

70.19   moor-ill . . . louping-ill   red-water, a disease of cattle; and a disease of sheep, symptomised by leaping. According to James Hogg, 'the *Leaping-ill*' severely impeded sheep-farming in the 18th century (see *The Shepherd's Guide* (Edinburgh, 1807), 75–82).

70.21   flying in the face of Providence   proverbial (*ODEP*, 270).

70.26   his bark is waur than his bite   proverbial (Ramsay, 87; *ODEP*, 30).

70.29   first skreigh o' morning   first light; crack of dawn.

70.39   speak truth, and shame the de'il   proverbial (Ramsay, 108; Ray, 163; *ODEP*, 807).

71.16   finely flung   well and truly cheated.

71.17   make mair fit   hurry up; move on faster.

71.41   Beelzebub   a Philistine god, but commonly used as an alternative name for the Devil.

72.6–7   what shapes . . . fright a body   it was commonly believed that witches and wizards had the power of transforming themselves into animals. In *Letters on Demonology and Witchcraft* (1830), Scott cites the spectacular 'confessions' of the Scottish 'witch', Isobel Gowdie: 'Metamorphoses were, according to Isobel, very common among them, and the forms of crows, cats, hares, and other animals, were on such occasions assumed' (2nd edn, London 1831, 278–79).

72.21   no canny   unnatural, supernatural.

73.16   liferenter . . . fiar   in Scots law a *liferenter* has a right to use and enjoy (without destroying or wasting the substance) some property owned by another, who is called the *fiar*. In the present case, Hobbie Elliot's grandmother would be liferenter of Wideopen in right of her husband, Hobbie's grandfather, with Hobbie as fiar.

73.17   heritable band   for *band* ('bond') see notes to 57.9 and 57.10. In Scots law a *heritable* bond was a written declaration to pay money with a conveyance of land to the creditor for his security.

73.17–18   annual rent   *Scots law* old technical term for the interest on a loan. Hobbie's vow to pay it 'half yearly' is not self-contradictory.

73.28–29   at Jeddart   as a royal burgh Jedburgh (Jeddart) had its own burgh court. It was also a circuit town for the High Court of Justiciary under the Courts Act 1672, c. 40, and as such a relatively important legal centre.

73.30   famous witnesses   *Scots law* witnesses of good repute.

74.4–9   motto   loosely following the published version of Samuel Taylor Coleridge's 'Christabel' (begun 1797, published 1816), lines 81–84, 89–90. Scott first heard the poem recited by Dr John Stoddart, *c.* 1800, and is here possibly quoting from memory.

74.19–20   To hear was to obey   this command had recently appeared in Lord Byron's 'The Bride of Abydos' (1813), line 44: 'Pacha! to hear is to obey'. In Byron's poem, which Scott had read with 'great delight' (*Letters*, 3.396), Giaffir is giving orders preparatory to telling his daughter (Zuleika) to marry the Bey of Carasman, whom she has never seen. More generally, the statement reflects the tone of command and instant submission found in popular oriental tales such as the *Arabian Nights Entertainments* and James Ridley's *Tales of the Genii* (1764).

76.16–17   over dale and down, through moss and moor   compare 'Hobbie Noble', stanza 13: 'He has guided them o'er moss and muir,/ O'er hill and hope, and mony a down' (*Minstrelsy*, 2.121).

79.30   young Marischal of Marischal-Wells   apparently a fictional character. The name and some aspects of his temperament suggest an affinity with William Keith (d.1712), ninth Earl Marischal, one of the Scottish opponents of the Union and a leading (if unreliable) Jacobite conspirator in 1708. According to George Lockhart of Carnwath: 'E M——l of *Scotland* was Master of a quick and lively Spirit, a great Vivacity of Wit, an undaunted Courage, and in short, of a Soul capable of doing great Things. But his Misfortune was, he could not seriously . . . apply himself to Business, being loose and irregular in his Measures, and too bent on his Pleasures. However, being a Man of Honour and Capacity, he was always faithful to his Prince and Country, did them both great Service, and merited much from them' (*Memoirs Concerning the Affairs of Scotland* (London, 1714), 181). Marischal's youthfulness and idealism, on the other hand, are closer to the circumstances of the Earl of Derwentwater (1689–1716), executed after the Jacobite rebellion of 1715.

'Marischal-*Wells*' was perhaps suggested by Wells House in Rule Water, Roxburghshire, built in Queen Anne's reign. The nearby estate of Abbotrule belonged to Scott's friend, Charles Kerr (1767–1821), whose erratic nature also invites comparison with Marischal; Abbotrule was also the starting-point of Scott's earliest excursion into Liddesdale. See George Tancred of Weens, *Rulewater and its People* (Edinburgh, 1907), 180–81, 198–209.

80.6   the Pretender   name give to James VIII by his Hanoverian opponents. For the political events alluded to here, see 'Historical Note', 200.

80.25–26   motto   *Othello*, 1.1.177–78.

81.8–9   honest to his principles   *honest* was a favourite catchword of the Jacobites, indicating loyalty to the cause.

81.10–11   tow on his distaff   business to attend to. Proverbial: see *ODEP*, 834.

83.3   Hie Te'iot   High Teviot: i.e. Upper Teviotdale, in Roxburghshire. The region is associated with the early history of the Scotts of Buccleuch, but was also settled by the Elliots (see *Border Elliots*, 93).

83.24   at sharps   with unbated (unblunted) swords; in earnest.

84.6   under-spur-leathers   subordinate attendants, menials beneath notice. Literally, a 'spur-leather' is a strap for fastening a spur; in referring to the non-gentry members of the conspiracy in these terms Ellieslaw is showing what a snob he is.

84.10–11   ripe for the sickle . . . reapers   see Revelation 14.15.

84.12–13   the more mischief the better sport   proverbial (Ramsay, 112; *ODEP*, 534). Lord Lovat is said to have used these words at his execution, on hearing that a collapsed gallery had killed many spectators. Lovat had been sentenced to death for treason after the failure of the Jacobite rebellion of 1745. See *Tales of A Grandfather*, Ch. 85: *Prose Works*, 26.391.

85.1   old Gilliecrankie-man   a veteran of the battle of Killiecrankie, fought in 1689, at which a predominantly Highland army loyal to James VII and II defeated the Protestant forces of William III. The form *Gillicrankie* is common in Jacobite songs celebrating the victory, both in Latin and Scots.

85.2   bought and sold   echoing the refrain of a traditional Jacobite song, best-known in Burns's version: 'We're bought and sold for English gold,/ Such a parcel of rogues in a nation!' (see *Poems and Songs of Robert Burns*, ed. James Kinsley, 3 vols (Oxford, 1968), 2.643–44, 3.1404). The widespread bribery of the Scottish nobility (a historical fact) was a common theme in anti-Union protest.

85.8 better soon than syne sooner rather than later: a variant of the old expression 'soon or syne' (see also *ODEP*, 752).

85.9 as Sir John Falstaff says a rather loose version follows of his speech in *1 Henry IV*, 2.4.478–81.

85.10 the old end of the ballad the quatrain that follows closely matches the chorus in Robert Burns's song 'McPherson's Farewell' (published 1788), though Burns acknowledged this part of his poem was not his (see *Poems and Songs of Robert Burns*, ed. James Kinsley, 3 vols (Oxford, 1968), 1.385–86, 3.1261–62). In his 1809 review of R. H. Cromek's *Reliques of Burns*, Scott stated that 'McPherson's Lament' was a well-known song 'many years' before its adaptation by Burns (*Prose Works*, 17.259–60). James MacPherson, leader of a gang of Highland cattle-thieves, was executed at Banff in November 1700.

85.26–30 motto *1 Henry IV*, 5.1.74–78.

86.10–11 Forster and Derwentwater Thomas Forster (1675?–1738), MP for Northumberland, and James Radcliffe (1689–1716), third Earl of Derwentwater, leaders of the abortive uprising in the Northern England during the Jacobite rebellion in 1715.

86.12 Douglas Robert Douglas, leader of a troop of volunteers in Derwentwater's rebellion: 'He was indefatigable in searching for Arms and Horses, a Trade, some were pleased to say, he had follow'd out of the Rebellon [*sic*] as well as in it' (Robert Patten, *The History of the Late Rebellion . . .* , 2nd edn (London, 1717), 63). Scott follows Patten's identification of him as a brother of the Laird of Fingland, in Teviotdale, in *Letters*, 3.246.

86.13 Luck-in-a-Bag Thomas Armstrong, a notorious horse-stealer in Cumberland, *c.* 1700 (see Scott, *Border Antiquities of England and Scotland*, Vol. 2 (1817), Appendix 13, xciv, xcvi). His nickname also occurs in an anecdote related by Robert Patten, concerning the reaction of an 'old Borderer' to news that 'the loose Fellows and suspected Horse-stealers were gone into the Rebellion': '. . . I can leave my Stable-Door unlock'd, and sleep sound, since Luck-in-a-Bag and the rest are gone' (*History of the Late Rebellion*, 2nd edn, 1717, 64). Patten glosses *Luck-in-a-Bag* as *'A Nick-name to a famous Midnight Trader among Horses'*, though no mention is made of him having held a command in Robert Douglas's troop.

86.28 battle of Sark a bloody engagement, fought near Gretna on the West Border in 1449, at which the Scots triumphed over the English.

86.38 Beneath the salt-cellar traditionally the salt-box stood near the centre of the table, dividing the guests from the retainers who sat below it. For notices on the custom and its origins, see the *Edinburgh Monthly [Blackwood's] Magazine*, 1 (1816), 33–35, 132–34, 579–82.

86.39 sine nomine turba *Latin* literally a crowd without a name; a group of people where there is no one of consequence or worth noticing.

87.7 all the delicacies of the season a phrase current in Scott's day. Compare *Blackwood's Magazine* on 'the habit of giving dinners, "with every delicacy of the season"' (21:122 (February 1827), 212).

87.13–16 P. P., Clerk of this Parish . . . Sir Thomas Truby characters from Alexander Pope's 'Memoirs of P. P. Clerk of This Parish' (published 1727). Allusion is made in particular to the following passage: 'I said within myself, "Remember, *Paul*, thou standest before Men of high Worship, the wise Mr. Justice *Freeman*, . . . the good Lady *Jones*, . . . nay, the great Sir *Thomas Truby*"' (*The Prose Works of Alexander Pope*, ed. Rosemary Cowler, 2 vols (Oxford, 1986), 2.111). Scott humorously likens himself to P. P. in *Letters*, 1.45.

88.5 when will you lift *lift* in Scots can mean to carry out a corpse for burial, to start a funeral procession.

88.6   the Knight of Langley-dale   compare Scott's lines in 'Jock of Hazel-dean' (1816): 'Young Frank is chief of Erington,/ And lord of Langley-dale' (stanza 2 : *Poetical Works*, 11.316). 'Langley-dale' also features in a poem communicated by Robert Surtees to Scott on 9 November 1809, glossed by Surtees as 'a beautiful vale' belonging to Raby Castle (Durham), and the site of 'an old tower . . . said to have been the residence of a Mistress of the last Earl of Westmoreland' (see MS 870, f. 30r). Langley Beck runs through the grounds of Raby Castle, joining the River Tees 10 km E of Barnard Castle.

88.17   of D——   presumably of Derwentwater, though strictly speaking the period is too early for the third Earl (see note to 86.10–11). The dash is characteristic of coded messages and 'secret histories' at this time.

88.19–22   What's he that wishes . . . doomed to die   Marischal appropriates elements from an exchange between the Earl of Westmoreland and King Henry in *Henry V*, 4.3.16–20.

88.30   leap the ditch   paralleling the biblical expression, to leap a wall (see 2 Samuel 22.30, Psalm 18.29).

88.33   qualified guests   i.e. those of higher rank, with better qualifications to be present. The term *qualified* was also used in the 18th century with reference to Scottish Episcopalians who had renounced allegiance to the Jacobite monarchy, and Scott is perhaps also playing on this special sense.

89.1   with a witness   with clear evidence, without a doubt (the phrase has something of the force of 'with a vengeance'). Compare *The Taming of the Shrew*, 5.1.105 ('Here's packing, with a witness, to deceive us all!').

89.14   old John Rewcastle   Rewcastle is a farm (once Rue Castle), 3 km W of Jeburgh. It became a fairly common surname in Hawick, perhaps rather more so there than in Jedburgh.

89.15   Jedburgh smuggler   the smuggling of English goods (e.g. cloth, grain, and small luxuries) over the Border was established on a fairly wide scale by the beginning of the 18th century, with little interference from the Scottish authorities. Jedburgh served as a major thoroughfare. After the Union of 1707, however, the existing English system of excise administration was extended to Scotland—a highly unpopular move since it was more efficient than the Scots system and made smuggling more difficult. See T. C. Smout, *Scottish Trade on the Eve of the Union, 1660–1707* (Edinburgh and London, 1963), passim.

89.20   Episcopal meeting-house at Kirkwhistle   Episcopal meeting houses ministered to by clergy who refused to take the oath of allegiance were kept up in several areas of Scotland after the establishment of Presbyterianism in Scotland by William III. At the time of Union, which confirmed the authority of the Kirk, Episcopalianism was the creed of most Jacobites. Kirkwhistle is apparently a fictional location.

89.27–28   Englified justice of the peace   the office was originally introduced into Scotland by James VI on the English model and was strengthened after the Union in 1707; but because of the different structure of local government, and the role of the Sheriff, it never achieved much importance.

89.30   Darien and Glencoe   focal points of anti-English sentiment. The ill-success of the attempted Scots colony at Darien (on the Isthmus of Panama), culminating with a disastrous expedition in 1699, was widely held to have been engineered by William III and the English trading interest. The massacre in 1692 of the Macdonalds of Glencoe, whose chief had failed to meet the deadline given to Highland clans for taking the oath of allegiance, was organised by hardliners in the Whig administration in Scotland acting under general instructions from William.

89.36   Green and the English thieves   Captain Thomas Green of the English ship the *Worcester*, executed on trumped-up charges of piracy, along with two of his crew, at Leith sands in 1705. Historians agree in seeing him as a victim of resentment against England in the wake of the Darien scheme (see previous note).

89.38   Cockpool and Whitehaven   on different sides of the Solway Firth. Whitehaven is in Cumbria, England. Cockpool, the site of an old Castle and now a tiny settlement, is close to the mouth of Lochar Water, 2.5 km W of Ruthwell, in Dumfriesshire.

90.2   cess, press, presbytery   the land tax, military service, and Presbyterian religion, all allegedly imposed on Scotland by William III. The three appear together in the Jacobite song, 'To daunton me': 'Eighty-eight, and eighty-nine,/ And a' the dreary Years since Syne,/ With Sess and Press, and Presbytry,/ Good Faith, this had liken till a daunton me' (*A Collection of Loyal Songs, Poems, &c. Printed in the Year 1750*, 70).

90.2   old Willie   William III.

90.6   Country-Keeper   see note to 44.6.

90.21   stone walls have ears   proverbial (*ODEP*, 864).

91.31   vogue la galère   *French* row out the galley; i.e. here goes, come what may. See [Alain-René] Le Sage and d'Oreneval, *Le Théâtre de la Foire*, 10 vols (Paris, 1737), Air 98: 'Et vogue la galère tant qu'elle'.

92.1–2   house of James ... now at Dunkirk   Scott is parodying the rudimentary codes used by Jacobite correspondents in the period. For the embarkation of the French fleet from Dunkirk with James VIII on board, see 'Historical Note', 200.

92.4   break bulk   to open the hold and take goods from a ship; to begin to unload.

92.9   Nihil   *Latin* nothing; perhaps echoing the aphorism 'ex nihilo nihil est' ('out of nothing comes nothing').

92.27–28   unprovided of men and ammunition   these words echo closely George Lockhart of Carnwath's account: 'The regular Troops wanted Ammunition and other Warlike Stores ... all the Garrisons were unprovided, and must have yielded at the first Summons' (*Memoirs Concerning the Affairs of Scotland* (London, 1714), 364).

92.32   go the vole   win all the tricks at cards; run every risk in the hope of great gain.

95.2–3   motto   James Thomson (1700–48), *Tancred and Sigismunda* (1745), 3.3.18–19.

95.37–38   every nerve bent up   compare *Macbeth*, 1.7.79–80 ('I am settled, and bend up/ Each corporal agent to this terrible feat').

99.1   fixed as Cheviot   the Cheviot (815m) is the highest point of the Cheviots, the range of hills dividing Scotland from England.

99.7   à très bon marché   *French* very cheaply, at little expense. The expression was used by Scott when writing to his friend, Charles Kerr, in May 1795 (see *Letters*, 1.39).

99.9–10   marry in haste ... repent at leisure   proverbial (Ramsay, 99; Ray, 43; *ODEP*, 515).

100.30–32   motto   see Edmund Spenser, *The Faerie Queene* (1590), 1.9.35.

104.4–5   cold-blooded Stoicism   the Stoic school of philosophy, founded in Athens in the 4th century BC, was noted for its doctrine of intellectual detachment from the vicissitudes of fortune. Ratcliffe's Stoicism is juxtaposed with the Cynicism expressed by the Dwarf.

104.11   fiat of Nature   i.e. the command of natural creation. The term *fiat* invites comparison with the pronouncement 'Fiat lux' ('Let there be light'), at Genesis 1.3 in the Vulgate (Latin Bible).

104.40   breaking on the wheel   an old form of execution; the prisoner was stretched tight on a wheel and the bones in his limbs broken.

105.24–25   year's close imprisonment ... manslaughter   *manslaughter* is the English legal term analogous to the Scottish term 'culpable homicide'. While a person convicted of murder would be sentenced to death, one convicted of culpable homicide would suffer a lesser penalty. The judge had discretion as to the length of a prison sentence, and there is no evidence to suggest that a 'year's close imprisonment' was a standard punishment.

106.10 heir of entail an *entailed* estate on the death of the possessor could be inherited only by lineal heirs. Stipulations might also be attached restricting the succession to heirs male (or, rarely, heirs female). In the present case, the deed must be supposed to have been in favour of Letitia Vere and her heirs male, in the absence of whom the estate was to descend to the next nominated heir of entail.

106.40−41 all violent passions ... madness Horace, *Epistles* (*c.* 20BC), 1.2.62: 'Ira furor brevis est' ('Anger is a brief madness'). The axiom is also quoted in *Timon of Athens*, 1.2.28.

107.27−31 motto *Timon of Athens*, 5.1.120−24.

109.2 rough deal wood in the form of deals (rough slices of timber).

112.24 motto *Much Ado About Nothing*, 4.1.67.

112.33 Abbey of Jedburgh an Augustinian abbey, founded by David I, and first colonised *c.* 1138; its church was completed about the middle of the 13th century. One of a chain of medieval foundations in the south of Scotland (including Kelso, Dryburgh and Melrose abbeys), Jedburgh stands close to the Border and was ravaged by the English on numerous occasions in the 15th and 16th centuries. The *dependency* at Ellieslaw bears some resemblance to the the chapel at Hermitage Castle, originally a religious settlement by monks from Kelso; though, unlike at Ellieslaw, the ruins stand apart from the present castle.

112.38−39 Saxon architecture describing here what is now usually termed early Norman architecture. For a comparable usage of *Saxon*, see *Marmion* (1808), note to Canto 2, stanza 1, and Canto 2, stanza 10 (*Poetical Works*, 7.94n, 100).

113.16 odour of sanctity a sweet odour said to have been exhaled by eminent saints at their death; the good repute of a holy person.

113.16−17 cowl and scapulaire a garment with hood, covering the head and shoulders, and a short cloak covering the shoulders; the vestments of a monk.

113.19 the Italian taste a reference to the baroque school of sculpture, in the style of Gian Lorenzo Bernini (1598−1680).

114.1−2 the violent expedients of the Romans apparently alluding to the rape of the Sabine women. The most obvious source is Livy's *History of Rome* (1.9), a standard text at the Edinburgh High School when Scott was a pupil.

114.11−12 canonical hours the hours between which marriage can be performed within the Church of England. Canonical hours officially did not apply in Scotland, where episcopal clergyman were forbidden by an Act of 1695, c. 15, to celebrate marriages on penalty of banishment or imprisonment: a prohibition which remained in force until 1711.

114.28 a tenth part of a scruple compare *The Merchant of Venice*, 4.1.324−25 ('the twentieth part/ Of one poor scruple').

114.28 fall back, fall edge 'whatever comes'; proverbial phrase (Ray, 189; *ODEP*, 242); apparently from *back* and *edge*, the blunt and sharp sides of a knife or sword.

115.35 down on thy knees compare *As You Like It*, 3.5.57−58.

116.24 grippie for grippie in a hand-clasp, with fists gripped together. Scott himself, also a *lamiter* (i.e. lame, through childhood polio), was noted for the strength of his grip. See James Hogg, *Familiar Anecdotes of Scott*, ed. Douglas S. Mack (Edinburgh and London, 1972), 130: 'The muscles of his arms were prodigious'.

116.34 supper him up   give him his last meal of the day (usually, in Scots, used of animals).

117.5 Loudoun   Lothian (see note to 60.13–14).

117.6 him they ca' Bang, or Byng   Sir George Byng (1663–1733), Viscount Torrington, appointed vice-admiral 1705, commander of the squadron which confronted the French fleet under Admiral Forbin in 1708. (Sir George is not to be confused with his better-known son, Admiral John Byng (1704–1757), executed after a court martial for cowardice.) The passage makes play of the Scots meaning of *bang*, as to 'beat', 'overcome', or 'thrash'.

117.8 auld Nanse   a nickname for Queen Anne.

117.20 let byganes be byganes   proverbial (Ramsay, 96; *ODEP*, 96).

117.25–27 kilt awa ... kilt himsel ... kilt him   a sequence playing on several meanings of *kilt* in Scots : 'hurry away'; 'take himself off'; 'string him up'.

118.24–25 motto   see *As You Like It*, 2.7.163–64.

119.18 a male fief   an entailed estate that can only be inherited by male heirs. See also note to 106.10.

120.16–17 monks of La Trappe   an order of reformed Cistercians, founded in 1664, and at first restricted to La Trappe and two other monasteries. Apart from prayer and contemplation, the monks devoted themselves to manual labour, and a rule of absolute silence was observed.

121.8–9 the mansion and the mains   the mansion house and the home farm of the estate; the demesne lands.

122.21 sowing the wind to reap the whirlwind   see Hosea 8.7.

123.18–19 His defence ... in the State Trials   the defence and last speech of the Earl of Derwentwater (see note to 86.10–11), along with five other leaders of the rebellion in 1715, are given in *A Complete Collection of State Trials*, compiled by T. B. Howell, 15 (London, 1812), 762–806.

123.21–22 Law's bank ... Duke of Orleans   John Law (1671–1729), son of an Edinburgh goldsmith, was forced into exile after fighting a duel in London in 1695. After the death of Louis XIV in 1715, the regent Duke of Orleans allowed him to open a bank and issue notes. Law's foundation of the Mississippi Company produced a mania for speculation in France, and was followed by his appointment as Finance Minister in 1720. In the same year his financial schemes crashed violently, leading to the ruin of thousands of investors.

123.33 Marlborough   John Churchill (1659–1722), first Duke of Marlborough, celebrated English general, who campaigned almost continuously on the continent during the War of the Spanish Succession (1701–1714).

GLOSSARY

This selective glossary defines single words; phrases are treated in the Explanatory Notes. It covers Scottish words, archaic and technical terms, and occurrences of familiar words in senses that are likely to be strange to the modern reader. For each word (or clearly distinguishable sense) glossed, up to four occurrences are noted; when a word occurs more than four times in the text, only the first instance is given, followed by 'etc.' Orthographical variants of single words are listed together, usually with the most common use first; in these cases separate references, divided by a semicolon, are given for each form. Often the most economical and effective way of defining a word is to refer the reader to the appropriate explanatory note.

a' all title-page etc.
a' body everybody 70.16
abune above 19.18, 21.12, 122.37
acquent acquainted 43.12
ae one, a single 19.12 etc.
aff off 54.30, 66.27, 72.35, 117.7
afore before 21.7, 26.29
aften often 12.17, 26.24
against towards, near 13.20
ahint behind 28.12
ain own 18.9 etc.
aith oath 49.20
alane alone 50.24, 55.16
alang along 46.11
amaist almost 27.35, 27.39, 29.3
amang among title-page etc.
an' if 11.23 etc.
an' a' as well, too 17.39, 65.13, 122.4
ance, anes once 28.11, 72.10; 31.36, 70.26
ane one 13.20 etc.
aneugh enough 63.9, 68.11, 69.27
anither another 28.13, 49.7, 49.8
at against, with 68.21
a'thegether, a'thegither altogether 47.1, 51.8; 72.43
a' thing everything 28.27
atween between 18.38, 24.1, 51.30
aught1 anything 68.19, 70.13, 101.38
aught2 own, possess 64.15
auld old 12.18 etc.
awa, awa' away 12.7, 23.31, 24.6, 117.25; 24.19 etc.
aweel well 12.36 etc.
awfu' awful, dreadful 72.20

ay, aye yes 51.43 etc.; 12.3 etc.
aye always 18.22 etc.; still 21.6
bairn child 26.20 etc.
baith both 12.32 etc.
band bond 57.9 (see note), 73.17, 73.18
band-stane bond-stone, a stone extending through the thickness of a wall 29.4
bane bone 43.19, 68.39
bang beat 117.6 (see note)
bargain dispute 23.39
barrow-man someone who carries building materials on a barrow 30.4
basto see note to 37.13
Baudrons see note to 60.37
bawbee see note to 13.10–11
bay reddish brown (horse) with black mane and tail 43.7, 68.40, 81.25
be see note to 18.4
belang belong 63.26
bent moor, open country 72.29
best-looked best-looking 36.25
bide wait 65.10, 66.32, 70.16; remain 25.27, 117.7; endure 39.26; wait for 68.25
bien comfortable 12.25
big build 28.26
big up rebuild 52.13
bigging building 26.43
billet note, letter 98.23
billie, billy brother, 68.32; 66.35; comrade, friend, 12.31
binna do not be 116.43, 116.43
birl at turn, cause to whirr 23.24

bit *goes with following word* indicating smallness, familiarity or contempt 21.6 etc.; spot, place 17.32 etc.; small piece (of) 47.20, 73.34

blackface see note to 12.13–15

blaw blow 25.26 etc.

blent mingled 59.35

blind poorly marked 54.26

blink short moment, instant 48.34

bluid, blude blood 26.25, 43.33, 43.34, 62.39; 43.19, 69.20, 116.24

blythe, blithe glad, cheerful 12.25 etc.; 17.31, 23.18

boddle small copper coin worth two pence Scots 69.6

bodkin needle 22.2

body person, man 31.34 etc.

bogilly ghostly, haunted by bogles 17.32, 18.41

bogle goblin, terrifying supernatural creature 23.6 etc.

bonnily well, satisfactorily 122.26

bonny, bonnie beautiful, pretty, fine 12.19 etc.; 19.3, 26.38, 116.33, 117.25

bouk body 21.42 (see note), 54.39

brae hillside, slope 71.42

braw fine, splendid 12.21 etc.

brent smooth, unwrinkled 59.34

bride's-cake wedding cake 73.35

bridesman bridegroom's attendant at a wedding 113.39

brither brother title-page, 47.17

broadsword cutting sword with broad blade 117.23

broke trained 46.15

brouze see note to 47.36

buff made of buffalo-hide leather 42.40

burn stream 122.27

burrows-town see note to 43.40

bye rather than 50.18

byganes bygones 117.20, 117.20

byre cowshed 48.28, 63.1

ca' call 13.5 etc.

cabal plot, intrigue privately (against) 15.22, 40.15

cadger see note to 25.38

calcine reduce to dry powder by burning 16.20

callant, callan lad, fellow 23.12, 51.29; 54.12

cankered ill-tempered 48.13, 50.15, 122.29

canna cannot 13.16 etc.

cannily carefully, quietly 48.40

canny skilful, shrewd, 44.10 etc.; favourable, lucky 48.5; good, kind 116.22; for 12.7, 32.21, 55.8, 56.7, 69.39, 116.31 and 122.4 see note to 12.7; for 72.21 see note to 72.21

cantrips magical tricks 70.11

carena care not 57.41, 61.8

carle fellow 116.25

carline old woman 17.41, 23.24; witch 20.16

carman carter, carrier 104.41

cauld cold 117.22

cess see note to 90.2

Chamberlain see note to 23.31

chare accomplish 48.25

chield, chiel fellow 20.8, 51.37, 70.24; title-page

chuse choose 39.7

clam-jamfarie disorderly crowd, rabble 61.9

claver talk idly, gossip 13.12, 18.22, 58.2

clavers nonsense 12.34

cleugh gorge 15.30, 17.33

clew clue 121.25

cloot hoof 63.4, 68.36

clout piece of cloth 26.7 (see note)

coif see note to 25.12

con offer, express (thanks) to 72.30

conscience consciousness, inward knowledge 36.31

corp corpse 66.17

couldna couldn't 47.19

cousin-german first cousin 24.8-9

cowl see note to 113.16–17

crack talk, gossip 12.33 etc.; for 13.22 see note

crane-berries cranberries 50.13

craw *noun* crow, rook 25.29

craw *verb* crow, boast 43.36

creish grease, lubricate 63.17

crib stall, cabin 71.14

cripple lame 50.15

crousely confidently, proudly 43.36

currie company, band 70.10

daffing teasing, foolery 24.6, 53.5

daft foolish, stupid 12.9, 51.29, 58.1

dauntonly bravely, defiantly 85.11

deal see note to 109.2

deave annoy, bore 51.32

de'il, deevil devil 17.35 (see note) etc.; 16.36

de'il ane not one, no one at all 52.9, 117.21

de'il's-buckie a perverse, obstinate person 50.16

depone testify, declare on oath 28.11

didna didn't 23.2, 51.35, 57.22, 57.37

din fuss, disturbance 116.36

ding knock, drive 69.33, 72.40

dinna don't 12.9 etc.

dirdum blame, punishment 66.18

distaff stick used in hand-spinning 25.18, 81.11 (see note)

divan council 80.4

doesna doesn't 65.11, 117.26

door-cheek doorpost 72.28

doublet see note to 41.25–26

doubt fear, suspect 13.17, 122.4

douce respectable, sober 70.2

dought *past tense* could 66.32

doun down 12.20 etc.

dour sullen, gloomy 73.36

dow be able 64.27

downa cannot 57.40, 64.27 (see note)

downcome downfall 66.21–22

drap drop 28.14

dreadnought see note to 11.11

dry-stane see note to 28.26

dune done 49.8

dung *past participle of* ding 69.33

dyke wall 12.18, 28.26 (see note)

ee eye 59.34

een eyes 19.3, 50.31

e'en1 just, simply 12.1 etc.; even 68.37

e'en2 evening 12.19, 28.10, 28.14, 44.5 (see note)

e'enow, e'en now just now, at the present time 54.18; 57.40

eilding fuel 62.20

empiric untrained medical practioner 120.1

eneuch, eneugh enough 50.17; 11.30

enow enough, in plenty 41.10

ewhow ah! gracious! 102.21

fa' fall 63.21, 66.18, 66.22, 70.18; for 26.21 see note

facetious witty, amusing 6.34, 7.37, 8.27

fain gladly, willingly, 42.4, 122.23; glad, happy 18.22

fallow fellow 20.10 etc.

fareweel farewell 57.39

fash trouble, annoy, 12.24 etc.

fauld fold, pen 47.14, 63.1

fause false, treacherous 16.43, 64.4

feind see note to 27.31

fiar see note to 73.16

fiat see note to 104.11

ficht fight 59.36

fie *exclamation* expressing disapproval or indignation 18.30, 18.30, 66.34

fief feudal tenure 119.18 (see note)

fit foot 68.39, 71.17 (see note)

flam trick 92.24

flow bog, marsh 21.33 (see note), 89.16

flung see note to 71.16

flyte quarrel, wrangle 26.5

forbye besides, in addition to 73.12

forehammer sledgehammer 61.24

forgi'e forgive 47.14, 72.5

forrit forward 23.25

fou full 52.13

founder strike down 65.39

frae from title-page etc.

frighted frightened 20.10, 26.4, 26.8, 26.11

fu' full 19.17

furze gorse 108.36

gae1 go 23.11, 23.18, 49.6, 63.15

gae2 *past tense* gave 116.33

gaed went 17.38, 85.12

gage pledge, security 41.32, 93.24

gait1 goat 47.3 etc.

gait2 way 17.31

gane gone 22.42, 56.37, 67.19

gang go 27.9 etc.

gar make 19.27, 22.41, 56.22, 116.21

gash sagacious, shrewd 23.23

gate way 12.34 etc.

gauger exciseman 90.4

gauging-stick see note to 7.10–11

gaun going 23.25, 27.32, 27.34

gear movable property, livestock, 43.21 etc.; wealth, possessions in general 19.18, 51.3

geaunt giant 59.31

gentle well-born 27.8, 47.42, 82.43

ghaist ghost 22.17 etc.

gie, gi'e give 13.14, 13.22, 24.12, 63.13; 20.39 etc.

gimmer young female sheep 47.3

gin if 18.5

girdle see note to 21.9–10

glaunsing glancing 59.34

gliff short while 64.41, 72.29, 72.33

gloaming fitful, shadowy 121.22

gowd gold 57.7, 69.34

gowk fool 65.8

grandame grandmother 25.20, 26.19

grandees nobility, persons of high rank or position 69.26

grane groan 73.37

grate grating, iron door 61.9 etc.

gree come to terms, agree (upon), settle 13.13 etc.

greet weep, cry 51.5, 54.14

grewsome horrible, disconcertingly ugly 70.25

grippie see note to 116.24

groat a small silver coin 62.41

grund ground 20.16, 47.19, 54.30, 72.5

gude *adjective* good 18.4 etc.

gude *noun* God 20.17

gude-dame grandmother 17.40, 18.22, 72.39

gude-sire grandfather 51.6

gudes goods, belongings 48.9

ha' hall 23.23

hadna hadn't 23.11, 117.22

hae have 12.7 etc.

haenna haven't 13.11

haffits face, temples 48.34

hail-draps pellets, small shot 20.9

hale whole 58.19, 65.9, 70.1, 70.10; unharmed 63.36

hame home 23.11 etc.

hanger short sword, usually hung from the belt 76.9

hantle great many, great deal of 12.14, 69.4

harry plunder, lay waste 58.21, 68.17, 121.37

har'st harvest 122.22

hasna hasn't 62.40, 68.30, 68.37, 71.15

hattock a little hat 54.2, 54.3

haud hold 27.6, 51.29, 54.16; keep, proceed 54.40; for 64.8 see note

havena haven't 70.7, 70.16, 70.27

hellicat noisy restless person, wicked creature 63.11

hen-cavey hen-coop 63.2

hersel herself 18.17 etc.

het hot 19.13, 21.9, 117.22

heugh steep bank 24.33

hie-lands highlands 11.29 (see note)

himsel himself 18.29 etc.

hind servant, farm labourer 48.10

hinny honey, dear 50.30, 64.30, 69.19

hirdie girdie topsy-turvy, in confusion 69.34

hirple hobble 21.9 (see note)

hist ss!, a sharp hissing noise to attract attention 48.20, 48.20

hout tut! oh dear! 12.23 etc.

hout awa nonsense, get away with you 12.7, 24.6

howe hoe 12.32

hunder hundred 13.10

huz us 122.25

ilka each, every 26.31, 63.7, 122.28

ill-fa'ard ugly 54.36

indweller inhabitant 26.24

ingle-side fireside 72.40

I'se I shall 13.22 etc.; I am 83.3

ither other 116.33

jealous suspicious, apprehensive 22.4

jeroboam a very large wine-bottle 89.24

jookery-packery jiggery-pokery, trickery 72.22

jow ring 19.27

kail cabbage soup 13.19

keb give birth prematurely to a dead lamb 16.17, 124.26

keepit kept 18.26, 64.12

kelpie see note to 17.9

ken know 12.31 etc.

kenn'd *past tense* knew 51.41, 57.11, 122.15; recognised 48.33

kenn'd, kend *past participle* known, known as 47.42, 70.14, 70.35; 18.3

kenna don't know 68.36

kilt see note to 117.25–27

kine cows 16.17

kintra country, district and its inhabitants 17.43, 18.3, 18.37

knapscap see note to 53.20

knicht knight 59.31

knowe knoll, little hill 12.19 etc.

kye cows, cattle 12.20, 54.4, 65.13

ladye lady 49.1, 65.31

lair learning 23.37

laird lord, landowner 6.35 etc.

laith loath, reluctant 62.39

laive rest, others 66.3

lamiter lame person, cripple 116.23

lang long 12.15 etc.; tall 72.14

lang-nebbit long-nosed, long-beaked 19.42

lap leapt through 117.23

leal loyal, faithful 53.28

led see note to 23.32

led-horse spare horse led by a servant 36.14

leddy lady 122.23

liferenter see note to 73.16

lift carry off, steal cattle 19.15 etc.; for 88.5 see note

liker more like 23.6

liket liked 122.29

lilye lily 59.35

ling coarse grass, heather 89.17

list please, choose 59.36

live-lang livelong 26.6

loaning grassy cattle-track 12.21; open pathway leading to a farm 24.32

loon rascal, scoundrel 73.12, 116.33; man of low birth or condition 82.43

loup leap 66.10

louping-ill see note to 70.19

low flame 25.27; fire 50.29

luckpenny see note to 13.14

lug ear 56.3

lunt light, torch 62.20

luve love 26.23

mains see note to 121.8–9

mair more 12.16 etc.; for 18.4, 51.26, and 71.17 see notes

maist most 18.5, 23.29

maister master 12.17, 12.36

mak make 59.33

mallenders dry, scabby eruptions behind the knee in horses 68.40–41

mammocks see note to 35.7

manna, maunna must not 46.27, 72.37; 27.35

march border 63.4

march-dyke boundary wall 29.5

mart market-place, emporium 5.24

maun must 12.1 etc.

mayna may not 26.2

mends revenge, compensation 18.27, 68.38

merk marks, currency worth 13s 4d Scots (1s. 1⅓d. sterling) 69.13

mickle, *see* muckle

mim demure, restrained 19.11

mind remember 19.21 etc.

misdoubt distrust, doubt 64.3

mislippen suspect 27.34

mis-set disconcerted 26.11

missive an informal writing conveying an offer or acceptance 73.28

mista'en mistaken 12.8

mistryst delude, lead astray 26.4; fail to meet with 27.32

mony many 18.3 etc.

moor-ill see note to 70.19

moor-pout a young grouse 6.40

morass bog, marsh 36.27 etc.

morning morning drink or snack 68.24

mort dead lamb or sheep 12.4

moss bog, moor 21.40, 28.12, 50.14, 76.16

moss-trooper see note to 53.15

muckle *adjective* much 13.16 etc.; large, big 52.11

muckle *noun* much, a great deal 20.1, 27.3, 60.24

muckle, mickle *adverb* much 12.8 etc.; 17.40

murrain a cattle disease 33.34; plague 63.10

musquetoon short musket, hand-gun 62.18

mutchkin *measure of capacity* ¼ pint Scots, i.e. ¾ pint Imperial (0.426 litre); 'a pint' 13.15, 13.21, 13.22

mutes professional attendants at a funeral 88.3

mysel myself 13.22 etc.

na not 19.1 etc.; no 26.4 etc.

nae no 18.21 etc.

naebody nobody 12.14 etc.

naething nothing 19.14 etc.

naig horse 66.26, 68.11, 68.40, 70.32

nane none 19.18

natheless notwithstanding 6.16

needna needn't 25.23, 116.34

negleckit neglected 122.25

neuk nook, corner 17.41

nicker snicker, laugh shrilly 66.16

no not 12.28 etc.

obeisance bow, gesture of respect 42.27

Odd God 13.8 etc.

ohon alas! oh! 50.28

onstead farm building 123.38

ony any 13.18 etc.

or before 52.13, 61.16, 70.12

ordinar see note to 50.12

oursels ourselves 69.17

out-bye out of doors 68.11; outlying 68.35

ower too 27.3 etc.; over 21.6 etc.

ower-maister overmaster 55.17

owerbye over there 44.11

owercome surplus, excess 13.37

paction pact, agreement 124.17

palfrey a small saddle-horse 41.41, 42.1, 71.4, 74.7

panada dish made by boiling bread to a pulp and adding flavouring 43.10

park field, enclosure 12.18 (see note)

partizan long-handled spear 116.19

peascod pea-pod 116.38

peel-house fortified dwelling 12.18, 123.37

peght see note to 26.18

pen-feather quill-feather 44.9

pen-gun see note to 13.22

pest plague, obnoxious feature 94.22

petted sulky 29.39

pick make an impression (upon) 61.24

pinch iron lever, crow-bar 61.24

ping droop, pine 72.40

pinners see note to 25.12

pipe-stapple stalk of a clay tobacco-pipe 61.26

pit put 21.6, 73.30

plack see note to 13.10–11

plea action at law, suit 13.17, 26.42

plenish furnish 69.35, 73.9

plenishing household equipment 52.12, 53.25

pleugh plough 12.22, 12.32

pot-sherd see note to 35.9

pow head 27.9

powney, powny pony 23.12; 47.38

preceesely precisely 13.16, 26.29

prent print title-page

press see note to 90.2

prick trace, track 54.26

proem introduction, preamble 5.7, 6.33

pu' pull 12.18, 56.3

puir poor 20.10 etc.

pund *currency* pound 13.10

qualified see note to 88.33

quarter-day see note to 7.32

quite free, rid (of) 59.33

raes roe-deer 17.38

rampauge rampage, rage furiously 22.41

rank row, line 18.8

rant romp, frolic 19.43

rash rush violently 116.43, 116.43

recruit restore, refresh 7.26, 84.1

red-wud wild, frenzied 17.38

redacter arranger, editor 6.20

rede *noun* advice, counsel 48.37

rede, redd *verb* advise, counsel title-page; 21.10

reek smoke 51.22

reest cure, smoke 62.8

reiver raider, robber 33.39 etc.

rig fit 18.13

rive tear 12.22 (see note)

rood see note to 29.5

roop see note to 68.41

rowel the spiked wheel on a spur 48.23

sae so 12.17 etc.

safe save 22.3

saft soft 21.12 (see note), 47.19

sair *adjective* sore, sad 55.4, 56.36, 73.37; harsh, severe 70.19, 72.35, 122.22

sair *adverb* very much, greatly 12.17, 27.39, 29.5

sairly badly, greatly 63.17

sall shall 64.4, 122.24

salvo face-saving expedient 86.42

sang song 47.19

saul soul 22.4

saulees hired mourners at a funeral 88.3

sax six 13.15

scapulaire see note to 113.16–17

scathe *see* skaith

scaur bank, edge 66.11

sclate-stanes see note to 57.12

scouther see note to 48.15

scutcheon shield with a coat of arms 113.12

sell self 72.41

sely innocent, harmless 59.32

semple low-born 82.43

sepulchral pertaining to the burial of the dead 120.12

sharps see note to 83.24

shaw wood, thicket 44.11; for 29.6 see note

sheeling-hill rising ground where grain was winnowed by the wind 24.11

shiel shell 116.38

shouldna shouldn't 47.4, 68.24

sic such 13.21 etc.

siccan such 12.34 etc.; what amazing . . . 29.3

siller money 57.9 etc.

sin since 47.37

sinsyne since then 26.42

sirs God preserve us! 64.12, 102.21

skaith, scathe harm, damage 48.8, 49.8, 62.41, 72.31; 26.20

skeel skill 61.15

skelp gallop, race 43.40

skep hive 122.23

skilfu' skilful, knowledgeable in medicine 70.14

skreigh see note to 70.29

slashed see note to 41.25–26

sled sledge 47.17, 47.38

sleuth-hound see note to 33.42

smeek smoke out 122.25
snapper stumble, trip 66.2
snaw snow 65.32
somegate somehow 70.40
sooth true, truthful 24.7
soutterain underground chamber 120.12
sowther settle, patch up 72.32
spadille see note to 37.13
spak spoke 59.31
speerings news, information 52.33, 54.11, 57.20
splore commotion, escapade 20.1, 48.33, 49.9
spunk spirit, mettle 19.11
spunkie see note to 17.9
stane stone 18.8 etc.
statuary sculptor 45.34
steading, steeding farm 50.28; 13.9
steek shut, close 63.16, 73.13
steer molest 116.21
stick stab 18.28
stievely firmly, 12.11
stirk young bullock 68.18
stocking cattle, stock 68.34
stoop see note to 68.41
stot bullock 68.18
stouthrief theft by force (typically in a dwelling-house) 68.30
streek stretch 70.27
subscrive subscribe, sign 73.29
suld should 27.8, 47.7, 47.11, 69.39
suldna shouldn't 28.9, 70.3
sune soon 62.22
supper see note to 116.34
surcingle girth for a horse 66.20
swatter splash, splatter 117.24
symbol token, coin 7.34
syne ago, since 12.34 etc.; for 85.8 see note
tablets notebook 49.27
tane (the) one of two 18.16
tap top 18.8
tasker see note to 52.11
tell'd, tauld told 12.17, 72.30; 26.24
tent attend to title-page
thae those, these 12.14 etc.
than then 20.8 etc.
thegither together 48.36, 70.36
themsels, themsells themselves 13.5 etc.; 28.9
thereaway that direction, those parts 54.22
thewes muscles, muscular strength 44.25

thought see note to 21.42
thraw turn 61.8; oppose, cross 55.14
thrawn perverse, intractable 122.29
threep assert, insist 55.37
thretty thirty 116.30
tittie sister 66.38, 122.36
token see note to 18.4
tolbooth see note to 69.12
toom empty 48.28
tother (the) other, second of two 18.17
toun, town farm, estate 23.29; 122.26
tow fibre for spinning 81.10 (see note); rope 117.27
trepan lure, inveigle 96.3
troth indeed 19.14 etc.; truth 63.14, 63.19, 64.7
trow believe 44.9, 51.35, 116.34
trunk-hose see note to 41.25–26
tryst, tryste agreement, appointment 65.13; 118.19; for 55.3, 57.41 and 58.5 see note to 55.3
twa two 13.7 etc.
tyke dog 24.19, 48.8
unco *adverb* very, exceedingly 12.4, 12.11, 12.29, 17.32
unco *adjective* weird, strange 70.1
under-spur-leathers see note to 84.6
upbye up there, yonder 17.41
uphaud affirm, warrant 22.39
vaticination prediction, prophecy 8.12
vizard visor, mask 67.33
vole see note to 92.32
wa' wall 12.18, 51.21, 68.17
wad1 would 12.17 etc.
wad2 wager, bet 116.24
wading see note to 20.28
wadna wouldn't 23.6 etc.
wadset see note to 57.10
wae sad 47.11; woe 66.7
wame heart, mind 70.37
ware spend, waste 13.21, 73.3
wark work 12.32 etc.
warld world 12.8 etc.
warlock wizard, male witch 39.21, 50.34, 55.17
warrant stand surety for, guarantee 24.18, 65.13
warst worst 52.32, 55.39, 55.39, 70.10
washy poor in condition, liable to sweat 68.40
wasna wasn't 67.1, 67.4

water-saps pieces of bread soaked in water 43.10

wauking awake 72.28

waur worse 30.3 etc.

weary wretched, dispiriting 18.7; for 26.21 and 26.23 see note to 26.21

wee little 19.1, 19.33, 28.23, 70.34; a short while, a moment 70.16

weel well 12.19 etc.; well! why! 18.21 etc.

weize aim, shoot 90.7

we'se we shall 52.14, 54.23

wether ram 47.14, 116.24

wha, whae who 24.26 etc.; 72.6

whaever whoever 31.33

whaup curlew 28.12

wheen few 18.8, 19.16, 26.5

whid move nimbly without noise 23.25

whiles sometimes, occasionally 48.40, 55.37

whin-stane whinstone, a slab or boulder of hard rock 76.42–43

whinger short stabbing sword 28.23, 54.39

whisht quiet! sh! 51.29, 54.20

whortle-berries, whortleberries bilberries 50.13; 89.18

wi' with 12.20 etc.

wide see note to 48.28

win get (at, through) 56.3, 73.13

wind blow 60.20

winna won't 26.4 etc.

woo' wool 13.4, 13.5, 13.7

worricow hobgoblin, demon 19.41, 20.11

wow wow! gee! 17.30

wrang wrong 18.35 etc.

wreath drift 51.21, 65.32, 124.27

writer lawyer, solicitor 69.14

writings legal documentation 73.19

wuss wish 12.26, 48.6, 73.30

wyte *verb* blame, accuse 57.35, 60.24, 63.8

wyte *noun* blame, responsibility 67.5

yaud horse 13.12

year-auld yearling 13.14

yoursel yourself 12.25 etc.

yowe ewe 12.1